SNAKE HUNT!

The defiant screams of the team's horses echoed off the high walls to either side of them. The slower-moving snakes were nearly there. Kelly had never noticed before what a terrifying sound their bellies made, slithering on the dry grass. Oh, a single snake could be silent when it was sneaking up on its prey, but dozens and hundreds of them made the grass hiss beneath them.

"Here! I need help!" Anne Boncyk shouted from behind the grain barn. She galloped into sight, waving an empty crossbow. "There's a mess of them sneaking around the barn!"

A young reptile, only about three meters long, whipped between the team's horses. Three spears jabbed for it all at once, but all missed their mark.

"Damn!" groaned Don, and shouted over his shoulder, "Anne, a three-meter coming through!"

"No, I'll take it!" Jilamey said. "I gotta get two!"

At first, the snake was too intent on catching its meal to realize it was being pursued. Encouraged, Jilamey galloped at it, trusty quarterstaff poised above his head. "Yeee-hah!" he yelled, bringing it down on the snake. It was a good, solid hit. The snake stopped dead and curled itself into a hurt knot. Jilamey had learned a lesson during his previous misadventure. Before the snake could coil about the staff, he discarded it and reached for the crossbow.

He never got the chance to use it . . .

CRISIS ON DOONA

ANNE McCAFFREY
AND
JODY LYNN NYE

ACE BOOKS, NEW YORK

This book is an Ace original edition,
and has never been previously published.

CRISIS ON DOONA

An Ace Book / published by arrangement with
Bill Fawcett & Associates.

PRINTING HISTORY
Ace edition / March 1992

ISBN: 0-441-23194-2

Ace Books are published by The Berkley Publishing Group,
200 Madison Avenue, New York, New York 10016.
The name "ACE" and the "A" logo
are trademarks belonging to Charter Communications, Inc.

PRINTED IN THE UNITED STATES OF AMERICA

10 9 8 7 6 5 4 3 2 1

CHAPTER

1

"MAYDAY, MAYDAY," A VOICE REPEATED OVER AND over again in Middle Hrruban through thick static on the audio pickup. "Anyone who is within the sound of my voice, Mayday! We require assistance. Our ship is down and damaged. Mayday!"

Todd Reeve and his friend Hrriss, at the controls of the Alien Relations Department scout ship *Albatross*, stared at one another in surprise. It was impossible to tell if the speaker was male or female, a Human like Todd, or a catlike Hrruban like Hrriss. The message repeated, sounding more panic-stricken.

"Where's that coming from?" Todd demanded, scanning the readouts on his control panel. They had just emerged from the second warp jump on their journey back to their homeworld of Doona from a diplomatic mission on the nascent colony world of Hrretha, and had not yet taken bearings on their position to initiate the third.

Hrriss's retractable claws extended as he reached for the controls. There was a low humming as the ship's benchmark program triangulated the distress signal and readings began to register. The readouts indicated they were positioned beyond the envelope of a star system whose blue-white primary glittered coldly on their screen. "Not too very frrr away. It comes from the vicinity of this sssystem's fourth planet," he said in a low, cautious voice that resembled a cat's purr.

"We've got to respond," Todd insisted at once.

Hrriss shook his head, his pupils widening over green irises. "Todd, we cannot. We bear the markings of a Trran ship, your Alrrreldep, and this system is interdicted by the Hrruban

1

exploration arm. It would be a violation of the Zreaty of Doona to enter this sssystem."

"But it's a Mayday! You have to answer Maydays," Todd insisted, staring at his friend in disbelief. "The oldest naval laws on Earth required it. Space laws can't be so rigid as to deny assistance in an emergency. Someone's in trouble! They need our help. Why is this one interdicted?" Todd demanded. "What's so dangerous about it?"

"Explorers from my people have claimed this system, called Hrrilnorr, for mineral exploitation, but also perhaps for colonization," the Hrruban explained.

In the Archives established on the Treaty Island back on Doona/Rrala, extensive records were kept of the status of various systems in each species' chosen sector of exploration. Though Doona was cohabited by Humans and Hrrubans, each race had committed to a Treaty specifying separate territorial rights to all other claimed systems.

"There are trace radioactive elements on the inner, solid worlds," Hrriss went on. "The Byzanian Glow Stones of the fourth planet have a curious, milky glow, most beautiful to look upon. They had a strange, mesmerizing effect upon my people, but even more odd upon the analysis equipment they carried. The glow affects short-term memory of both people and things. Until the effects have been proved hrrrmless, no one may enter here."

Hrriss regarded Todd, his closest friend of either species anywhere in the galaxy. They both knew how Treaty Law read. Violation of a system claimed by the other species was an overt act of hostility, which could end in war. The penalties for infractions started with grounding of the ship, and could end with them in prison on a hardship mining colony, or worse yet, remanded to Earth and Hrruba, separated forever.

Todd set his jaw. "If we start ignoring fellow beings' cries for help, we're no better than Rralan snakes. Someone's in trouble. We heard it. The voice said 'our' ship. 'We' require assistance. So there's more than one of them! We have to help."

Hrriss shook his head slowly, clearly uneasy. Todd took charge.

"Look, it's my responsibility. The ethics of my culture

require me to act." He prodded his chest. "I'd never forgive myself for ignoring that call and letting people die. Besides, we're in this sector of space and we could be in bigger trouble for ignoring a Mayday—if someone else comes by."

Hrriss regarded his friend somberly. "This is not a very well travelled area and the system is interdicted." Hrriss then saw how Todd's jaw was set and the implacable expression on his face and knew that his friend would not yield. So the Hrruban gave a slow nod of acceptance. "We have both heard the Mayday. I will say that I insisted on answering though you argued that the system was interdicted!" The Hrruban dropped his jaw in his distinctive grin. "It is better thus. The initial blame is mine, for this is a Hrruban system. I convinced you we must respond."

Todd's expression cleared immediately and he gripped his friend's shoulder in relief and approval. "I'd rather acknowledge my own errors, Hrriss, but your idea makes too much sense in this instance. So, just this once, I'll let you carry the can for one of my bright ideas. Anyway, the ship's recorders are . . . Wait a minim . . ." He tapped the small illuminated dial on the panel between them. "Log's not recording, Hrriss. No movement whatever on the VU meter. Those flaming Hrrethans . . . I told them the *Albatross* had been serviced before we went out on this jaunt . . ." As he grumbled, he lifted himself out of his chair. "I'll go see."

"That recording is important, Zodd." Hrriss called after him.

"Don't I just know it?" Todd hurried down the narrow companionway to the engineering compartment, growling Hrruban curses under his breath.

Duplicate meters to those on the pilot's consoles were attached to the front of each panel in the rear section. Todd dashed past the standing cases that operated space drives, life support, landing gear, food service to a blue and pipeclay cabinet. The feed switcher in the center of the panel was on the correct output. The dials were jumping, following the audio of the Mayday call still blaring over the speakers. Obviously the power was running. Only one set of dials wasn't working, the one attached to the holographic log recorder at the foot of the panel.

"Wouldn't you just know? Those Hrrethans aren't worth the leather they belt with!" Todd groaned. Every system had been in perfect working condition before the Hrrethans insisted on the mechanical-overhaul courtesy.

Frustrated, Todd kicked the front panel of the device and turned to look for the toolbox. With a wowing sound like a bear waking up from hibernation, the recorder started to move again, its disk turning and needles moving. Surprised, Todd glared at it and stalked disgustedly back to the pilot's chair.

"The good ol' reliable correcting kick. Try it again, Hrriss."

"A-OK now."

"Them and their 'courtesy,' " Todd muttered, watching the VU activity as the Mayday was now obviously being recorded. That "courtesy" had been yet another delay when he was fretting to get back aboard the *Albatross* and out of the tight uniform he had to wear on such occasions. Sometimes the courtesy appearances that he and Hrriss had to undertake as representatives of their respective cultures were unredeemed boredom as well as too much spit, polish, and restricting clothing: This latest jaunt to open a new transportation facility at Hrretha being an excellent example. "Wonder how long that Mayday's been bleating?" From his training in space flight, he knew the fate of spacers whose life support ran out. Recorders on passenger liners kept on until power was exhausted. Others ended when no more activity was recorded by the life support systems. "I'd hate to think we'd jeopardized everything for a cargo of corpses."

"We will assume rescue is required," Hrriss said. He transmitted a reply. "Stranded ship, this is the *Albatross*. We rrreceive your message and are coming to help. I will make the course correction," Hrriss added, working without looking up.

As they passed through the heliopause, a wild wailing made the cabin speakers vibrate unpleasantly. Hrriss's ears flattened against his head, and his eyes narrowed.

"Perimeter buoy," he said, wincing. "I knew we ought to be close to one. Can never dodge them. Good engineering. Records even the most fleeting pass," he said, reading the control panel, "and our entry. It will also broadcast a rrrecord of the intrusion to the Zreaty Island beacon," he reminded Todd, his tone gloomy.

"So? It's not as if we didn't expect one," Todd said, his eyes on the screen. "We're committed now." His remark was more statement than a request for agreement.

The blue-white sun was a dwarf, much the size of Sol in the Earth home system. The *Albatross* had come out of its jump directly above it, so that the computer-plotted ellipses of its seven planets spread out below the ship like ripples in a pond. The Mayday originated from the fourth planet from the sun, a small, solid sphere with a ring of eight small and irregular satellites. The triangulation crosshatches appeared on the viewscreen and closed down on a point near the planetary equator, and just passing into the night meridian. Anxiously they watched the blip disappear around the planet's curve. Todd adjusted the *Albatross*'s course to meet its orbit at the earliest possible moment.

Though it took a long time for the scout to cross the distance to the fourth planet, neither Todd nor Hrriss moved. Todd leaned forward, elbows on knees, watching the planet and its moons grow on the viewscreen. Unconsciously he rubbed at his neck where the tight formal tunic had rubbed the skin. Even though he was now in the comfortable one-piece shipsuit, he still felt the constriction. Another reason he loathed these formal occasions. Why they never made the collars or sleeves with sufficient material to encompass one's neck or biceps Todd could not figure out.

Hrriss sat, apparently at his ease in his impact couch, but his tail tip switched back and forth, revealing tension.

"That buoy was alive and kicking, so no smart marauder has tried to blank it and get in for a quick decco. Of course, if any of those stones turn up on the market, the vendor's in real deep kimchee," Todd said, shooting Hrriss a mischievous grin. "Or maybe they'll try to tell us that their equipment's malfunctioning and they didn't 'hear' the buoy." His grimace was mocking as he shoved a finger in his ear, pretending to clear it of a deafening obstacle.

"I am still uneasy myself about entering here," Hrriss admitted. "Zomezing makes my hackles rise." He shook his maned head and then extended both long arms in a gesture of futility. "But we have no choice if lives are at stake."

"This shouldn't take that long," Todd said reassuringly,

making sure the *Albatross* was on course. "Not more than a few hours. In any case, a rescue is surely a defensible reason for breaking prohibition." He sighed, once again easing the soft collar off the back of his rubbed neck. "I'll be glad when we can slough this sort of duty off on someone else. I hated leaving home while all the Treaty Renewal debates are going on. I was needed there," and he jabbed a finger in the spatial direction of Rrala, "not there!" A second jab, contemptuous this time, was for the system they had just left. Todd's eyes locked on the viewscreen showing the fourth planet, and he began to tap his fingers impatiently on the console.

"Will only your two hands hold back the flood tides of disaster?" Hrriss asked him teasingly, to relieve the tension.

Todd turned red and laughed sheepishly. "Hope there's no flooding at all. But you gotta admit, Hrriss, I speak the best formal High Hrruban of anyone on the Treaty Island."

"That I do admit," and Hrriss's eyes glowed warmly. "Did I not help teach you myself?"

What Hrriss did not add was that, in many eyes, Todd was the first real Doonan. The experts said you couldn't true-teach another language to an adult, but a very young child could assimilate one as if it was his mother tongue. Todd, with his booming voice, far-ranging ways, and quick mind, was the first Terran totally at home on Rrala, the Hrruban and official name for Doona. Life on Earth was too confining, too rigid for the six-year-old he was when he arrived on Doona. He was thirty-one now. His swift adoption of Hrruban ways and language, and his innate courtesy, made him, when he came of age, a natural choice for Alreldep's diplomatic service. Over the years, Todd had been careful to be most punctilious about courtesies and laws, schooling himself to ignore slights and insults that often roused his hot temper and begged for retaliation.

"I feel as you do about the Zreaty negotiations," Hrriss said firmly. "The arrangement must continue. I cannot conceive of going back to Hrruba. My life is on Rrala. My career, my family, my hrrss . . . and my best friend." His grin exposed awesome teeth.

Todd grinned back. "Mine, too. Well, you'd think that twenty-five years of peaceful coexistence between Human and Hrruban on Rrala would convince them," Todd offered. "The trouble is, we're the ones living with it. I'm worried about the politicians, too far removed from the situation, who have power over it. They're liable to dissolve the Treaty without considering the effect on the people already involved."

"Zat is undoubtedly trrue," Hrriss acknowledged. "We have been on enough diplomatic missions to see where the distant governments have made purely political decisions that are irrrelevant to the true needs of the colony. Theirr continued meddling without sufficient investigation borrrderrrs the rrridiculous."

"In the words of an unknown but often quoted Terran philosophist, 'ain't that the truth!' "

As the first successful attempt at colonization of a nonmining, pastoral world, Doona was the natural focus of much curiosity and speculation on Earth. The Space Department and the Colonial Department of the Amalgamated Worlds were beside themselves with pride and worry lest the experiment prove to be a failure, after all, leaving them without sufficient funding or approval to send more missions and colonists into space.

Spacedep, as represented by then-Commander Al Landreau, had suffered humiliation in the Amalgamated Worlds government when the first Terran colonists found a Hrruban village on Doona across the river from their own landing site. No habitation had shown up in any of Landreau's scans, but the village was discovered very much an inhabited site. Because it was Ken Reeve—and his six-year-old son, Todd—who had managed to prove that aliens were, in fact, resident on Doona, Landreau resented the Reeve family more than any of the other eleven original colonists. Not only did the mysterious appearance of an alien species on Doona seriously compromise the Phase I operation under Spacedep, and Commander Al Landreau; but also the repercussions reverberated through the Colonial Department (Codep) for permitting Phase II to be initiated and colonists placed on the planet. The most stringent rule of the Terran Colonization Plan was to avoid planets which harbored another sentient species.

Landreau was not actually at fault. The Hrrubans had not been "in residence" at the time of his extensive survey. By matter transmitter, the Hrrubans had moved their entire village back to their home planet of Hrruba, since the winter months on Doona/Rrala were long and harsh. But Landreau neither forgot nor forgave the humiliation of being wrong.

However, the visionary leaders of both species had decided to make the best of this coincidental colonization: to prove that two alien species could interact without exploitation or contamination. Doona/Rrala became the vital test for Human and Hrruban.

The original colonists of both species were allowed to stay, and more of each species joined the project, under the loosest of control by their respective governments. Both races were determined to make this project work and prosper. And they were scrupulous in keeping to the rules laid down by the momentous Decision at Doona, where a six-year-old boy translated the relevant clauses.

The original twenty-five years of that Decision were nearly over and renegotiation soon to be discussed. Both Todd and Hrriss knew of the recent incidents which they were certain had been arranged with the express aim of creating dissension between Hrruban and Human, rupturing the Treaty, and, more important, preventing a renewal of the unique settlement on Doona/Rrala.

Over 100,000 settlers, Doonan and Rralan, now lived on the beautiful planet, year in and out, benefiting from their complementary skills and strengths, and surviving the intense and bitter winters by mutual support. If the Treaty was not renewed, the settlers would be forced to return to homeworlds with which they were no longer in charity. More heart-rending, staunch friends would be forever separated: like Todd and Hrriss.

All the while that Hrrubans and Hayumans lived in harmony on their planet, space exploration had exploded in all directions—always aware that each species was forbidden to explore sectors clearly marked with space buoys of the other.

Although Landreau never forgave either species, he had gone on to discover so many other systems and planets useful to his own kind that he quickly achieved the rank of Admiral. In a way he owed that to the Decision at Doona, which had brought him to the notice of his superiors. His own efforts had kept him in a highly visible situation. Judicious manipulations on his part, the tacit assistance of powerful companies interested in acquiring rich planets, moons, and asteroids, and diplomatic overtures to high-ranking government officials had resulted in his promotion to the head of Spacedep, twenty-two years after the Doona affair.

Landreau had looked for, and found, others who shared his dislike of the Doona Decision. Some purists had always argued that a treaty promulgated through the linguistic precocity of a kid had to be defective. Certainly that most honest and unambiguous of treaties proved troublesome to some ambitious and aggressive Humans.

Landreau carefully cultivated such officials, always seeking a way to burst the Doonan idyll—and avenge himself on the Reeves. Subtly, of course, for he would not risk his current high status: especially one which allowed him the facilities of Spacedep's far-flung resources and highly skilled and trained personnel. If some of the immense budget available to Spacedep's Commander in Chief was siphoned off to explore a way to achieve personal vengeance, it was admirably hidden in the morass of official reports, payments, and analyses.

There was, however, another covert reason for subverting the Doona Experiment: Hrrubans and Humans, dissimilar in form, needed similar worlds to colonize, and for the same pressures. If Doona failed, all terms of the Treaty were null and void. The forbidden sections of space would be open once again to Admiral Landreau's mighty vessels and well-armed fleets, and if the rich world was already inhabited by a Hrruban colony, tough on them! A few well-placed germbombs and the Cohabitation Principle was invalid. Unless, of course, other factions of Earth's government could be persuaded how archaic the principle was and rescind it. How much easier would life be on Earth if one could ship out the unwashed masses to fend for themselves on new worlds with viceroys to skim the riches off the top.

The Doonan settlers were certainly aware of Admiral Landreau's hatred, and his machinations, and there were many adherents on both home worlds that did their best to neutralize some of the worst of Landreau's subtle campaign in various government offices. Though Ken and Todd had never vocalized it, they knew that they were Landreau's particular target. Landreau regarded Todd as an incorrigibly wild brat who went native with distressing speed after landing on Doona. Todd's assimilation of the formalities of High Hrruban diplomacy at the age of six, Landreau dismissed as a fluke.

Hrriss, now nearly thirty-five, always had a cooler way of interpreting a situation than his tall friend. Hrrubans were unassailable by any power from Earth. By Treaty agreement, the arm of the galaxy which the Hrrubans chose to explore was off limits to Terrans. Hrruba's home system was protected by the same Treaty. Any incursion into either sphere would be an act of war. Even Landreau in his obsessive hatred for the Reeves would hardly start a war between the species to get at a single family. Though Hrruba was run by a bureaucracy of great antiquity fully as cumbersome as that of Earth, it was directed gently by one mind whose interests allowed expansion and alliance to proceed. Hrriss and his family were unlikely to be removed from their home for any reason less serious than war. It brought Hrriss's need to defend to two foci: Zodd and the Rrev family.

"I know Landreau's working every angle to spoil our chances if he can," Todd said. "But the Doona Experiment is doing incredibly well, and everyone on Earth knows it. There would have to be an awful stink raised to bring the Experiment to an end at this point."

"A diplomatic insult, perhaps?" Hrriss suggested delicately. "A wedge need not be a large one to drive two elements apart. On Rrala, Terra, or Hrruba, it makes little difference."

"Well, if Landreau thought he could start one on this latest diplomatic mission of ours, he failed." Todd grinned. "Rogitel of Spacedep sounded like he wanted to start an argument with me at the banquet on Hrretha, but I pretended to be bogged down in protocol—fardles, I know all the moves better than he does," Todd said with a snort, his eyes on the screen. Their quarry had reappeared on their side of the planet, and its orbit remained unchanged. "So I got him talking about exploration in the Eighth Sector—safe enough topic."

"I told you it would be useful to know those details," and Hrriss dropped his lower jaw in the Hrruban grin. "He tried me later. I refused to be insulted when he called me a would-be

Hayuman. If he wishes to create an incident, he will have to try harder." Hrriss's wide pink tongue now licked his upper lip, a further sign of amusement. "Varnorian of Codep asked me if it was true that you were applying to join a Hrruban colony to escape penalties from Earth. As if that would not be a Zreaty violation."

"Glad you batted that rumor out of court. I heard a smitch of it, too, and disavowed it with all the innocence at my command." Then Todd snorted. "Anyone who knows me knows better than to try something that simple on me."

The *Albatross* had closed to within thousands of kilometers of its goal. It was easy to swing into orbit from planetary north. The scout had been designed to pass through atmosphere as easily as it did through the frozen void of space. It swept low, across the top of the envelope of atmosphere, above the mass of clouds enveloping the small planet, angling toward the signal.

"If you keep a sharp watch portside, Hrriss," Todd said, his own eyes on the starboard, "maybe we can catch it first time round and not waste too much time in-system."

It was Hrriss who first set eyes on the source of the distress signal.

"Zzhere!" he hissed, pointing with one of his extended claws. Todd marked the trajectory of the floating craft, perched just on the edge of orbit. It was too far away for the cameras to discern much detail about the ship itself, but one thing was clear: any passengers would soon become cinders. The orbit had decayed so much that in only a short time, their ship would be inexorably caught by the planet's gravitation and fall, burning, into the atmosphere.

"Hey, what if we dip below them and drop a tractor cable?" Todd suggested. "You know, that's awfully small for a ship, even a scout."

"And bigger than the average escape pod," Hrriss said, his tone thoughtful.

The size didn't seem unnatural. Hrruban and Hayuman exploration teams flew variously sized scout vessels. The difference was that the Human teams were larger, or doubled up in specialties. Hrrubans sent out the minimum crew needed to make a primary judgment on a planet. When they found one that warranted a full-team investigation, they dropped a one-way transportation grid to the surface and then 'ported in the appropriate personnel. "It must be Hayumans, then, or they would not still be here calling for help. Standard procedure for Hrrubans is to drop a temporary grid and 'port home safely."

The *Albatross* used the gravity well of the Hrrilnorr IV to brake its speed. The next time it passed within visual range, Todd was able to plot a course to follow their quarry.

"I have initial telemetry readings. No atmosphere leak from the surface of the craft," Hrriss said with relief, reading from his scopes for traces of gas.

Though the craft had been able to retain its structural integrity, it was in grave difficulties. Rather than describing a smooth orbit, the speeding vessel jerked and stuttered its way around the fourth planet, as if pulled this way and that by divergent gravity fields. It passed over the day side again. Hrriss and Todd were blinded by the glare of planetary sunrise.

"Attention, the ship," Hrriss spoke urgently into the comunit, using Terran, broadcasting on all frequencies. "We are the scoutcraft *Albatross*. We are here in answer to your Mayday. Can you read us?" He repeated the hail several times, and then in Hrruban. There was no answer.

He pushed up the gain on the receiver. Nothing came from the speaker but atmospheric noise and the repeated Mayday message.

"They could have lost all communications but the beacon," he said, plainly worried. "If their life support is already gone . . ." Hrriss trailed off and pointedly did not look at Todd.

Todd blanched at that possibility and bent over his controls, trying to keep his face expressionless. "We can spring the tractor line on the craft and haul it in. Passengers could use life suits to access the *Albatross*'s lock." Hrriss nodded approval of the strategy. "Hope it's not too late."

As if taking the pilot's words as a challenge, the small dot on the horizon appeared to fall out of orbit, heading like a meteor for the brilliant white layer of clouds below.

"Oh, no, you don't," said Todd, seizing the manual controls.

Todd drove the scout hard after it, hoping the damaged vessel would not pick up too much speed from the gravitational pull until the *Albatross* could swoop in on it. He toggled the magnetic tractor net into alert status. They were dragging through the top of the atmosphere now as the *Albatross* pursued its quarry, still kilometers ahead. His hands were a blur on the keyboard. Hrriss kept calling out to the ship in both languages, hoping for a reply from the craft ahead. With the sun reflecting off its surface, it was impossible to see more than a vague shape. Hrriss kept requesting on all frequencies for details of the damage the lone ship had suffered.

In the midst of the dense clouds thousands of meters below, Todd at last urged the *Albatross* ahead of the speeding hulk. There was a powerful jerk that bucked them around in their seats when the net of magnetic lines engaged the metal hull of the other.

"Gotcha," Hrriss said, his teeth snapping in triumph.

"Great. Now let's just tell those guys to drag ass over here."

Once Todd headed the *Albatross* back into space, the two men turned the external camera onto their prize, and irised down the lens to counteract the glare. There was a silence and an air of angry disbelief as they stared at the object the tractors had brought in. It was cylindrical in shape, the length of their own scout, and not unlike the escape shuttle they had mistaken it for. What their efforts had acquired was a full-sized orbital beacon, an unmanned buoy similar to the ones hanging above and below the proscribed system, still screaming out its Mayday message on the *Albatross*'s receiver as they stood staring at it. The needles on the VU meters leaped back and forth in their glass settings.

"So we've been suckered into an interdicted system by a recorded Mayday," Todd said, unbelievingly. "I'll report this illicit use all the way to . . ." He paused, since the top of Spacedep was Al Landreau and he knew what short shrift that report would get. "We have fallen into deep kimchee, my friend. I should have listened to you."

"No, friend Zodd, you listened to a distress call and acted conscientiously," Hrriss said with a heavy sigh. Neither needed to discuss the ramifications of this.

"Let's get this sucker hauled in and see if we can salvage that Mayday beacon. That'll add credibility to this incident."

"Good thinking, Zodd," and Hrriss programmed the winch for a slow wind while Todd monitored the progress from the external camera.

"Hold it!" Todd held up one hand. "There's something attached to it. Oh-ho! Double trouble. Did we record the capture? Good. Unless I'm vastly mistaken there's a device riding along a very suspicious-looking thickening of the longitudinal spar. That thing is rigged to blow on contact!"

"Rrrreelease," Hrriss said, almost spitting in disgust at the stratagem. "Can you get a close recording of that section?"

"I have so done." Todd was immensely satisfied by that much of this episode, but as Hrriss plotted their course out of the area, his elation drained from him. "Someone's been getting awful clever, Hrriss. Our course was known from the time we left Doona, so there was plenty of time to set this up where we'd stumble into the trap on our way back from Hrretha."

"All too trrrue." Hrriss nodded, his expression as bleak as his friend's. Even the markings on his intelligent felinoid face seemed to have faded in his concern.

"I could wish boils on the hide of whoever perpetrated this. We could have been killed!"

"Waz that the object? To kill us? Or to lure us into interdicted space?"

The eyes of the two friends met—the yellow-green and the clear blue.

"I know someone who wouldn't shed a tear at my demise," Todd said grimly.

"I have similar well-wishers," Hrriss replied, tapping the console with the tips of his claws in a rhythmic fashion.

"Our deaths wouldn't mean as much as our broaching interdicted space," Todd began, rubbing his chin. Stubble was developing, and there were moments, like this, when he wondered what he'd look like with a full beard, or at least sufficient face hair to make him more Hrruban.

"But not only is there prrroof of our samarrritanism, but also I, Hrriss, made all the vocal contacts."

Todd dismissed that notion. "Everyone knows we're together, so I've certainly been wherever you were, legal or not. What I don't understand is exactly why the tactic was planned in this fashion. Was killing the real end? Or discrediting us?"

The two exchanged few words on the rest of the journey back to Doona. Both of them were deep in thought as how best to mitigate their situation. Violating one of the main stipulations of the very agreement they were hoping to see renewed this year was not good, however inadvertent.

"Have you convinced yourself that the recording is enough, Hrriss?" Todd asked after they had identified themselves to the Doona/Rrala buoy.

"Our people will believe us."

"Let's devoutly hope that's enough. Too bad that false beacon didn't blow up. We could at least have brought a section of it home as additional proof."

"We *do* warn everyone that there are bogus Maydays out there!"

"That is obligatory. Bogus or not, we were in the right to investigate," Hrriss said one more time. "A cry for help from other space travelers is not ignored with impunity."

As soon as they landed the Albatross back on Doona, they contacted the tower. Linc Newry was on duty.

"Can you rustle your stumps, Linc?" Todd asked. "We got an official report to deliver."

"Official? Huh? Nothing to do with the Hunt, is it?"

"Not really, but it'd be great if we could get through landing procedures and decontam and get the Hunt properly organized," Todd said with an encouraging grin.

"I'm coming," Linc said, and obviously switched to a handset for he continued talking. "As you're just back from that Hrrethan shindig, I think it'll be okay if I just seal the lock on the Albie and we can do the decontam and stuff when the Hunt's over."

So Todd and Hrriss gratefully disembarked, watched the seal be affixed to prevent entry, and, thanking Linc for his courtesy, hurried off to find Ken Reeve and detail the Mayday incident.

"Genuine or not, you have to answer a Mayday signal," Ken agreed, though the affair obviously troubled him. He smoothed his hair back with a resigned hand. His thick, dark hair had receded above his temples, and lines were beginning to etch the fair, sun-weathered skin near his eyes. He and Todd were of a height now, but often, when he was confused and worried, as he was now, Todd felt himself still the small boy and Ken the adult. Maybe he relied too much on his father's wisdom where experience and the study of law didn't provide the answers. Hrriss sat beside him, his yellow-green eyes unwinking as he stared at the floor between his feet. Ken could tell the Hrruban was worried, but he was not as prone to outbursts as his son.

Todd's eyes were fixed hopefully on his father's face. Ken shook his head and sighed. "Wise of you, Hrriss, to handle all the oral transmissions. Let's hope that the pictures of that device and the possibly explosive ribbing show up." He gave his head another little shake. "Such contingencies will have to be written into the new Treaty, allowing for legitimate rescue efforts and specifying penalties for abuses. I shall suggest the modification myself to Sumitral at Alreldep. But I cannot be easy that the incident was there, waiting to trap the unwary." He paused again, holding up his hand when Todd opened his mouth. "Were there any other representatives at the Hrrethan ceremonies likely to have taken the same warp jumps you did?"

Todd looked abashed. "Dad, I just wanted to leave. My neck was rubbed raw and it was bad enough those Hrrethans insisted on giving the *Albatross* a clearance . . ."

"They insisted?" Ken asked, his expression alert.

"Yes, and we told them that Spacedep had already cleared the *Albatross* . . . Oh, I see what you mean. The recorder could have been tampered with there. You think we were to be the victims?"

"We were not the only ship likely to pass that system," Hrriss said in a slow thoughtful tone. "I will inquirrre. It is worrth that much. And discreetly." He dropped his jaw at Ken. "When one *is* hunted, one generally senses pursuit."

"Then I can leave you to mention this to Hrrestan?" Ken asked. Hrriss nodded. "I shall inform Hu Shih. That will satisfy the necessary protocol. Investigations can be initiated . . ."

"Just don't let that sort of time-wasting stuff interfere with the Snake Hunt, will you, Dad?" Todd was clearly apprehensive. "It's only two weeks away and we've a lot to do."

Ken smiled. "The Snake Hunt is too important to the Doona/Rrala economy to have its leaders absent. I'll handle all the necessary reportings. And inform Sumitral. He warned me to expect trouble from unlikely areas. Cunning of our detractors, isn't it, to start a controversy over a samaritan issue! And it has the flavor of something the segregationalists would try."

"The group that think Hrruba is only being friendly to get their claws into the best star systems?" Todd asked with patent distaste.

"Or perrrhaps," and Hrriss let his fangs show, "it is those who sense we are arming ourselves for the conquest of your home planet."

"No one takes that foolishness seriously," Ken said quickly. "You don't even know where Terra is."

"Nor you Hrruba," and Hrriss winked.

Ken and Todd both laughed with their friend, whose full-throated chuckle would have sounded to many like an ominous growl. Laughter eased the tension lines from Ken Reeve's face.

"Go on, the pair of you. We'll deal with the matter after the Snake Hunt. Which is going to be brilliant this year, isn't it?" He pinned the two friends with a mock-stern glare.

"Absolutely!" The friends chorused that assurance and left Ken's office.

In only a fortnight's time, Doona would be inundated by foreign dignitaries and guests eager to witness, and participate in, the famed Doonan Snake Hunt. Hundreds of people would converge on the First Villages for the semiannual migration of the giant reptiles, and Todd and Hrriss were in charge of coordinating the Hunt. Which was not so much of a hunt as a controlled traffic along the snakes' traditional path.

While there had been intense arguments both for and against annihilation of this dangerous species, the conservationists— many of them colonists—had won. The immense snakes were unique to the planet, but their depredations, which affected only one area of the main continent, could be controlled. The reptiles ranged in size from two-and three-year-old tiddlers of three to five meters in length to immense females, nicknamed Great Big Mommas, growing to twelve to fifteen meters. They had incredible speed and strength and, although they ate infrequently, they had been known to ingest an adult horse or cow in one mouthful. Their vision was so poor that they could not see a man standing motionless a few feet from their blunt snouts, but they would strike at any movement: particularly one that gave off an enticing odor.

Their traditional route from the sea to the plains just happened to lie by the river farms of the settlers where quantities of livestock grazed, too numerous to be shut up during the migration. So the settlers had devised a method of herding the snakes, making certain by a variety of means that few escaped to wreak havoc among the herds and flocks.

At first the settlers resorted to crude methods of keeping the snakes in line, destroying far too many for the conservationists' peace of mind. Then hunters from other planets learned about the drives, as they were originally called, and begged to join in for the thrill and excitement of adding such a deadly specimen to their trophies. These men also had some excellent suggestions to give the Doona/Rralans, gained from similar drives of dangerous species to which Ken Reeve, Ben Adjei, the colonists's veterinarian, and Hrrestan listened with interest.

"Make it into a real Hunt," they were advised. "Attract the thrillseekers and you'll not only make some money out of it, but you'll have enough help to keep the snakes on the right track."

So the Hunt became an organized sporting feature; one which put considerable credit into the colony's treasury and one which became safe enough to advertise as a spectator sport for those who wanted titillation without danger.

At first, Ken and Hrrestan, with Ben's advice, organized the Hunt, but gradually, as Todd and Hrriss showed genuine aptitudes as Hunters and leaders, the management had been turned over to them. Much had to be arranged to insure that injuries were reduced to a minimum; that visitors were always teamed up with experienced Hunters or in safely prepared blinds; that the horses hired out were steady, well-blooded animals, accustomed to snake-stench and less likely to plunge out of control and drop their riders into the maw of waiting Big

Mommas. There were hundreds of minor details to be overseen by Todd and Hrriss before Hunt Day.

When Todd and Hrriss got to their office, they found that much had already been put in hand by their assistants, based on assignments and duties from the last Hunt. Scouts had been given their posts in the salt marshes from which the migration began. Every homestead within ten klicks of the long-established route had had fences, walls, and buildings reinforced. "Sighters" who would fly above the swarm and monitor its progress had been chosen and their aerial vehicles serviced. "Lures" had volunteered. Mounted on two-wheeled motorized rough country bikes, they were specially trained to lead maverick snakes back to the main swarm and to kill snakes that could not be turned. Lures usually performed what had become a rite of passage for young Doona/Rralans: capturing or killing two snakes on a Hunt, or succeeding in stealing a dozen eggs from the marsh nests. In fact, this rite had become an honor sought after by hunters of every system. Many now came just to win accolades as proof of courage and to have their names added to this new legend.

Those who did not wish to expose themselves to physical danger were accommodated in snake blinds, built along, but back from, the river trail. From these, spectators could enjoy this unique sight and excitement. The blinds were sturdily constructed of sealed rla wood, strong enough, though in truth any Great Big Momma Snake could have knocked one into splinters with its powerful snout. However, experiments with various odors had proved that a heavy citrus smell liberally poured on the outside of the blind covered the scent of the juicy morsels within and was a powerful deterrent to the snakes.

Twelve Teams of from twenty to forty horsemen and women rode in escort of the snake swarm. Clever riders on the quick, well-trained horses could head off renegades or stragglers, for some of the tiddlers were always breaking off the main group, looking for something to eat. These were considered fair game for Hunters wishing to kill, or capture, in proof of their prowess.

Approved weaponry—for the Treaty did not permit heavy

weapons in the colony—were projectile rifles, metal-headed spears, compound bows and arrows, and any sort of club (though bludgeoning a snake to death, even a tiddler, was extremely dangerous.) Crossbows were the most popular for a quarrel could penetrate right through a snake's eye to its brain. The only problem was to then keep out of the way of the thrashing body in its death throes.

The worst headache for Todd and Hrrestan was still the composition of the Teams, for they had to intersperse novice and experienced Hunters without jeopardizing team effectiveness. There were also some "solo" or small Teams of off-world hunters but they had to produce qualifications to hunt on their own: proof that they were experienced riders and projectile weapon marksmen; preferably letters from other authorized Hunts or Safari Groups.

As Todd scanned the list of those on his Team One, he noted with satisfaction that Kelly Solinari was on it. So, she'd be back from Earth! She'd be a good team second, even if she had been away from Doona for four years learning how to be a good diplomat at Alreldep. Another name, scrawled so badly that he couldn't quite decipher it, was new to him but documentation showed that this J. Ladruo had participated in several well-known Safaris. Well, Team One had to take its share of novices.

He put that minor detail from his mind and went on to designate the places where they'd have to place charges that could be detonated to startle the snakes back into line. Usually the Beaters managed that, with drums, cymbals, flails and small arms fire, but he pored over the accounts of the last Hunt, to see where breakthroughs had occurred and how he could prevent them. He almost suspected the snakes of rudimentary intelligence the way some evaded Teams and Beaters. He'd begun looking at meteorology reports, too, for a wind from the wrong direction would make a shambles of the most careful plans. Drafting contingency plans for windy conditions was his next task.

"The first Hunters have arrived," Hrriss told him, coming in with their documents.

Todd looked up, startled. "So soon?"

"Zooon?" Hrriss dropped his jaw in a grin. "You've been

working too hard, my Zodd. Only two more days before the deluge!"

Todd groaned as he took the papers from Hrriss and checked the names off against the Hunt application list. Then he brightened. "Two more days and Kelly'll be home."

Hrriss' grin deepened. "You'll be happy to see her?"

"Sure, she's the best second I ever had." He didn't notice the odd look his friend gave him.

Of the many people making their way to Doona for the Hunt, Kelly Solinari was probably the most excited. She couldn't wait to breathe fresh air again on Doona. On Earth, you felt that taking a deep breath was a crime against your fellow humans and besides, it didn't smell good so why contaminate your lungs with government issue. She knew that Earth's air had improved with stringent reductions of pollutants and the careful control of waste products but her lungs didn't agree. She was also looking forward to eating "real" food again: the absolute calorie rationing on Earth was nothing short of a sophisticated form of starvation. For a born Doonan such as she, these four years were a prison and she was about to be set free.

There had been a lot of change on Earth since her father and mother had left the stagnant, crowded planet: and they'd been considered radical for wanting to emigrate. Now there was an active desire, especially among the young, to break away from their crowded, depleted home planet and go out to settle among the stars. New opportunities had created an aura of hope, lightening the general gloom of the population. The success of the Doonan experimental colony begged the question of when more planets would be made available. Without the Hrruban element, of course.

In the back of every mind lingered the warning of Siwanna, the awful memory of the destruction of another race. In Kelly's diplomacy courses, the Siwanna Tragedy was brought up again and again to warn the eager young diplomats-to-be that such an error could be repeated. It had been an unforgettable and tragic shock that the Siwannese had suicided as a race when the colonists from Earth encountered them. They had been a gentle people, with too fragile a culture to survive contact with another intelligent species. Siwanna was empty now. Codep had erected a memorial to the race there, and had forbidden anyone to settle on the world whose inhabitants had been accidentally destroyed. And that was the beginning of the Noncohabitation Doctrine. No Human colony could be initiated on any planet already inhabited by sentient beings.

The Hrrubans' strong culture and identity made them, in the administration's eyes, a statistical rarity. The Doona colony was an exception, where colonization teams from two cultures had met accidentally. The first-contact groups were to regard all new races as fragile and potentially self-destructive. Depending on which teacher you were talking to, this meant Hrruba was Earth's partner in the great task of opening up the galaxy for exploration and colonization. Or, conversely, Hrruba was an obstruction to Earth's efforts. Kelly, who had been born on Doona, and had more Hrruban than Earth-born friends, was always ready to defend her Hrruban mates, and no one could match a Doonan in an argument.

Younger Terrans and her classmates generally shared her views. They wanted to see Humans allowed to live and prosper on new worlds. In the back of their minds was the idea of meeting and making friends with new alien races, though that thought was rarely voiced, not with so many older folk with ingrained habits ready to report them to noise monitors for loud talking. Who could have a decent argument in whispers?

It was so good to be home, even if Doona was crowded this season! Well, crowded for Doona, but only marginally inhabited compared to Terra. Kelly stared out of the hatch at the swarming mob on the landing field waiting for friends and family. It looked as if every single Human on Doona, all 45,000 of them, must be waiting to greet someone. There was even a cluster of Hrrubans, who enjoyed the spectacle of homecoming for its own sake.

She searched the crowd eagerly, hoping to see her own loved ones after her long absence. She'd be unlikely to see them, lost as they were in the mob of welcoming committees waiting to greet the important visitors who had traveled with her from Earth for the Snake Hunt. It had meant more ships coming in, a cheaper fare for her in consequence. And, to judge by the shuttles bearing the markings of other systems,

Doona was already awash with those eager to be part of this primitive event.

One of her fellow passengers, Jilamey Landreau, had bored everyone at their table with his simulated-hunting triumphs. He considered that it was essential to his consequence to be at the Doonan Snake Hunt and kill "one of the big ones." Preferably from horseback, to prove his prowess against a living target. Even as they were making their way down the gangplank, he was still blathering on about it to anyone who would listen.

Kelly, who had hunted snakes on horseback herself, had been the patient listener many a time. She'd recognized his name and decided that it was smarter for her to play it cool in his presence. Her diplomatic training had taught her how to hold her tongue. She was also too kind to make fun of someone who had so far defeated only computer-simulated prey.

She turned her back on him gratefully when her mother and father, Anne and Vic Solinari, approached her from the other side of the field, crying out their welcome, gesticulating for her to notice their position.

"Sweetheart!" Anne said, gathering her into her arms. "Oh, Kelly, welcome home!"

"Oh, Mom," Kelly said, hugging her mother and suddenly feeling like a little girl again. "I missed you. Hi, Daddy."

"You look so grown-up," Vic said, embracing his daughter in turn. "I wasn't sure we'd recognize you. You look just fine. How was the trip?"

"Long," Kelly said, wrinkling her nose. "Cramped. Very smelly. All they had was canned Earth air."

Vic laughed. "It's the second thing that's kept me from taking a trip back to Earth: the first is living in the crowded conditions. I sure don't miss those little granite boxes! Well, come on! Your brothers and sisters are waiting to hear all about what you've been up to. All voice and video this time, not taped transmissions."

"Am I okay for Team One, this year, Dad?" Kelly asked urgently.

Her parents laughed. "Formal notice came last week," her father said, ruffling her hair. "And Michael's kept that Appie mare of yours exercised and has kept your snake-skin in her stall so she won't disgrace you, us, or Todd."

Kelly breathed out a huge sigh of relief. "I was afraid we wouldn't land in time."

"Afraid Todd wouldn't remember to put you on his team?" her mother said with a raised eyebrow.

"Oh, mother!" Kelly was glad of the excuse to go search for the luggage the handlers had just dumped on the tarmacadam.

Kelly finally found and threw the bags into the back of the family's power sled. It was exhilarating to be back on Doona. It couldn't just be the weaker gravity or the invigorating pure air that made her feel so light. She was happy.

As they flew toward their ranch, her mother and father pumped her for data about her life over the last four years. She didn't stop talking for one moment all the way home. The weather was gorgeous, and Vic kept the top of the sled down so they could enjoy the sun.

Then he was turning the sled into the gate of the family ranch, some klicks distant from the original First Community buildings. The new town had been built some distance from the original colony site, out of the path of snake migration. Their ranch abutted the Reeve farm on one side and the Hu property on the other. Behind them was the red sandstone back of Saddle Ridge, no-being's-land except for the wild animals native to Doona. Beyond that and the river was the Hrruban First Village. Every landmark came rushing back to her like the tide coming back up the Bore River from the distant sea.

She knew her mother and father were struggling against laughter as she kept inhaling and exhaling until she was hyperventilating. But she couldn't seem to get her lungs cleared of all that stinking canned air. And she couldn't keep from swiveling her head about her, wishing it were on a 360-degree socket. The sheer space, just loose and lying around, was a sight for her eyes.

Student housing allotment on Earth was very cramped, even for a junior diplomat trainee in Alreldep. No special treatment was given one who had graduated with honors or taken the advanced degree in only a year. She had had to endure the same tiny quarters as any other beginner in what she liked to call Diplodep. She had missed having room to stretch out, and the view of faraway horizons. She had longed for that almost as much as she had missed her family. And Todd. And today was the Hunt.

They were nearly at the ranch house now, and Kelly felt her heart pounding for pure happiness. Two of the farm dogs paced the sled, barking their heads off. Kelly leaned out, calling their names and trying to pet their heads as they ran. Vic coasted the sled to a stop in between the house and the barn. When he turned the ignition off, he gave Kelly one more quick hug.

"Welcome home, sweetie. Hey!" he yelled at the house. "Lookit what I brung home!"

Joyfully, Kelly leaped out of the sled and into the arms of her brothers and sisters. The two smallest, Diana and Sean, tried to jump into her arms. The dogs raced around them, barking and jumping and trying to lick her face.

"Hello, coppertop," she hailed her brother Michael, who waved from the door of the barn and hurried up to meet her. Michael was a year her senior, but they had always pretended to be twins. Their faces were very much alike, with broad foreheads, wide golden hazel eyes, and strong pointed chins. His hair was as fiery a red as hers and just as thick. Their mother always said they reminded her of two matches in a box. Their father, more kindly, merely called them autumn-colored, to suit their autumn birthdays.

"Hi, hothead," Michael said with a broad grin on his face, swinging her around in a circle. He was a very junior veterinary resident, working under Ben Adjei at the Doona/Rrala Animal Hospital. Michael was still clad in his white tunic, but was stripping it off as he steered her toward the house. "Hurry up and change into your gear. They're going to start Gathering the Hunt at twelve hundred hours. Go scrub the ship stink off your skin, or the horses'll run from you, not the snakes. Unless you're too tired to participate?" he asked teasingly.

"Not a chance!" Kelly said, wriggling free and heading toward the house. "It's what I hurried home for! Oh, how I've missed Calypso."

"That's what Todd said you'd say." Michael nodded, helping her carry her bags. "Still horse crazy after those years of horseless Earth?"

"Thank goodness, he and Hrriss got back from that Hrrethan

assignment," Kelly said, ignoring her brother's jibe. "Wouldn't be a proper Hunt without them leading it."

As soon as she had showered in unlimited hot water and dressed in comfortable well-worn clothes, Kelly raced out to saddle her bay mare, Calypso. The mare gladly accepted the present of a couple of carrots and nuzzled her mistress's hand. Kelly just hoped that she hadn't forgotten too much in her years away. But Calypso would take care of her: she usually did. And there was just time left to get down to the Assembly Hall.

Vaulting into the saddle, Kelly kneed Calypso forward, toward the fields leading to the village common. After living on earth for a time, it was hard to readjust to so few people per square kilometer. By law, there could be only as many Humans as Hrrubans. After the Decision came into effect, more Humans had had to be imported to equal Hrrubans, and four more villages' worth of Terran colonists—out of the millions applying—had come to Doona/Rrala. Even so, the combined population made little impression on a planet whose diameter was three thousand kilometers greater than that of Earth.

Kelly was proud that her mother and father were two of the original colonists. Over the quarter century since that historic Treaty, Admiral Sumitral of Alreldep had continued to negotiate with Hrrestan, Hrriss's father and chief of the Hrruban village elders, to make room for more Humans who wanted to leave overcrowded Earth and more Hrrubans with a similar desire. The talks had been successful, and the population of Doona had increased a thousandfold. Men and women who had lived in cramped, crackerbox-sized apartments on Earth had built homes and ranches in the fertile river valleys and settled down with room to stretch out.

No limit had actually been set on how much land each settler could claim, so long as waste, pollution, and senseless destruction of resources were avoided. As well as the native urfa, Vic Solinari, who had come to Doona as the storemaster, had elected to raise sheep and goats, his share of the precious breeding stocks sent from Earth. To keep the grasslands healthy, he rotated their pasturage every season to another part of their land. Typically Doonan, he also had a stable of horses, Kelly's favorite animal as well as cats and dogs.

It had been four years since Kelly had seen a living animal except Humans and Hrringa, the lonely Hrruban minding the transmitter grid in Alreldep block. Elated and exhilarated, she screeched greetings to a flock of goats milling around in a pen, and sighed with happiness as a cluster of young colts galloped in play across a fenced meadow not far from the house. It was wonderful to be home. Kelly legged Calypso into a canter down the hill toward town, revelling in the rhythmic gait and the joy of being back in the saddle again.

CHAPTER

2

DR. BEN ADJEI HAD ESTIMATED THE DAY THIS year—and he hadn't been wrong in twenty years—when the great reptiles would migrate from the salt marshes to the low-lying desert fifty kilometers inland to lay their eggs. Only off-worlders bet against him, the local population shrewdly inciting them to do so.

A Sighter had landed her small copter behind the Reeve ranch house early in the morning to alert Todd that the egg-heavy female snakes were arriving in the desert and beginning to burrow into the dunes. Immediately, Todd called a meeting of leaders of the Hunt at the colony Assembly Hall. They had gathered from all over Doona and had been staying in or around First Village for the last few days, in case Ben Adjei's estimate was off a bit.

For the past fifteen years, Todd and Hrriss had been in the first line of hunters. Their rapport was instinctive: they seemed to read each other's mind. They never took unnecessary chances or risked lives, theirs or others. Their impressive tally of kills and captures of the dangerous reptiloids had reached legendary totals. As they grew to an age when their parents would permit it, they came to lead the Hunt and had done so now for ten years.

"You could see them in the underbrush, swarming toward the sands," Lois Unterberger informed the leaders who had congregated at the Reeve residence, the usual Hunt head-quarters. Excitement made her brown eyes wide, showing white all around the irises. Her dark hair was intricately braided and pinned tightly to her scalp. "Hundreds of them, like a river, pouring onto the dunes and disappearing into burrows.

I followed the leading edge all the way from the salt marshes. Hrrel is still in his copter over the dunes, watching until I get back."

"This is it," Todd said excitedly. "Lois, you fly back and keep an eye on the snakes. We've got to know the minute they start to leave. Dar," he instructed another Sighter, "go and check the snake blinds along the way to make sure everyone knows the snakes are coming and to stay inside. Take two of the Lures with you, and drop them at the vulnerable points we discussed."

"Gotcha! I'm away," Dar Kendrath said, dashing for his small craft.

"And keep in touch!" Todd called after him. "We need to know the moment the snakes start to move out!"

Dar threw him a salute from the seat of his copter as the vehicle took off.

"We're ready," announced Lou Stapley, who was in charge of the Beaters, who helped to keep the snakes in train by thrashing the undergrowth with flails or beating drums and cymbals.

Wranglers, very experienced riders, were in charge of each horse platoon. Their main concern was spotting the nervous rider who could panic his mount. Or a horse who suddenly decided he had had quite enough snake hunting in his lifetime.

Hrrula, one of the Reeves' oldest friends, was both the leader of Team Two and a Wrangler. "Everrryone is prrrepared," he assured them.

"Great," Todd said, checking them off on his list. All the preparations were falling together nicely.

"We've got the pass blocked toward the Launch Center," Jesse Dautrish said, scratching his jaw. "Let's hope it looks impassable to snake eyes. But it won't take long to clear it after the Hunt's over. The bridges have thorn barricades as well as mines, just in case the snakes try to cross the easy way." Though the snakes could swim, the banks of the rivers upstream were too sheer and deep for them to get a belly-hold. "I need another shower," he added, scratching his waist. "Damn dust settles in every pore."

Jesse's assistant, Hrrol, brushed at her short, tan fur, sending up clouds of dust. "All the charges are laid near rrrsidences and rranchess," she said. "Here's your copy back, Hrriss."

"Well done," Hrriss told the attractive Hrrol, and passed the list to Todd.

"Okay, okay," Todd said, calling the Hunters to order. "Let's go. Spread the word, we gather the Hunt at noon, and we'll ride out as soon as we get the word from the Sighters. Robin, see you at the feast later."

"Right, Todd!" called Todd's youngest brother, running for his horse. "Good hunting!"

Todd and Hrriss saddled their mounts and rode to the Assembly Hall to wait for the rest of Team One. Horses were still the primary form of individual transportation on the colony world. Doonan-bred horses were one of the colony's most important assets and trade goods, especially on Hrruban-settled worlds. Hrrubans were fascinated by the gentle quadrupeds, and were natural riders. The breeding of horses, rescuing the beloved animal from near extinction by careful genetic husbandry, was done on nearly every ranch on the planet, both Human and Hrruban. The Doonan style of saddle and bridle included gems and other valuable pieces easily obtained from the planet's generous storehouse of precious minerals.

The style, which echoed the formal wear of the Hrrubans themselves, seemed unbelievably ostentatious to denizens of Earth, to whom a single one of these gems represented additional comforts not yet purchased. When gems could be picked up in riverbeds and rift bottoms and polished with little effort by the finder, it was difficult for young Doonans to take the awe and greed over such trinkets seriously. Todd was proud of the way his gray gelding, Gypsy, looked in the new tack he'd made, aglitter with gilding and pretty stones, many of which had no commercial value, but some of which were worth enough alone to buy a change of status on Earth.

The colony folk had also rediscovered handcrafts. Doonan/Rralan crafts were so well thought of that goods of that origin commanded a good price off-world: pottery; needlecraft; weaving; stone, metal, and wood sculpture; jewelry; and leatherwork. An object made of the porous rla wood could be dyed in rainbow colors before it was painted with rlba sap to seal and harden it to the consistency of stone without the weight. Todd's saddle frame was made of rla, giving him a sturdy seat that required no effort for his mount to carry. He needed to travel light, because the Hunt was hours of hard riding.

Gypsy danced beneath him as other Hunters and their horses gathered around them on the common. The gray gelding had caught some of the excitement Todd was feeling. The hard work of the last two weeks was about to pay off. He and Hrriss exchanged grins of relief.

"Do you know, for a while I was afraid no one else was coming when the shuttles were late arriving?"

"Not coming!" the Hrruban echoed, mocking disbelief lighting his eyes. "Many spend the time between Hunts looking forward to the next one."

A slender horsewoman on an Appaloosa mare rode down the hill toward the square, standing in her stirrups and waving. Todd recognized the flame-bright hair on sight and vigorously waved back.

"Hey, Hrriss, Kelly made it back!"

"Good!" Hrriss said, raising his own long arm to return her salute. "One more good backup rrriderr to keep order among the aliens."

"Hey, gal, welcome home," Todd shouted when she was near enough to hear him over the pounding of Calypso's galloping hooves. "Mike said you were trying to make it in time for Hunt. And you haven't changed at all!"

She plumped back in the saddle, to signal the mare to halt, and eased her between Gypsy and Rrhee, Hrriss's mare. Now, grinning, she snapped her fingers, her expression mock-wistful. "Gee, and I worked so hard to create a new image."

"Don't bother," Todd replied, grinning back. "The one you got's not bad enough to put anyone off. Exactly."

"Oh, you! Hrriss, how are you?" and she turned to the Hrruban. "Heard you guys got drafted on that Hrrethan 'do.' "

Todd and Hrriss exchanged quick glances. How had Kelly heard of that? But then, she was an Alreldep trainee.

"Verry well," Hrriss answered, dropping his jaw. "The speeches lasted many hours. If it were not for the pleassure of having a functioning transportation grid, the people of Hrretha would most gladly have forgone the honor of having so many eminent speakers."

"Spacedep and Codep both sent representatives," Todd added. "I was a little surprised to see Varnorian there himself, instead of sending a deputy as Spacedep did."

"A good thing you went to keep them honest," Kelly said, making a face. "I've been hearing all about the two of you from my little cubbyhole in Alreldep block! You're considered to be quite a pair of heroes there."

Todd waved her words away embarrassedly.

"You must tell us all about your experriences, as soon as the Hunt is over," Hrriss said, showing his fangs in the widest Hrruban smile.

"Absolutely!" she promised them.

Kelly's mention of Alreldep brought back to Todd the full memory of his ship's passage into the interdicted zone around Hrrilnorr, and the fact that two weeks had gone by and there hadn't been the least hint that their "rescue" had been recorded, or even mentioned to the Treaty Council.

He would be interested to know if she had heard any rumors: especially one that might suggest the beacon had been planted by factions unsympathetic to the Doona Experiment. This was not the time to bring up such a sensitive topic. Riders needed their wits about them in the Hunt. Plenty of time to take her aside and get her reactions later on.

"That medical kit been renewed lately?" Todd asked her, nodding at the roll neatly strapped to the cantle.

"You bet. Mike made it up special," and Kelly gave him a wry sideways glance, "in case you fall off again!"

Todd snorted. "And when was the last time you saw me fall off?" he demanded in mock outrage.

"You have two to your credit," Hrriss said, his eyes narrowing slyly. "Did not Ken say it takes thrrree falls to make a rider?"

Todd laughed and patted his sides tenderly. "More like two hundred, friends."

The rest of Team One began to close up to the leaders. Two more old friends, Hrrin and Errala, from one of the distant Rralan villages, rode up behind and greeted them happily. The three shook hands with the Hrruban mates. Todd checked them off his list.

Places in the teams were always reserved for friends and friends of friends. The prestigious first six Hunter teams had to open further to admit high-powered guests whose inexperience sometimes tested the experience and skill of their hosts. But their presence meant a healthy contribution to the success of the Hunt and thus had to be tolerated.

Hrrubans and Humans in equal numbers joined the ride every year. Though Hrrubans required slight alterations to the standard saddle to accommodate the difference in their skeletal structure, they were keen on any opportunity to ride their beloved hrrsses. Ocelots, gifts to the Rralans from their Human friends, prowled alongside their masters' mounts, waiting for the signal to go. The spotted hunting cats were among the few animals that were fearless in the presence of snakes, and kept down other pests that troubled the settlements. The more skillful, working in teams of four or five, even brought down young snakes and killed them.

Hrrula skillfully guided his horse to join theirs, followed by the rest of Team Two. The sudden crowd caused Hrriss's two pet ocelots, Prem and Mehh, to go on guard. He swung off his mount to soothe them. Hrriss found that he did not recognize most of the Hrrubans who made up Team Two. They were undoubtedly visitors, probably from the new colony worlds. Hrrubans who lived on Rrala did not have such a wild, predatory look when discussing the Hunt, and those who still lived on Hrruba were revolted by the thought of slaying fresh meat. Though understandably excited about the pursuit and kill, Rralans were more concerned with staying alive throughout the Hunt. Hrriss calmed Prem, who seemed to have caught his agitation. The fierce little cats had been a gift from Todd and had already proved themselves in battle with the snakes. It seemed they were as eager as he was to confront them again.

Each team leader checked in with Todd as soon as he or she arrived in Assembly Square. Inessa, Todd's younger sister, hailed them from Team Six, waving a throwing stick. Hrriss poked his friend in the elbow and pointed to Inessa. They both waved. Since their older sister, Ilsa, had married and returned to Earth, Inessa and her two younger brothers, Dan and Robin, took it in turns every year to ride with the Hunt or help guard the family ranch. Hrriss, the only offspring of his parents, used to envy Todd his many siblings until he found that they regarded him as an extension of Todd.

Suddenly Todd groaned. "Will you look at that? Spare me!" He tossed his head in the direction of the Assembly Hall, to their left.

Obediently Hrriss and Kelly glanced that way. From the doorway, a young man swaggered out wearing the very latest in hunting pinks, and boots that had to have cost the equivalent of starfare between Earth and Proxima Centauri. He swung a six-foot length of polished wood between his fingers.

"Don't they ever read the advisories we send out on what kind of protective clothing to wear for rough riding?" Todd said in a low but disgusted tone.

"But, Todd, he's trying. I heard him tell me that he researched both hunting garb and polo accoutrements and decided on this compromise as being appropriate," Kelly said, her eyes brimming with devilment. "I heard him every mealtime, in fact."

"And you didn't warn him?" Todd shot her an aggrieved glance.

"What? And ruin our fun?"

"He was on the ssshuttle with you?" Hrriss asked.

"Indeed, and at my table. That, dear hearts," Kelly said, amused, sitting back in her saddle to watch their expressions, "is Jilamey Landreau, Spacedep's nephew. He's harmless."

"I'll give you any odds, Kelly dear old thing, that he's going to be trouble for whatever Team he's on," Todd said, summing up the stranger with a practiced eye, as Jilamey mounted the horse chosen for him with a modicum of expertise, though the quarterstaff proved an immediate encumbrance. "I don't like the stable he comes from."

"It is not the stable he comes from that should concern us, Zodd," Hrriss assured him, his eyes glinting mischievously, "and his trouble will be in conzrolling his hrrss. He will not be in our way."

"Ah, but he said he's on Team One," Kelly replied, delighted at the shock on Todd's face.

He fumbled for the Team list in his pocket. "I've got a J. Ladrulo . . . Oh, no."

"I wondered at him being on Team One," Kelly said, her face full of mischief. "I thought you knew what you were doing. However, don't worry about him. I'll make him my responsibility. I owe him a couple." Now her eyes took on a gleam similar to Hrriss's, her expression bland. "For aspersions cast like bread upon the surface of our table."

"You're mixing metaphors again," Todd said, ready for the banter they always enjoyed. "Didn't they teach you anything useful at Alreldep?"

"How to manage little men like Jilamey, sweetheart," she said, giving him a coy and insincere smirk. But she sighed as Jilamey urged his animal over to Todd and Hrriss.

He threw them a jaunty salute and banged the quarterstaff painfully against his knee. The horse snorted, flicking an ear at such an unusual appendage. " 'Lo, Kelly. Didn't think I'd have the pleasure of your company so soon again, much less with Team One. Jilamey Landreau, at your service. Nearly missed my chance—shuttle was late. I've heard all about your local menace. Read up on the subject, too. I'm expecting great things of this day. I want to catch a really big snake. I'm assured that you're the best. My friends"—he threw a sly glance over his shoulder at his ship companions—"could only get on Teams Three and Four."

And why he wasn't with them, instead of complicating Team One, Kelly did not know. She'd have a small talk with the village elders later, she assured herself. Punctiliously, she introduced Todd, Hrriss, Hrrin, and Errala to Jilamey. At least he had enough manners not to gawk at the Hrrubans.

"Landreau, you say?" Todd asked with cool courtesy. "Not any relation to Admiral Landreau, by any chance?"

"The Admiral's my uncle. That's why I got on your team." Jilamey grinned amiably.

"Isss zat so?" Hrriss said, taking up Todd's lead. "I find it amazing that he would perrmit one of his kin to take parrt in a Snake Hunt."

"Why not?" Jilamey appeared surprised. "Supposed to be the best hunting available."

"The Admiral told you that?"

"He didn't need to. Everyone knows that," Jilamey ingenuously assured them.

The three old friends exchanged glances. The boy couldn't possibly be so naive. Or was it simply that no one had ever dared tell him how his uncle was linked with the Doonan snakes? Quite possibly. The settlers had escaped Landreau's attempt to dispose of witnesses to his humiliation by driving a swarm of snakes down on the barn where he had imprisoned the colonists. He had never returned to Doona, nor would he have been welcome. It was amazing enough that his nephew had been allowed to come. However, now that Landreau was head of Spacedep, in charge of space exploration and defense, he was also not someone to antagonize. If his nephew had inveigled a place on Team One, there might be reasons not yet known to Todd and Hrriss. But it galled Todd to have to protect a Landreau from snakes. Inwardly he also winced at the comments likely being made by other teams about Team One.

"Read up on the Hunt, you say?" Todd asked.

"Everything I could find about the great snakes of Doona," Jilamey replied, grinning at everyone.

Could the fellow—Todd pegged him at the mid-twenties— really be so naive? Or was he disguising a covert assignment for his uncle with this behavior?

"Team One is only one of many, then, you realize. There are dozens of teams," and Todd gestured broadly to the various groups around the village green, awaiting the reports of Sighters. "Each team supports each other . . ." Jilamey nodded his head as Todd made each point. " . . . and we may be called upon to break off and go to another team's assistance if they're in trouble."

"But Team One takes the most chances, doesn't it?" And Jilamey looked anxious.

"Always," Hrriss assured him. "You will have the best of sporrrt with us!" His eyes glistened.

A Sighter's craft suddenly appeared and made an almost impossible swing to land in front of the Assembly Hall in a cloud of dust. The pilot leaned out of a hastily opened window.

"We've spotted the main swarm! They're starting to come out of the hatching ground! Should be due east of here in two, three hours at the most. We've left watchers with handsets in the brush along the way."

The announcement charged the atmosphere with eager antici-pation. Only the uninitiated shouted and whirled their horses in glee at the coming test of courage. Todd and Hrriss trotted their horses over to the man, demanding details. The snakes could move along with unbelievable speeds. The best way to minimize the danger to livestock and Human was to intercept the swarms as far to the north of the main settlements as possible.

Don and Jan, a husband and wife from one of the Amal-gamated Worlds colonies, galloped across the village green, slowing only when near the sled.

"I was afraid we wouldn't make it," Jan panted. "We rode all the way from the Launch Center."

"Your timing's as good as ever," Todd said. The pair were good friends to Doona. "We're just getting ready to go. You haven't missed a thing."

Don and Jan had moved up steadily from the other teams over the years, and were genuine assets to Team One. A slen-der woman woven out of whipcord, Jan was a fine rider who had worked with the rare horses on Earth, and also a skilled hand with lasso. Don had keen vision, and was a dead shot with a rifle. With their arrival, Team One's complement was filled. To Todd's relief, there were no more duffers assigned to them.

Team leaders made their way to preassigned positions, marked out on the maps Hrriss had distributed the night before. Transmitters of featherweight Hrruban design were now being handed out to riders. If anyone became lost or injured, he or she was to call for help immediately. No place could be guaranteed as safe from adolescent snakes.

"I don't want to carry a radio set," Jilamey complained when he was handed his unit.

"It doesn't weigh much," Kelly said, snapping hers to a belt hook.

"But I don't wear a belt with this garb. It spoils the sit of the jacket. I'm already wearing this silly safety helmet."

"Mr. Landreau," Todd said, resisting an impulse to tell the young fool simply to belt up and go home, "the transmitter is not elective wear. It could mean your life, or the safety of oth-ers." Could Landreau have deliberately planted this imbecile in the hopes that he'd be killed and the Admiral could blame

Doonans? Todd shook his head. That was too farfetched. He pointed a finger at Jilamey. "When you asked to hunt, you also signed an agreement, did you not, that you would abide by our rules?" Startled, Jilamey nodded. "If the sit of your jacket means more to you than your life, and others in this team, you don't have to wear the radio." Jilamey brightened. "But you'll have to stay in one of the snake blinds until it's over."

"Not a chance!" Jilamey protested, his eyes opening wide as he finally realized that Todd meant exactly what he said. "Oh, all right. I don't see what all the fuss is, anyway." With ill grace, he slung the transmitter belt bandolero-style across his chest.

The giant reptiles of Doona made their way to spawning grounds on the plains once a year, but for some reason returned from the sea along the river. They were fearsome to behold one at a time, but when they swarmed, as they did during this season, it was a sight beyond terror. The largest ones, "Great Big Mommy Snakes" in Doonan parlance, were the stuff of campfire stories to terrify small brothers and sisters on moonless nights. The most horrifying thing about the stories was that they were true. The snakes could reach lengths of twenty meters, with maws that could ingest a full-grown horse. Their smooth-muscled bodies were as large as tree trunks and covered by tough protective scales. Fortunately the snakes were not invincible.

Biologists had arguments over whether or not the snake stench stunned smaller creatures. Or whether, after all, the snakes were smart enough to hunt upwind of their intended prey. The young snakes, the two-year-olds, making their first return trip to the plains, were the most dangerous, because they weren't canny enough to avoid trouble. The small ones were only small by comparison. Even in their second year, they measured three meters, usually more. The combination of their youthful energy and inexperience and their pangs of wild hunger made them deadly adversaries. A young snake could bring down one of the fierce mdas all by itself. Weaker animals were snapped up as tidbits.

Doonans and Rralans had the advantage of knowing their terrain, the horses they rode, and of having witnessed many

Hunts. But for outworlders who arrived with more bravado than training, the objective could be fatal. The prey was tricky and very dangerous. The contest was even weighted somewhat on the side of the young snakes. After all, none of the Hunters were five meters long and muscled in every inch. Then some wit decided to add an extra fillip, awarding "coup" points for using the least technology or hardware possible in making the capture.

Every year, a few of the would-be heroes got hurt while trying to capture a young snake that was too big or too wily. Todd didn't remember who had started the newest nonsense, but it had come to be a big headache for him and the other Hunt team leaders. He sympathized belatedly with the original masters, who had been in charge when he passed the adulthood ritual himself years before. He had pulled off a highly pointed coup by using a fire-hardened lance and a garrote to finish off the snake, and carried home more eggs than anyone else that year.

Every ranch had its own defenders, well prepared with bazookas, rifles, even shoulder-mounted missiles to discourage reptiloid invasions. It was preferable to deter entry rather than kill. Some said that snakes remembered where they'd been deflected and stayed away.

The snake stench was fierce along the river embankment, where the snakes had passed on their way to the spawning ground. The Appaloosa mare rolled her eyes and twitched, but showed none of the other signs of hysteria displayed by the younger mounts. Kelly patted her neck and settled into the comfortable saddle. Kelly favored the style invented by the gauchos of old Earth, which protected rider from horse with layers of soft padding between each and the saddle frame. The fluffy sheepskin which Kelly bestrode on top of all made the contraption look heavy and ridiculous. In reality, it was lighter than most leather saddles, and held her so snugly it was almost impossible for her to fall off. She was grateful for her choice, feeling her tailbones where she had lost her saddle calluses. If she rode a day on leather now, after four years' absence, she'd be crippled for a week. Chaps, like the ones worn by Todd and most of the other Hunters, protected her legs from trees and scrub.

Fastened by her knees, she had two small crossbows, loaded with the safety catches on, and half a gross of quarrels, some of them explosive. She also had a spear with a crosspiece for protecting her hand at close quarters, and the traditional paint-capsule gun for marking troublesome snakes she couldn't reach, for the next teams to pick out.

Kelly noticed that Jilamey had an almost dainty-looking slug-throwing revolver slung on the horn as well as a number of the approved weapons and that cumbersome quarterstaff. Clicking her tongue at his naivete, Kelly smiled. Wait until he saw one of the Great Big Mommy Snakes. His pistol would do no more harm than flicking sand at a leviathan would.

They passed one of the snake blinds that lay next to the path. The reek of the citrus perfume, like citronella, was powerful enough to divert humans as well as snakes. Kelly was glad to see that the newer snake blinds were situated close to thick, climbable trees. If one of the Hunters got hurt, there was a quick haven available.

Above them, Saddle Ridge was nearly invisible through the trees. As soon as they reached a landmark rock, they turned inland away from the river path and cut through the forest into hilly grasslands. Todd was leading them up as close as possible to the dunes without breaking cover. Once the snakes finished laying their eggs, they headed in whatever direction they thought led to food on the way back to their territories. The job of the teams was to cut off their other options, riding alongside the bulk of the snake swarm, guiding it back to the sea without giving it a chance to stop.

"The safest thing," Todd reminded the guests, "is to expedite the snakes' passage. There's plenty for them to eat in the water. We try not to kill the snakes that are willing to go peacefully. We want the wild young ones that endanger other creatures. It'll be easy to pick out the rogues and mark them if we run with them. We have to keep our distance from the main group, though, or they'll just gang up on us and eat us all."

Kelly could almost have repeated his speech word for word. It was the same one he had been giving for years. She smiled impishly at his back, which he held straight in the saddle, wondering what he would do if she chimed in. She was fond of Todd, and equally fond of Hrriss. Of course it was nearly impossible to think of one without the other, they were so inseparable. A pity. She couldn't help but think that their united front was what had kept both of them single all these years.

Ahead of them, a streak of brown and gray as quick as a blink broke out of the undergrowth and showed them a patterned back. Jilamey let out a yell, and Errala jumped, making her horse dance back out of the way. The snake, a tiddler at four meters, seemed just as surprised to see them. It doubled in its own length and scooted back into the brush.

"That one is afraid of us," Hrriss said, holding up a hand to forestall pursuit. "It may already have eaten, or it has learned discretion in the last years."

"I always like a Hunt that begins with a well-fed one," Jan said grimly, calming her mount. The radio crackled into life: Teams Six and Seven were in pursuit of snakes that had left the spawning grounds in the opposite direction, but the majority were coming Team One's way.

More snakes followed the first one, but these attempted to slither past the horses without stopping. The snakes were normally solitary creatures, but at this particular moment of their life cycle, they did seem to understand safety in numbers. When pressed too closely, they split up and headed in several directions, hoping to elude pursuit. The team formed a wall with spears and flashing lights, heading off snakes and scaring them into the direction they wanted them to go. The Hunters and Beaters stationed along the way would repeat the actions, keep them moving toward the river route. Suddenly a Mommy Snake, not one of the GBMSs, but still more than respectable in size, appeared between the outcroppings of rock. It was followed by a swarm of smaller snakes that quickly outdistanced it.

Yelling into his radio, Todd wheeled his horse after them and kicked the animal to a canter. "We got some biggies on the road!"

The others followed, falling into position behind him. The team formed a cordon along the front edge of the swarm, following it downstream into the trees, keeping it contained with pain and noise. With the blunt end of spears, flashguns, whips, even brooms, they pushed, prodded, and drove the snakes back into line. The Hunters had to stay spread out, since their quarry ran anywhere between twice a man's height in length and fifteen meters long. A single snake could endanger several riders. Somewhere behind them, as the stream of reptiles advanced forward, Teams Two, Three, and Four were joining the wall of Hunters. The river acted as a natural barrier on the other side, saving manpower. Still more teams were spotted in the forests and meadows, driving stragglers that broke out between the teams where the Beaters' threshers couldn't go.

"Now we ride them into the sea," Jilamey crowed, brandishing the staff above his head like an Amerind he must have seen in the Archive Pictures.

"It is *not* that easy," Kelly yelled back, losing her composure at last. Really, Jilamey was just begging to be killed. Or thrown. His mount really didn't like all that brandishing.

A tiddler, probably returning from its first spawning, catching the scent of the lathered mare, slithered toward her with amazing speed. Calypso saw it coming and swapped ends to buck, lashing her hind feet out at it. Kelly hung on. Calypso might be accustomed to the stink but she retaliated in proper equine fashion to the direct assault. Landreau, thinking he was being heroic, spurred his mount toward it and slammed the staff down on its nose. Abruptly his horse ran backward as the tiddler reared up, ready to lunge forward, jaws wide and eager to swallow horse and rider in one gulp.

Cursing Landreau and her horse in one breath, Kelly swung Calypso about with the strength of her legs alone and leveled one of her crossbows at the predator. The snake was all bunched to strike when Kelly discharged the bolt. She'd lost none of her marksmanship in her four years away. The quarrel struck right through the creature's forehead. Sheer momentum kept the snake moving toward its prey while Jilamey's terrified mount managed incredible speed backward until it was jarred to a halt by a tree. Then, with a squeal of fear, the horse jumped off its hocks to one side and took off in a panicked run, Jilamey clinging desperately to his saddle. Then the tiddler fell sideways, a wavy line that quickly disappeared under the mass of snakes. No doubt one of the other reptiles would stop and eat the corpse while it was still twitching. Team Two or Three would have to deal with it.

Kelly and Calypso resumed their position as they passed one of the pairs of margin Hunters, who waved them a salute with spear and flashgun. They were positioned well, on a small natural upthrust of rock overlooking the well-worn river path. The snakes disappeared from Kelly's view briefly as the Hunters looped around the far side of the ridge and the snakes followed their own old road. It was to the Hunters' advantage that their quarry preferred to slither on smooth dirt and stone rather than over the uneven floor of the jungle. Kelly guided Calypso among the huge, ridged rla trees, keeping her eye on the young snakes. Before and behind her, flashguns popped, distracting the snakes who might break out of line.

Snarling yips and growls erupted behind them, amid the sound of two horses whinnying in fear. Kelly risked a quick glance over her shoulder. One of the bigger reptiles was coming up behind them, followed by a pair of horses crashing through the undergrowth. Two of the Hrruban visitors from Team Two had earmarked a Mommy Snake and were riding it down, without regard for the organization of the Hunt or their own safety. They wore only their equipment belts and helmets, without a stitch of clothing over their furred limbs and tails to protect against the branches whipping at them.

Their quarry had slipped out of line and was now on the outside of the Hunters' cordon. The experienced riders in Team One knew that the snake was only waiting to get far enough ahead of its pursuers to turn about and strike. Hrrubans had superlatively fast reflexes, but they were slow as falling snowflakes compared with the teeth and coils of a Mommy Snake. Only experience countered speed.

The snake was tiring. The species was made for sprinting and quick striking, not long-distance runs, and it had recently laid its eggs. The Hrrubans had probably surprised it coming directly off the hot sands through the narrow gap. It was in search of a wider place where it could make a stand. Kelly didn't like the situation she could see developing. Couldn't the Hrrubans see that those meter-wide jaws could engulf one or both of them?

Todd turned his head and exchanged glances with Hrriss. The Hrruban abruptly edged his horse out of the line and slipped between and ahead of the two endangered Hunters.

Kelly was sure she hadn't seen either one of the leaders lift
his radio. It was this sort of instantaneous cooperation which
gave them their reputation for telepathy. Todd raised his rifle
to his shoulder and fired.

He was using an explosive shell. The shot went off against
the ground in front of the Mommy Snake. It slid to a rapid halt
in a heap of coils to see what had kicked up the dirt just as
Hrriss gathered himself in his saddle and sprang.

It was an amazing leap. He landed on the back of the snake's
neck. Its head went up to dislodge him, but he had sunk in
his claws, the advantage Hrrubans had over Hayumans. Kelly
judged the creature to be a good fifteen meters long, and the
snapping teeth were as long as her hand. The Hrruban would
be just a mouthful if he slipped. With one strong arm and his
prehensile tail wound around the snake to hold on, Hrriss took
the knife from his belt. The snake was unable to reach him with
its teeth, but it had miles of muscled coils upon which it could
call. It bucked and twisted, trying to dislodge him. A length
of tail snapped around Hrriss's leg and squeezed. The Hrruban
let out a snarl of pain and hung on. Kelly came level with him,
then rode past him, looking over her shoulder in horror. She
found she was riding next to Todd, who had slowed down.

"I'm going back," Todd called, wheeling his horse. "Keep
the line in order."

"Right! Quick kill, Todd," Kelly replied. She turned her eyes
forward. Behind her, she could hear Todd barking directions
to the other two Hrrubans on how to attack the snake without
further endangering Hrriss.

Jan and Don had spread out to make up for the short-
age in personnel. Don was on the radio to the other teams,
keeping track of the stragglers who strayed out of the cordon. He waved encouragement to Kelly, as did the other
two members of Team One. Then Jilamey drew level with
her, babbling something, his sweaty face red with excitement. Did he think he needed to help Hrriss and Todd? Idiot! She waved him on, to fill in the line behind Don. She
lifted her radio to her ear and picked up field coordination
where Todd had left off. He and Hrriss were already out of
sight. They'd handle the Mommy: they were clever Hunters.

Todd galloped his horse back to where the Mommy Snake coiled and writhed, trying to dislodge Hrriss. Hrriss's now-riderless horse, cannoning between the others, had scattered the two strange Hrrubans' mounts in opposite directions, keeping them from reaching the Mommy Snake's open maw, and probably saving their lives, though the ungrateful Hunters would be unlikely to realize it.

Hrriss clung to the nape of the great reptile's neck, even though his leg had to be paining him. Repeated thrusts of his knife blade were scattering drops of ichor as the snake flung its head from side to side, trying to get rid of the agonizing pest on its back. Hrriss kept on striking powerful blows but the snake almost seemed to anticipate his targets and he hadn't hit anything vital yet. The blade bit again.

The great length of the snake coiled and writhed in fury. The two Hrrubans who were responsible for this disaster controlled their hysterical horses at a distance from the giant reptile, watching Hrriss, clearly not knowing what to do. Todd cursed. The Hunt was against killing any of the wildlife that hadn't gone rogue. Once one had gone berserk, the Doonans had no choice but to kill it to save their own lives. It was just like these senseless strangers to incite one to terminal frenzy and then sit back to watch the fun. No, that was unfair—they really didn't know what one of these snakes was capable of. But that wouldn't help his friend.

By now, Hrriss's two ocelots had joined the battle, tearing at the snake's sides to help their master. Long gouges were ripped from the skin, oozing ichor that was churning dirt into a hideously viscous mud. The snake bent its powerful neck to try and bite at the two little pests on the ground, but as it bent for one, the other would rake at it from the other side, turning its attention away.

Recognizing that he was unlikely to get a clear shot at the head of the furiously thrashing snake, Todd put up his rifle and reached for the lasso. He began whirling the rope just above Gypsy's head, keeping the noose small enough so as not to tangle in the branches above him. Despite his care the rope snagged on a bush and he had to start over.

Shouts alerted him that Team Two was closing in on them, following the next flux of snakes very near to the river path.

Out of the corner of his eye, Todd could see that one of the riders had his own rope circling above his head, just shy of the canopy of leaves. Hrrula shouted to show he was ready. Hrriss ducked as low as he could go against the snake's back without flinging himself into its coils. Teeth gritted, Todd gave the signal, and both of them threw at once. As soon as the other man's noose dropped over the snake's head, he yanked back on his horse's reins, causing the animal to dig in its hooves in the soft mold and pull the rope taut. Todd pulled back, too, and the snake fought between the two lines, unable to reach either of its mounted tormentors. Struggling wildly, the snake released Hrriss's foot. The Hrruban grabbed hold of one of the ropes with a clawed hand and slashed repeatedly at the reptile's throat with his blade. It flung loops of itself forward to protect its vulnerable underjaw but not soon enough. Too much damage had been done by Hrriss's blade. Its loops lost strength and its head hung in the nooses, dying.

One of the strange Hrrubans, evidently deciding that the danger was over, rode forward and plunged his spear through one of the snake's eyes into its brain. The writhing of the coils became more frenzied, and gradually died into infinitesimal twitches. Todd let his rope drop slack and started to gather in the lengths, urging his horse forward with his knees.

The Hrruban visitor's triumphant cry echoed through the forest.

"I have killed the great one!" he crowed, flexing his claws over his head.

"The kill is Hrriss's," Todd said flatly. Hrriss was beginning to climb free. Todd swung off his horse to help him to his feet. Hrriss signalled that he was not seriously hurt, though he was favoring the leg. "If he had not acted when he did, the results might have been very serious for you."

On Hrrula's hissed orders, a Team Two rider went off into the brush to retrieve Hrriss's horse. He reappeared shortly, leading Hrriss's Rrhee, then rode off to rejoin his own team, now far ahead in the jungle. Hrriss spoke softly to calm the ocelots, mad with bloodlust, who were still tearing at the twitching corpse of the snake.

"But I plunged the spear through its brain! It is dead, by my hand. I claim the kill," the visitor insisted.

Todd let his eyes meet those of the strange Hrruban. The visitor possessed a very broad back stripe, indicating that he held a position of rank in Hrruban society.

"With the greatest of respect," Todd said, dropping into full formal Hrruban which forced him to suppress the fury he felt, "there can be no doubt that the creature was already dying when you rode forward."

The broad stripe was somewhat taken aback by his host's use of the formal language. Since that was used only during events of the greatest importance, it was ingrained in the Hrruban not to disagree with the speaker without considerable forethought. Hrrula, an old ally of Todd's, waited silently nearby.

"Perhaps we will discuss the matter later," Todd said politely, gesturing to the Team Two leader. "We must complete the Hunt. Time is pressing."

"Quite right, honored guests," Hrrula said, having slathered the snake slashes and scale pinches with vrrela salve. "With your permission, Zodd Rrev, we must catch up with our team. We are needed." Before the strangers could protest, the Hrruban grabbed the rein of one of the horses and pulled it after him. The animal obediently followed the lead mount. In a moment, all three of them were out of sight.

Todd mounted up again. He sent a concerned glance toward Hrriss. "There's a snake blind only a hundred meters ahead, if you need a rest."

"I am all right," Hrriss assured him. "Truly. There is no real damage. The circulation will return to the leg in a short time. It could have been worse."

"Could have been much worse," Todd said. Then, with a wicked grin, he added, "It could have been your tail!"

"Team Three leaving the spawning grounds," his radio announced. "They're moving slow this year. Vic just herded a couple of tiddlers that were trying to leave the grounds from the wrong side. Look out for 'em. They're mad."

"Fardles!" Todd put his heels to his horse. Hrriss's episode had taken only a few minutes from start to finish.

The sound of hoofbeats pounding up behind her made Kelly swivel about in concern. One, no, two horses returning. She relaxed and smiled as Todd and Hrriss passed her.

"Hrriss did it in!" Todd called. Hrriss was leaning to the right, obviously favoring his left leg. "Good kill. Mommy Snake! Fifteen and a half meters or I'll eat it. But he'd better not get a big head, or he won't get through the trees!"

"You're lucky to be alive," Kelly said to Hrriss, at the same time pulling a face at Todd. "That was a magnificent tackle! I hope those two Hrrubans realize you saved their lives."

"Those foolish ones were made to understand that by Zodd," Hrriss assured her, his tail tip lashing to one side of his saddle. The others cheered and shouted encouragement to him as he resumed his place in the line. Todd moved ahead and raised his radio on high as a signal to move out. Kelly told the other team leaders that Todd was in charge again and clipped her own box to her belt.

They were moving swiftly up on the most dangerous part of the Hunt. The team was about to leave the jungle and move out on featureless grasslands. Without the trees to restrict them, the snakes often attempted to escape from their shepherds and go in search of landbound food. The task of keeping the swarm together the rest of the way was made more difficult by the local landowner.

Twenty-five years ago, when the Treaty allowed more Humans in, to match the Hrruban population, Codep had added four families to the original eleven in the First Village. The Boncyks were one of those four. In spite of warnings from the established colonists that the snakes used this area as a thoroughfare twice a year, Wayne claimed the fertile plain not far from the marsh for his family's holdings. On top of that disregard for local wisdom, the Boncyks compounded their problems by running herds of cattle and teams of pigs, China and Poland. Naturally the snakes, especially the hungry tiddlers, found the smell of live meat irresistible. The larger ones, with the larger hungers, would go berserk if the wind shifted to tantalize them with the odor of edibles.

To prevent wholesale slaughter, this was when the teams had to be most alert. The Hunters were already tired. Fortunately the snakes were wearing out, too, but they became more cantankerous and tricksy. Once the tantalizing Boncyk farmlands were past, the salt marshes were not far, and once the snakes reached them, they would disperse while the teams remained on guard to drive back any who might decide to return to dry land—and fat cows and pigs. When the last of the snakes were back in the salt marshes, hunting the rodents, waddlers, waders, and other such tidbits, the Hunt would be declared over and the triumphant teams would return to the village common, except for the skeleton force that remained on guard until the next morning.

Jilamey had had his eye on a pair of young adolescent snakes almost since he rejoined the run. With the bare treetops of the marsh wood in sight, he was going to have to move quickly to capture his quarries before they vanished into the fetid waters. Kelly watched him measuring the distance to the edge of the marsh.

With a now-or-never expression on his face, Landreau spurred his horse toward the pair. He had his quarterstaff well balanced in his right hand, confident that he could knock the snakes on their blunt skulls, stunning them, and secure them alive.

In theory, it was a good idea. However, it failed utterly to take into account the nature of snakes. As soon as Jilamey thumped one of the fleeing tiddlers in the back of the head with the heavy staff, it turned. As quickly as patterned lightning grounding through a rod, the snake swarmed up the quarter-staff, hissing furiously. It wrapped its wrist-thick coils around Jilamey's arm and struck at him. The long, white teeth snapped on nothing as the youth ducked and thrashed at his assailant.

Letting her crossbow dangle, Kelly drew her knife and kicked Calypso to the rescue. The snake struck again, this time penetrating flesh. With a screech that ascended into the soprano register, Jilamey warded off the snake and started clubbing the reptile over the head with the butt of his little gun, which he had grabbed in desperation. To the surprise of those observing the fracas, the snake dropped limp across the saddlebow. In the berserk frenzy of panic, Jilamey kept battering the twitching body even after the others had called to him to stop.

"Now, don't that beat all!" Don exclaimed, laughing. "That micro-sized popgun did some good, after all!"

"Well, gather him up before he slides off your lap!" Kelly ordered Jilamey, reining in next to him and expertly digging her fingers for a firm hold on the slippery scales. With her free hand, she fumbled for a snake bag and passed it over. "I don't think you remembered one of these. Cram it in and be sure you tie the neck of the sack as tight as possible. They've been known to wiggle free if they've any space."

"I did it, didn't I? I captured one!" Jilamey's red face was now suffused with incredulous triumph and his voice broke a bit on the "captured."

"If you remember to get it in the bag," Hrrin called, teeth showing under his feathery brown moustache. Although excitement made his hands shake, Jilamey managed to stuff the limply uncooperative and slithery coils of snake into the bag and securely fastened the tie. "Congratulations. You're halfway there!" Hrrin added.

Still holding the bag, Jilamey looked about him, not certain what to do with his prize. Jan took pity on him and helped him secure it to the saddle on rings embedded in the saddle tree for just such a purpose. Eyes shining, Jilamey galloped to rejoin Team One. Jan followed more sedately, an indulgent grin on her face.

Just inside the boundaries of his ranch, Wayne sat on his horse, flanked by his wife, Anne, and their eldest son. Nearby, on a pair of nervously curvetting horses, were Wayne's guests for the Hunt, a couple from the Hrruban home world. They were all armed with crossbows with explosive quarrels, ready to deal with any reptiles escaping from the cordon. The younger Boncyk hefted a bazooka on his right shoulder while his horse shifted under him, trying to balance itself against the weight. Wayne posed another problem to the teams: he was a notoriously bad shot. He had a tendency to detonate the ground right in front of a Hunter's horse more often than the snake it was pursuing. Todd's horse had been spooked by one of Wayne's bombs the year before, dumping him in the pigpens, so he kept one wary eye on the stockman as they passed him.

Kelly could feel the wind shifting as they came up the hill. That was the worst thing that could happen. Instead of a following breeze that swirled the heady snake musk around them, a new stench filled the air, as potent as snake, blindingly putrid as well as sickly sweet.

"Faugh," Kelly said, averting her head and wondering if it would do any good to jerk her scarf over her nose.

"Oh, no," Todd groaned. "Pig air!"

Not only pig was in the air but also the delectable aroma of livestock, blown directly from the Boncyk herds and teams into the noses of ravenous snakes. In a maneuver as planned as a dress parade, the snakes turned, a great river of rippling, leaf-patterned hide across the Hunters' cordon, rolling uphill toward the farm buildings. With no river, hill, or wood between the snake thoroughfare and the farm, there were no barriers to deflect the snakes' inexorable approach.

The moment the pig stink came his way, Todd called for the Sighter crafts to pick up Lures and make a drop near the marsh in an attempt to divert the main bulk of the reptiles. Then he called for any available Beaters and Hunters. The teams spread themselves out across the field to try and contain the flow and regain control. Kelly could hear the screaming farm animals, their cries reaching up the scale to pure panic. They seemed to sense their danger despite the shift of the wind. Boars might have stood and faced the reptiles, but not the gentler China and Poland pigs who were milling about their sturdy pens with no refuge from the approaching menaces. Even if the pressure of the terrified animals broke down the pen bars, they hadn't the speed to outrun snakes. The only hope of saving them was to head the snakes off again, with full firepower if need be, before they reached the pens.

"Stop them!" Boncyk called, galloping up, waving his crossbow. "My pigs!"

"Damnit, Wayne, you've been told year after year to get those pigs out of here before spawning season!" Don snapped.

"The sows are farrowing this month! I can't move them when they're birthing; they're too set in their ways."

"They're not the only ones," Don grumbled under his breath, but Kelly heard him and grinned.

The stockman and his retinue galloped after Team One, haranguing Todd all the way. Todd had one object in mind: to stand between the threatened sties and the onrush of snakes, firing to turn them away. It was unlikely that they could save all the animals, but he meant his team to try.

The wooden enclosures were too far apart and too big for the Hunters to surround. The team hauled their horses to a halt, giving them a breather as they assessed the best vantage points before the swarm arrived.

Todd and Hrriss decided that they'd best guard the narrow path between the two barns that lay between the snakes and their prey. Bottling them up in that space would make them easier to turn, with some scud bombs to halt them and give the ones behind pause. The older and bigger snakes were smart enough to sense the danger of such tight quarters and turn back to look for easier pickings in the marshes.

Wayne and his family flanked the edges of the buildings, concentrating on the reptiles who would avoid the main route and try to slip around. Still watching the way the wind blew, Kelly realized that the wind carrying the pigs' scent was blowing directly toward the worn pathway, and not back into the main mass of reptiles. If the wind shifted, they'd be surrounded in minutes. And goodbye, Boncyk Bacon.

The defiant screams of the team's horses echoed off the high walls to either side of them. The slower-moving snakes were nearly there. Kelly had never noticed before what a terrifying sound their bellies made, slithering on the dry grass. Oh, a single snake could be silent when it was sneaking up on its prey, but dozens and hundreds of them made the grass hiss beneath them.

"Don't worry about tiddlers," Todd cried. "It's the big ones that we need to turn back. They can swallow a sow whole."

"Here! I need help here!" Anne Boncyk shouted from behind the grain barn. She galloped into sight, waving an empty crossbow. "There's a mess of them sneaking around the barn!" Kelly swiveled her head. Two of the infiltrators were lying contentedly in the gravel, engulfing the bodies of their deceased comrades without a care for the crossbow quarrels sticking straight up, but half a dozen others were making straight for the farrowing pens.

With a sharp command, Hrriss sent his ocelots to Anne's rescue. Gathering their haunches, the spotted cats pounced onto the back of the two largest reptiles, four meters long, and dragged them thrashing like severed air hoses out of the pens. With a quick bite behind the flat heads, the cats dispatched their prey and went for two more. The respite gave Anne time to reload both her crossbows.

A young reptile, only about three meters long, whipped between the team's horses. Three spears jabbed for it all at once, but all missed their mark.

"Damn!" groaned Don, and shouted over his shoulder, "Anne, a three-meter coming through!"

"No, I'll take it!" Jilamey said. "I gotta get two." He wheeled his horse about and pursued the young snake.

Rolling his eyes at such bravado, Todd gestured for Kelly to follow Landreau. If the boy had been sent to embarrass Doona by getting killed in the Snake Hunt, Todd was determined the plan would fail. Jilamey had managed the first catch, somehow, but anything could happen here, with snakes all too close to valuable stock.

At first, the snake was too intent on catching its meal to realize it was being pursued. Jilamey drew his miniature gun and shot at its back. He hit it square, but the low-caliber slug just bounced off the scaly hide. But the snake felt the impact and turned to see what had hit it. Seeing Jilamey bearing down, it slowed a trifle.

Encouraged, Jilamey galloped at it, trusty quarterstaff poised above his head. "Yeee-hah!" he yelled, bringing the long stick down on the snake. It was a good, solid hit. The snake stopped dead and compressed itself into a hurt knot. Jilamey had learned a lesson during his previous misadventure. Before the snake could get a coil about the staff, he discarded it and reached for the crossbow.

He never got a chance to use it. The snake sprang around the horse's leg, lashing out with its tail to encircle a hind leg and bring the animal, and rider, down. The horse, instinctively lashing out behind, then reared and stumbled, falling across a young Mommy Snake which had broken through the cordon. The Mommy was stunned and the tiddler got mashed. Todd and Gypsy came round the corner, chasing the Mommy, Todd with his crossbow cocked. If Jilamey fell now, the Mommy would take him in one gulp.

. But Jilamey's mount was an old campaigner, and once he felt his legs free, he danced backward as fast as he was able until he was stopped by the rails of the sty, where once again he reared, striking out with his front legs. The Mommy reared up, too, just as Jilamey, roaring commands at the rearing horse, slid off its rump, over the rails and straight into the sty, landing with a splat on his back in the muck.

"Augh!" the youth cried, flailing his arms and legs. "Help me! I can't get up!"

Jilamey couldn't see the danger he was still in, with the tiddler rousing from its mauling, and the Mommy equally interested in this convenient quarry. Todd shot a defensive charge under the Mommy's tail: pain and noise alarmed it enough to divert its path so that it swerved into the tiddler. A second explosive burst in front of them, and both shot away, Todd in pursuit.

Trying very hard not to laugh, Kelly swung off Calypso and, keeping a good hold on the reins, reached through the fence rails into the pen. It took an effort, but she got the young man to his unsteady feet and guided him back onto solid ground.

"You're out of the race, Master Landreau," Kelly said, trying not to take a deep breath. The sour miasma of pig excrement made her gag. Calypso kept backing away from the stench, pulling Kelly's arm nearly out of the socket. "Unless you can clean up real quick someplace."

As Jilamey, disgust and horror contorting his features, tried to scrape muck off his body, Kelly managed to catch his horse and then had trouble getting the horse to approach its erstwhile rider.

"My snake? My second snake? What happened to it?" And to Kelly's surprise, he started to run back to the place of his near demise, darting about, looking for the reptile.

"That one's long gone, Jilamey."

"But what'll I do?" Jilamey looked so pathetic that Kelly nearly laughed aloud.

"What we do is get you to the nearest blind and check you for cuts. You don't want muck-infected wounds, I assure you."

"But I've got to get the second one," Jilamey insisted.

"Like that?"

He tried to approach his horse, who kept backing away snorting.

"It's not far to the nearest blind, Jilamey. We'll clean you up and maybe then the horse'll let you on him."

"But they're all going that way!" he said, dazedly looking back at the melee in the Boncyk yard. More riders were reinforcing Team One by that time, and the pigsties were well cordoned off from the snakes. "I must have my second snake."

"You're lucky you got one!" she said, beginning to lose patience. "And we've got to clean you up. Then at least you can *ride* back to town."

The prospect of walking that far clearly won his attention. So, while Kelly on Calypso led his horse, they made their way to the nearest snake blind, which was not far away, but back in the woods away from the Boncyk farmyard. As she led him, she hoped that his stench would not entice a tiddler or Mommy to investigate his delightfulness. On the way, they met the backup riders who were going out to help Todd.

"He took a fall," Kelly said, over and over again, as her friends threw her puzzled glances. "Good hunting! Good hunting!" Wish I could finish it with you, she thought. Nerd-sitting is such a nuisance. Having to sit a Landreau was close to insult in her lexicon.

Once the four spectators inside the tiny building got a whiff of Jilamey, there was no way he would be given room. Not even the heavily scented hunting box could overcome the odor clinging to the young man. There was, however, a barrel of rainwater just outside and it was the will of the many that Jilamey might have use of all of it. As there was no window on that side of the blind, he went outside and stripped off his sodden clothing. When he was safely inside the barrel, Kelly took a shovel and scooped up the stinking remains of the once sporty outfit. She left the knee boots because her brother knew how to neutralize the odor on leather. Spare clothes were donated and a sort of a towel, and pretty soon, Jilamey, smelling considerably more like a Human, was allowed back into the blind.

Then Kelly could check for wounds. Once the muck had been scraped off, she found several. Nothing major, but scrapes, one shallow cut, and many bruises, the worst of which blossomed on his left cheek and ear. If it hadn't been for the regulation helmet, he might have crushed his skull on the fence post.

"I have never had anything like that happen to me in my life," Jilamey said, over and over, as she dabbed at his injuries with disinfectant and rubbed a styptic to stop the bleeding. "I thought that snake was going to eat me!"

"You were a very handy morsel," Kelly replied, carefully smearing vrrela from her medical kit on the scrapes. She reached for one of the flasks at her belt. "But Todd doesn't allow snakes to feed on his team members. Have a drink of this."

Jilamey uncorked the mlada and took a tentative sip. He followed that taste with a more enthusiastic tot and sighed happily as the warmth of the liquor hit.

"Not too much," Kelly warned him, taking the flask away and recorking it. "It's strong."

"Strong is what I need right now," he pleaded. "One more?"

"Well . . ." Kelly studied him and decided what he'd been through was worth one more drink. His bruises would probably hurt more as they developed.

"All right," she said, pouring him another.

"Todd saved my life," Jilamey remarked thoughtfully. He sat up on the edge of that remark and winced, settling back again in the low chair. "My uncle, the Admiral, has always held a poor opinion of the Reeve family, though he never says why. Even when I asked him after I knew I was going on this Hunt. I shall tell him how wrong he is. If he had seen Todd today, he'd be ever, ever so impressed."

"Todd was only doing his duty as team leader," Kelly said carefully. She was amused as Jilamey had regained his affected manner of speech as soon as he was comfortable again. "But he is quite an impressive person."

"I agree!" Jilamey said, both hands clutching the small hammered metal cup. "It was most daring of him to sweep down like that, right in the face of the G—what did you call it?"

Kelly smiled to herself. Undoubtedly he would regale his friends endlessly about his Snake Hunt. He might even tell the truth. It certainly wouldn't hurt Todd's reputation to have the story go around. "GBMS. It stands for Great Big Mommy Snake. Nearly all of the big ones that come out for spawning are the females."

"And he drove them both off just before they could reach me. He saved my life. I admire him ever so. I know better than to believe everything my uncle has been saying about his family. He's wrong when he says that Reeve is out of his element here, and should be returned home for his own good. If the father is at all like the son, well, I've never seen anyone better suited to a wild venue." The young man chuckled self-deprecatingly. "Certainly I'm not. I know I'll only play at it the odd weekend or two." He raised his eyebrows entreatingly and extended the cup toward Kelly. She had been listening intently ever since Jilamey had mentioned his uncle.

"Oh, well, one more won't hurt you," she said, pretending reluctance, but eager to hear more. She poured the cup full. "It's all organic, you know." Any gossip about the great Landreau interested all Doonans personally. Having just returned from Earth, she was more aware than most of the tensions surrounding the upcoming Treaty Renewal, and the disagreement between the factions pro and con. "So what did your uncle think of you coming here for the Snake Hunt, Jilamey?"

CHAPTER

3

THE WRITHING, SQUIRMING CARGO WAS HAULED back triumphantly to the center of the Human settlement. Hunters who had successfully passed their rite of passage with the capture of two snakes were congratulated and toasted with splashes of mlada, some of them directed internally. With understandable satisfaction, Todd saw the two Hrrubans who had endangered Hrriss ride back into the square, hunched over their saddlebows in pain. They had the telltale swellings or rroamal inflammation under the fur on their arms and legs. At some point on their wild ride they had passed through trees bearing the toxic vines. Because the inflammation wasn't far advanced, a quick application of vrrela would swiftly cure the agony, but Todd couldn't help but think of their suffering as a measure of justice.

The heavenly smell of cooking greeted them all. Meat was turning on spits in roasting pits, which were also filled with freshly picked corn on the cob and newly dug potatoes. The combined aromas made the returning Hunters half frantic with hunger.

"Not a bite until you clean up!" Pat Reeve shouted at her dust-covered son. Todd grinned and pointed to the carcasses of the small snakes thrown across the rump of his horse. She returned the grin and held up her joined hands over her head as a gesture of victory. The snakes' meat would be thrown into a savory stew to simmer with root vegetables and fresh herbs. Some of the traditions of Snake Hunt were a lot more delicious than others.

"Where's Mrrva?" Todd called back over the clamor. "Hrriss got his leg squeezed by a Mommy Snake."

Pat's eyes widened in concern. "She's inside," she said, gathering up the small carcasses and hurrying toward the door. "I'll warn her. You get him inside."

Hrriss protested that he was all right. "I have been pressed worse between my hrrss's body and the stable wall," he pleaded.

"Come on." Todd ignored his friend's protests, knowing that the leg had to hurt a lot more than Hrriss was letting on. He helped Hrriss off Rrhee and shepherded him toward the Hall. "If your mother doesn't kill me for neglecting you, mine will."

Once Hrriss was in the capable hands of his mother, Mrrva, Todd checked on the other members of his team.

The hunting parties, still congratulating each other, finally separated to wash and dress for the upcoming celebratory banquet. Medics took charge of the injured. There were numerous wounds and bruises due to inexperience with the vegetation of Doona/Rrala and a long horseback ride.

Nonparticipants clamored for firsthand stories and adventures from the heroes, and sympathized with the disappointed Hunters who had returned empty-handed. Todd congratulated several young friends who had passed their ritual, and checked on the various small wounds that some of his team members and friends had sustained. There had been no deaths in any team during this Hunt. The unusually hot weather had somewhat slowed the snakes' usual split-second reflexes. Todd felt they'd been extraordinarily lucky, considering how many amateurs had ridden out. He walked Gypsy and Rrhee down to the paddock to unsaddle and turn them loose, enjoying the post-Hunt atmosphere, listening to everyone comparing brags about the size of the ones that got away. Soon, he was able to work his way to his own quarters and the long-awaited and much-needed shower.

There were preparations for the usual all-out blast of a party going on in the Assembly Hall. It was the biggest building on Doona/Rrala, bar the Archives Building on the Treaty Island. It lay on the Human side of the Friendship Bridge halfway between the new construction which replaced the first Human village and the first Hrruban village. It took the place of the much smaller mess hall, which had been the chief building of the original settlement. The support beams and wide windows of the Hall were of extruded plastic, but the white walls and roof were formed of the same sealed-rla wood as the bridge. The many ornaments and statuary on and within its walls had been donated by craftspeople from both races and every village on the planet. It was surrounded by gravel walks and pathways that rambled in a pleasing knotlike pattern among gardens containing rare plants from Earth and Hrruba, proudly maintained by volunteer gardeners. During other times of the year than Snake Hunt, the entire sentient population of the planet could fit within the walls of the Assembly Hall or in its landscaped grounds, for speeches or celebrations. The Hall doubled as the social center whenever visitors came.

The five days following each Snake Hunt were designated by Doonans as New Home Week, recreating an Earth custom of reunion, but as Dot McKee, one of the senior settlers, pointed out, for their new home, instead of their old one. If at all possible, everyone returned home for New Home Week. Unless they were on exploration missions, no great effort was required of the Hrruban settlers, for every Hrruban had access to transportation grids. But the Human Rralans had to make sacrifices of time, effort, and money. Either way, both species came home some way or other. So Kelly hoped to see several of her primary-school chums back from long-term exploration missions for Spacedep and the colonizing arm of the Hrruban government. She hoped that Todd's brother, Dan, would be among them. Right now, she had to find Todd and report what Jilamey had said.

The Doona/Rrala Ad Hoc Band was tuning up in a corner of the Assembly Hall when Kelly entered. She smiled at Mrs. Lawrence, the leader of the band, and then began to circulate. The Hall had been beautifully decorated for the feast. Floating wicks burned in glass sconces containing scented oil. The sconces hung on the walls between bright festival decorations. Long tables draped with white embroidered cloths had been set up perpendicular to the head table on its dais. Kelly wandered about, searching for Todd and Hrriss, and finally saw them sitting together at the opposite end of the Hall. Hrriss glanced up and caught her eye to wave her over.

"Who'd ever guess you've been chasing snakes! Give us a twirl!" Todd said. "Very pretty!" he added approvingly, as she executed a neat turn on her heel to show off her dress.

She'd brought it specially for tonight, a confection of shimmering blue and gold with a fluffy knee-length skirt. "Glad you approve, citizen," Kelly replied pertly, ducking into a graceful curtsy. "I'll have you know that this is the very latest style from Earth in evening informal—to distinguish from casual, which this most definitely is not. Notice please the wide skirt, to show an insouciant disregard for the tightness of Corridors and Aisles. The very height of fashion, or should I say width? Can I sit down or is there something else I'm supposed to do right now?"

Todd gave a snort. "We do the Hunt. Others do the food," he said. "Mother, Mrrva, and Mrs. Hu have that in hand." He reached out and, grabbing her hand, neatly pulled her onto the bench beside them.

"Hrriss, is your leg all right?" Kelly asked, wondering if that was why the pair were so indolent in the busy Hall. She saw no bandage, though she caught the astringent odor of vrrela.

"Oh, zat!" Hrriss dismissed it with a negligent click of lightly extended claws. "It was nozzing, as I told Zodd. I am only bruised. We are sorry to have missed you on the rest of the ride," he added regretfully.

"Me, too," Kelly sighed. Despite the rain barrel, Jilamey had exuded a pong that she was afraid might cling to her and spoil this evening. "I dropped my nerd off at the medical center for a full check-over, and took a double-long shower to get the pig smell off. Did I miss anything good?"

"You left just before the best part," Todd said, grinning broadly at the memory. "We were afraid that once the mass of snakes caught up to us, they'd make short work of all Wayne's stock, but we didn't count on the sows. When the tiddlers started coming through the slats into their pens, they turned as aggressive as you could have wished. Wayne was delighted."

"Really?" Kelly wondered if Todd was teasing her, but a quick look at Hrriss confirmed that this master dissembler was telling the truth.

"They stomped the snakes flat. Hell hath no fury like a sow whose piglets are in danger," Todd chortled. "Those sharp hooves chopped lengths off the tiddlers that got through. The others turned around and fled."

"So we concentrated on the Mommy Sssnakess," Hrriss added. "By the time the Beaters arrived, we were able to get the swarm back into line. The boars were snorting war cries by the time we started zo clear out of there."

Kelly applauded, laughing. "Let's have a Pig Brigade next year."

"That's what I suggested to Wayne," Todd said, grinning with malice. "Since he won't move them out of the way, we might as well get some help from them. They're as good as ocelots for chopping up tiddlers."

"Nearly as good," Hrriss corrected him mildly. Todd favored his friend with an openmouthed stare of feigned astonishment.

"Don't compare chickens and brrnas," Kelly said, playfully putting a hand between them. "I'm glad I got you two alone before everything got started," she continued in an undertone, turning so her back shielded her words. "I tried to find your father, Todd, but he's out showing some diplomats around the model stock ranches. Young Jilamey got talkative when he got mlada'd up in the snake blind. I don't think he realized what he was implying, in his chummy confidences about Uncle Landreau's opinion of the Reeve family." So she repeated Jilamey's exact words.

"Dad and me out of our element here?" Todd demanded, more indignant than insulted. He left out a harsh bark of laughter. "Earth never was *my* element!"

Kelly grinned, a sparkle in her eyes. "Well, you've won one staunch adherent in Jilamey today. Jilamey admires you tremendously for saving him from the very jaws of death. And he's going to tell his uncle how quick and clever you were."

Todd snorted. "Much weight that'll carry with Al Landreau. Candidly I was thinking that maybe the Admiral sent the kid into the Snake Hunt to get him killed and make the Reeves look worse."

"It failed, didn't it?" Hrriss said, but the tips of his claws were showing as he rattled them on his knee.

"As the Mayday failed?" Todd said softly.

"What Mayday?" Kelly asked, wondering if she'd missed something.

Todd's brows drew down over his nose. He stared off across the room, blank-faced. His hands twitched, showing the tension that he wouldn't allow his face to reveal. Kelly knew the signs. Todd was revving up to full anger even if he never let it go public.

"Landreau has absolutely no grounds to pull any of us out of the colony, no matter what his personal opinion—and grievance against us—might be."

Hrriss scowled, pulling his eyebrow whiskers together. "There were ominous undertones at the Hrrethan celebration we attended," he said. "We are all aware that pressure of some kind would increase now that the Treaty Renewal talks are so close. Two of the Hayuman speakers who were on Hrretha are here now, too, Varnorian and Rogitel. Rrev has seen them, but I think he has not spoken with them."

"At least you're aware of undercurrents," Kelly said, deciding that now was the time to reveal her own budget of suspicion and anxieties. "I caught more than that on Earth," and to give herself time to organize her thoughts, she filched nuts from one of the appetizer bowls next to her on the long table. "Jilamey's comments today merely support the innuendos. I was going to talk to Ken and Hrrestan in private, but, with the shuttle's delay, I barely arrived home in time to ride out on Hunt.

"As you two should know, Alreldep is completely pro-Doona, but I wish I could say the same for the other two space services. I feel almost endangered when I have to carry a message to Spacedep offices. Now that there are plenty of thriving colonies, there is a feeling that Doona is no longer needed. The experiment was 'interesting,' that's all. The Treaty may just as well be voided, and we can all go our separate ways."

"Has public sentiment gone that far against us?" Todd asked sadly.

"The public? No!" Kelly hurried to assure him. "They voted on allowing Doona to be colonized, and from what I can tell, none of them have changed their minds. The government agencies are what we have to worry about. To the average man or woman in, say, Air Recycling or Food Services, Doona is still the shining star, the pastoral world that opened up space travel and revitalized Earth's economy." Kelly plastered an imaginary banner on the sky with a sweep of her hand. "Even if those people're unsuited to colonization, they're making sure that their sons and daughters are taking specialized training so they'll be qualified one day. And every child who visits Alreldep on a school tour wants to be the one to find the next Doona. It's the old flatheads in Spacedep who want us to go back to square one and pretend that a cohabited colony never happened. Especially not one independent from the government of Earth and on which the Earth language is subordinated in favor of the co-inhabitor's. Having to speak Middle Hrruban when they come here is one of the things that really rankle with them." She smiled and shook her head, taken aback at her own frankness. "Listen to me go on! Do you know how long it's been since I've been able to talk like that? It's not approved for diplomats to be heard spouting judgmental statements. Unfortunately I've got no proof of opposition except gossip and the unwelcoming mien of Spacedep menials. You'd just have to trust my powers of observation, such as they are."

"How long have we been friends?" Hrriss said, speaking in the Low Hrruban of a familial group. "We have trusted you since you were able to ride a Hunt."

"Before that," Todd replied in the same vein.

Two Human women passed them, carrying a huge basket of bread between them. Hrriss looked about cautiously before replying, and glanced at Todd for permission. He and Todd had discussed the matter and decided that Kelly had to be told what had happened. With her connections in Alreldep, she'd have access to offices and ranking officials that they did not.

"Unfortunately we have perhaps precipitated an event which would ssserve Spacedep's purpose well, though we do not yet know who is responsible for engineering it."

Kelly's eyes went wide. "What happened?"

"This is confidential, you understand," Todd said, still in Low Hrruban, which would make what he said unintelligible to many. Kelly grinned at his tactic and nodded for him to continue. "On the way back from Hrretha, we received a Mayday signal, coming from an uninhabited, interdicted world," Todd went on, twisting his shoulders at their naivete. "We responded to the call, only to discover that it was coming from a beacon drone. We found no trace of radiation or ion drive to tell where the ship that dropped it came from. Anyone passing that way could have heard the Mayday, but unluckily it was us."

"The fact remains that we crossed into a forbidden zone for no purpose," Hrriss finished, his purring voice low.

"But you'd have the log record of the Mayday . . ." Kelly began.

"We nearly didn't," Todd replied sourly. "A slight malfunction . . ."

"Corrected by a kick," Hrriss said, grinning.

"In the holographic recorder," Todd finished.

"Loose circuit?" Kelly asked, even as she wondered why she was trying to find logical explanations of the malfunction.

"More likely"—Todd managed a fine approximation of an Hrruban growl—"it got *over*serviced when the Hrrethan space station insisted on being *sure* the *Albatross* was in perfect working order."

"Even though we assured them that our own people had serviced it before we started out," Hrriss added, letting one claw escape its sheath.

"So no idea who put the drone out there?" Kelly asked, knowing the answer even before Hrriss shook his head.

"There were others who would make their second warp jump at those particular coordinates," Hrriss said, "but everyone knew we were anxious to return speedily to Rrala."

"So it was set up to catch you two." Her remark was more statement than question.

"That's the most logical assumption," Todd said, "in the present circumstances, but we *have* a recording of that Mayday, which I don't think we were supposed to have."

"And you let Hrriss do all the talking, didn't you?" Kelly asked briskly, and looked relieved when both nodded. Then her shoulders sagged. "But it's just the sort of incident Spacedep would contrive, an unnecessary breach of the Treaty and by a Doonan."

"And a Hrruban!" Hrriss reminded her.

She did *not* like the inferences that even an idiot could draw, let alone an anti-Doona faction. "Who else knows about this?"

"Our fathers," Hrriss said, "Hrrestan and Rrev. It was decided to defer the matter until after the Hunt."

"Sensible. No one on Doona'd let you escape your Hunt responsibilities," Kelly said, and then to insert some levity into the conversation, "including me. And," she added more brightly, "since this is Doona, you'll be believed. It's on Earth that I wouldn't give a cracked egg for your chances. If we can only limit the incident to Doona—once the visitors have left and can't get their noses into something as juicy as an interdiction breach."

"In any case, I'm the one at fault," Todd said in his characteristic forthright manner. "I was piloting the ship, and I insisted that we respond to the Mayday, even if it meant passing an interdiction buoy. It's serious but it oughtn't to damage the Doonan Treaty."

"Hear him. He would have us suffer even before being found guilty," Hrriss said wryly, nudging Todd in the ribs with the back of his hand. "First it must be proved to the Treaty Council that we acted out of malice. If sanctity of life cannot supersede borders and barriers, then we may not call ourselves civilized."

"Well, let's not borrow trouble from tomorrow, huh?" Kelly said, cocking her head at them. "I'm not without resources, you know. Just let me know when to call in favors, and where, and you know I'll do it." Then, seeing a swarm of guests crowding into the Hall, she reverted to Standard. "It's party time, lads," she said, rising to her feet, giving her skirts a practiced flirt. "And I intend to party!"

Since by tradition and Treaty, there was no hotel, guests were assigned space in the old plastic cabins of the original village. Many visitors found them a diverting change from the usual sterile accommodations. The more prestigious were billeted with Doonan host families, and the overflow used canvas tenting shelters. However, Doonans, Hayuman and Hrruban alike, provided visitors with Friendly Native Guides to keep them company and, more important, to show them the dangerous vegetation and keep them from unexpectedly rousing the ferocious bearlike mda. Such individual contacts with those from other worlds had improved good opinions of Doona over the past twenty-five years.

This year, the Shihs, Phyllis and Hu, leader of the First Human Village, were pleased to have the honor of hosting the Fifth Speaker, the Hrruban Minister for Health and Medicine. The Hrruban's stripe was noticeably broader and his mane was whitening around his face, but he was solemnly kind to all who approached to greet him. He caught Todd's eye and smiled. They had met on Hrretha only a few weeks before. Most likely, the venerable Hrruban was still seeing the small boy dressed in mda fur with a rope tail tied around his waist instead of a grown man in normal Earth-style tunic and trousers. Responding to that memory himself, Todd straightened his tunic and squared his shoulders as the Speaker and Hu neared him.

"A fine Hunt, and, it would seem, a fine party to come," Hu Shih complimented Todd, reaching up to pat the young man on the shoulder, and nodding amiably to Hrriss. The venerable metropologist's eyes were shining as he took in the decorations and the happy crowd filling the Hall. "No Hunters with more than scrapes and bruises and"—Hu's eyes twinkled—"depressed ambitions. Very well done, indeed."

"Thank you, sir," Todd said, politely dropping into Middle Hrruban, since the Fifth Speaker was here in a social capacity. "Have you heard about the Boncyk sows?"

"Indeed we have," Hu Shih replied, his usually composed face becoming wreathed with laughter.

"The tale will return with me to Hrruba," the Fifth Speaker replied, his deep black eyes sparkling. "It is, of course, the greatest pity that the scene was not recorded, but the various narrators seem to agree on so many details that the truth will not suffer much in the retelling."

"We are considering the addition of a Sow Brigade to next year's Hunt," Todd went on, dropping his jaw in a Hrruban-style grin.

He saw Hu's start of surprise but the Fifth Speaker grumbled his throat chuckle and Hu relaxed. Todd had always been on special terms with Hrruban Speakers and could dare where protocol would have strictly forbidden such banter. Todd was not surprised when Hu deftly eased the Speaker toward the dais and the special chairs where the elders would observe the proceedings.

"I will expect a full report of their performance next year, Zodd," the Speaker said, allowing himself to be shepherded away.

The Ad Hoc Band began to play incidental music, loud enough to be heard through the low roar of conversation but not loud enough to drown it.

Todd looked around for Ali Kiachif, one of the oldest friends of the colony and its most faithful proponent. The swarthy, drink-loving old Codep captain had missed few New Home Weeks since the beginning, attending anytime he could arrange his schedule to be there. He wasn't in the Hall yet, and Todd couldn't remember having heard anyone mention that he'd arrived. Todd was a little disappointed, but he could well understand it if Kiachif wasn't able to make it back to Doona. Kiachif was a busy man these days. His rounds had grown a hundredfold since the colony's inception, and had earned him a small fleet of ships serving under him, plying the expanding spaceways, carrying cargo and passengers. Doona was still one of his favorite stops. He always claimed it rested his eyes from the sometimes horrific conditions on mining planets, which far outnumbered the agricultural planets, where people lived in miserable conditions in the stale air of domes or in the unremitting toil of prison facilities. While he never mentioned Doonan grog, everyone knew that it was more to his taste than methylated spirits cooked over a Bunsen burner.

In their festive best, everyone looked cheerfully ready to enjoy themselves to the fullest. The threat of being overrun by the great snakes had once again been averted. In the true spirit of Doona, some of the native Humans wore Hrruban dress, and some of the Hrrubans affected "Trran" trousers, skirts, or dresses. The various diplomats were attired more formally but not repressively so, while their young wards and the other guests were dressed in the latest styles from Earth or Hrruba. Evidently the fashion industries of both cultures had been stimulated by the contact, and styles had merged, mingled, and then evolved to become highly individualistic.

Oddly enough, though most Terrans still spoke in murmurs, their clothes shouted in the most vivid of shades, enhanced by additives that caused iridescence and luminosity, sometimes rather shocking to the eye. Todd felt almost conservative in

the green casual trousers and darker green silk shirt sent to
him by his sister Ilsa. She had gone back to Earth for higher
education and had married a man she met at school. Byron
worked as a consultant to Spacedep, so he was occasionally
on Doona to visit the Treaty Island, as he was for the Hunt. He
was a fair stickman, playing his turn with the band, bobbing
his head to the rhythm as he beat the drum skins. He threw
a sideways grin toward Todd.

"There's Hrringa," Kelly said, smiling at a tall, almost
chestnut-maned Hrruban in crisp formal attire. "I'm glad they
sent someone down to spell him at the Hrruban Center. He'd
have hated to miss the fun." Todd nodded to the catman, who
was serving a term as the transportation grid operator in the
Hrruban consulate on Earth. Hrringa was a member of Hrriss's
clan. Though his friend never made much of it, his family was
of a fairly broad Stripe.

"They always do. He was on Team Ten in the Hunt, you
know. Did you see much of each other?" Todd asked Kelly.

"Quite a lot. Most people on Earth don't speak the language,
so I'm sort of a tie to home. So few people realize that he
speaks fluent Terran: and there are always those who try to
talk pidgin Hrruban with him." She rolled her eyes at such
an insult to her friend. "Then there's the opposite extreme
with those silly men in Amalgamated Worlds Administration
treating him as some sort of sacred shaman."

Hrriss made a noise like a snort. "What do you expect from
them?"

Kelly's expression turned sheepish. "I tried to wangle a ride
home through the grid instead of flying out," she admitted.
"Hrringa would have obliged me, I know, but they don't like
us junior types to use the grid when the senior diplomats can't
get access anytime they want to. They waved me off. It was
no use my explaining that Hrringa and I were raised together,
or that I had a right to go to Doona." She clicked her tongue
regretfully. "Well, I'd better go be a good hostess. My mother
said if I wasn't on the front line shaking hands . . ." She left the
threat unspoken, with a broad grin to show she knew it wasn't
serious. "I'll find you later, Todd. Keep your ears open."

"You, too." Todd blinked as Kelly was swallowed up
immediately by the swirling crowd. He couldn't believe how

fast the Hall had filled up. He looked at Hrriss, who was also looking a bit dazed.

"We were so intent, we were not paying attention," the Hrruban said. "Meanwhile, the party has created itself."

"Yeah." Todd craned his neck for one last look at the girl. "Kelly looks beautiful, doesn't she?"

"Her grace is one with her beauty," Hrriss said approvingly. "Come, Team Leader, we have other duties even as she does."

Young men and women warily carried full trays of drinks and nibble snacks past them into the main room. As the kitchen doors swung to and fro, Hrriss and Todd caught sight of Mrrva. Hrriss's mother could be seen standing over a huge simmering pot with a spoon to her lips, tasting the contents for spice. Mrrva held the Hrruban equivalent of five college degrees in physical health science, and was director of the Rralan Health Services, but she also enjoyed the simple tasks of hospitality that entertaining on Doona required. Her eyes widened when she saw her son and Todd enter.

"Go out therrre," she ordered, pointing with her spoon toward the doorway. "Why are you here? We do not need help from such as you. The Masters of the Hunt should mingle with guests, not serve like cubs and youths."

"But, Mrrva . . ." Todd began, his voice wheedling as he edged toward some of her famous pastries.

She slapped his hand with her spoon and immediately threw him a cloth to clean off the sticky liquid.

"You will be served in due courssse," Mrrva said in a tone which brooked no further discussion. She made a sound between a hiss and a growl. "When will we ever put the manners of a man and Master on you, Zodd!" Then she turned on Hrriss. "I know you have been taught. Go now and exercise the teaching."

Abashed, the two returned to the Hall. Leading the Hunt had been a pleasure. Hosting the party was a chore they would gladly have missed. The throng had swelled to hundreds in the great room. Todd passed among them, shaking hands and returning kisses. While on the one hand he was glad to see the friends that reappeared year after year, on the other, there was never any time to catch up on any details—of their success in

the Hunt let alone what they'd been doing the past year—
before someone else claimed attention.

He and Hrriss finally made their way to the dais and stood
in front of the main table. Before the feast could officially
begin, the long-awaited blooding ceremony for the successful
Hunters must proceed. As Master of the Hunt and master of
ceremonies, Todd was required to make a short speech of
welcome to the sea of guests. He would speak in Terran,
with Hrriss repeating it after him in Middle Hrruban. He had
a feeling of déjà vu. It had been only a few weeks before that
he stood and listened to the governor of Hrretha offer similar
greetings to his guests. There had been many like events in
the last few years. They were beginning to blur into one
another. He began by offering his gratitude to all the people
who had aided in organizing and running the Hunt, and went
on from there.

"To old friends and family, I welcome you home, and to
new friends and first-time visitors, I hope you'll enjoy your
stay, and that you'll return to us again in the future," Todd
said, winding up the necessary remarks. "I won't hold up
dinner long. The cooks would throw me into the stew with the
snakes!" There was a small murmur of appreciative laughter,
and Todd held up a hand. "However, there are some people I'm
happy to call to your attention. They've earned this moment.
As I call your name, will you come up on the dais, please?"

The Hunters who had passed their initiation rite that day by
capturing a brace of adolescent snakes were called up one by
one, to stand shoulder-to-shoulder before the audience. Some
of them were shy and directed their smiles down at their feet
as Todd congratulated them on their successful passage. One
among them—a young woman from the mining colony of
Ellerell IV—had chosen instead to bring in eggs. She had
saved all her extra pay for five years to be able to make it
to Doona for Snake Hunt. When first laid, snake eggs were
almost too soft to move. By the time they had hardened enough
to transport, there was a real danger that they might hatch on
the way in. She had brought in twelve of the soft and leathery
head-sized eggs in a specially designed fluff-lined sack brought
all the way from Ellerell. Her thoroughness and care impressed
even the Doonan judges, who had seen a lot of inventive

approaches to the problem over the last two decades. She was invested with the small gold medal from which depended two wiggly streamers. Some of the children squealed when they saw the ribbons, which looked amazingly like the tails of miniature snakes. She and the other Hunters wore their awards proudly as they were given a standing ovation.

Jilamey Landreau was called forward with the rest of the almost-successful who had captured a single snake. He shook hands with Todd and Hrriss to the accompaniment of encouraging applause from the audience.

"Thank you, Todd," the young Landreau said, clutching his medal with the single streamer. "I wish there had been a chance to take the second snake. I was so close!"

"Next year," Todd suggested. "Your first was a good capture. We can hold that snake 'on credit,' so to speak."

"Hey, you could?" the youth exclaimed, his eyes shining. Todd recognized that the Hunt craze had claimed another adherent. "Can I get the hide to take back with me? I want to use the stripe as a fashion accessory! That'll really make 'em look twice at me!"

"I'll see to it," Todd said, slightly amused at the young Landreau's naive delight. He clapped Jilamey on the shoulder encouragingly before moving on to congratulate the next participant.

The feast was then officially begun. As the Hunters, both successful and unsuccessful, sat down, Byron played a roll on the snare drum to get everyone's attention. It segued into a compelling, irregular beat on tom-tom. Clad only in their knife belts and ornamental necklaces, several young Hrrubans ran in and began a stomping, swirling dance: obviously a Snake Hunt. Two lithe female dancers, acting in tandem as if they were part of the same body, portrayed the snake. They snapped imaginary coils toward the Hunters or recoiled fearfully from their spears. It was a compelling sight, as the rear half of the snake curled herself on the floor behind the body of the other and switched her tail fitfully as the front half swayed, striking at this dancer or that with her fangs. The Hunters catapulted past the reptile to attack, missing and hitting the floor beyond. With great energy, they rolled upright to their feet like kittens and renewed their attacks on their foe.

The upright dancer was so skillful that she didn't appear to have a solid bone in her body. Her undulations had a hypnotic quality. It was a shock to the watchers when one spearman sprang forward, past the snapping jaws, and plunged the weapon into the snake's breast. The serpent gave one tremendous convulsion and subsided to the floor gracefully to quiver into stillness. When the snake had "died," a complimentary silence held the audience. Then a burst of thunderous applause awarded the dancers. They sprang up, acknowledging the praise, and then gathered to either side of the doors leading to the kitchen.

The band stayed on its dais long enough to play a fanfare to announce the arrival of a massive cauldron borne aloft on a tray by eight young men and women clad to the ears in heatproof towelling. The huge kettle of savory snake stew was presented to Todd as the Master of the Hunt. With intricately decorated ladles, Todd and Hrriss served the special guests on the dais, after which the cauldron was brought to the long sideboard. From then on, buffet style was the order and everyone served themselves from the seemingly inexhaustible supply of stew and the other viands brought out from the kitchen. Todd caught sight of Mrrva sitting down at the end of the table near Hrrestan: she had shed her apron to display gorgeous filmy robes spangled with jewels.

As the party began in earnest, toasts were offered to the Hunters and the prey. For many of the guests, the feast was a double reason for celebration. For some this would be the first time they had eaten "real," unprocessed or nonsynthetic food. For others, this was a high point of gastronomic enjoyment. It was true that every year, more real fruit, vegetables, grain, and meat were being made available to the people of Earth from its farming colonies, but the majority of homeworld meals still came from synthesizers. Hrriss nudged Todd in the ribs and indicated a child at one of the front tables. He was suspiciously and most reluctantly taking a tiny bite of fruit from a spoon. The tot sniffed it first, not in the least willing to trust the curious substance in front of him. With much coaxing and much gesturing to others tucking into their food, the child's mother got him to accept the morsel. After a very tentative chew, the boy grabbed the spoon out of his mother's hand, finished the bowl in front of him, and reached for his mother's as well.

When all had eaten sufficiently, the party went on to its next, and inevitable, stage. The Ad Hoc Band resumed its place on the dais and started to play dancing music. A few took advantage of the music, but most sat contentedly, letting the meal settle. Gradually, drinks in hand, diners began to circulate the Hall, pausing to chat with old friends or welcome newcomers, or congratulate the new Hunters.

Todd and Hrriss excused themselves from the dais and began more protocol rounds just as the Ad Hoc Band started to play a perky song, based on an ancient Earth chantey. It was a joke among Doona/Rralans, but it had never been played at a New Home Week before. Todd guessed that Sally Lawrence, who had written the new lyrics, wanted a broader audience. He hoped that the listeners would accept it for the facetious tweak it was, and not take it seriously. Sally's eyes were twinkling as she struck a chord on her guitar and began to sing.

"My mother was a human girl from Doona Village Four
She loved a handsome Hrruban boy who lived
just next door
Their love bore offspring, one, two, three
A kitten and a werecat and the third was me.

"Now my brother Hrrn and I, we were raised up
quite all right
But my sister Mrrna Joan, she was different day and night
Smooth-skinned at night, by day her fur grew
She was a true Doonan through and through.

"Yo ho ho! A Rralan true
Takes the best of both as all should do."

It was a familiar tune to the locals. Some joined in the chorus, roaring a lusty "Yo ho ho!" Nearly everyone else seemed to get the joke, to judge by the shouts of approval and calls for an encore. Todd noticed that some of the Human diplomats looked annoyed, and a few of the Hrruban homeworlders looked positively ill at the thought of Hrrubans and Humans interbreeding. Todd couldn't think how to explain that the thought had never seriously crossed the mind of the songwriter.

"Maybe this is the moment to start the dancing?" Kelly said, coming up behind Todd and poking him in the side with a finger.

"I'm not very good at it," Todd said apologetically, but he gestured to the bandleader, who immediately struck a fast step.

Immediately the floor was full of couples, whirling and jigging about in circles.

"Neither am I!" Kelly seized his hand. "Let's go anyway!"

Jaw dropped in amusement, Hrriss leaned toward him. "If she promises not to step on my tail, I get the nexxxt dansss."

"It's a deal," Kelly called as she dragged Todd into the crowd.

Kelly had told a fib when she said she was a poor dancer. With her hands bunched in the folds of her skirts, she swayed and stepped with grace to the lively melody. Todd knew the steps, but he felt as awkward as a wooden mda trying to keep up with her. He was relieved when that music stopped and a slow dance began. Kelly melted into his arms, stretching up one hand to his neck. That was oddly delightful. They had grown up together, but he had never realized before that she was so much smaller than he, so delicately built—or, to be more honest, that she was a girl at all. She had just been one of the capable people he depended on, until she went away. Kelly had never balked at fences, and she could wrangle snakes or horses with the best. He could barely connect the tomboy who had grown up literally next door with the sparkling vision in his arms. Unconsciously he tightened his hold a trifle, and she rubbed her cheek against his chest. The music drifted to a halt, and Kelly turned her face up to give him a brilliant smile, her golden eyes aflame in the festival lamplight.

"Thank you," she said. "That was lovely."

Todd didn't know how to reply suitably. "Um, thank you. Isn't it Hrriss's turn now?"

"Only if I promise not to step on his tail," and Kelly's look was enigmatic but she allowed him to lead her from the floor and find Hrriss.

He stood watching for a moment as Hrriss, rather too expertly, Todd thought, spun Kelly out into the dancers, his tail wrapped around one leg, well out of the way. Not that Kelly would put a foot wrong, Todd realized.

"Hey, young Reeve," called out Captain Buckman, a former Spacedep marine. He had joined the colony on Binar 3B-IV and was now its governor. "Where can I get some mlada?"

"Allow me," and Todd located the case of mlada bottles stashed under one end of the dais draperies. As he served Buckman, he thought the man's eyes were already a little red. His breath smelled so strongly of alcohol it might ignite spontaneously. "You'd better watch your intake, sir. Too much of this stuff results in potent hangovers."

"Hmmph," said the old man, watching Todd refill his glass. "But you pour generously, boy. So this is how you impress the diplomats, hey? Is yours the last face they see before they pass out? Where's Pollux?"

"Who, sir?"

"Where's Pollux, Castor?" Buckman asked, prodding Todd in the middle. "Your twin, your inseparable pal, your other half, boy."

"Hrriss is on the dance floor," Todd replied a little stiffly. "Did you want to speak to him?"

"No, no. So the two of you aren't joined at the hip? I'll be danged. Come back and refill this in about, oh, a quarter hour, won't you?"

Todd nodded and moved on to the next group, clustered at the farthest end of the room from the band. This was an informal roundtable discussion by the Jacks of All Trades. That much-sought-after designation meant that a colonist had enough flexibility and training in such a variety of skills that he could turn a hand to any task that needed doing or problem that had to be solved. Codep preferred that there be at least one JOAT in any colony group. Both men and women could ship on in that capacity. Ken Reeve's own designation for the Doona colony project had been that of a JOAT. As an unofficial chair and host of the JOATs present, he was directing the discussion among those from several nascent colonies that had recently earned their Amalgamated Worlds status. Many of them had been born or raised on Doona. The billy-JOATs and nanny-JOATs, as they liked to call themselves, unofficially, of course, were now gleefully engaged in a loud argument about the best way to set up barrier screens against pests. Todd checked and refilled each guest's glass and picked up empty dessert plates for transport back to the kitchen. Before leaving, he exchanged winks with his father.

The band was taking a much needed break, and near the kitchen doors, Sally Lawrence was having a private discussion with Varnorian of Codep. Todd bowed over her hand as he refilled her glass.

"So why do you object to my song?" Mrs. Lawrence demanded of the Codep chairman. "On artistic principles?"

"Scarcely on that score, my dear lady," said Varnorian, loosing his not inconsiderable charm. "Your artistry is remarkable." He wasn't the friend to Doona that the late Chaminade had been, but he was at least a graceful guest. He had very pale blue eyes with dark lashes. There was something both attractive and cold about eyes like that. "My objection is purely contextual. I feel that such an idea should not have been voiced, let alone mocked. Totally unsuitable lyrics, if you could by any extension of poesy call them that."

"Mr. Varnorian, Doona's a hard world and we have developed our humor to leaven the hardships. If I care to make a joke, it's my world, and most of us got the joke."

"Forgive me, but the taste of the joke is but a little questionable in terms of the larger aberration, my dear Mrs. Lawrence," said Varnorian, and he smiled again with that facile charm. "The real aberration is Doona. The cultures here are too different, too mutually exclusive. East in East, you know, and West is West. Never the twain shall meet." He lifted his refreshed drink to her, certain he had had the last word.

"Oh, Shakespeare?" asked Mrs. Lawrence, fluttering her eyelashes at him. Todd knew as well as she that it wasn't. Everyone on Doona was more familiar with Kipling, who seemed to "know" so much about their unusual situation. She continued to sip coyly at her glass.

"No," said Varnorian patronizingly. "Not at all, madam. I believe it might be Strauss. Nineteenth century, not seventeenth."

"Really? How clever you are," Sally said, and linking arms with him, moved him out of Todd's vicinity.

"What is Ssalllee up to now?" Hrriss asked, appearing at Todd's elbow. Todd looked around for Kelly. "Oh, I left her in good hands. Is that Captain Buckman beckoning for you?"

"He's had too much mlada already," Todd said, not too pleased with matters.

"That is undoubtedly true," Hrriss agreed after a moment's consideration. "And here is someone else in even worsse condition."

Jilamey staggered up to them with a determined expression on his face. The mlada he had begged of Kelly in the snake blind was only the start of his libations, though neither Hrriss nor Todd realized that. But he had consumed considerably more with his meal, which Todd had observed. That he was still standing spoke highly of his capacity. The young man was dressed in the most precious of modern styles. His tunic had appliquéd gems arranged in a crisscross pattern at the neck to stimulate lacings, and he wore frivolous boots with knee-high tops turned over to show their long fringes, which were also jeweled. "I've been looking for you for hours, Todd, to talk about snakes."

"It's a little early to talk about next year, Jilamey," Todd said diplomatically as he touched the single ribbon on the youth's medallion.

"Next year?" Jilamey blinked at him. "Ah, yes, next year! Of course. I'll be back next year. I'm one snake up. Have a drink on that."

"No mlada, I thank you," Todd replied, smiling to defuse any insult. "I'll stay with the punch."

"Punch? On a night like this?"

"Frankly, Jilamey, I don't really like it. It leaves a taste in my mouth of something long dead. I've got fresh raspberry-apple punch here if you'd like some. Homegrown fruit."

Jilamey shuddered. "Thank you ever so, no! Mlada for me. How about you?" The youth turned to Hrriss.

"Neither do I drink," the Hrruban said, dropping his jaw in a grin. "I have felt what mlada can do. Wait until you feel your head tomorrow morning. It will seem as though a ripe melon had replaced your cranium, and that every borer worm on Rrala is trying to drill through it."

"That's enough about worms," Jilamey said, grimacing horribly. "I've seen the big kind too closely today. I almost couldn't eat the meat at supper, but it smelled so good I got over it. That pretty Kelly told me I wasn't gripping tightly enough to the saddle with my knees. I will exercise mightily, and next year, my knees will meet inside the horse before I fall off in front of a snake!"

"That's the spirit," Todd responded.

Jilamey took a steadying drink and held out his glass to be topped up. "You went through this how many years ago?"

"The first Snake Hunt on Doona—well, more of a snake drive—happened when I was six." Tactfully Todd avoided mentioning how it came about. "We've had to wrangle snakes past our farms every year since then. We had to organize it because we were losing too many head of livestock to the snakes."

"No, no," and Jilamey waved a forefinger unsteadily. "I mean the coming-of-age ritual. You caught a big one and brought it in. Pete's been telling me and my friends all about it." He swayed as he pointed over his shoulder to where Peter Ivanovich, leader of Team Three, lay sprawled in a heap of cushions, snoring.

"Right," Todd said. Something in the young Landreau's tone alerted Hrriss, who appeared suddenly behind the swaying youth. He caught Todd's eye and looked a question. Todd shook his head very slightly. "The first one was only a tiddler. Eight meters. You saw a number of those today. The second one was a real whopper. Twelve meters and a little bit over."

"I was there and saw it," Hrriss put in. "A huge creature. It provided many days of meat for the settlement, and useful skin for other purposes."

Jilamey's eyes narrowed. "I don't believe it. How did you catch something like that? It's bigger than a house!"

"Careful planning," Todd said, maneuvering Landreau toward a chair before he fell over. "This is a good time for a yarn. Let me tell you all about it." Jilamey listened carefully through to the end of Todd's narrative, and then sat up very straight. He stared his fellow Human in the eye. "You've been rehearsing your story with the others. It's a falsehood. That snake is almost as big as the one that tried to eat me. I've never heard such a load of ballast in my life.

It's exactly what Pete recited to me, almost word for word."

"I give you my word of honor that the story is true," Todd replied, shrugging away Jilamey's disbelief.

"Space slag!"

Todd shrugged again. "It's too much trouble to lie."

"Twelve meters! Impossible!" Jilamey exploded.

"Well, it's still on record," Todd said, not wanting to get into an argument over what was a fact. Then he grinned at Jilamey. "I had to, you see. Hrriss caught a real big Mommy the year before. I couldn't let him get an edge on me, now could I?" Surreptitiously he winked at his friend. "I broke his record but only by a few centimeters."

"If you don't believe him," Hrriss added silkily, as Jilamey still looked skeptical, "see if you can find anyone who has heard it told differently. There are many still awake who were here when it occurred. And there is the computer link in the corner! The records are available from the Treaty Archives for anyone to read. The Hunt and its results are documented."

Muttering, Jilamey poured himself another glass from the mlada bottle which Hrriss had managed to water down. Then he took himself off.

"What a head he's going to have tomorrow!" Todd said, shaking his head sympathetically as he watched Jilamey's wavering path toward the Archive room. "He didn't contest *your* record." Loyally Todd considered that omission a slight on his best friend.

"I expect no one mentioned it to him," Hrriss said uninterestedly. "No one tells the story of the second-place Hunt. Listeners want to hear only about the first-place achievement."

Sometime later, when Jilamey came back, Todd courteously extended the jug of watered mlada.

"No, no more for me, thank you ever so. I believe I have had sufficient for this evening," he said, slurring words which were nevertheless courteous. "I must seek my quarters. How can you possibly look so . . . so hearty?" His manner abruptly turned accusing.

"Clean living," Todd said jokingly. "But I assure you that when I finally see *my* quarters, I shall not move for two days."

"Yes, well, I checked your record—just to know the facts,

you see," the Terran put in quickly, with a shamed expression. "I apologize. I will never again doubt anything you tell me. Twelve point four three meters! How I wish I'd seen that fight."

"It was a good one," Todd said with quiet satisfaction.

"It must have been." Jilamey smiled with genuine good humor. "You're too much to be true, Todd Reeve, but I'd rather you beside me in the Hunt than anyone else I've ever met on any world."

"Thanks," Todd said, shaking the hand Jilamey held out to him. "It'd be an honor."

Landreau shook hands with Hrriss, too, and staggered off toward the guest accommodations.

"I could wish that another of his stripe would reassess our honor," Hrriss said.

"Let's just hope that one suddenly doesn't appear on any panel of inquiry you and I have to face," Todd replied. "He doesn't think much about Reeve honor and that's all we've got: honor."

CHAPTER

4

A LOUD CLATTERING AND THE FEEL OF ROUGH hands woke Todd from a sound sleep. There were men in blue uniforms leaning over him, shouting in loud voices and shaking his shoulders. It revived an old nightmare he had had the first time he'd seen those uniforms, twenty-five years before. They were Spacedep marines, the same units that had accompanied Landreau to Doona, to round up the colonists so they could be sent back to Earth. For a moment he was six years old again, the giant snakes were being herded through the village under Landreau's order, and his family was in danger. The Hrrubans, including Hrruna, the greatest, most important of them all, were behind him. He had to hurry to save the other Humans. He raised his hand to keep the soldier from grabbing him again to hustle him away to the convoy ship. An adult arm interceded, and the marine stepped back. Todd stared at the arm. Was it his father's? No, it was his own. In a moment, reality reasserted itself, and Todd calmed down. He was grown-up and could protect himself. There was no need to assume immediately that anything was wrong. The marine was waiting a few feet away from the bed. His fellows stood in the doorway. Todd could see his mother and father just behind them. Pat looked worried, and Ken furious.

"Todd Reeve," the marine said, reading from the plastic film containing his orders. "You are instructed to accompany us to the presence of the Treaty Councillors."

"Certainly, gentlemen," Todd said, throwing off the blanket. "Allow me a moment to dress?"

Todd had gone to bed only an hour before sunrise. Once the remaining guests went home with their hosts, he and the

83

other volunteers who could still stand had spent several hours cleaning up. The Hunters among them had had no sleep since the night before, and they were weary. Hrriss had been reeling with fatigue when he mounted up to head toward the bridge to go home. Todd was glad that he lived so close to the Assembly Hall. Much farther, and he'd be spending the night curled up where he dropped from exhaustion. He barely managed to strip off his new silk shirt and hang it up before falling into bed. His good trousers hadn't fared so well, hiking to his knees under the blanket when he thrust his legs down. He had been too exhausted to straighten them out before he dropped off to sleep. The guards waited impatiently while he splashed some water on his face and shaved quickly.

It would seem that matters had taken a turn for the worse while he slept. A marine guard meant that the Treaty violation was now being addressed. He hoped truth would be all the defense he and Hrriss would need before a panel of inquiry.

The sky still wore the pale, moist veil of early morning when Todd reached the pad where the *Albatross* stood. Hrriss was already there, standing under the chill sky between his father, Hrrestan, and Commander Rogitel, assistant director of Spacedep. Ken Reeve had wanted to accompany his son, but the marine sergeant had denied him. Todd was relieved to see that at least Hu Shih, as leader of the Human settlers, was present. The old man's clothes were rumpled, as if he had hastily grabbed the nearest to hand. He was talking in a low worried tone with a small woman wearing a long robe tagged with the insignia of a Councillor. So, Todd thought, one of the Treaty Councillors had been called away from the crucial negotiations to be present when the ship was opened. From her weary expression, she had been waiting a long time. She was a small, elderly woman with dark skin and dark gray-shot curls which clustered closely around her head. Treaty Island was not so much an island as a minor continent which lay in the southern oceans a third of the way around Doona, which made this hour midday for her. Todd could have wished it were midday here and he'd been able to get enough sleep to keep his wits about him.

Hrriss looked expressionless, which meant to his old friend that he was deeply concerned. The glance he exchanged with

Todd emphasized the fact that the situation was as bad as it could be. It would have been much better for both Todd and Hrriss had they been able to approach the Treaty Council of their own volition—which they had planned to do once the Hunt was over. But, despite his feelings of foreboding at the precipitous manner, he and Hriss had the truth to support their actions. It was only that Landreau, and others, had been waiting for just such an incident. The presence of marines magnified the incident out of proportion.

The presence of Rogitel, one of Landreau's senior lieutenants on hand, meant that the Council had to convene an inquiry: just as Kelly had warned.

"Councillor Dupuis," Rogitel said, bowing slightly to her, "the perpetrators are now present."

"It has only just come to our attention," Councillor Dupuis said in a withering tone, "that this ship has violated the Treaty."

"Hrriss and I reported the incident as soon as we landed, Councillor," Todd said politely. "Accordingly, the vessel was sealed."

"The Treaty, as a condition of the Amalgamated Worlds charter, requires all ships to be inspected after out-systems flights upon landing. Postflight inspection is a requirement under the law, if for no other reason than fumigation and irradiation, and inspection of the ship's log."

"Madam," Hrrestan began politely, holding up a hand to stay the marine's action, "if this is merely postflight inspection, why have the soldiers been brought here and why is this gentleman present?" The Hrruban indicated Rogitel.

"We received information that this ship did not undergo a postflight inspection, that it has been sealed for two weeks, and may be involved in a Treaty violation," the Councillor said. She answered Hrrestan in the formal Hrruban of diplomacy, a courtesy which boded no good at all. "Naturally Commander Rogitel as Spacedep's representative is present. The violation is alleged to involve an uninhabited satellite of a star system."

Todd felt his spirits sink to a new low. Leaving the *Albatross* sealed was no crime, and indeed, such postflight inspections were not always completed in a timely fashion. As long as the ship had been sealed, the inspectors didn't much mind. Ken and Hu Shih had been informed of the incident; they had told Hrrestan, who was scarcely likely, even under the stringent codes of honor under which Hrrubans operated, to jeopardize his only child. No one else should have had that information. Ken and Hu might have been annoyed that the two friends had told Kelly, but she'd've told no one, knowing how very serious this could be. So who could have leaked that information? Clearly only those who had set the trap into which Todd and Hrriss had fallen.

"A serrious charrge this is," Hrrestan said, also in the formal tongue. He sounded calm, but his pupils were slitted to mere lines, a sure sign that the older Hrruban was deeply troubled.

"Serious, indeed," Councillor Dupuis said. "I require a deposition from the ship's crew before the ship is unsealed."

"I trust," Commander Rogitel put in so suavely that his manner alarmed Todd, "that there has been no tampering with that seal?"

"Examine it yourself, Commander Rogitel," Hu Shih said, very much on his dignity at hearing such aspersions cast.

"Hmm, it looks untouched," Rogitel said, taking a long time peering at the seal, though he didn't touch it.

"Reeve! Hrriss!" The Councillor waved them forward to the sealed hatch. "Do you swear and affirm that you took nothing out of this ship besides articles of clothing and personal effects?" They nodded solemnly, raising their right hands simultaneously. "That the contents listed here on the landing manifest were signed by the landing supervisor at the time of disembarkation?"

"I do," Todd said with a formal bow.

"I do," Hrriss echoed with an equally formal bow.

With a gesture, the Councillor ordered the marine sergeant to break the seal. As he touched the control pad, the hatch slid back, and a whoosh of stale air made those nearest, including the Councillor, recoil. Todd thought that that was one mark on their side as he saw Dupuis recognize what that implied. Lights came up inside the *Albatross* and the sergeant stepped politely aside as the ramp extruded the few feet to the ground. The port workers swarmed aboard to do the fumigation routine.

They were as quick as they were efficient and very shortly left the ship with a nod from the foreman that their task was completed.

The Councillor acknowledged this and then gestured for Todd and Hrriss to follow her into the *Albatross*. Rogitel followed them, still wearing that blandly smug expression. While he wasn't like his superior, Landreau, who blustered when angry, Rogitel was coolheaded and very quiet, a dangerously misleading trait, which tempted the unwary to talk in his presence under the delusion that he wasn't listening. Rogitel missed little, and he shared Landreau's bitter feelings about Doona. Kelly's warning about him was all too timely.

"This is a very serious matter," the Councillor said as they followed her to the cabin of the *Albatross* while the ventilation system sucked away the fumigation mist. "We have incontrovertible information, gleaned from the orbiting buoy around Hrrilnorr system, that a ship, now identified as the *Albatross,* passed through the perimeter of that system. Both of you should know," and she paused to make plain her point that they should know, "that Hrrilnorr is a proscribed system and may not be entered. *Do* you have any explanation that will justify such a violation?"

"Yes, we did enter that system, ma'am," Todd said without the slightest apology in his tone. Rogitel raised an eyebrow very slightly and sucked in his pale cheeks at such an open admission of guilt. "In response to a Mayday message broadcasting over the emergency frequency. Our log tape shows a holo of the object broadcasting that Mayday and we both felt justified, in that circumstance, to enter a proscribed system and render such aid as was needed. In view of the proscription, Hrriss, as a Hrruban citizen, answered the appeal. If you will view the log tapes, Councillor, I'm certain you will agree that our action was justified." Todd gestured for her to precede him to the cargo bay.

The Councillor pursed her thin lips, but there was an element of surprise in her manner as she moved down the short corridor, with Todd, Hrriss, Rogitel, and the marines following. "Then of course I will inspect your log tapes. If you were answering a Mayday, this puts an entirely different complexion on the matter. But it would have been wiser," and she pinned them with a harsh stare, "to have reported the matter sooner, rather than later."

"The Hunt, ma'am, is of great importance to Doona, and Hrriss and I were responsible for its success," Todd said, not so much in apology as in explanation.

Dupuis raised her eyebrows in an expression of disagreement of his priorities.

"What a clever explanation for breaking interdict at Hrrilnorr," Rogitel said, his eyes cold. "Have you an equally glib explanation for these?" At the commander's gesture, a marine lifted off the panel on the front of the drives cabinet, revealing a number of small packages. Rogitel tore the wrappings off one and held it up. "Would you mind telling me what this is?"

Astonished, Todd stared at the hand-sized lump. It looked like a free-form rock swirled with multiple colors, like sunshine on oil. He'd seen something like it on educational tapes in school, when they studied the biology of other alien species. "It looks . . . like a cotopoid egg case." Todd felt sick. Cotopoid egg cases were priceless and rarely available on any legitimate market, since they were artifacts of another interdicted system.

"Now, tell me how it got there, behind your engine control panel."

"I don't know," Todd said, staring disbelievingly at the equipment cabinet. "It wasn't there when I last inspected the engines."

"When you last inspected the engines. And when was that?" Rogitel asked. "Remember, you are speaking before the Treaty Councillor."

"Before we took off from Doona," Todd replied, his mind racing. When had these incriminating packages been inserted in the control panels? On Doona where a mechanic in Spacedep's pay would have had access to the *Albatross*? Or on Hrretha during that second, totally redundant "servicing"?

"And these?" the Spacedep official demanded. "What about these?" There seemed to be dozens of small artifacts shoved between the elements of the machinery. When the marines removed other panels, still more bags and bottles were revealed.

Some were opened to expose objects of great value and rarity, also from interdicted systems.

Part of Todd's bewilderment reflected a droll amusement at the sheer volume of purloined valuables that Hrriss and he were supposed to have assembled. But any amusement was soon drowned by the obvious fact that a lot of trouble had gone into framing them with such a widespread cache of illegal treasures.

"I have no idea where any of this came from," Todd said in staunch repudiation as he suppressed the rising anger he felt at such long-planned treachery.

"Such a display would have taken weeks to gather. We did not," Hrriss said with stiff dignity, his tail tip twitching with indignation. He turned to the Councillor. "We answered a Mayday call. The tapes will verify this."

"Then how did those get there?" Rogitel demanded as yet another cache was discovered.

"We are not responsible for their presence on the *Albatross*," Todd said, his tone as expressionless as Hrriss's. "There were no such illegal items on board this ship when we left Doona. I oversaw the check myself."

Rogitel's heavy lids lowered over cold blue eyes. "Then where did they come aboard?" Rogitel asked in a poisonously reasonable tone.

"The Hrrethans insisted on a complimentary service of the *Albatross* while we were attending the ceremonies there," Todd said, making no accusations. "When we landed, we reported the incident to my father. The postmaster's deputy, Linc Newry, had properly affixed the seal."

"That is the lamest explanation you've yet advanced, Reeve," Rogitel said. "The seals on the hatch were intact. They were placed there not half an hour after the ship had landed, according to the portmaster's log. It would have taken far longer than half an hour for anyone to secrete all these items. Therefore, you two are the only ones capable of concealing the artifacts on this ship—sometime between your departure from Doona and your return, via the Hrrilnorr system!" Rogitel was winding himself up to a good display of outraged anger. "Councillor Dupuis, these young men, so

trusted by their parents, have been using their privileged position as trusted messengers of Alreldep to pillage treasures from
interdicted planets. Alreldep will be shocked at the abuse of
their trust."

"I am not Alreldep," Hrriss said coldly. "I am a Hrruban,
a citizen of Rrala, on whose behalf I made the journey with
Todd Reeve to Hrretha. I answer to the Hrruban High Council
of Speakers and to the Treaty Councillors. Not to Spacedep."

"I stand reproved," Rogitel said with noticeable sarcasm.
"You shall indeed answer to the Treaty Councillors and your
own High Council of Speakers."

Just then, one of the marines pulled the panel from the last
cabinet, the ship's log recorder. Behind the metal sheet, some
of the equipment had been moved to one side to make room
for an ovoid white stone, at least a meter high. It resembled Terran alabaster, except that it had an inner illumination
of its own. The Spacedep official regarded it from a safe
distance.

"The very presence of such a gem," and Hrriss extended
his forefinger, claw fully sheathed, at the luminous Byzanian
Glow Stone, "supports our innocence. They are only found
deep inside the caverns of the planet. The log will show how
little time we spent in that system: far too short a span to have
landed, searched, and found a Glow Stone of that quality.
Further," he went on, holding up his hand, "they are why the
system is proscribed. The effects of the mineral's emissions
are not yet fully investigated."

"But their possible danger makes them all the more collect-
ible," Rogitel said, an air of triumph in his stance. "Arrest
them!" he ordered the marines who bracketed Hrriss and Todd,
weapons drawn.

"We are innocent," Todd said, standing erect and ignoring
his escort.

Hu Shih stepped forward to block the exit. "I protest, Madam Councillor. I have known these young men far too long to
entertain for one moment that they are guilty of transgressing
a Treaty whose terms they have scrupulously obeyed and
upheld for twenty-four years. Or," and Hu Shih straightened
his shoulders in denial, "jeopardize themselves and the world
they hold dear by pilfering baubles."

"You call that," and Rogitel pointed at the Byzanian Glow Stone, "a bauble?"

"It is in *my* eyes," Hu Shih said in measured contempt.

"Perhaps," said Councillor Dupuis, "but this matter has gone from a minor infraction to systematic robbery and the arrest is to proceed."

"To that I must concur," Hu Shih said, bowing to her, "but an armed escort is unnecessary and insulting. I can speak with full confidence that neither Todd nor Hrriss will resist the due process of law."

Councillor Dupuis accepted his statement and gestured for the squad leader to have his men reholster their weapons.

"These . . ." and Dupuis waved at the array of incriminating evidence, "are to be impounded, identified, and placed in the highest security."

"Remove that Stone with care," Hrrestan said to the two marines who were about to lift the Byzanian Stone out of its hiding place.

"Yes," Rogitel said, stepping in front of Hrrestan and ostentatiously taking charge of the removal. "Don't touch it with your bare hands or let it touch unprotected skin. Treat it as carefully as you would radioactive substances. And it's heavy."

"What, sir?" asked one of the marines, a glazed expression on his face. He had been standing right beside the Stone since the panel had been opened. Now the light seemed to pulse, drawing every eye to it.

Shading eyes with one hand and stepping quickly around Rogitel, Hrrestan pulled the man away from the white light. The marine shook his head, looking puzzled.

"He has been affected by it already. We must all leave before the Stone's effect spreads," Hrrestan said. "The most noticeable effect it has is an interference with short-term memory."

As Hrriss and Todd dutifully proceeded with their escort, Todd caught a glimpse of Rogitel, disconnecting the flight log recorder. He carried it out of the ship cradled in his arms like a bubble made of glass.

Once the group was outside, technicians sealed the ship once more with fiberglass wafers, and Councillor Dupuis affixed her own seal. Hrriss and Todd were hustled to a shuttle which had landed while they were inside the *Albatross*.

"That Glow Stone," Hrriss murmured as they were led to seats, "affects more than men."

"Quiet there! No conversation between criminals," Rogitel said, no more the suave diplomat but the acknowledged jailor.

"Criminality has yet to be proved," Hrriss said as he was pushed into a seat while Todd was taken farther down the aisle before settled. They were advised to fasten their safety harnesses and were then studiously ignored by the marine guard.

During the entire journey to Treaty Island, no one even offered them anything to eat or drink, although Rogitel and the marines ate a light meal.

Perhaps, Todd thought, sunk in a negative mood, it was as well he and Hrriss could not speak. Rogitel would construe it as collusion to be sure their "explanations" tallied before interrogation. But Todd did not need to speak to Hrriss to know that his friend would be as puzzled as he that dozens of illegal items had been secreted on the *Albatross*, a ship used almost exclusively by themselves on official tours of duty.

And the positioning of the Byzanian Glow Stone indicated a good try at jamming the recorder. His kick must have tipped the Stone sufficiently to restore the function, but had the Stone's radiation erased the tape? Would the all-important Mayday still be recorded? Surely machinery was a little less receptive to the Glow Stone's effects than a human? And the Mayday was the only proof of their innocence right now.

Once the shuttle landed on Treaty Island, the two prisoners were hurried inside the huge Federation Center. Hrriss had only a glimpse of the high, white stone façade before they were rushed up the stairs and through a maze of identical hallways. There was no sound but the clatter of boot heels on the smooth surface of the floors. The sergeant stopped before a door, its nameplate blank and status sign registering "empty."

"You'll wait here until the Council is ready for you," the sergeant said. "Food and drink will be brought in a bit."

"That is most considerate," Hrriss said in Terran Standard.

The numbness of shock had receded sufficiently to make him aware of an intense thirst and, less insistent, some hunger.

"You're a Treaty prisoner and the courtesies are observed," the sergeant said, but Hrriss could see that the man approved of his use of Terran.

Hrriss knew that the military arm of both parent governments was made up of fierce patriots who preferred their own culture in all ways. It was one of the reasons there was no standing force of any kind on Doona, the symbol of compromise. As the Treaty Organization was trying to maintain a separate but equal method of expansion in trading and colonization, each culture needed to remain independent from the other. That would make a Doonan "army" an unacceptable third force.

"Hear tell you all had some party last night," the guard said, sounding almost friendly. "What's keeping you?" he added, looking down the hall just as Todd, between his guards, reached the room. "In you go." The escort stood aside to let Todd enter. "Food and drink coming."

"Thanks, Sergeant," Todd said, and his stomach rumbled. Whether the sergeant heard that or not was irrelevant, for he closed the door firmly. Both Hrriss and Todd heard the lock mechanism whirr, and the bulb over the door lit up redly. They also heard the stamp of boots as someone stood to attention outside the room.

The two prisoners turned to view the room. No more than three meters on a side, with a long window running along the wall opposite the door. A broad table was set underneath the window, a tape reader on its surface but no tapes in it or blanks ready to be used. There were three padded chairs against the wall: a cheerless functional cubicle.

"Are they likely to listen in?" Hrriss asked.

"I doubt it," Todd said, glancing at the door. "Looks like a research room, not an interrogation facility, in spite of that tape reader." He had been listening to the sound of his voice. "It's soundproofed. Scholars insist on that as an aid to deep thought and concentration. Fardles, despite what they hauled out of cabinets and crannies on the *Albatross,* we're still only alleged Treaty breakers, not actual criminals.

"We might as well be, Zodd, with all the treasures Rogitel pulled out of hiding," Hrriss said gloomily.

"Hu Shih didn't believe we took them. Neither did your father!" Todd began to pace with some agitation. "All the way here I kept trying to remember every time we've left the *Albie* unguarded and open. Suffering snakes, Hrriss, that stuff could have been planted anytime the last few years."

"Not if proper service checks were carried out, Zodd, and you supervised the last one yourself," Hrriss reminded him.

"Yeah, so I did. Then the junk has to have been planted during that phony servicing on Hrretha. There'd've been time to platinum the hull. Furthermore," and now Todd whirled on Hrriss, pointing his index finger at his friend, "Rogitel was on Hrretha, and lurking close to us all the time. To prevent us from going back to our ship to see just what sort of servicing was being done?" When Hrriss nodded agreement with that thought, Todd continued, "Furthermore, we filed our flight plan, same as always, and, despite that short detour to Hrrilnorr system, we weren't much behind schedule landing back on Doona, were we?"

Though Hrriss recognized the validity of that logic, he knew that Todd was talking himself out of despair even as he offered the same hope to Hrriss.

"We always register flight plans," Hrriss said. "We leave and arrive on time at all destinations."

"So," and Todd stopped pacing long enough to whirl back to Hrriss, "where do they think we had time to pick up all those juicy little rarities? Cotopoids are found on only three planets in two systems, if I remember rightly, and none of them on any route we've taken recently. I can't identify half of the other stuff but," and now he sighed, "that damned Byzanian Glow Stone is genuine and there's only one place you can come by them and we were orbiting above it."

"All our flight plans are on record," Hrriss said, finding reassurance in that fact, "and they will prove our innocence. Come, stop pacing. It suggests a guilty mind."

Todd plopped down next to Hrriss and shoved the third chair a short distance away so the two of them could share it to prop their feet. Hrriss disposed his tail comfortably through the opening in the rear of his chair and composed himself.

"There's something nagging at me," Todd said after a few moments. He circled his hand in the air, trying to catch hold of an elusive thought. "Something Councillor Dupuis said, that they had received information that the *Albie* had been identified by the Hrrilnorr beacon. Isn't it a little soon for such to reach Hrruban Security? That beacon didn't dispatch a robot probe when we passed it, which is the only way that the data would get here short of a month. It shouldn't have been picked up for another few weeks even by digital rapid-transfer. That's why my father thought that the matter could be deferred until after Snake Hunt."

Hrriss yawned broadly, showing fangs, incisors, and grinders that Todd always found an impressive array. "We both know how interdict beacons operate. But there were other people using Hrrilnorr as a warp-jump coordinate. Perhaps they collected the message and reported the infraction."

"Whose side are you on?" Todd demanded, half joking. Hrriss often played devil's advocate when they had to reason through a problem. "A little too coincidental to please me, especially with the Treaty Renewal imminent."

Hrriss yawned again.

"Who else was using the Hrrilnorr connection, Hrriss?"

"I do not remember, only that some were."

"But I thought most of the top brass came by transport grid. And Rogitel is not the type to plan practical jokes. Nor is Landreau, and this thing was planned."

Hrriss was working his bottom into the padded seat, trying to make himself comfortable enough to sleep. Todd often wished he had the Hrruban propensity for sleep. Despite their generally high level of activity when awake, they could, and did, take naps anytime opportunity offered.

"I agree," Hrriss mumbled. He caught himself in the act of falling asleep. "We were promisssed food and drink. I could sleep better with a full belly. But I need sleep to make sense out of this situation. I had only an hour in my bed whenever this morning was." He sat up, suddenly anxious. "I hope my mother will feed the ocelots when evening comes. If they're not fed, they will go in search of food and raid my neighbor's ssliss coop again."

"You'll be home to feed them yourself," Todd said.

"I hope so but the ocelots do enjoy ssliss eggs."

"Don't talk about eggs. I'm starved." When Hrriss yawned even more broadly than before, Todd regarded him in disgruntlement. "And, damn your lousy furred pelt, you can sleep. I can't when I'm starving."

"Then wake me when the meal comes," Hrriss advised, and settling himself, his chin dropped to his chest, his hands, so oddly more human than the rest of him, relaxing in his lap while his tail hung slack behind him, the tip only occasionally twitching.

Todd sighed, settling back, legs stretched out in front of him, crossed at the ankles on the supporting chair, and began running over the day's happenings. *Who* had placed those incriminating items on the *Albie*? He turned to ask what Hrriss thought. Hrriss's breathing had slowed, become steady and shallow. The gentle oscillation of the tip of Hrriss's tail attracted Todd's attention. Its movement was hypnotic and soothing. As Todd watched it, his own eyes grew heavy. After a while, despite his hunger, he dozed off.

"As you can see, Madam Councillor," Rogitel continued, running the recorded flight log back to the beginning, "the so-called rescue mission to Hrrilnorr was only the last stop in a series of piracies these two young reprobates committed." Landreau's aide was able to act as prosecutor before the Treaty Council only because noncolonizable Human-claimed planets were kept under the aegis of his department. Entries in the log of the *Albatross* suggested that the ship had visited at least three in that category.

The log went through a further playback, projecting its holographic images onto a platform while sound was broadcast through wall speakers. Hu Shih, Hrrestan, Rogitel, and Ken Reeve glowered at the images while Councillor Dupuis's expression was impassive.

That morning, as soon as the marines had left with Todd in custody, Ken had persuaded Martinson, the portmaster, to let him go to Treaty Island via transport grid, for Martinson had also been called to give a deposition. Now Martinson sat nervously hunched over his folded hands. Allowing the *Albatross* to go uninspected for so long was a black mark on his record.

He, too, was risking censure, even dismissal, if a crime resulted from negligence even by his subordinate, Newry.

"No fewer than eight landings are recorded between the date the scout ship left Doona and the date on which it returned here," Rogitel said. "Eight! And only the one on Hrretha legitimate. Here." He stopped the tape and rewound it. "Here is their so-called rescue, after they had passed through the perimeter of Hrrilnorr." The hologram showed the nose of the ship as it approached a distant sun. An audio signal for help crowded by static came out of the speakers. The audio monitors then erupted with the siren call of the interdict alarm, but the ship passed without stopping. Hrriss's voice could be heard responding to the Mayday message. The print update on the screen showed Hrrilnorr's identification number and location. Then the ship's nose penetrated the cloud layer of the planet's atmosphere.

"Naturally," Rogitel's insidious voice went on, "the system's buoy did not record the Mayday, since it did not exist. That could so easily be patched into the log by either conspirator. Both have the necessary qualifications."

Then the camera eye upturned for landing, to show the stern of the ship as it touched down on grassoids flattened by the exhaust from the engines.

Councillor Dupuis looked down at her notes for a long moment. Her face showed inner conflict. "This is far more serious than a simple violation. There is no choice but to make an exhaustive formal inquiry into this matter."

"I heartily concur," Ken Reeve said so emphatically that Rogitel regarded him in stunned amazement. "A formal inquiry that will clear my son and Hrriss of every one of these ridiculous accusations."

The Treaty Controller slammed his gavel down on the bench. He was the ranking Hrruban on Doona, and had been nominated to his post by the Third Speaker of the Hrruban High Council. It was a bad time for one of Third's minions to be the senior Councillor on Doona; Third had been against the joint colony from the day Humans were discovered. Ken tried to take comfort in the fact that the Controller was reputed to be a just personage who tried each case on its individual merit.

"Please be silent, Mr. Reeve. We take the log tape in evidence." He addressed the holographic recorder. "This hearing is to decide whether Todd Reeve and/or Hrriss, son of Hrrestan, have violated the Treaty of Doona, and to what degree."

Testimony was then taken from Martinson, who explained that the *Albatross* had gone unsearched two weeks ago due to extenuating circumstances. "They were Snake Hunt Masters and I know how much time and planning that takes to prevent trouble. They told the duty officer that they urgently needed to take advice on a protocol matter. Since the ship was sealed and its papers in order, Newry granted their request."

"And is this laxness typical of your administration of your post as portmaster?" Rogitel inquired acidly.

"No, Commander, it is not," the portmaster said, eyes flashing. "I've been in this job fifteen years, and I've known Todd and Hrriss all that time. I had no reason to suspect that there was anything out of the ordinary about this landing."

"Whose advice were they in such a hurry to obtain?"

"Mine," Ken spoke up, and was relieved as he succeeded in making eye contact with the Spacedep official. Ken held that contact, trying to look the disgust he felt. He had never ceased to dislike and distrust bureaucrats, and Rogitel was nearly as bad an example of the type as Landreau.

"And when were the seals on the hatch cut?" the Treaty Controller wanted to know.

"Not in my presence," Martinson said in an aggrieved tone. "My assistant, Lincoln Newry, was deputized in my absence, but in something as serious as this I should have been there! I have no idea who else was there. When I did arrive, the ship was already open, with troops pouring all over it."

Next Ken Reeve gave his evidence. Under irritated prompting from Rogitel, Ken repeated the story that Todd and Hrriss had told him two weeks before.

"I believe them," he insisted at the end. "They were genuinely distressed when they realized they'd been tricked into violating an interdicted system."

"We have asked you to draw no conclusions," the Treaty Controller said ponderously. Ken nodded, angrily swallowing the rest of his opinions, and sat down.

The Council proceeded thereafter to take evidence from the sergeant of the Spacedep marines who had searched the *Albatross*. Rogitel testified that he had received information from a confidential source, whom he declined to identify, that there might be contraband aboard the ship.

"Furthermore, I wish to put on record my disgust that two such untrustworthy men were allowed the unsupervised use of a scout ship!" he finished in a voice trembling with outrage.

"I have studied the records of the defendants, Commander Rogitel," Madam Dupuis said, sternly raising her voice above Ken's as he erupted from his chair to protest the slander, "and find absolutely no proof to support a claim of dishonesty or irresponsibility. You will kindly retract such an unsupported remark."

If Rogitel did so with an ill grace, at least he did so and it would be in the record.

"We will see"—Madam Dupuis hesitated—"the two young men now."

Ken Reeve took that as a good sign: the Councillor was by no means convinced of Rogitel's damning evidence.

Todd and Hrriss were brought in then, and sworn in as witnesses. As one, they turned to face the table. As accustomed as they were to diplomatic events, facing the full Treaty Council with little sleep and only a dry sandwich to eat was not auspicious. The holographic tape was run once more in their presence.

The first landing was shown, and the two young men were stunned.

"This can't be our log," Todd protested. "We made no landing. This must be a mistake."

"Silence!" the Treaty Controller demanded, rapping his gavel. "Continue."

Todd and Hrriss watched, incredulous, as the holographic replay continued. At each entry and departure, the ID signal repeated on-screen. There was no question that it matched the *Albatross*'s code. When the tape finished, the Treaty Controller turned to them.

"As the log shows, you visited several off-limits worlds, and took therefrom prohibited materials, and in some cases, precious and valuable items of historical worth. I must say, your thefts were nonpartisan. My notes show that some of them came from Hrruban-marked planets, and some from the Amalgamated Worlds. What can you offer as your defense?"

"Sir, something's skewed," Todd said agitatedly. "We passed into only one prohibited system, Hrrilnorr, and only to respond to a Mayday message. That much of this tape is accurate. The rest has been added. We made no entries into other interdicted zones."

"But why is there no Mayday message recorded in the alarm beacon orbiting the system?" Rogitel asked. "Such beacons are designed for that purpose, to record transmissions that originate within its range of sensitivity."

"I have no ready explanation . . . sir," Todd added after a pause. "A flaw in the mechanism? The in-system sensor malfunctioning? Plenty of buoys are damaged by space debris. But Hrriss and I heard the call for help. We diverted from our planned route to respond. All we found was that buoy, orbiting the fourth planet."

"A marker buoy, as you say," Rogitel intoned coldly. "You broke Treaty Law for an unmanned probe?"

"We did not know it was a marker buoy at the time we heard its message," Todd replied, trying to keep his voice level.

"It is what we found," Hrriss said coolly, "broadcasting the distress message." The Hrruban extended a pointed claw and replayed the section of the log.

"Mayday, Mayday," said the tape. "Anyone who is within the sound of my voice, Mayday! We require assistance. Our ship is down and damaged. Mayday!" The message began to repeat, and Hrriss shut it off. "Every pilot of whatever species must respond to such a message. As Zodd said, we could not ignore a Mayday. It would be uncivilized."

Rogitel stood up. "Please tell the council directly: where did you find the buoy?"

"We found it orbiting Hrrilnorr IV."

"The Buoy Authority lists no such installation in orbit around Hrrilnorr IV. There are no extraneous beacons orbiting in that system. There are only two assigned to it, each one AU perpendicular to the plane of the ecliptic above and below."

"There was a third one," Todd said in weary rebuttal. "The buoy was broadcasting the message for help that's recorded on our log. It still sounds genuine. We couldn't and didn't ignore it."

Dismissively Rogitel switched off the audio. "Anyone could have recorded that message in your ship's memory. The voice is broadcasting in Middle Hrruban, the language of Doona. The static could have been made by crumpling packing material near the microphone. You put it in yourself. Without correlation, the message must be accounted as false."

"I respectfully suggest that an analysis of the voice patterns of Hrriss and Zodd be made," Hrrestan said. "Analysis will prove if one of them recorded the Mayday message."

Councillor Dupuis made a note, nodding acknowledgment of Hrrestan's suggestion.

"We didn't make that spurious recording," Todd said, turning his head to meet the eyes of the seven Council members, "and we most certainly did not collect or secrete those artifacts in the equipment cabinets."

"Simple lies to assuage your guilt," Rogitel retorted.

Todd's eyes flashed hotly. "I do not lie." He half sprang from his seat, but Hrriss pulled him down.

"Councillors, may I speak?" Hu Shih rose somewhat stiffly to his feet. "We have before us two reliable young men, considered rather more than unusually truthful by their elders and their peers. Let a full inquiry establish what is fact or fiction."

"So ordered," the Treaty Controller said, banging his gavel.

The Spacedep subdirector shrugged dismissively. "That can take months. We have before us right now recorded proof that differs greatly from their verbal accounts. Surely this is sufficient to deprive them of positions of high responsibility and trust. The flight recorder has been placed in evidence. It shows landings preceding and following their landing on Hrrilnorr. Their posted flight plan showed that they skimmed the space between the Human and Hrruban arms of the galaxy, so it is possible to have visited all these worlds in the time they were gone. In every case, they broke interdiction. In only one did they attempt to justify the falsehood with a tale of rescue. Look at the evidence"—Rogitel swept an arm to indicate the table where most of the contraband lay—"taken only this morning from the ship they alone seem to use."

"The commander forgets one detail," Hrriss said. "The flight plan we filed with portmaster Martinson is the shortest possible journey we could make between Hrretha and Rrala. There was not time for us to have landed on all these worlds and collected these things in the weeks we were gone. Especially since our log-in and log-off times were verified."

As if they had placed themselves in further jeopardy, Rogitel called up the holo again and pointed out the time/date designations. "The flight recorder says that the time was available to you. We have run it through compcheck. Though the timing is tight, you would have had the time."

"Only if we knew exactly where all these artifacts were," Hrriss protested, "with no allowance for any time to search. How could we know where they were? It would have taken months to research archaeological and geological data from the Treaty Island banks. Or are you suggesting that some of the researchers on Treaty Island are guilty of collusion and deception, too?" Hrriss asked softly.

"The matter will be investigated," was all the commander would say. He addressed the Council. "Clearly the defendants are guilty of deviating from their registered flight path. Spacedep, as the body in charge of security and defense for the Amalgamated Worlds, demands that this matter be examined as well."

"Tell me, Commander," Todd demanded, leaning across the table toward Rogitel, "just why would Hrriss and I wish to steal rarities like that? Much less something as dangerous as that Glow Stone? Where could we possibly fence our loot without being detected? Especially as we are not scheduled to take any off-planet trips in the next year?"

"We are innocent," Hrriss added, his tone more growl than speech.

Rogitel did not quite flinch, but his body inclined ever so slightly away from the Hrruban. "Machines cannot lie," Rogitel said flatly. "Only people can, and it would appear in this case, very poorly. And you"—he pointed his finger at Todd— "you admit entering the Hrrilnorr system. You have just said that you recognize the danger of a Glow Stone and that you know it is found only on Hrrilnorr IV. There are many other unscrupulous persons in this galaxy who could use the Glow Stone's peculiar properties to excellent advantage. And those" —now his finger swung to point at Hrriss—"are particularly well known to Hrrubans."

"We adjourn for due consideration," said the senior Treaty Councillor, rising to his feet to end this session. His colleagues were equally solemn. "This is a matter of unprecedented gravity."

Every face was solemn and, in some cases, sad. This was the first time in twenty-five years that there had been any infraction of the provisions of the Treaty. The ramifications were profound, and could result in punishments ranging from exile for the two defendants, up through war and/or disbandment of the colony. The negotiations among them for renewal of the Treaty had been under way for several years. All knew that the twenty-fifth anniversary would be a crucial time—a time when the Treaty could be easily swept aside. A violation of this magnitude might obliterate two and a half decades of hope and dedication.

Two of the Council, Madam Dupuis and Mrrorra, were representatives of Doona/Rrala, and were both second-wave settlers from the First Villages. They were upset and puzzled, because they knew Todd and Hrriss well. Neither could find credence in the facts that suggested these two, whose friendship had created the Decision at Doona, could willfully destroy the colony. Their interspecies friendship had been held up as a symbol for Human/Hrruban cooperation all over the galaxy.

"Therefore," the Treaty Controller said heavily, "until the inquiry has been conducted and a decision reached, the two defendants are under house arrest. They are to be kept separated at their places of residence, and interim communication denied. This matter is adjourned pending investigation." The gavel banged once more. It might have been the report of a gun. Todd and Hrriss both reacted as if it had been, startled, shocked, deeply hurt by even the mere thought of such a separation.

But they were honorable young men, and although they held each other's eyes for a long, long moment, they did not speak. Then, distressed and saddened, they turned away from each other. No solitary confinement could have been harder to bear.

Especially when they needed each other's support to prove their innocence.

Ken Reeve was out of his seat a split second after the Council had filed out of the chamber. He rushed around the table to his son. Hrrestan was as quick to go to Hrriss.

"Rogitel seems to have pretty damning evidence against you, Todd," Ken said, wearily shaking his head. "But I know you've told the truth, so we'll beat this."

"What motive would we have for stealing such dumb stuff?" Todd asked his father, his hands spread in a helpless gesture of disbelief. He felt numbed by despair.

"Did either of you enter any or all of these interdicted systems?" Hrrestan asked.

"Why would we? We always come straight back to Doona, where we belong," Hrriss answered his father in the familial form of Hrruban.

"You know how we hate those damned missions, Dad," Todd added. "And one thing more, that damned beacon with its phony message had a destructive band. We were tractoring it up to the *Albie* when we saw that. Contact stuff from the look of it. Blow us and it up."

"Why didn't you mention that earlier?" Ken demanded.

"Hell, Dad, I only just remembered it," Todd said, scrubbing at his tired face with hands that nearly trembled.

Ken looked at Hrrestan. "A detail that might be useful. A convenient shot would explode the beacon."

"So it could," Hrrestan said, his tone thoughtful. "We will begin our own covert investigations. Little could we have imagined that a minor infraction of the Treaty would be subsumed by a larger and horrendous charge of piracy and smuggling. I will initiate inquiries for your defense on Hrruba."

"I've still some contacts on Earth through Sumitral," Ken said, noticeably brightening as actions became obvious. "His daughter is here on Treaty Island doing some research. I'll talk to her after I see you on your way home. I don't have all that many friends or allies on Earth, but I know we can count on that family."

"Let's just hope none of our former Corridor or Aisle neighbors get wind of this," Todd said, trying for some levity. It wrung a sad grin from Ken.

"You were never born for Earth, Todd, but you've always been a natural here on Doona," Ken said, "but I promise you, I'll holler down the doors if it'd help."

"Someone must know where that beacon came from and who put it there."

When they left the chamber, Todd and Hrriss were hustled through the bare corridors to the transport grid, which was located in another part of the building. Both were sent separately back via grid to the main continent with an escort of armed guards. The last glimpse Todd had of his best friend was Hrriss, standing too quietly between a guard lieutenant and Hrrestan. His fur seemed to have lost all its luster and his tail dragged in the dust behind him. Their eyes met, and Hrriss nodded once to him. Todd often felt that he could almost read the Hrruban's mind but there was no such feeling between them now.

The image seemed to disintegrate into mist, and then Todd was in the midst of the Hrruban village, facing the Friendship Bridge. Once he crossed it, he wouldn't be allowed back over until his innocence was proved. The thought made his feet feel heavy.

The guard accompanied him to his family ranch house, where Pat Reeve was waiting. In the living room, Kelly stood up when they came in. Todd was a little surprised to see her, until he realized that it had been many hours since he'd been taken away. She had probably come over this morning to continue the talk the three of them had been having the night before, and found he was gone.

The marine sergeant gave both women a sharp salute and then withdrew, taking his squad with him. Pat hovered for a minute, looking from Kelly to Todd, then went out toward the kitchen.

"You must be hungry. I know we are. I'll fix us all a snack."

"An armed escort? What happened?" Kelly asked, worried by the beaten expression on Todd's face.

"It's worse than I could have dreamed," Todd said. "This isn't a simple case of an interdiction infraction. Oh, no, nothing simple or easily explained like answering a Mayday call. Hrriss and I seem to have been to many planets in many interdicted systems, doing a fine job of smuggling rarities and classified items, all of which we have been secretly stashing around the *Albie*." He grinned sourly at the gasps that elicited. "We're big-time looters and purveyors of illegal artifacts, and up on charges of smuggling and contraband, using our prestigious position on Doona/Rrala to perpetrate crimes against Hrruba and Terra, and half the planets in between. That log entry we felt would clear us has had some very interesting additions." He rubbed his eyes with one hand. "I don't know how they got there. One thing is certain: neither Hrriss nor I put them there. Then Rogitel kept insisting that we falsified the Mayday signal to get into the Hrrilnorr system, to steal a Byzanian Glow Stone."

"A Glow Stone? A real one?" Kelly asked, her voice breaking with incredulity. "They've got one of those in the remote-handling research lab on Hrruba. They're considered ultra-dangerous. And," she added with a facial grimace, "they are only found on Hrrilnorr IV."

"Well, one was found in the communications cabinet," Todd said. "And whatever else it does, it deleted the short-term memory of the marine standing nearby. So Hrriss and I are not only smugglers and looters, we're stupidly dangerous pirates." His mother opened her mouth to protest and closed it, her eyes sparking with suppressed anger and resentment. "At that we got off lightly. The Councillors placed Hrriss and me under house arrest while they're investigating. We're not supposed to communicate at all." At that point, Todd's broad shoulders sagged, and he looked as dejected as a small boy, all the droll defensiveness and outrage gone. "We haven't been separated since I started wearing rope tails."

Pat Reeve could restrain herself no longer. "This whole thing is ridiculous. Why, neither you nor Hrriss have stolen so much as a . . . brrna." She spat that out after a good long hesitation as she tried to remember any other incident of petty crime. "How can they possibly accuse you and Hrriss of piracy or smuggling? *Any*one else could have done it. *Any*one on the launch pad could have access to your ship."

Todd had sunk to a chair, elbows on his knees, head in his hands, diminished more by the separation than the absurd charges. Sighing, he propped his chin on his hands and told his mother and Kelly about the additional landings and launches noted in the log, and the even stranger omissions concerning the orbiting alarm beacon. Kelly stood by him, not quite touching him, alert to any cues. When she moved toward him he caught her hand, squeezed it once, and then dropped it as if he shouldn't hold it—or her.

She was perplexed by that gesture, sensing it to be a "keep off" signal. She backed off. This was so unlike the resilient Todd she'd always known, but if he felt himself ostracized, perhaps he didn't wish her contaminated by his disgrace. That, too, was unlike the Todd she'd always known. But then, Todd had never been under such vile suspicions before and shouldn't be now, Kelly thought in seething outrage.

"This whole affair is ridiculous," she said, dropping her hands helplessly. "It's absurd to think of you two as smugglers! The Council must all be strangers, to let Rogitel get away with an accusation like that."

"The Treaty Controller this term is one of Third Speaker's nominees," Todd said in a dull voice. "I recognized him as soon as I came into the chamber. You both know him; he'd let us get into a war if it would remove the Human threat to Hrruba."

Irritably Kelly shook her head. "Surely we have some friends on the Council. I hoped Madam Dupuis would be on your side. She used to live around here."

"She's got to go by the evidence, the same as the other Councillors," Todd pointed out. "Any way you present it, it's damning. She had no option. That log tape was tampered with! Very cleverly, by someone who knew exactly how to match holo images perfectly." He sounded more like himself and then suddenly slumped again, scrubbing at his rumpled hair. "I don't know how we can prove that. *Why* didn't I open the recording unit when the log tape jammed! I'd've found that wretched Glow Stone then and we'd've known we were being set up. That was a costly kick." A flash of Todd's usual spirit accompanied that remark. "And whaddya bet," he went on in a bitter tone, "the Hrrilnorr warning beacon will show we spent far more time in that system than we say we did."

"What about the beacons at the other planets you're supposed to have visited?" Pat asked, grasping at the possibility.

"Surely, if you're supposed to have been at so many other worlds, all of those beacons can't have been got at?"

Todd regarded his mother almost pityingly and shook his head. "This was all too well planned, Mother, for them to neglect that sort of verification. Remember, it's Spacedep involved and they have the resources to do just this sort of documentation."

"Look, Todd," Kelly began in a firm tone, being as positive as she knew how, "you two have an enviable reputation on Earth. Much better than Rogitel's. There's going to be a lot of talk when he comes up with this sort of a crazy charge. And I don't care how much evidence there is against you. *He* doesn't have as good a reputation as you and Hrriss, and Doona, have. I'll see what I can find out. I'll talk to everyone I know about this ridiculous accusation. Furthermore," and her smile was malicious, "Hrringa can start the action. He'll do it for me. And"—her voice rose in triumph now—"I'll enlist Jilamey Landreau!"

Todd gave her a frankly contemptuous look.

"Don't be so skeptical, pal," she said. "He's been following me around all afternoon in hopes of finding you. He only gave up an hour ago. He's got a superlative hangover, but he's still raving about you saving his life. I'll send the rumor about your entrapment home with him. Yes, entrapment!" For Todd had looked up with some glimmer of hope in his dull eyes. "What else would you call it? You and Hrriss were framed. To ruin the Treaty negotiations. We'll beat this, er, rap," Kelly exclaimed, her eyes flashing.

"This what?" asked Pat.

Kelly grinned. "Well, I'm studying ancient colloquialisms." She leaned over, grabbing Todd by the shoulders, and kissed his cheek. "It's okay for one of your other good friends to visit you again, isn't it?" Immediately, she regretted her choice of phrases because a shadow crossed Todd's face: the friend he most wanted to see was forbidden him.

"It's okay for you to visit, Kelly, anytime you want," Todd answered, putting as much welcome into his voice as he could. He touched his cheek where she had kissed it. "Soon, please?"

"I'd better go now. I'll be back again tomorrow, and we'll have a council meeting of our own." She started to go, but turned back a few steps from the door. "Think you should know, Todd, how many people have said how much they enjoyed Snake Hunt and the feast last night. I'm not the first to tell you that you did a good job." She gave him a wry smile and wrinkled her nose. "I won't be the last and you'll feel better when you know how many people are solidly on your side. Anyway, the Hunt was the greatest."

Todd managed to smile back. "Thanks, Kelly. That Hunt seems to have happened years ago, not just hours," he said, then rallied, sitting up and straightening his shoulders. "But it was a good one. Thanks again for all your help."

"I intend to repay that in kind," she said, grinning wickedly. "You wait and see!" She waggled her finger at him, and that brought a slight grin of remembrance for all the times he had used that gesture and spoken that phrase to her. "I gotta go now, Todd, Pat. We're expecting dozens of Home Week visitors and Mother'll shoot me if I don't put in an appearance soon."

Todd closed his eyes against the thought of the dozens of Home Week visitors his family generally entertained after the Hunt. Everything good about his life seemed to have been ripped away in a single morning: his best friend, his reputation, and his honor. He heard the front door close softly and Kelly clattering down the steps. Then he felt his mother's gentle hand on his shoulder and he patted it.

"She's a staunch friend," his mother said, then she added in a teasing tone, "and still as much the tomboy as ever."

"Not quite," Todd said, forcing himself out of despair. He looked up at his mother with a lopsided grin. "Not at the Hunt party she wasn't."

"Oh?" Pat rolled her eyes facetiously. "You noticed?"

"Of course I noticed," Todd said, hearing an edge of irritation in his tone.

Pat put up her hands to ward off an imaginary attack. "I'm not, I swear I'm not," she said. "But she *is* a staunch friend and she'll do all she can to help. She's smart. Anne says Kelly graduated second in her class, even with all the discrimination against 'colonial types.' "

"I didn't know she'd got that high," Todd said, impressed. "But why didn't she make first?"

"Oh, you," and Pat play-batted at him. "She'll call in every favor she's owed on Earth. You just wait and see."

"Oh, Mom, how did we ever get ourselves in such a mess!" He dropped his head and began digging with the heels of his hands at eyes that hadn't seen the danger. Pat dropped beside him, her arm supportively about his shoulders. "When did that stuff get hidden on the *Albie*?"

"We'll find out, son, we'll find out," his mother said. "You've always been motivated by conscience, by truth, and you've always respected the rights of others and your responsibilities to them. No one who knows you and Hrriss will believe this vile canard."

"What about those who want to? Who want to see this colony disbanded, discredited?" Todd said in a soft but caustic tone.

"We both know such people exist and they have caused this entrapment," his mother said. "But there is a way out it. The truth, and we'll shove the doubting faces into that truth. Just you believe we will!"

Todd uncovered his eyes, reddened by his rubbing and the tears he was trying to repress. "I wonder if we haven't been a little naive here on paradisiacal Doona."

"That's a possibility, but we're not too long in the tooth to protect what we've earned by hard work and fair dealings. You'll see!" She gave him a firm clap on the back, wanting him, he knew, to buck up.

"Yes, Mother, we will!" he replied with as much feeling as he could instill in his tone.

"Now, I've always found that the best way to work out a problem is to work! Since you've obviously been struck off the diplomatic lists, you can just go help Lon Adjei round up the horses for their annual injections. Since Mark Aden went off-planet, we've been a little shorthanded. Not that he was much help as a stablehand when he spent so much time mooning over Inessa. She and Robin are already out there. I'd go but we've had New Home Week callers all day long." She gave him a second, playful thump on the back. "Go on, hon. Have a shower to clear your head."

Todd gave her a grateful glance. "That's the best idea anyone's had all day."

He went to shower and change. Wrangling horses would get him away from the house and give him something to occupy his mind. But, even as he showered, his mind kept whirling around the morning's bizarre events.

"Machines can't lie," Rogitel had said. The phrase kept running through Todd's mind. No, they couldn't lie, but they could be tampered with. But when? And how? And by whom? No face filled the void when he tried to figure out who had set a trap for them. If only he and Hrriss could sit down and think this mess through . . . The two of them could discover the answers in no time, he knew they could. They had solved countless puzzles together over the years. Not to be able to communicate with Hrriss, as he had done every day since he was six years old, made him feel empty and lost. He jerked the shower control over to cold and steeled himself to accept the chill.

After a hard day's work, Todd returned home. As the evening stretched interminably out before him, again and again, Todd found himself starting out the door to go over the bridge to the Hrruban village, as he had done nearly every day for the last quarter of a century. Quelling that urge, he sat down at the computer unit and almost typed in Hrriss's comp number. But that would be a violation. Could he send his brother Robin over the bridge with a note? Just to let Hrriss know he was thinking about him? No, not even that solace was permissible until the accusations were dismissed. No communication meant just that, and Todd had given his solemn word. He had never broken it. He and Hrriss were honor bound, and honor meant everything to them. Someone was playing on that to keep them apart. Divide and conquer. Well, Todd was determined that no one would conquer without facing a fight.

CHAPTER

5

"YOU'LL BE WELCOME AT HOME FOR A CHANGE, my cub," Mrrva said kindly, bringing Hrriss inside as the guards withdrew from the door.

Hrriss still felt himself torn apart by the harshness of the restriction. He had never thought of himself as complacent, or smug about his reputation for honesty, but to have it so smirched and casually disregarded shocked him.

"There is considerable physical evidence against us, Mother," he said wearily. From their front window, he could see the Friendship Bridge, built so long ago by Hrrubans and Hayumans in the spirit of cooperation. Across it, not very far, lay Zodd. He forced himself to turn away. "It is false evidence, but they must believe what they see. I know only that if we were allowed to be together we could solve the mystery in half the time. We could discuss it until we understood it. It is so difficult to have a lifelong companion torn away from one's side, Mother."

Mrrva's heart went out to him. "I am sorry to learn that you and Zodd must be separated but it will be only temporary. In no time they will see that Zodd and you are innocent of any crime, and you will be together again." She guided him through the house and out through the back door. "Wait here for me, little love." She settled him under the arbor in the garden behind the house, and hastened out to the dining area to bring cool drinks for both of them. It was a fine day, and the sun warmed the colors of her sprawling flower beds. She had nearly forgotten how solitary a cub Hrriss had been. Only the explosive arrival on the scene of the lively Hayuman boy Zodd had demonstrated how lonely he had been.

"Don't dwell on the apartness," Mrrva said, urging him to take the cold drink. She had pitched her voice to intimate levels to give her words more weight. "You will only make yourself ill. Later, when you have relaxed, you shall explore the facts. For now, let yourself relax. It is so seldom I have you all to myself."

The herbal drink loosened some of the tightness in his throat. "Have I neglected my duty to you?" Hrriss asked sadly. "I offer apologies to you and Father."

"No, no! Not at all," Mrrva assured him in a purr. "We are more than proud of the way you have grown up and the way you hold yourself in honor. Since you first met, Zodd has been welcomed daily as your friend. And ours. He is nearly my second cub. The tasks which I have set you over the years have been done twice as quickly by two sets of hands instead of one." Mrrva let her jaw drop ever so slightly. "The only way in which you have perhaps slipped in your duties is in the begetting of an heir to the Stripe. Have you forgotten that you are Hrrestan's only cub? When will you choose a mate? I have waited for the matter to occur naturally to your mind." She paused, blinking solemnly.

Hrriss lowered his head, abashed. "I have not thought of a mate. My life has been so full up until now that there has been no urgency."

Mrrva gave him an understanding sideways glance. "Please to consider it now, then. I wish for your happiness, but it would increase your father's if you do not allow the Stripe to pass to another's offspring."

Hrriss flinched. He couldn't allow the line succession to die just because he was too indolent to find a mate. It would be easy, he thought, merely to mate with a willing female and produce an heir, but, without affection, such a union would be sterile. Matches based on duty were no longer common in Hrruban society, though they did still exist. But the example set by his parents, who were bound by mutual respect and admiration, was one he hoped to emulate. Hayumans chose their mates based on mutual appeal and affection. When they'd been just approaching manhood, he and Zodd had often talked about mating, but in a clinical fashion, comparing the difference imposed by the physical variations of their separate species. Once they had been able for the duties of adult males, they had both been too busy for wives and children. The time had come to review the situation. In several aspects.

Since the sordid accusations this morning, the previous tenor of his life and ways had been drastically altered. He had never imagined a different style of life. Certainly not a life without Zodd in it every day, going out on missions, or taking care of their tasks at home, but now that he thought of it, there was an itch he hadn't bothered to scratch. Who knew how long he would be kept from acting as an emissary of Doona, and whether others would ever again consider him to fit that post. A Stripe without honor had no place in society. He must be cleared and pronounced innocent, or his life was over!

Since there was nothing more he could do that day to clear his name, Hrriss seriously considered his duty to his Stripe. Now was the time to find a suitable female. More than time. He was already much older than his father had been when he was born. It wasn't that he'd missed female companionship. He had joyfully given relief to many charming partners during their seasonal heats, vying with other young males to serve their need. No male Hrruban would touch a female without her permission, but many females had made their preference for his attentions quite blatant. Centuries of civilized behavior hadn't quite reduced that primal urge, though in these modern times, many females used contraception remedies when procreation wasn't an objective.

Hayumans were not as natural as Hrrubans about sexual matters. It seemed strange to Hrriss that a society which was so much like his own often ruthlessly repressed their natural urges and behaviors. Even when Hrruba had been reduced to crowded quarters for each den and new litters were no longer blessings, the traditional openness about sex had remained.

Mrreva left him alone in the garden with his thoughts. It was so quiet that the tiny breeze brought distant voices and the faint clatter of hooves and machinery from the property beside theirs. Turning over his mother's suggestion in his mind, Hrriss began to examine the possibilities of the females he knew. And came right up against a very important consideration: would she understand his friendship with the Hayuman? Would she like Zodd? More important, would Zodd like her?

"I suppose I shall have to trust to my own judgment alone for this," Hrriss said out loud, and laughed.

Many of the females in this and other villages had sought him as their lifemate, and tempted him to commit while in their estrous cycles. There was never anything as crass as a demand for long-term relations, only a sighing and sensuous persuasion. While the attractions were obvious, Hrriss felt there needed to be more to the perfect image than a sexual being. He wanted a woman who thought, and created, and laughed. The image which kept coming back to his mind was the lithe, cinnamon-furred snake dancer at the feast. Her delicately graceful movements repeated in his memory again and again. He remembered her name was Nrrna, a soft and pliant sound. She worked with Mrrva in the Health Center. He wondered if she was willing. The last time she had gone though her fertile cycle, she had let him know that she would welcome him, but he had had to go off-planet then. When he returned, she had said nothing to him about what had gone on in his absence.

There was also Mrratah, a weaver whose textiles were wearable art. Last year, after Snake Hunt, they had spent a wild night together. The heavy musk in the air and the excitement of the chase had stirred him. She had been out on Hunt, too, and was as aroused as he by primal bloodlust, the beat of the dance band's drums, and the scent in the air.

Hrriss's eyelids lowered as he remembered that night, let his body sway with the rhythm in his memory. There was a high-pitched snarl that was so like the voice of Mrratah in excitation that he opened his eyes. His female ocelot, Mehh, loped out of the house past him, with the male, Prem, in determined pursuit. Mehh was young, no more than two Doonan years old. She was coming into full heat for the first time. Her attitude toward Prem was playful but firm. She intended the order of things to proceed as she pleased, not the way the male chose. That was right, according to the Hrruban way of life.

The spotted cats dodged back and forth through the bushes Mrrva had planted around the green for privacy. They were not concerned with hiding what they were doing. Simple urges moved them. Sometimes Hrriss wished that he was not a thinking being. These creatures were acting out his unspoken dream.

Mehh skidded and rolled to a halt in the grass before him. Prem followed, and tried to mount her before she was upright again. A quick blow across the nose from a paw full of razor-sharp talons let him know that Mehh was not ready yet. Prem withdrew a few paces and waited, making a soft, urgent rumbling sound low in his throat. Mehh flipped onto her belly and crept insouciantly, provocatively, into the mating position with her tail high and to the side, presenting her nether quarters to the male. She was blatant about what she wanted, and her urgent throaty growls made it certain that she wanted it now. Without hesitation, Prem was on her back, teeth gripping the female's scruff as he mounted her.

With an odd sense of detachment, Hrriss watched them. The female snarled and rolled over, driving Prem a paw's length away, and just as swiftly invited him back again with raised tail. Prem crooned, a mild sound when compared with the green fire in his eyes. Hrriss, shaking his head to break the fascination, felt a creature sympathy for Prem. Right now a relationship, wild and abandoned and fun, would take his mind off the ache in his heart, and the anger in his mind. Both Nrrna and Mrratah could be extremely exciting in estrus, but they were good companions away from the mating dance as well.

His mother had made a valid point. It was more than time to seek a lifemate. While he was in this enforced separation from Todd, it might ease his loneliness to choose a mate. He would not be abandoning other aspects of his life, but filling in the parts that had too long remained empty.

Through the house, he heard a knock at the front door. Hrriss started to get up, but he heard his mother's soft footfalls emerge from the other wing and go toward the door. A short time passed, and she came out to him.

"Hrriss, I will be going out later. Pat Rrev has said that she wants the four of us, Hrrestan and me, and Pat and Rrev, to speak together this evening. She is as convinced of your innocence as your father and I."

Hrriss nodded eagerly. "Tell Zodd . . ." he began, and then swallowed the rest of his words, hanging his head and letting his hands fall limp to his sides. "I may give no message for him. It is a matter of honor."

"Poor Hrriss. He knows, my little one," Mrrva said sympathetically. "He knows."

Hrriss cleared his throat tentatively. "Mother, you know Nrrna, don't you?"

"Yes," the Hrruban woman said, clearly surprised. "She works at the Health Center in the laboratory where I conduct my research."

"Has she ever come to this house to join our evening meal?" Hrriss inquired.

He thought the pupils in his mother's eyes widened just slightly. "She has, from time to time. Her company is excellent. I shall inquire if she is free to join us."

Then she turned and left the garden in a rather abrupt fashion that made Hrriss wonder if she was displeased in any way with his suggestion.

The afternoon was fair, and the air had a fresh crispness that was far more relaxing to Todd's jangled nerves than the tropical warmth of Treaty Island. He rode Gypsy down the narrow trail that circled around the fruit orchard at the edge of the Reeve Ranch. The fruit trees were fenced in for protection, though many a clever horse stretched his neck far enough to nip ripening apples off the nearer trees. Apart from the orchard, Lon Adjei, as manager of the ranch, gave the horse herds plenty of room to graze in, but the open land made it harder to find them.

Todd was after a foursome of colts who had hightailed it this way, avoiding capture as if it was a new game invented for them to show off. He lost sight of them among the clumps of shrub and mature trees. He and Hrriss had always worked together on this sort of a detail: the Hrruban had keener eyesight and sense of smell. He could find yearlings no matter where they hid themselves.

A scented breeze shifted, and blew directly into Todd's hot face. Gratefully he took a deep breath and was nearly unseated as Gypsy slammed to a halt under him.

"What's the matter, boy?"

The gelding propped his front legs, refusing to move forward. Gypsy was a sensible animal, so if he was scared to move, he had reason. Possibly there was a small ssorasos in the woods, which Gypsy had smelled when the wind changed. When surprised, the knee-high mammal attacked like a juggernaut. Todd dismounted and sidled cautiously a few feet up the path. In front of him was a clump of red-veined plants. Todd recognized them instantly. Ssersa. It was toxic enough to humans, but absolute poison for horses. Gypsy had smelled the poisonous weed.

"Smart horse!" Todd said over his shoulder to reassure the gelding. Ssersa was nearly as bad a contact-toxin as rroamal. Most animals were wary of it while it was unripe. When it matured and dried, it lost its bitter aroma and smelled sweet and appealing. It was death for livestock, especially those of Earth origin. Ranchers assiduously cleared it from their pastures or they lost stock. The trick was to get it before it dried and left its seeds for the unwary animal. Ben Adjei, Lon's father, called ssersa "silent death." Ranch hands automatically pulled it up wherever they saw it.

The radio at his waist crackled. "Todd, where are you? I've lost sight of you and I've got two more for you to hold for their shots."

"I'm on the trail behind the apple orchard, Lon," Todd replied into the radio. The horse snuffled his ear and he pushed him gently away. "I was chasing a pair of yearlings and Lady Megan's twins. Gypsy got wind of a patch of ssersa back here. I'm uprooting it and bringing it in."

"Ssersa!" Lon's voice exclaimed. "Damn, I was sure I cleared the whole place of it. And before it could seed."

"Never mind. Probably some bird seeded it," Todd said. "Be with you as soon as I pull it up and catch those yearlings."

Pulling on the hide gloves from his belt, he yanked the plant up and beat its roots on the ground to dislodge the dirt. Then he squashed it into a ball, which he shoved into his saddle bag. The stink of ssersa sap made Gypsy restless and quite willing to move away from it.

Todd lifted the gelding into a canter. The trail was wide here and the surface firm enough to safely maintain a stiff pace. The colts were well ahead of him but, as he recalled it, there was a grassy meadow up ahead that would certainly cause them to stop and graze.

An eerie scream—like a horse in agony—made him dig his heels into Gypsy's ribs and they galloped over the breast of the hill. Two of the colts were skittering around the pasture nervously. The third was standing over the fourth, which lay still in a patch of bracken. He whinnied shrilly.

Todd brought Gypsy to a dirt-kicking halt and was out of the saddle at a run to the young horse on the ground. The remaining twin nudged its fallen brother with its nose, puzzled by its unresponsiveness.

"No more games for this lad," Todd said sadly. He still had his gloves on, so he turned back the upper lip to see the livid magenta of the membrane. "Poisoned. Damn it. There can't be more ssersa." Fearing for the other youngsters in this meadow, he looked all around him, and then at Gypsy, who was standing calmly. Turning back to the dead animal, he opened its lips again and saw what was stuck in the colt's teeth—the twigs of dried ssersa. Sitting back on his heels, he radioed Lon.

"More ssersa?" Lon demanded disbelievingly. "Where? I cleared that meadow. I know I did." There was silence and a sigh from the speaker. "Leave it. I'll get the flyer and bring the corpse in for burning. We can't even use the hide. The toxins will poison whatever it touches. Todd, there was no mature ssersa in that field, I promise you!"

"Then where did it come from?" Todd said, aggravated. Lon was a good farm manager. If he said he'd cleared ssersa weed, he had!

He remounted Gypsy and rounded up the other two. He had to lasso the mourning colt to get him away from his dead twin but gave him a few feed pellets to make up for the insult. Whooshing the others in front of him, he kept his eyes peeled for any further sign of ssersa. It was an active seeder, like many Doonan plants: so where there was one, there'd be others.

Then, just as he herded the colts over the lip of the ridge, he spotted a burned patch in the grass on the one level place on the entire field: a patch just about the size of a small transport shuttle.

Todd got his charges back to the barn without further incident. Lon examined the three young animals and entered the control numbers in their freeze brands into a hand-held computer unit. Todd saw Robin and Inessa in the paddock, dragging one unwilling horse after another into the chute for inoculations.

"That's a hundred forty-three," Lon said, slapping the last one on the rump as he sent it running into the corral, "counting that poor poisoned colt. I think that's all we're going to find. We've combed the landscape."

"Shouldn't there be more like a hundred sixty?" Todd asked.

"Yeah, should be," Lon said, scratching his ear with the edge of his comp. "I put in a call to Mike Solinari at the Veterinary Hospital, and the foreman on the Hu spread, just in case any of our animals have hopped the fence."

"Not bloody seventeen of 'em," Todd replied grimly.

"With that ssersa you found today, that might account for some, but we haven't even found any bodies. Not even mda will touch a ssersa carcass." Lon gave a disgusted snort. "My dad told me that if I can't hand-pull fields, I deserve to have such losses but, honest, Todd . . ."

"Didn't Hrriss and I spend"—Todd made himself continue despite the pang that the reminder of happier days gave him— "a whole week helping you? But I'll tell you something else I found—a burn-off mark on that one level spot in the big meadow."

"A shuttle burn-off?" Lon's tanned face paled. "There's been no emergency landing in that section. D'you think . . ." He stopped, not liking his own thoughts.

"Rustling does present itself as an explanation," Todd said, not wanting to believe it either, "especially if there've been no bodies found."

Since Doona's wealth was its stock, not minerals or mining, rustling was the sovereign crime and punishable by immediate transport to the nearest penal colony. To keep track of all stock, each animal was branded with freeze-dry chemicals as soon after birth as possible: a painless process that left a permanent ID, naming its ranch of origin, breeding information, and control numbers. The brand was unalterable so that it was easy to keep a record of inoculations and vaccinations throughout an animal's lifetime. It made illegitimate transfer of ownership impossible. It also made rustling—on Doona—an unprofitable occupation.

Despite rigid psychological tests devised by Lee Lawrence, the colony sociologist, sometimes unsuitable personalities slipped through. People eager enough to get off Earth were known to equivocate about their open-mindedness as regards living with aliens, or their willingness to learn and speak an alien language. Their bigotry was generally discovered soon enough to do no lasting harm and they were sent off Doona, either to Earth or to see if they would fit into a totally Human colony.

Other new settlers became overwhelmed by the responsibilities of caring for a whole, stocked ranch, let alone a house set in the midst of more uninterrupted land than anyone on Earth had ever seen. Some could not adapt to the lack of laborsaving devices which were felt to be superfluous or environmentally dangerous. Fossil fuels were avoided, and natural power, windmills, river barrages, or battery cells charged by solar panels supplied what power was required. Some settlers learned to cope, others requested transport back to familiar constrictions.

Those unwilling, or unable, to take responsibility for themselves in a pioneer society posed the worst problem. Sometimes, folk who had been told all their lives what to do couldn't adjust to making their own decisions. Or, once they realized that behavior monitors had been left behind on Earth, they began acting as if they could behave any way they wanted. And take anything they wanted. Rustlers generally emerged from that group.

"We haven't had any rustlers for years," Lon said. "And how could there have been a shuttle landing when we've got satellite controllers?"

"Have we got any newcomers from Earth who've gone possession crazy? You know that syndrome."

"How could I forget?" Lon asked grimly, spitting into the dust. "It was my father's new mares that were stolen. A guy named Hammond did it. I've a hard place in my mind for anyone named Hammond. Since then I've learned to judge people. I've a good record at picking those who won't make it through their first season."

"You helping Lee with his testing these days?"

"He has only to ask. Now, let's double-check the ones we do have so I can send in the brands of those we're missing."

Together they checked the withers of each animal that came out of the chute, entering the brand and updating the inoculation record.

"Yeah, we're seventeen shy. I'll just send the IDs on to Vet. They'll forward the list to Poldep. Once the word's out we've done that, we might just find those seventeen missing horses back in their home pastures."

Squinting at the sky, Todd shook his head. "They might not be on Doona anymore."

"Oh, come on, Todd. The security satellites would have reported any unauthorized transport in orbit," Lon said, scornful of that suggestion. "No, we'll find out where they got stashed on this planet. Might take a while, but we'll find 'em on Doona."

Todd did not argue the point now, but he was annoyed that seventeen animals were missing. Seventeen! At the current market price, that was almost half the value of a good farm. Doonan horses were a valuable commodity, not only as transportation and a constant source of fertilizer but for the end product of meat, hide, and bonemeal.

"I'll look into it, find out if the neighbors have any inexplicable losses, and I can make that report to Poldep." Even as he spoke, Todd realized he was no longer the person to make reports to Poldep.

"No, I'm farm manager. I'll make the report," Lon said, almost too quickly. "I need your help more out here in the pens," he went on, stumbling to get the words out. "You've a longer attention span than those two flibbertigibbets," he said, nodding toward Todd's two siblings.

It was obvious that the ranch foreman knew the details of Todd's house arrest, even if he had the tact not to comment on it directly. Most of the neighbors had radios, so Todd could ask his questions without leaving the ranch. But he could see that keeping his word was going to complicate life considerably.

"I'll radio them, Lon," he said quietly. "And thanks."

"The Reeves have been having a run of bad luck lately," Lon said stoutly, turning his head to spit in the dust. "I figure you don't deserve it. Count on me if you need help—off the ranch."

"Me, too!" said Robin. At eighteen Terran years of age, he was the youngest of the Reeves' five children. He and Inessa climbed out of the corral as the last of the foals galloped free. "I don't think I'm grounded. Am I?" He turned wide ingenuous eyes to his brother.

"No, it applies to me."

"And Hrriss," Inessa said in a low angry tone, then she turned to Lon. "We've put the five that need to be observed in the stable. Don't think any of 'em are contagious but they need a bit of hand feeding. So I'm through."

"Nobody is through until you put the rest of the medicines away and clean out the inoculators," Lon ordered, shouting down their protests. "And last time I looked that pen hadn't been mucked out. Hop to it!"

With affected groans, the two young Reeves shouldered the vaccination equipment and staggered dramatically toward the medical outbuilding behind the foreman's house.

"What a pair of actors," Todd observed.

"Eh," Lon said, slapping him on the back. "You and Hrriss were the same at that age." Then he ducked his head at the ill-chosen reminder and spat again in the dust.

"Hrriss?" Kelly tapped on the partition of the Hrruban's room. "Your mother said I'd find you here. Are you very busy?"

"Not too busy to see you," Hrriss said, and Kelly chuckled at his gallantry. He rose from his computer console and they brushed cheeks affectionately.

"You okay?" Kelly asked, looking him over with sisterly concern. "Do you need anything I could bring in for you?" She knew she'd be stir-crazy if she had to stay in one room too long. How she'd gotten through school on Earth without dropping out had required every ounce of self-discipline she possessed.

"I'm okay," Hrriss said, but ruined it with a sigh. "I may move about the village, you know. But it is frrrustrating to be restricted. I want for nothing but I will think of something to give you the pleasure of visiting me again." Then he clamped his lips so tightly that his eyeteeth were visible under the tightly drawn flesh.

"He misses you, too," Kelly said softly. "And that's not a message," she added angrily, "that's my personal opinion. I'm entitled to speak for myself."

Hrriss nodded understanding and his muzzle relaxed across his teeth.

"So, what've you been doing with yourself?" Kelly asked, hoping that she could carry on some sort of a lighthearted conversation that wouldn't constantly remind both of them of the third person who should be here and must be nameless and messageless—all for honor!

"A little research into matters of concern to my mother," Hrriss said, his eyes twinkling. "I have also been monitoring the official zranscripts of the Zreaty negotiations, and sending out correspondence to friends on other colony worlds. I hope to locate someone with contacts among the purveyors of illicit artifacts. If we could find out where the articles found on the *Albatross* were purchased, and by whom, we could prove our innocence." Hrriss felt a wash of shame every time he thought of the harsh-voiced prosecutors who dismissed his sworn word of honor as meaningless.

Kelly sensed his disquiet. "That's a damned good idea, Hrriss. In fact, I'm doing a bit of research along those lines myself." Then she made fists of her hands and frowned angrily. "How anyone could be daft enough to think you and . . . to think you could be a pirate and a smuggler is beyond my comprehension. I want you to know that!"

"Thank you," Hrriss said.

"And I'll bet no one in this village believes it, either," Kelly went on, wound up by indignation.

"A Hrruban does not bring disgrace to his Stripe . . ."

Kelly rolled her eyes skyward. "You are not in disgrace, Hrriss, any more than Todd is. You're just . . . just pending investigation. You're sure I can't get you something?" she asked in a milder tone, rather surprised at her own vehemence. But the idea of an honorable person like Hrriss even thinking the word "disgrace" infuriated her.

"Nothing I can think of," Hrriss said, dropping his jaw at her energetic defense. He was as much touched as amused by it.

"You have already brought me something I appreciate greatly: yourself. Will you please visit again when you may?"

"Of course," Kelly said, giving him a big hug as she turned to go. "Hang on, Hrriss. This won't last long."

Ken found Emma Sumitral in a research room in the Treaty Center. She was a tall, slim woman of thirty, with large, smoky gray eyes and dark brown hair. She had the same formal carriage as her father the Admiral, which somehow made even the casual smock she was wearing look elegant.

"I am very troubled by what you've told me," she said after Ken had detailed the seizure at the *Albatross* and the findings of the hearing. "You may count on our support. My Father will certainly want to help you, but I'm not sure what he can do. I'm not sure if there's anything I can do."

"You can help me find out who informed Rogitel that the *Albatross* was stuffed with contraband. Naturally he refused to reveal his source. The Treaty Controller doesn't know, or won't tell. The rest of the Council refuses to talk to anyone other than Hu Shih or Hrrestan. And they're probably only speaking to Hrrestan because he's head of the Hrruban contingent. I hate like poison being ignored, Emma." And Ken managed a weak smile at that defect in himself. "I've got to find out who planted that junk, especially that blasted Byzanian Glow Stone, because they admitted being near Hrrilnorr IV. But no one there believed that they'd heard a Mayday. *I* believe!"

"I personally find it very hard to believe that either Todd or Hrriss could be smugglers or pirates. But it is most unfortunate that they did not have the *Albatross* inspected as soon as they landed. Especially in view of that Mayday."

"I reported that to Hu and Hrrestan myself. You know the boys were Masters of the Hunt, that that trip to Hrretha meant they'd have to work day and night to get the Hunt organized. Newry saw no harm in sealing the ship and letting the boys get on with crucial Hunt details." He hissed out a sigh, sounding more Hrruban than Hayuman, letting his hands go limp in his lap.

"But Treaty Law had been violated," Emma reminded him in a gentle voice. She was a noted expert on the topic.

"A Mayday should be considered extenuating circumstances, Emma, not a crime. And there was no one else capable of organizing the Hunt. That could not be cancelled, and that's why I thought it was permissible for the formal inspection to be deferred. Just for two weeks." Ken raised his hands again in a pleading gesture. "You know yourself that we have to have the Snake Hunt, whether we dress it up as a tourist attraction or New Home Week or whatever. Those snakes would swarm whether or not there were any Hunters to restrict them. Hu and Hrrestan agreed with my analysis of the situation—Doona *has* to be profitable and the Snake Hunt provides a large hunk of our income. If anyone is guilty of not insisting on that inspection, it's me. I should be taking the blame."

Emma looked very grave. "Ultimately you may have to." Then, having startled him, she went on. "From what you have told me, Ken, it is not just that delay, it is also all those valuable items that were found on the *Albatross* and the tape record of landings and launches within the framework of that Hrrethan journey."

"Neither Todd nor Hrriss is untrustworthy or a pirate or smuggler."

"No, they are not the type. However, the fact that blame is being attached to those two young men may yet work in their favor. They are much admired on Earth. Their friendship is legendary. I think you could say that it epitomizes Doona in many people's minds."

"Will it? After all this has been broadcast about the galaxy?" Ken asked bitterly.

Emma looked at him sternly. "If there is any rumor, gossip, slander, or libel about this investigation before it has been completed and its report made, there will be far more trouble for the loose-mouthed than they can swallow! The boys are under house arrest, not incarcerated in a Poldep facility. Unless they break their bond, they are safe from slander. Now, let's see what we can find." She turned to her desktop console.

She initiated a search based on the boys' names and the name of their ship, the word "Hrrilnorr," and the names of the artifacts that Ken could recall. "Now we wait."

When the computer eventually spat out a list of file names, Emma briefly scanned each one, and instead of data, found she was looking at a moiré graphic with a blinking square in the center requesting a confirmed password.

"Classified! In the last two weeks, every one of these has acquired a special clearance password. They're locked!"

Ken swore softly. "Damn it, I'd hoped you'd be able to get through. I got the same graphics. Not a single code I knew got me any results. Do I need to start standing on desks to get cooperation?"

"Not yet . . . I hope," Emma admitted with a wicked light in her eyes. She bent over the board. "I've got Father's code-key number. They wouldn't dare classify these files too high for the head of Alreldep to access."

To Todd's surprise, his father arrived home for dinner with a very attractive woman whom he introduced as Emma Sumitral.

"How do you do, Miss Sumitral?" Todd asked stiffly, and then the name registered. "You wouldn't be related to Admiral Sumitral, would you?"

"Indeed I am, Todd Reeve," she responded, squeezing his hand warmly. "I've heard a great deal about you from my father." She had a brilliant smile that lit up her gray eyes. Then she crooked her neck to look behind him.

Suddenly his formality deserted him and he burst out laughing. "I gave up wearing that rope tail a long time ago, Miss Sumitral."

" 'Emma,' please," she said, and he gestured for her to take a seat. "My father used to regale me with stories about Doona. I was only five when the first wave of settlers left Earth for Doona, so this world has always been special to me. I always wished my father didn't work for the government so we could have come, too," she admitted. "I'm glad now that he does. His position has opened otherwise locked doors for me as a researcher, and now I believe it may help you, too."

"What?" Todd said, grasping at whatever hope was offered him.

"Todd, we'll wait until Hrrestan and Mrrva arrive. This concerns them, too, you know." Ken's expression was so concerned that Todd wondered what they could have found out that would upset his father—more than he was already.

Hrrestan and Mrrva arrived at the Reeves' house shortly before sunset. Todd greeted them courteously. He had to bite his tongue on "How's Hrriss?" Even with the parents of his friends, he would not break his given word.

Hrrestan and Mrrva nodded gravely to their son's dearest friend, their liquid eyes saying what they, too, would not say aloud. Both Hrrubans already knew Emma Sumitral.

"I've chased out the other children for the evening," Pat said, trying to set all her guests at ease. "An adult evening. Kelly ought to arrive any minute now."

Todd looked up, somewhat surprised, but Kelly hadn't smothered him with sympathy earlier and she'd scarcely do it in front of guests. "She is?"

Pat glanced at him, worried. "I thought you'd want her input. Isn't that all right?"

"Sure," Todd said hastily.

As deftly as her father would, Emma led the discussion away to other matters, and held forth on the subject of trade among the colony worlds. Todd found her not only charming but intelligent. He rather thought she and Kelly would like each other.

Kelly arrived only minutes behind the Hrrubans. They greeted each other warmly. "It's nice to see so much of you these days," she said ingenuously.

Todd couldn't help but gawk at her, for she couldn't have more plainly told him she'd visited Hrriss, too.

"Well," said Pat, surprised, "you did learn some diplomacy, after all."

Then Ken introduced her to Emma and offered drinks all round. For the first time, Todd found that the simple courtesies he usually enjoyed extending struck him as unnecessary time-wasters. Once Hrrestan and Mrrva were settled, Emma began to detail the files she had unlocked.

"It's turned out to be more than just trusting my father's opinions of you and Hrriss," she said. "I think we may have stumbled onto a very complex and highly organized smuggling operation." She waited patiently until everyone stopped demanding details. "I found some, all right. And more data from the beacons orbiting the other prohibited worlds is still coming in. So far, all of them show the identification number of the *Albatross* as having entered those systems shortly before or shortly after the ship visited Hrretha. The information is not yet complete. There are still four buoys circling interdicted systems left to be heard from, and that data will come in within the next few days."

"I can't believe that they all have the code number from the boys' ship," Pat said.

"Now, the beacons identify the *Albatross* as being the ship that crossed their barriers in each instance. The codes as you know are complex, not easy to duplicate."

"As I told you, Emma," Ken began, his anger building, "someone's gone to a lot of trouble to make it convincing."

"For a researcher like myself, there's just too *much* corroborative detail available to be coincidence or accident," Emma went on, and although Ken started to protest, Pat touched his arm, her eyes watching Emma's face. For Pat was beginning to see what Emma was driving at. "So far we have thefts committed by two young males who lack for nothing. They're psychologically normal, without any history of kleptomania or harmful pranks. Healthy in every way." Todd blushed at her frankness and she smiled gently at him. "It was necessary to take a glance at your medical profile," she said. "There's nothing in it to be ashamed of. To continue, they're respected by their community, and their future is bright if only they continue to behave as they have. This series of crimes requires a motivation."

"I know the motivation," Todd said in a flat voice that showed he was controlling his anger. "This issue would make a terrific fulcrum for the lever to pry Doona apart."

"I'm inclined to agree," Hrrestan said, nodding his head in agreement with Todd's opinion, "but if we have the motivation, can we also discover the perpetrator?"

"Landreau has to be involved in this somewhere," Todd said angrily, his eyes flashing blue fire. "Rogitel's presence at the Hrrethan affair was unnecessary. Both . . ." Todd halted then plunged, "I felt he was nearly splitting with anticipation and it couldn't have been for the inauguration of another grid facility! He was there, keeping track of . . . of us . . . on Landreau's orders. The Admiral would do anything to discredit Doona this year and to disrupt the crucial talks that are going on. A scandal like two notable citizens of Doona turning out to be pirates and smugglers could tear everything apart. Only how did it get done?"

"The opinion of the Ssspeakrrrs," Hrrestan added, "favors the idea of a conspiracy, aimed at you and our son, to discredit the Rralan Experiment. They have informed me that they are conducting their own investigations into these charges as they know that never have you or my son behaved in a dishonorable fashion. As Emma Sumitral has ssaid, there is far too much evidence against them. There are elements on Rrala who also wish this Experiment to end in disarray. These are being scrutinized. True guilt lies elsewhere but it will be discovered."

"And I," Kelly said, looking inordinately pleased with her contribution, "am handling the unofficial Tcrran Investigative Group. You didn't know you had one, did you, Todd?" She grinned at him. While she had admired Emma's clear-minded statements, she hadn't quite liked her tone, nor the way she had smiled at Todd. Sort of, well, proprietary and perhaps a little patronizing. Whoa! Kelly thought, yanking hard on her own mental reins. Who was acting proprietary now?

"May I remind all of you," Emma put in, "that it is essential that all investigations be done as circumspectly as possible so as not to prejudice the official one?"

Ken leaned forward toward Emma. "We must all be wary of how we proceed. But, in spite of the need for caution, I've started some inquiries through the Alreldep office, and I discover, to my relief," and he grinned at his son, "that the memory of Todd as he was has been replaced by the record of a hardworking young man."

"Which reminds me, Dad, this hardworking young man did some rounding up today with Lon. And we found out something I like even less than I like my present anomalous position. We're minus seventeen horses, mostly yearlings and two-year-olds."

"Seventeen horses gone since the last count?" Ken repeated, staring at his son in disbelief. As if he didn't need this, too, on his plate.

"One was dead of ssersa poisoning and I helped Lon clear that field myself. There were other ssersa plants where there shouldn't be a one."

"Ssersa does not have legs to walk," Hrrestan said, shaking his head as he knew how careful the Reeves were about hand-pulling the toxic weed from all grazing areas.

"There was also this burned-out patch on the one flat space in the field," Todd went on. "Shuttle-sized, I'd say."

"Rustlers!" Ken nearly bounced from his chair with indignation.

Hrrestan hissed. "That is a most serious crime. There have been no instances of animal theft in years."

"Lon reported to Poldep. We sent a list of the brands to Michael," and Todd turned to Kelly, who was as surprised and angry as any stock rancher would be. "One or two of 'em may have jumped the fence."

"But not seventeen," Ken said, still absorbing the shock. "We'll have to hang on to some of the breeding stock, then, Todd."

"Dad, I'd ask around to see if there's anyone new here who's had a sudden embarrassment of credit. I'll just put it about that there'll be no charges pressed at Poldep if that little herd wanders home, wagging tails behind 'em."

"Could snakes have caught them?" Pat asked. "You had that breakout at the Boncyks'. What if a Mommy or two got past you?"

"None did," Todd replied flatly, frankly upset that his mother even asked such a question.

"Well, it was a possibility," she said apologetically.

"What else could go wrong?" Kelly asked, more rhetorically than expecting any answer.

"What else?" Emma asked, her expression clearly reflecting her dislike of adding to the current problems. "I think I'd better be the one to tell you. Admiral Landreau has arrived. He gridded in just before I left Treaty Island."

CHAPTER

6

ADMIRAL AL LANDREAU HATED DOONA. INITIALLY, when the bright blue pebble with its light cloud coverage had swum into his viewscreen, he thought it looked peaceful and pleasant. When he had been assigned to explore it for a preliminary search, it had seemed the perfect Earthlike world, class M in the old parlance, atmosphere, near-normal gravity and all, the very epitome of what Spacedep was searching for. It was full of possibilities, and the key to fame and better departmental financing for him.

Ever since the first colonists landed there, though, it had been one long headache for Spacedep and Landreau. He lay the source of all his troubles squarely upon the backs of the Reeves. A family of malcontents, by all accounts from Aisle and Corridor monitors, always disturbing civilized people with their noise and antisocial behavior. They had made a public fool of him. They, or specifically, Ken Reeve, had blamed him for not noticing their mythical cat people or the nightmarish giant snakes in time to prevent the colonization. As if there was any way he could have known about them, in spite of that ape Sumitral's insistence that the clues were all there. Reeve had made a fool of him, claimed he jeopardized the colony.

Well, the colonists had been in the wrong. They had violated the Siwannese protocol, had resisted being removed from the planet in spite of their feigned horror over that violation, and had been compounding that transgression anathema for a quarter of a century. Now was the moment to eradicate that mistake, put it behind him. He fully intended to do so. His opportunity had been handed to him, calligraphed, signed, sealed, and set under a glass bell. To make it the sweetest possible revenge, Todd Reeve, the hysterical, bilingual boy child of Ken Reeve, was to be the key to ending this quarter century of humiliation. The Treaty Council was buzzing: rumors of resignation threats already abounded. Landreau was looking forward to hearing Rogitel's full report.

There were cat people all over the building where he gridded in. Their hairy, fang-toothed faces made him shudder. The Hrrubans were an abomination against nature's plan. Cats shouldn't walk like humans. They should go on all four legs like the basically feral animals they imitated.

When the mist of transfer cleared, he was facing one of the very creatures he abhorred. The animal operating the grid center opened its mouth at him and showed its teeth, casually displaying its bestiality. The horror was that it thought it was smiling. He nodded curtly and stepped down.

It was outrageous that these Hrrubans should have stumbled on any technology as powerful as the transportation grid. While the grid was convenient, having to use it frightened him: he preferred to be in control of the mechanisms used in travel. What if the operator hadn't been well enough trained, and Landreau was trapped in the grid, neither one place nor another? Supposing someone with a grievance against him took a bribe and sent him to the wrong destination, even a fatal one? He would have preferred to have the one facility on Earth destroyed, and its operator returned to its homeworld. Wherever that was. If Landreau could only find it . . . That damned Treaty neatly blocked that aspiration. However, the cats were not fooling Admiral Al Landreau. He had long since deduced their real objective. This transport grid of theirs: a single grid, like the one on Terra, could be quickly built into a giant one, capable of moving armies. Yet the blockheads and simpering idiots in positions of power on the Amalgamated Worlds refused to see the threat inherent in the cats' technology. But he had made allies, supported causes in return for the support of his. This year would see the end to the Hrruban threat before it became a nightmare reality.

The grid operator said something in the ridiculous collection of grunts and growls that served the beast race for a language. Sounded like bad plumbing. And that was yet another insult:

that Human beings were to imitate such filthy noise instead of good, clean Terran.

"Commander? I'm Nesfa Dupuis," a low voice at his elbow said in the Terran language.

Startled but relieved, Landrau turned. The speaker was a small Human woman with dark skin and glowing brown eyes. She stood next to the grid station, her hands folded quietly into her voluminous sleeves.

"Treaty Councillor," Landreau said smoothly, with a gracious nod and a quick handshake. "I want to see everything that you have on this vexing matter. When may I meet with the Council? It is important that I see them immediately."

The small woman held up a hand. "Not today, I'm sorry to inform you. We're in the midst of deep negotiation on space rights, Commander."

"Hmmph!" Landreau snorted. "Isn't such a negotiation irrelevant in the face of the crimes reported to you? You're wasting time. Might as well address yourself to immediate and germane issues. Save yourself the bother."

Landreau realized immediately that he had misjudged this one. She was a Doona colony sympathizer. Another fardling New Ager. He sighed and turned on a charm that never failed to work. "I'd like you to consider me a friend in this case, Councillor. My lifelong ambition has been to promote the improvement of the quality of life for Humanity. I'll do everything in my power to help expedite a successful conclusion to this disgraceful incident. Then the Council can continue its more important responsibilities."

"You are so cooperative, Admiral," Dupuis said aloud, her schooled expression not revealing her true feelings, but she had long since taken the Admiral's measure and was aware of some of his machinations. "The Council is, of course, grateful for any assistance in bringing this unfortunate situation to a swift conclusion. You will doubtless wish to confer with your assistant. An office has been set at your disposal near the one Commander Rogitel is using. This way, please."

The deep male voice crackled over the speaker in the airfield control tower. "Tower, this is Codep ship *Apocalypse,* on final insertion through orbit. I'll be down there in a minute."

"Can't you be more specific, Fred?" Martinson asked, clapping one hand to his headset and checking the screens which displayed telemetry from the orbiting navigation probes around Doona. "Good to hear from you. Pad eight is open for your use. Got two mechanics on duty this morning if you need any refitting. Happy landing."

The transport ship appeared as a ball of fire in the sky as the retros ignited in atmosphere and slowed the descent velocity. Below, the roof of number 8 bay was rolling open. *Apocalypse* set down expertly in the ring encircling the number on the fireproof surface of the launchpad. There was one final burst of fire and a belch of black smoke as the engines shut down. Martinson arrived alongside the *Apocalypse* in a flitter, with a fumigation team and a customs official in tow.

"Hello, Martinson. Sorry to have missed New Home Week," the burly trader said, descending from the ship as the team crowded him on its way up into the passenger compartment. "Probably cost me a lot of business, but you can only go so fast in space, eh? I've got bushels of test seed designated for the farms here. Say, what's all this?" He glanced at Newry, the customs agent, who took his manifests out of his hand and marched around to the ship's cargo hatch.

"Sorry, Fred," Martinson said. "Every ship has to be gone over with a fine-tooth comb. Orders."

"I've got my orders, too!" Horstmann boomed. He was a big man with a big voice, and pale hair buzzed short in a spaceman's clip. "Got customers waiting! You'll get your duty fees. I've never shorted you. So what's the scramble for?"

"Only takes a few minutes," said Martinson, refusing to discuss the matter. He was determined not to be caught bending the rules again.

Horstmann stood, impatiently tapping his hand on his thigh until the customs agent returned with the clipboard. "Is everything all right? I've got business to do! You can't stop the Horstmann of the *Apocalypse* from his ride forever! Ha, ha, ha!"

"All clear," Martinson said, ignoring Fred's traditional joke. Newry handed his chief the clipboard full of manifests. He nodded over his shoulder toward the flitter. From the passenger seat, the thin form of Rogitel arose and approached the trader.

"Ah! Commander," Horstmann said, extending his hand. "Nice to see you. I've got your little package for you, tapes from the governor of Zapata Three. Kept it next to my heart. Got a real fine collection of seals from a lot of places I didn't know existed . . . ?" He cocked his head, hoping to be enlightened.

"Just pass it over," Rogitel said, ignoring the query and Horstmann's extended hand.

With a shrug, Horstmann drew the package out of one of his sealed shipsuit pockets. Rogitel took the parcel, examined it briefly, and handed a credit chit to the captain.

"And thank you," Horstmann said, with overblown mock courtesy as the Spacedep official turned and walked off without another word. "Huh! What's the matter here? Doona's usually a hospitable place. Couldn't he waste an extra syllable to be polite? Some people!" The Codep captain shook his head ruefully. "Well, credits are credits." Horstmann tucked away the chit in his pouch. "Bobby! Come on! Customers are waiting!"

He walked into the Launch Center's warehouse, where stalls were set up for traveling traders across from the permanent trading booths for the Doona Cooperative of Farmers and Skillcrafters. These facilities, originally the odd table or two set up for the display and sale of merchandise, had evolved into tidy shops, complete with display cases and specialized lighting. The exchange of goods and money became comfortable and convenient for traders who didn't need to establish an on-planet trading route at every stop, and for their customers, who could browse about the wares displayed. Ali Kiachif had suggested the improvements. His ships carried trade goods from one world to another. Now the port attracted persons of both species from all over Doona, to sell their own goods and buy what traders might have on offer.

"Give me a moment to unload the merchandise, good folk!" Horstmann pleaded. "Ah, today's a good day to do business."

A couple of Hrruban ranchers from their Third Village had a string of pack ponies with them for sale. As the *Apocalypse* had suitable facilities for animal transport, Horstmann prowled around the little animals, lifting a hoof, examining teeth, before he made an opening offer.

Ken Reeve arrived at the warehouse in time to see Rogitel stalk away in the company of the portmaster.

"Hello, Horstmann," he called over the heads of the crowd.

"Well! Reeve, good to see you," Horstmann boomed, coming over to greet him. His huge hand engulfed Ken's in a companionable grasp.

"What was the commander after here? He usually doesn't grace a launchpad with his presence."

"I'd a special delivery for Ol' Skinny Shanks. Bird from Zapata Three passed it on to me for him. Since I'm not due on Terra for another couple of weeks, I could make the detour here. I got paid for it. Feels like tapes er something. Sealed up from one end to the next from places I've never visited." Then Horstmann lowered his voice. "You looking for information, eh?"

"Just curious," Ken replied, equally circumspect. "Rogitel and Landreau have been on Doona for a week, and they've stayed on Treaty Island. Not like Landreau to waste time before jumping down our throats on some damned fool petty issue."

"Hmm," Horstmann rumbled sympathetically. "Heard some spacescud I didn't like. I don't believe for a millisec that Todd'd be dealing in irreplaceables. If he was, why didn't he notify me? Everyone knows I offer the best prices on curios. What else can I tell you?"

"When is Kiachif due here next?" Ken asked.

The big trader laughed. "Soon, I hope! I'm supposed to meet him here in a few days, and I want to be on my way ASAP. Codep's got some new rulings about trading, and he wants everyone to hear them from his immortal lips. But I've got a schedule to keep."

"Having a profitable season?" Vic Solinari asked, coming over to greet Fred.

"Oh, I've made a few credits in commissions. Went through Zapata Three like wind through the trees. Almost thought they'd never seen an honest trader before." Horstmann patted his credit pouch with an air of satisfaction.

"And have they seen one now?" Vic Solinari asked, winking broadly at Ken.

"Vic! That cuts me to the quick," Fred said, his huge hands crossed dramatically over his heart. "How many times have

I given you fellows the shirt off my back?" Then he made another abrupt change of mood. "In fact, I did once, when no other size I was carrying would fit one of the miners on Zlotnik. Poor devil. Gave him a pretty good deal, I might add. Say, perhaps you'll be interested in these. Zapata's doing a good line in metal chain, all grades and gauges. Bobby!" he shouted to his young son, who served as his supercargo. The boy, who was driving a loader full of merchandise, stopped when he heard his father shout. "Roll out some of that chain! I brought them a galvanizer last trip, and the results are fine. Won't ever rust. You got my personal guarantee. They're starting a line of ergonomic hand tools that I'll bring along next time. Fit the hand. Save the blisters. You'll be interested in those."

The two Hrrubans came over to discuss the ponies and ended up taking part of their price in narrow-gauge metal chain. They shook hands and Horstmann arranged with one of the Humans from First Village to have the beasts boarded until he was ready to load up and leave. Ken looked over the metalwork and other goods which Horstmann's son placed on the long tables. The trader himself passed among them, shaking hands and arranging deals quickly. Some Doonans paid in credit vouchers; others with goods, such as rough or cut gemstones or finished craftwork.

Pottery, textiles, ready-to-wear tunics and overalls were placed out by Horstmann's crew for inspection. A large, floppy bundle came out on the next skidload, and Fred pounced on it.

"Well, these have come a long way. Hey, Reeve," he called. "Here's horsehides with your ranch markings on them. Sell them, they get ridden and eaten, and the hides end up back here for craftwork. Now, that's recycling."

"My brand?" Ken asked curiously, making his way over to look. "That's my brand, all right. Where did you say these came from? Zapata? I didn't sell this many to anyone on that world. At least I don't think so."

"Well, you must have," Horstmann pointed out. "I'd know the Reeve Ranch markings anywhere, and Zapatan provenance is with 'em."

Ken flipped over one hide after another. Twenty still showed his freeze mark but he couldn't remember having sold a full score of horses to Zapata Three. He'd easily recall a sale that would have fed his family for a year or more. Then he clicked his tongue on his teeth. Could he be looking at hides of animals that had gone missing? Over a period of years, there'd been a fair number of inexplicable disappearances. Some he could chalk up against hunting mdas, disease, or ssersa: a few would be a normal enough loss for any rancher. But twenty? Maybe Todd was right. Rustlers had returned to Doona and taken the animals off-world in spite of satellite surveillance.

Hides kept a long time. They could be accumulated and then sold when enough time had passed to dim memory of loss. Someone had blundered, letting the rustled hides make their way back to Doona. The general method of making profit from rustling was to take the animals to a pastoral world that wasn't yet cleared for animal residence, where colonists were desperate for breeding stock and fresh meat. Thriftily then the colonists traded cured hides to other planets for goods. Probably swapped hides for some of Zapata's new chains.

Now if he could just trace the hides back, to Zapata to the colonists and then to the men who'd sold them the animals, he could pass that information on to Poldep. Having them come back in a lump proved it was one person who'd been responsible all along, not several different gangs. That'd be a good fact to pass on to Poldep.

"Fred, who sold you these?"

"Why?" The trader squinted at him suspiciously. "Something wrong with 'em? You know damned well, Reeve, I don't deal in stolen goods and I've the Zapatan provenance."

"So you do," Ken said reasonably, "but I'd be grateful if you could give me a name."

"Truth to tell, I can't. I was shaking hands and changing credits so fast that I have no face to attach to the goods." Horstmann looked genuinely regretful. "I'd've checked if I'd thought it odd, but I know you sell off-world."

Ken suppressed his frustration and asked with a friendly smile, "How long will you be on Doona?"

"I've got to wait for Kiachif, 'come frost, fire, or flood,' as he says," Fred replied, grinning. "I'm supposed to take a shipment for him into the Hrruban arm, and he hasn't caught up with me yet. I got a message on the beacon that this time

I'd better stay where I am. Not that I wouldn't. Don't tell him, but I'm fond of the old pirate."

"Good," Ken said. "Fred, I know you got the provenance so don't take this wrong, but I've got a feeling that these animals were stolen from me. Would you let me take the hides to check against the sales records?"

"I'd like to, Ken, I really would," Horstmann said, bobbing his head from side to side in his reluctance, "but I might be able to sell 'em. Can't sell 'em if the buyer can't see 'em, now can I? Why, my wife hear about me doing something like that, even to a good honest man like yourself, and she'd skin me and put *my* hide in with the. rest."

"I understand, Fred, I really do," Ken said, hiding his exasperation. "But look, there's a computer outlet right here in the Hall. Just let me have a chance to check the brand numbers. Won't take long and these could be evidence."

At the word "evidence," Horstmann froze. Poldep investigations were the bane of any licensed trader. They meant unavoidable and unlimited delays. He narrowed an eye at Ken. "Well, so long's it's only just across the Hall. But I didn't get 'em illegal. You know we don't deal in bad merchandise."

"I know that, Fred. Thanks." Under Horstmann's baleful gaze, Ken switched on the terminal and keyed in his user code. Ken watched the trader out of the corner of his eye until he got involved in a deal and temporarily forgot about Ken and evidence.

If these were horses that had gone missing over the past few years, then he—and other ranchers who said they'd had periodic losses—might be able to break up this new spate of rustling. That is, if they could also solve how the rustlers were getting past the security satellites. Having solid evidence to show Poldep would ensure their cooperation. And prove ranchers hadn't just been careless in pulling up ssersa or keeping proper track of their stock.

Ken had to think hard to remember when he first lost track of a horse for which a carcass had never been found. Even mdas left the skull and hooves and occasionally scraps of hide and bone fragments. It had to have been five or more years ago. He called up his records for a date ten years back when the horses were rounded up for their annual checkup. Now he remembered. In late summer, one of his stallions hadn't come home, a big powerful bay who'd sired a fine few foals before he disappeared. Buster he'd been called. Ken initiated a search for that name.

The screen blanked and was replaced with the "One Moment Please" graphic. Ken twitched impatiently while the search went on. In a few minutes, the screen cleared, then filled with name, description, and freeze mark. Ken jotted the number down and started flipping through the hides, trying to find a match. He didn't.

"I'm doing this backward," he told himself. He blanked the screen and began to type in the numbers on the Zapatan hides and asked for matching data.

The program, in the way of all computer inventory programs, was painfully slow. Each query consumed several minutes, having to access data from the master mainframe on the other side of the planet. Fretfully Ken drummed his fingertips on the console and glared at the cheery graphic. When the screen changed, he pounced on the keyboard.

"There! Cuddy, two-year-old, sired by Maglev out of Corona, black and white pinto, gelded." Ken slapped the hide, pleased. "Six years ago, eh?" He hit the key to copy and print the document, then flipped Cuddy's hide over to the next one. His hand was arrested in midair as he glanced from the hide to the screen and back again. This was an Appaloosa hide, leopard Appaloosa at that, small black flecks on white. "Wait a minute! This didn't come off Cuddy." Undeniably the file said pinto, but the skin was white flecked with black.

Ken sat back in the chair with a thump. Not that a pinto could change its spots to leopard Appaloosa. He checked the brand numbers again but the figures tallied. Could Lon or Todd have entered the freeze brand to Cuddy's file? He felt a spurt of righteous anger over such sloppiness. But neither Lon nor Todd was prone to be slipshod. Not about recording the correct markings. He frowned. He didn't have many Appies. Kelly's father liked the breed. But the freeze mark was his, not Vic's. Perplexed, he turned to the next one, a bright bay with a white saddle mark shaped like a parallelogram just below the freeze brand.

The brand designated a two-year-old chestnut with no saddle mark. Could there be a glitch in the system? Could the computer be scrambling his files? He'd have remembered a leopard Appaloosa and a bright bay with such a distinctive saddle mark. These were totally unfamiliar animals. He needed a control.

He entered the markings from a horse he knew better than any other animal on Doona, his mare Socks. She was Reeve Ranch entry #1. Socks was elderly now, but still willing to go out for a ride in fine weather. Data scrolled up, and Ken went straight to the description of the animal. This one was all right. It was the mare, all the way down to her four white socks. So what was wrong with the other files?

He brought up again the first two he had tried, wondering if solar flares had interfered with the satellite transmission of data from Treaty Island Archives the first time. To his chagrin, they remained unaltered and the hides still bore marks of horses he didn't recognize.

One by one, Ken compared his records with the freeze-dry markings for each hide in the bundle. When he was through, not one of the hides matched the color description of the horse that should have worn it. It was as if someone had lifted the brands from his horses and transferred them onto someone else's, a removal that he knew was, if not impossible, then certainly achieved by a heretofore unknown process.

"You get what you want, Reeve?" Horstmann asked cheerfully, coming over in between a spate of deals to slap the other man on the back.

Ken shrugged. "Yes and no, Fred." A very clever operator was making a profit on selling rustled animals on Zapata Three and, probably, elsewhere. And with Zapatan provenances, surely there was a way of finding out who that clever person was. "When Ali Kiachif arrives, I'd like to talk with him. Had any bids on these hides?" Ken didn't want them scattered, but he also couldn't block a sale for Fred just to keep the evidence in one place.

"Well, the Hrruban in the Doona Cooperative of Farmers and Skillcrafters booth sounded interested in them."

"Look, I'll give you a deposit. . . ."

"Against the price? Or just to hold 'em?"

"To hold 'em, Fred. That provenance might be forged."

"Didn't look forged to me!" Fred's eyes widened at the mere suggestion that he'd been conned.

"Nevertheless, you don't want to sell and then find out the provenance was counterfeit, if you know what I mean." Ken deliberately used Ali Kiachif's favorite phrase.

"I know what you mean: fines! Okay. Under the circumstances, Ken, I'll waive the deposit and put these damned things to one side where no one'll see 'em. That help you?"

"It surely does, Fred, and I appreciate it more than I can say." Ken smiled gratefully but he rather suspected that Horstmann might be cutting some sly deals on the side that he didn't want the senior Codep captain to know about. Normally such a favor cost a lot more than just the breath it took to ask it. "Don't forget to tell Kiachif that I need to see him."

Armed with his curious findings, Ken arranged an interview with the Poldep chief in charge of Doona's quadrant of the Amalgamated Worlds. Poldep, the enforcement arm of the Amalgamated Worlds Administration, had jurisdiction on every planet which had signed the charter. Sampson DeVeer listened politely to Ken's theory about rustlers somehow evading the security satellites, but clearly he was finding it hard to believe.

"It's a very interesting theory, Mr. Reeve," he said blandly. He was a tall man who had been called good-looking by many women behind his back, because his diffident manner kept them from approaching the man himself. He had broad shoulders and an intelligent face. His wavy hair and moustache were nearly black. "I'd need proof to proceed, you understand. Not just speculation."

"I have proof," Ken said, producing the film copies. DeVeer's casual attitude was beginning to get on his nerves. DeVeer was rumored to be anti-Doona, though he wasn't an active antagonist to the colony. He claimed he was just trying to do his job, and the presence of unknowns like the Hrrubans made it more difficult for him. "These hides have been altered in some way."

DeVeer tented his fingers, peering through them at the hard copy that Ken had spread out on his desk. "That's very unlikely, Mr. Reeve. It's more probable the records were changed. In my twenty years serving Poldep, I have never come across any-one, or anything, that can produce an undetectable alteration to the freeze-dry-process brands." His tone was unequivocal.

"Well, someone has," Ken insisted, indicating the leopard Appaloosa hide which ought to have been black and white. "I don't run Appies. But that's my freeze brand. And you know a horse has never been known to alter its hide."

"Perhaps the skin was dyed?"

"If the leopard Appie had turned black and white, I'd say that was possible, but not probable. There is also no trace of dye according to this chemical analysis of the hide." And Ken tossed that flimsy across the desk to DeVeer.

"Mr. Reeve," DeVeer said again patiently. "These are nega-tive proofs. You have the hide of a horse that you say you never owned with a brand to an animal you did." He held up a hand to forestall an outburst. "I know that rustling has been an ongoing problem on Doona. I've investigated several cases myself. The freeze-brand system was developed to prevent rustling. I'd say it has. Now you come along, wanting to contest the validity of that excellent system. Frankly I don't think this is a case of rustling. Maybe you should look a little closer to home, where some people might have a chance to duplicate your brand on strays that they can legally sell off-world. Doesn't your son have regular access to spacegoing transport?"

Ken barely kept himself from reaching across the desk and planting his fist firmly in DeVeer's face. "Are you suggesting that Todd has rustled horses from the ranch he will one day inherit?"

"Inherit might be presumptuous, Mr. Reeve, but the oppor-tunity is there . . . Now, now, look at this objectively, Mr. Reeve. I'm trying to clarify a perplexing set of facts. I'm not speaking with any intent to offend. Let me put it to you this way. If, for example, you had a horse, a living one, with a brand matching one of these stolen hides, I would have a lead to investigate . . . a duplication of numbers, which is a possibility. An honest error at branding time when you got to handle a lot of foals. Or if you know who had bred this leopard Appaloosa, I'd have another lead. And if you knew how these brands could be altered, which is something I've never heard of, then we really would have a cause for an immediate and intensive inquiry. As it is, we have nothing to go on but unlikely speculation and possible data base errors." He stood up, indicating the interview was over. "I assure you that, if you come to me with something concrete—even one piece of evidence—I'll be glad to listen."

Ken got most of his anger blown out of his system on his way back to the ranch. Any Poldep inspector worthy of his rank would have seen the anomalies in hides with inappropriate markings. Data base errors! Duplication of freeze-brand numbers! *That* had never happened, not in the twenty-four years he'd been breeding horses. Nor had it happened to any other rancher, Hayuman or Hrruban.

That sly dig about Todd inheriting being presumptuous. Presuming what? That Todd would be found guilty and sent to a penal colony and denied the right to inherit colonial land anywhere?

Ken made himself calm down and warned himself not to even consider such an outcome. It was dark when he reached the ranch and the lights blazed out a welcome on the flower beds Pat had labored so long to surround the house. He was glad to see Kelly had been invited over for dinner again, but he hoped Pat wouldn't be silly enough to push Todd. That lad didn't push! He stood his ground and he was doing it now with courage and fortitude. Ken was prouder than ever of his son.

The moment Ken started recounting his discovery, Pat put dinner on hold and, instead of the meal, the big round table was spread with the hard copy. Ken had talked Fred into letting him take two of the hides home and he'd stopped by the vet lab to borrow a microscope for a good look at the hide marks.

"This is a real stumper," Todd said, looking up from his turn at the microscope. He gestured for Kelly to take a turn at the eyepiece. "There's no shadow of an original freeze mark. I'd swear this one was the first one, and genuine. Only it can't be. 'Cause Cuddy was a pinto, not a leopard Appie."

"Could they have used a chemical to neutralize the original brand mark?" Pat asked, studying the printout of the descriptions of the horses whose numbers had appeared on the wrong hides.

Ken shook his head. "There's no chemical that can do that."

"A laser?" Robin asked brightly, sure he'd come up with the logical solution. "That looks like chemical burns sometimes."

"Black magic is the more likely answer," Kelly said in a gloomy tone, leaning back from the microscope. "I'd swear that was genuine and the only mark that hide had ever worn."

"You raise Appies, Kelly," Ken began.

"Yeah, but we don't sell our leopards. You know that. And if one of ours had gone missing, you know that Dad and Michael would have combed the planet to find it."

Ken knew that was true enough.

"Todd, I got a job for you," he said, placing an arm about his son's shoulder. "We've got to get all the other ranches to let us do a read-only search of missing stock and the brands they wore. If we find a missing horse wearing one of those brands," and he pointed to the lists, "we'll have some solid evidence to give DeVeer."

With a wry grin, Todd said, "The old fogey didn't suggest that your son might be using his ol' dad's legitimate brand marks to sell stock off-world, did he?"

Ken wasn't quite quick enough to mask his annoyance and dismay at Todd's droll query.

"What'll they think of next to hang on Todd's neck?" Kelly demanded indignantly. "As if you could fit one horse in the *Albatross*, let alone seventeen or twenty!"

Ken snapped his fingers. "Damn, now why didn't I think of that factor?"

"You were probably far too mad to do so," Pat said, raising her eyebrows in amusement.

"You're right about that. Now, let's get back to work. Robin, have you had a chance to find out who's missing stock?"

Robin produced a flimsy from his pocket. "And Mr. Hu said a rancher named Tobin's been complaining that some of his stock has run off."

"Let's get details on those animals, then, and not just freeze brands, but full descriptions and markings."

"Maybe Hrriss could . . ." Inessa began, and then clapped her hands over her mouth, her eyes big with regret at mentioning that name in Todd's hearing.

"You can ask him, Inessa," Todd said evenly. "You're not under any restraint. Find out if Hrruban ranches are missing horses, too. Maybe the rustling's only aimed at Hayumans."

"You can't possibly mean to imply that Hrrubans would stoop to rustling?" Kelly asked, regretting the statement the instant the words were out of her mouth.

"They'd be the last to rustle hrrsses," Todd said, whimsically using Hrriss's pronunciation. "But someone might like to make it look that way."

"Good point, Todd," Ken said. "Now let's . . ."

"Let's have dinner," Pat interjected, "before it's spoiled. The hides will keep."

After dinner, in which theory and speculation were rife, everyone went off on their designated searches. Robin took the family flitter and zoomed away to visit the Dautrish farm. Kelly went off in hers, promising to do a thorough search of the Solinari records and see if perhaps the leopard Appie had been bred by another rancher. Ken used the office system to double-check his records at source and Todd settled in at the computer terminal in his room.

He put up a mail message to the hundreds of ranches on Doona, asking permission to do a read-only on their stock files, and leaving his user number and name as the signature. Then he put a control list of the numbers and · hides that his father had gone through. Before he finished that, three ranchers had flashed back permission. First he listed missing stock, by number and description. He set up a separate file to isolate description matches. When he thought of going to Main Records to obtain numbers of hides returned to Doona for leather processing, he used the ranch number, in case his was unacceptable to Treaty Island. He berated himself for the growing paranoia he sensed as a result of his house arrest, but he needed this information too badly to wish to be denied access.

He didn't dismiss the possibility that someone had made illicit use of the Reeve Ranch freeze-mark files. And although rustling had been an ongoing problem for ranchers, that sort of illegal entry smacked of a very long-term effort. Rustlers were in and out, making a quick profit from their hauls. They certainly wouldn't plan so precisely how to confuse records and an entire, viable industry. Or would they?

It was that leopard Appie hide with a blatantly Reeve brand that really baffled him. He knew he couldn't rest until he'd found where that horse had been bred and who had owned it.

As he was to discover in the next few days, lots of people had missed horses that they never traced, never found the carcass of, and had never bothered reporting. Every rancher expected to lose a few to natural calamities. But the more he looked, the more he came to realize that no ranch had lost as many over the past ten years as the Reeves.

Branding an animal with some other ranch's ID simply wasn't the sort of practical joke ranchers played on each other. Not by the dozens, certainly.

While one bay hide could look like another bay hide, swirl marks were taken when an animal was registered. Broken-color horses were far easier to identify from their birth diagrams, which plainly indicated the shapes of the darker hair.

Then a thought struck him. Maybe these weren't Doonan horses at all. At least the ones whose hides Ken had found. Maybe that was the deception: horses stolen from another planet marked with Doona brands to satisfy innocent purchasers. No wonder there was a Zapata provenance. When he discovered how many colonial worlds bred horses, with vast herds far too large to be individually marked, Todd decided he'd leave that option till last.

He'd look first for those animals which had been discovered dead. The cause of their demise would be in the records . . . and there were quite a few. All with the initials *MA* for Mark Aden, Lon Adjei's former assistant. *SS* meant ssersa poisoning, *MS* for snake, *M* for mda, *A* for accident—broken leg or some other injury which resulted in euthanasia. The unexplained disappearances, however, began to increase over the last few years.

The fact that the Reeve Ranch suffered the most losses and that the spurious hide marks were all Reeve brands as well worried Todd. Admiral Landreau was back on Doona. Any example of incompetence, any whiff of dishonesty that could be charged against the Reeves, could be seized on and used by Landreau and others to try and get them deported, could work against the welfare of the entire colony. This was too precarious a time for him to be trapped by a home arrest, out of circulation, out of action when he was most needed. Anger suffused Todd. Ever since he set foot on Doona, he had defended the ideal it exemplified—harmonious cohabitation. He knew to the marrow of his bones, the cells of his blood, the lungs that breathed clear Doonan air, that Hrriss felt an equal dedication.

Why had he decided that they had to answer that Mayday? He answered himself. Because, being who he was, reared as he was, he could have done nothing else. And someone very clever had counted on that! He couldn't quite see Admiral Landreau being so psychologically astute. Rogitel, now, he might. But Todd had had little intercourse with the commander—only that one meeting on Hrretha. Not really time enough in desultory formal responses for even a trained psychologist to have taken that kind of measure of anyone.

Another file for a missing horse recalled him to the task at hand and he punched the print button. The stack of films beside him was growing.

He'd had to make a joke out of DeVeer suspecting him of doing the smuggling for profit. And yet, with all those valuables found on the *Albatross*, it wouldn't be so hard for someone else to accept that possibility. But for anyone to think that he, Todd Reeve, or Hrriss, son of Hrrestan, Hrruban leader of Rrala, would sully all they had lived for, worked for . . . that was very hard to swallow. The beautiful dream that was Doona was inexorably slipping away from his grasp, deny it though he might. Ilsa had never understood his passion for Doona. And really, neither did Robin or Inessa, but they had never lived under the restraints of Earth society, so they'd no idea what they'd lose. He wished for the millionth time that he could talk to Hrriss. If it wasn't for the support of his family, the often stumbling reassurances of old friends, the wisdom of Hrruvula, his counsel and Kelly's daily visits, he would find that unendurable.

The cheery "One Moment Please" graphic appeared on the screen again. Todd felt another rush of hot rage, which he fought to dispel. It didn't do any good to tear himself up, but he was frustrated and angry. Instead of being out there, offering support for the ongoing Treaty talks which would cement permanent relations between Earth and Hrruba, ensuring Doona's continuance, Todd was being used as a pawn to break the colony and the alliance. Every time he answered one charge or began to solve one problem, another cropped up to claim his attention. It was curious, because everything seemed centered on him or his father. And that incontrovertibly led to Admiral Al Landreau as the most likely origin of this complex conspiracy. He had no proof nor the freedom of movement to secure any.

Why did animosity consume Landreau to the point where his revenge on the Reeves, father and son, embraced Doona, and all the good that had been achieved over a quarter of a century?

Todd searched his memory of those early days on Doona. Of course, he had arrived after Ken and the other ten colonists had struggled through an unbelievably long and cold winter to build homes for their families when the ship arrived in the springtime. Eleven men, placed alone on a supposedly uninhabited planet, had to make all the decisions of socialization and civilization that would frame a new world. They courageously faced physical hazards and the incredible moral obligation. When Ken had discovered the Hrruban village, they had been ready to leave in obedience to the prohibitions which had been hammered into their heads almost from birth: cohabitation with another species could only result in the destruction of the other species. But the Hrrubans were no gentle, vulnerable, sensitive ephemerals.

Circumstances had swept the Terrans along at a furious pace, and they had found themselves cohabiting, with no way to adhere to their decision to leave Doona. Todd grinned, wishing he had been more aware when his father had lost his temper at the various bureaucrats who had blamed the colonists for the untenable situation. Once the mutual benefits of this trial cohabitation had been understood, Alreldep, with Admiral Sumitral, and Codep had accepted with fair grace. But Landreau, the Spacedep representative, never forgot and showed no hint of forgiveness.

Todd took a break from the computer and got up to stretch. He raised his arms over his head and heard the crack as muscles protested being forced to remain too long in the same position. At some point, his mother had quietly left a pitcher of juice, some buttered bread, and the final wedge of the dinner pie on a tray on the worktop. Gratefully he poured a glass of juice and, with the pie in one hand, walked to the window. He was thankful every day for the abundance of real and tasty food. He still remembered the metallic taste of childhood meals, the sameness of each supposedly nutritious meal. He had always felt hungry.

He pushed open the window and leaned his elbows on the frame. The sun was starting to drop behind the trees over the river at the bottom of the pasture. He wished he could be out and doing, back at his job, able to visit his friends. Even when he was a small boy, he had hated confinement. Never mind that his prison was the many acres of his father's ranch: his freedom of movement had been severely curtailed and he was unused to that. It was, however, better than a genuine incarceration in a four-by-four-meter cell. The only times he had been allowed to leave the ranch over the last two weeks had been to appear on Treaty Island, for more questioning. Each time, he had hoped for a glimpse of Hrriss, but their visits didn't coincide. The prosecutors were being careful to keep them strictly apart.

The incriminating evidence of illegal artifacts found on the *Albatross* was quite enough to convict them of criminal activities inconsonant with the positions of trust both he and Hrriss had held. With Landreau and Rogitel briefing their attorneys, this could call into question the success of the Doona Experiment of Cohabitation. That would be a rather farfetched allegation, since one Hayuman and one Hrruban were involved, not two members of the same species working against the interests of the other.

Their defense attorney was Hrruvula, a brilliant Hrruban advocate of the same Stripe as First Speaker but young enough to be light-furred, a shade that the horseman in Todd named buckskin. His stripe, while still narrow, was a dark accent to his fine hide. His Standard was as fluent as a native-born Terran and indeed he had assiduously studied both the language and the legal systems of Earth as well as those of his home planet. He had one assistant, the physical opposite of his tall muscular self, a diminutive dark-haired, dark-complected Terran named Sue Bailey, a name Todd thought inordinately appropriate for a legal clerk. During all the sessions Todd had attended, she said little, rarely glancing up from the square portable over which her fingers flew in taking down their conversations.

Hrruvula made no bones about the fact that the evidence—tape and objects, and most especially the Byzanian Glow Stone—damned Todd and Hrriss. Todd suggested that Poldep had not investigated any of the anomalies or made any attempt to question other suspects.

"When they have you and Hrriss, with your fingers in the till as it were," Hrruvula said, revealing a fine understanding of old Terran metaphors that would delight Kelly, "they have no motivation to look for anyone else. But you two have no motive that I have been able to discover. You both have the reputation of indisputable honor and dedicated responsibility. You both have a splendid future on Doona, and only fools, which neither of you are, would jeopardize such a future so near to its real inauguration: the renegotiation of the Treaty of Doona."

"Have you discovered anyone else with such motive?"

Hrruvula lifted his shoulders. "As you suggested, Admiral Landreau's public animosity toward Doona as well as his frequent assertions that he would 'get the Reeves' have been verified. Documentation has been provided by many eminent personages. But there is no proof . . ."

"There has to be . . ," Todd had interrupted.

Hrruvula held up his first digit, claw tip showing. His jaw had dropped slightly and his eyes sparkled. "Yet." Then Hrruvula had asked if they had any more information about the hides.

The Treaty Council members sat looking austere and troubled, facing Commander Landreau over the Council table. The head of Spacedep was flanked by Rogitel, his assistant, and by Varnorian of Codep, who looked bored by the whole proceeding. Landreau sat hunched slightly over his clasped hands, like a moody predator bird, as he reiterated the charges against Todd Reeve and Hrriss.

Todd and Hrriss were not present for this introductory session. They were, naturally, represented by Hrruvula, with Sue Bailey tapping quiet fingers on her keys. With a Poldep officer on guard, the illicit artifacts were displayed, the Glow Stone in a heavy plastic case. Sampson DeVeer was also present, seated next to the recording secretary at the foot of the table.

"The accused, Todd Reeve and Hrriss, both colonists of this planet, have been granted numerous unusual privileges," Landreau began. "Among them, exclusive use of a scout-class spaceship and almost unlimited access to the Archives and other records."

"These 'privileges' were warranted by their extra-planetary duties which they have faultlessly executed to the benefit of their native planets and their adopted world," Hrruvula replied. "They were elected unanimously to fulfill the position of travelling emissaries for Doona/Rrala."

"Yes, and see how they reward the trust put in them," Landreau spat out. "Illegal invasion of space, piracy, smuggling!"

"We are by no means convinced, Admiral Landreau," Madam Dupuis said in a stern tone, "that the defendants are guilty of piracy and smuggling. They have both separately maintained that neither of them placed the artifacts on the *Albatross*, nor could the one have done so without the other's knowledge."

"But their own log claims otherwise." Landreau made his voice sound reasonable, even saddened by the clandestine activities of Todd and Hrriss. "I am not at all satisfied by the so-called confessions that your interview extracted from the, er, defendants."

"My clients would be happy, in fact delighted, to answer these allegations under oath," Hrruvula replied.

"How good is the word of such deceitful parties?"

"Objection!" Hrruvula said, shooting to his feet.

"Sustained," Madam Dupuis said, shooting a repressive look at Landreau.

The Admiral took a deep breath and, with a fixed smile, continued. "Oaths in a case such as this are not good enough," Landreau said, and began enumerating his reasons. "They claim there was a robot beacon orbiting Hrrilnorr IV. Admiralty Records emphatically proves that no such beacon ever existed. *On* the off chance that a rogue beacon from some other system or passing vessel had entered the system and been drawn to Hrrilnorr IV, a scout was dispatched to search. No trace of any mechanical devices was found except the ones assigned to that system. But," and now he waggled his finger, "an astonishing assortment of illegal objects *and* that Byzanian Glow Stone were unquestionably found secreted aboard the *Albatross*, and those two . . . young men"—his tone made that designation an insult—"deny any knowledge of them." He paused dramatically. "I insist on guaranteed veracity. They must submit to interrogation—by qualified technicians, of course—under querastrin."

An agitated murmur rumbled through the Council chamber, although Hrruvula, whom Landreau was watching, appeared unmoved by such a drastic course. Querastrin was by no means a new truth drug, but it was a harsh one. It stripped the person under its influence of both privacy and dignity. Suicides following querastrin interrogation were frequent: more often in the cases of those proved innocent under such a drug than those convicted of crimes they had denied.

Hrruvula fixed his deceptively mild green gaze on Landreau and allowed the pupils to slowly contract. Landreau shuddered inwardly.

"But why should it be needed in this instance, Admiral?" the counsel asked. "Querastrin seems rather an extreme measure. Both Terran and Hrruban courts permit suspects of all but the most bizarre crimes to retain their dignity and give evidence under oath. My clients, on the occasion of the inspection in Councillor Dupuis's presence and separately during every interrogatory session, have explained the circumstances of their entry into the Hrrilnorr system. Their account has not varied in any particular during any repetition."

"But their 'account' does not tally with the physical evidence supporting their arrest. The future of an entire colony is at stake here, don't you understand that?" Landreau asked plaintively, meeting every Councillor's eyes in turn. "Does that not count against the well-being of two single citizens? As a Human, I am appalled that one of my kind invaded a sector which you Hrrubans claimed as your own territory. A deliberate and premeditated abrogation of a specific Treaty clause, and that is the least of their acts against the Treaty. Surely you must wish such unscrupulous persons removed from this society to prevent them tainting the minds of your young folk who have, I am told, become accustomed to following the lead of . . . these two young men. Doona does not need such role models." Landreau allowed his dismay to be clearly seen.

The Treaty Controller nodded slowly as if agreeing with that assertion of opprobrium. Landreau's eyes narrowed slightly and the hint of a smile pulled at his thin lips. The common good was a sensible tack to take in ramming home his points. A nice wedge, neatly driven in to make these idiots reexamine their values.

Hrruvula dismissed that with a wave of his hand. "Who are we to consider to have tainted whom, Commander?" he asked.

"*Cui bono,* Counsellor," Landreau said. "Who profits from the crimes? In the testimony given to this august body, the suspects failed curiously to address several interesting items which I have uncovered. Then, too, I have recently come into possession of evidence, just brought to my attention, on another matter entirely. The government of Zapata Three felt obliged to submit this directly to me. This includes not only these financial records," and Landreau extended a sheaf of flimsies for the court steward to present to the Councillors, "but a description of a male, one point nine meters tall, with dark brown hair and blue eyes, calling himself Rikard Baliff, the named depositor. This so-called Rikard Baliff has had a most lucrative and active account for the last ten years. The date of the first deposit, by chance, happens to be only two months after that scout, *Albatross,* was assigned to Todd Reeve and Hrriss, son of Hrrestan. The most recent deposit was made only three weeks ago."

"I fail to see the relevance of these documents," Hrruvula remarked with a slight, exasperated sigh of boredom.

"It's obvious enough to me, to any thoughtful person," Landreau replied, piqued. "Young Mr. Reeve has been building a stake himself, should the Doona Experiment fail. A new life, with a new name—financed, in part, we may now surmise on this new evidence—by the sale of horses bearing Reeve Ranch freeze marks as well as the rare artifacts found on the *Albatross.* I have depositions," and he fluttered more sheets for the steward to hand over to the Councillors, "that this Rikard Baliff was always accompanied by a Hrruban. Plainly the two have been in collusion for a long time."

Madam Dupuis disguised her anger only by a great effort of will. Despite this new and most unsettling evidence, she could not imagine Todd Reeve as a conniving rustler and smuggler any more than she could see Hrriss being led around by the nose as an accomplice in such a nefarious undertaking. Why, Todd would have been barely twenty-one at the time he allegedly started this galaxy-wide enterprise. Furthermore, someone in those ten years would surely have recognized Todd and Hrriss at some point during their visits to Zapata and commented on it. Especially if Todd and Hrriss were at the same time representing the colony at an official function. She eased from one buttock to another, compelled by her oath as a Treaty Councillor to hear out this remarkable fabrication of Landreau's and fretting the way evidence upon evidence was being piled up.

When Landreau began to read from the documents, as if the Councillors were too infirm to do so for themselves, she interrupted him. "Have you any witnesses who can testify to the presence of Todd Reeve and Hrriss on Zapata to conduct these transactions?"

"Only scan the frequency of deposits, Madam Dupuis, and you will see"—Landreau's smile broadened—"that the dates match the times—on List B-2—when Reeve and his Hrruban partner were logged off Doona on official visits."

Madam Dupuis turned to her colleagues. "I would like to see their flight plans and log records for the past ten years."

"That is List B-3, Madam Dupuis," Rogitel said helpfully.

"It would seem that they have become deft at altering the *Albatross* log to delete unauthorized landings at Zapata, and on other worlds," Landreau said.

"If I may interject a word here," Rogitel said, "since the assistant sealed the *Albatross* immediately upon its landing four weeks ago, they did not have time to alter the log on that journey. The need to do so would account for why they were so insistent on postponing the obligatory inspection of their craft until such time when they could return and delete the incriminating portions."

One of the Treaty Councillors rattled the deposit sheet. "A lot of credit's flowed through this account. Where did the withdrawals go?"

"Why, to purchase illegal and smuggled items, sir," Landreau said as if any fool could have deduced that. "And undoubtedly to secure silence from any who might inform on their clandestine activities."

"Frankly, Admiral, I find that allegation harder to believe than any other evidence you have presented to this court," Madam Dupuis said. "Both young men have worked ceaselessly to ensure that the Doona Experiment continues."

"Ah!" and Landreau raised his hand, his face alight. "That is why their duplicity is so monstrous. Especially where the Reeve family is concerned, for it is well known that they would not be welcome back on Earth. Therefore, seizing an opportunity to be sure that he and his family would live in comfort somewhere else, Todd Reeve used his position and privilege to accumulate the necessary credits."

Hrruvula managed a chuckle and in a very human gesture, covered his eyes as if unable to maintain the dignity such a hearing required.

"Your humor is ill timed, sir," Landreau said, stiffly drawing his body to its full height in the chair, "for all of you must remember that ten years ago, demonstrations occurred on both Hrruba and Terra demanding that the Siwannese Noncohabitation Principle be upheld and the Doona colony abandoned as a violation." Then he gave Hrruvula a smug glance of satisfaction for that unequivocal fact.

"Those demonstrations subsided and an inquiry proved that the agitation had not been spontaneous as claimed but had indeed been subsidized by unidentified conservatives from both planets."

"That is on record," Madam Dupuis said. "More to the point, at no time during the period were any colonists permitted off-planet."

"Exactly, Madam Dupuis!" Landreau shot to his feet in triumph. "And shortly thereafter Reeve and Hrriss began their 'goodwill' appearances."

"To dispel any lasting doubt as to the validity of the Doona/Rrala Experiment," Hrruvula said.

"And just look how that privilege has been abused by Reeve and Hrriss!" Landreau exclaimed. "To smuggle and steal in order to provide an alternate life-style in case the Doonan

Experiment should not prove successful at the end of the Treaty period. The Reeve family has a well-documented history of dissidence and anarchy."

"That is libel, Admiral," Hrruvula said. "They are self-motivated, hardworking, disciplined colonists with achievements any Stripe would be proud to acknowledge. And do!"

"I insist that the defendants submit to interrogation under querastrin," Landreau said, his face flushed, his eyes flashing, and his manner uncompromising. "That is the only way in which the truth of the past ten years can be unraveled."

"I protest the need for any such extreme measure!" Hrruvula was on his feet.

The Treaty Controller gave a sharp rap of his gavel.

"That may not be necessary," he said, though his phrasing caused other Councillors to regard him in surprise. "The defendants will be interrogated in court in the normal manner as to the violation of the interdiction of Hrrilnorr and their possession of illegal objects found secreted on the ship solely used by them. The defense attorney is to have time to review the new evidence presented to this court today and prepare a defense."

Madam Dupuis regarded the Controller in a fixed stare, for he intimated that he didn't believe there could be a defense adequate to clear the charges. She noticed that Hrruvula was quick to catch the innuendo.

"If those proceedings prove inconclusive," the Controller went on, "time enough to administer querastrin."

Landreau covered his jubilation. He had become worried at the Controller's silence, for it had taken a long time for his colleagues to place that nominee of the bigoted Third Speaker in the senior position. He had to deal with Hrrubans, to be sure, to effect that end, but at least they had been Hrrubans who felt as he did—that the Doonan Experiment should be disbanded. He tossed Hrruvula a challenging look. Just let that cat try to discredit the evidence that had been so carefully obtained. Just let him try!

And after discrediting the Reeves, such sterling examples of Doonan colonials, he was quite willing to start an interspecies war to depopulate Doona. Those plans needed only a few more little twitches to provide ample excuse for the protective preemptive strike he felt was necessary against the danger of a Hrruban invasion of Earth. Soon that twenty-five-year-old mistake would be exonerated.

The gavel startled him out of his reverie.

"Due notice of the trial date will be forthcoming," declared the Controller. "This session is adjourned."

Admiral Landreau sprang to his feet as the Councillors filed out, well pleased with the events. He failed to notice either their thoughtful expressions or the bland expression of Hrruvula.

"Well, that's a horse of a different color, if you get what I mean," Ali Kiachif said, startling Ken, who had been disconsolately stroking the leopard Appie hide. "I thought so when I shipped it. Alive, alert, and akicking, it was. Freddie lad told me you were looking for me. I've got another sled or two of your hides, myself, if you were interested in having them. Chance of a drink for a dry man? Some of your pussycat punch around, if you know what I'm talking about, eh? That mlada's a powerful temptation."

Ken looked from the hide on the table to the merchantman's friendly face. "Sure thing, Ali," and he swung out of his chair to get bottle and glass from the cupboard, "but are you saying that you remember this one horse in particular, out of all the hundreds you've carried?"

The captain lifted his shoulders expressively. "Thousands, Reeve, thousands!" He knocked back the generous tot Ken had poured. "Horses are what Doona ships the most of. But that leopardie Applousa was a real looker."

"Leopard Appaloosa," Ken corrected automatically.

"Don't see many of them, if you know what I mean. Er, I'm a bit dry."

As automatically, Ken splashed an even more generous portion and set the bottle down in front of the wiry old spacefarer.

"Tell me all you remember, Captain, please! I'm going half crazy trying to find out where the horse which wore this hide came from. My records come up blank and we're having to cross-check it against every animal ever bred here."

Ali Kiachif had been lowering the level of mlada in the glass slowly but steadily as Ken spoke. Now, wiping his wild whiskers with the back of his hand, he sighed with relief. "Ah, that cuts the spacedust and sifts the sand, with a vengeance. I remember perfectly because one, the unusual hide on the beast, and two, it was the first time I'd seen an animal with your freeze mark being exported. Looked like a nice animal so I couldn't understand why you'd sell it on. I take a fairly friendly interest in your family, from far away back. Got another reason to remember yon spotted laddie because I was taking your stablehand, young Mr. Aden, out into the great beyond with it! He was going to one of the new places to ply his trade." Kiachif scratched his beard. "Though I can't rightly remember what that trade was. He had a lot of tricky toys and equipment with him, but it was all his. He had a manifest, money, the works. A lot of money, I was thinking, for a young lad who never did anything but manage horses all his life. He was off to a grand start with all those gadgets wherever he was going."

"Now, that's the best thing I've heard in weeks, Ali," Ken said, but his smile was grim. "And it—partially—explains who knew so much about my ranch and freeze IDs."

"But that Appie laddie wasn't rustled. He was sold proper by that Aden feller."

"Who's part of a conspiracy to frame me and my son."

"What's that?" Ali Kiachif paused, hand on the bottle neck.

"I never bred a leopard Appaloosa, Ali. The Solinaris do. Those are, undeniably, my ranch markings but they should be on a two-year-old pinto."

"Well, I can swear that they're on the hide of the animal I loaded. That animal!" And Ali stabbed a stubby stained finger at the hide in front of him.

"You'd be willing to swear to that?"

"In front of anyone and as often as need be. But it's not one hide that's got your drive revving."

"No. So far I've found nineteen other hides, provenanced from Zapata, that don't tally with any horse I ever bred and marked. Poldep is saying it's Todd who's been rustling from his own father, amassing a fat credit account off-world." Ken could feel the frustrated anger building inside him again just having to repeat the foul accusations. "And there're more rumors that Hrriss is either coming along for the ride or sharing the take." At the astonished and disbelieving expression on Ali Kiachif's face, he reined in.

Ali did not. He poured a quick tot to steady himself, for his face had turned an apoplectic red.

"Not those boys!" he said, pounding his fist on the table, a separate bang for each word. "Charge anyone else from any planet anywhere in Terran space or even Hrruban space and I might agree, but not Todd and Hrriss."

"The Council and Poldep do not share your faith in their honesty. And damn it all"—the boost which Kiachif's instant defense had given Ken dissolved as quickly—"the facts, the evidence are against them."

"Facts! Facts? Evidence?" Ali narrowed his eyes, the shrewd trader, not the spirits-guzzling reprobate. "Facts can be altered, even evidence can be counterfeit to suit needs. But I'm a man who's dealt with all kinds, all over this arm of the Milky Way," and he waved expansively, "and I've never been wrong judging a man in my life. And I'm not wrong about that lad of yours who wore a rope tail to look like his best buddy. Anyone else, of any creed, color, conformation, or character, might do the dirty on his own dad so we'll have to find out who did!" Ali waggled his stained finger at Ken. "And by fire, frost, and every ounce of faith in this old bod, we'll prove it."

His wrath was so great he began to choke on the accumulated spittle in his mouth and Ken had to pound him on the back. Still strangling, Ali Kiachif held up his glass for a refill.

As she had promised, Kelly brought the ranch files to Hrriss's house. He came out to meet her.

"I thought I recognized the distinctive beat of Calypso's pace," he said warmly, greeting her. "Nothing's wrong, is it?"

"Not with Todd," she assured him, dismounting and throwing the mare's reins over the rail at the door. "But we got another small problem. Ken Reeve thought maybe you could help on the Hrruban end of things. Give you something to do."

"Constructive work is always welcome," Hrriss said, gesturing for her to precede him. "What is the task?"

Kelly outlined the story of the mismarked and unidentifiable hides. Hrriss scowled deeply, grasping the implications immediately.

"Zo, now we are alzo rustlers!"

To her surprise, Kelly actually saw the hair of Hrriss's stripe rise in resentment.

"Ken Reeve saw a leopard Appaloosa hide in a bundle Fred Horstmann brought in. The puzzle is that the Reeves don't raise leopard Appies. We do. But the freeze mark was a Reeve Ranch that was put on a two-year-old pinto."

"Neither pintos nor leopards change their spots," Hrriss said thoughtfully. "Had the freeze mark been altered in any way?"

"No. Ken had the hide analyzed and we've all had a look at it through a microscope. Dad doesn't show a record of any missing leopard Appies. But we need to know if any Hrruban rancher might be missing one."

"What good would that do? A freeze mark cannot be altered."

"But a duplicate number could be put on another stolen animal, couldn't it?"

"Ah, that is a different matter. And no reliable trader would export animals which did not bear the brand of a reliable rancher."

"Todd's already working on a read-only scan of Hayuman ranches but it takes so long on this antiquated computer net that if you could handle the Hrruban end of things . . ."

"Of course," Hrriss said, patting her knee to reassure her. "I will begin at once."

"I would like to help in any way I can," said a soft voice as a female Hrruban slipped into the room. "I have computer skills."

Kelly tried hard not to gawk at the unexpected presence of a female in Hrriss's company. "I'm so sorry. How very rude of me not to ask if you were already occupied, Hrriss." She started to rise but Hrriss gently pushed her back down on the divan.

"I am Nrrna," she said, coming straight to Kelly and holding out her hand. She had a short, fluffy dark beige pelt, evidence of her youthfulness, but her stripe was broad and dark, suggesting she came from a very good family. She wore a braided cloth in aqua shade, looped in decorative swags from her shoulders, waist, and ankles that offset her delicate form and beauty.

"I remember you," Kelly said, cordially gripping the slender hand, for Nrrna's face markings were familiar. She glanced at Hrriss and saw the glowing look in his eyes, not the least bit fraternal. Nrrna returned his glance in the manner of one who has developed considerable rapport. "We took a language class in High Hrruban, though I admit it's been years. Aren't you working for the Health Services these days?"

"Yes," Nrrna replied with shy friendliness, sidling slightly closer to Hrriss. "I heard of your academic success from my parents. Yours must be very proud."

Hrriss moved imperceptibly closer to the dainty female. "Nrrna and I will become lifemates this season," he said, looking proud and self-conscious at the same time.

"You will? Lifemates? Oh! Oh, I'm so happy for you!" Kelly leaped up to seize Hrriss and rub cheeks with him again, then turned to offer both hands to Nrrna, squeezing the delicate bones very gently.

Considering how Hrrubans mated, Hrriss was likely using the word "season" advisedly. Nrrna would know her cycle, and was planning carefully so they would have time for a joining ceremony before estrus began. Kelly felt that her face was cracking with her delighted smile.

"So this is the research into matters of interest to your mother, Hrriss! How wonderful! May you have every joy!" She snapped her jaws closed before she said what was in her mind, and didn't know where to look in her dismay.

Hrriss reached for her hand and pressed it between his. "When Zodd and I are able to resume our association, Nrrna and I will tell him together."

Kelly sighed. "Your news would cheer him up, but I can quite imagine how his knowing such a private arrangement could be construed. I may pop out in spots of anticipation but I won't mention it. That's one thing I've learned at Alreldep— how to know and not know. Just please let me be there when you do break the news. I want to see him really smile, from deep down," and she touched her diaphragm, "instead of just his lips."

"You have my word . . ."

"Which is worth a lot, believe me," Kelly said, her tone suddenly fierce.

Hrriss nodded solemnly and his eyes glowed at the strength of her conviction. Once again he took her hands but this time to seal their agreement.

"Well, I do feel better, Hrriss, I really do."

"And these records? Have you arrived at any style to conduct the search?"

"I have," Kelly said, and opened the packet. "It's such a boring job, takes forever, but if you can both help . . ."

"Nrrna, your parents may not wish you to involve yourself in an investigation of this nature."

"Locating missing hrrsses?" She raised her delicately marked brows at him, her emerald eyes wide with surprise. "It is to help the friend of your heart, Hrriss. And I am my own person. I may make my own decisions." Now she gave Hrriss a certain look that caught Kelly's breath. Undeniably the twinge of regret she felt at seeing such unselfconscious love was partly jealousy for what they already shared.

Hrriss turned back to Kelly, his jaw lightly parted and a mischievous glint in his eyes. "You see, she will have her way if she knows the rightness of the path."

"Are you and Zodd not on the same path?" Nrrna asked. "Hrriss has told me how much you are trying to help revoke those ignoble accusations."

"Ah, yes, well, Nrrna, that's another matter."

Nrrna's delicate laugh came out a soft purr. "It is so easy to tell when bareskins are embarrassed. Oh, I do not mean to offend with that term . . ."

"We are bareskins and I take no offense from such as you, Nrrna. Never," Kelly said. "And I blush far too easily for my own good."

"Especially when Zodd is the subject," Hrriss said, cocking his head to join in the teasing. Then he turned to Nrrna. "Hayuman females do not have your advantage."

"I wish I did," Kelly said with complete exasperation. "I don't mind telling you two—and talking about Todd is not a violation of that stupid ban you two are under—but I love the guy and he doesn't seem to see me as anything more than his 'trusted Hunt second' and the girl next door."

Hrriss regarded her with eyes that glowed now with a slightly different but equally tender regard than the one he gave Nrrna.

"He danced more with you than with anyone else, Kelly," he said. "And he kept his eyes on you wherever you were. And if he was not aware of it, he did not look at you as a trusted Hunt second."

"And I know he's annoyed because Pat and Ken keep inviting me over for dinner and I don't think he wants me to come. When I only want like blazes to help any way I can."

"Ah, but you do not know Zodd as I do, Kelly."

"No, I don't. That's why I'm asking you, and I really shouldn't belabor you with personal problems right now, but you do know him."

"Right now Zodd would be careful to shield you, as I tried to shield Nrrna," and he looked lovingly at her.

"Who refuses to be shielded," Nrrna said on a purr, "just as Kelly does."

"I most certainly am capable of taking care of myself," Kelly said vehemently. "Oh, Todd and that damned awkward sense of honor of his! Well, he wouldn't be Todd without it."

Hrriss contented himself with a nod. "Be yourself. Be helpful, be cheerful. And now let us all be helpful and see what we can learn." He glided across the room to the computer station and flicked it on with just the nail of his first finger. Sitting down, he logged on his user number. "I shall begin with Hrrula's ranch. He mourns every time one of his hrrsses goes missing. It is a personal affront to his care of them. I will drop a note to obtain permission."

Nrrna and Kelly watched while the data base brought up the user message board. Hrriss had his fingers poised over the keyboard when the screen cleared to show the last user number accessing the file.

"I cannot continue," Hrriss said, his voice sad and reluctant. "That is Zodd's number at the bottom."

"But if he's not on the net now, surely . . ."

"Not now. The time indicates that he logged off thirty minutes ago."

"Then go ahead."

"I cannot. It might be construed as an infringement of our oath not to contact each other. What if it was suggested that he left messages in a file for me to find and erase?"

"Sometimes . . ." Kelly raised hands above her head in pique, then lowered them, accepting such a scrupulous interpretation of their restriction. "You're becoming as paranoid over this as Todd."

"Thank you," Hrriss said solemnly. "In that context, it is a compliment."

Kelly rolled her head and threw up her hands again, this time turning to Nrrna for guidance. "Well, then, Nrrna. It's up to us. We'll investigate on our own, won't we?" Nrrna nodded enthusiastically. "So move out of that chair and let either me or Nrrna log on. Get you out of the room so you cannot be tempted, scaredy cat," and Kelly made shooing gestures with her hands at Hrriss. "If you're so concerned about our involvement, we may or may not tell you what we learn. Your place or mine, Nrrna?"

"Stay here!" Hrriss said, his tone just short of pleading. "I will not look." And he went to sit on the pillows farthest from the computer station.

"You can be in the same room with us while we're jeopardizing our reputations in helping you?" Kelly said teasingly.

"You both do us honor," Hrriss said gravely, and picked up a tape viewer, turning his head away. "But please tell me when you have located that leopard Appaloosa hide."

CHAPTER

7

KELLY FOUND ALI KIACHIF IN THE PUB OF THE
Launch Center, weaving to a circle of his captains a story of
derring-do during an ion storm in which he and one of his men
had rescued the ship, getting the cargo and everyone on board
to their destination with nary a scratch. The Codep captain's
talk was punctuated with alliterative triads and circumlocutory
references, but he had a knack for making a story come to
life. When the others drifted apart to discuss the merits (and
veracity) of his tale, Kelly approached him.

"Captain Kiachif?"

The spacer looked up. "What may I do for you, little lady?"

"My name's Kelly Solinari. I'm a friend of Todd Reeve."

"That's something we have in common," he said kindly.
"Come and commune, with a cup of cheer?"

"No, thank you," Kelly said, declining the offer of a drink.
"I don't really feel very cheery. His father said that you offered
to help clear him of these accusations against him."

"I've been of that mind, if you understand me."

Kelly dropped her voice to a discreet whisper. "It is Admiral
Landreau, isn't it, who hates Todd and his father enough to
frame them?"

"Hates 'em lock, stock, and block. Always has since they
made a fool of him. Only he made more of a fool of himself.
They didn't have to help much, if you see what I mean,"
Kiachif said. Having spoken his mind in as guarded voice
as she had used, he took a deep drink and let out a sigh of
satisfaction as he put the glass down.

"You don't happen to remember any other distinctive horses
wearing Reeve markings?"

Kiachif screwed his face. "I remember that one, like I told Ken. But perfect pat and plain, Miss Kelly, I didn't think much of that incident. You see, that Aden feller, their manager, was doing the shipping, so it seemed natural that all the horses had Reeve Ranch marks. That leopard-spotted one just stood out so much among the bays and browns."

"But it did have a Reeve brand on it, then?"

"Yup, it surely did."

"But how could it have?" Kelly's voice went squeaky as she tried to keep it low and couldn't repress her outrage.

"Well, now, the freeze brand is not supposed to be alterable. Technique's practically perfect. But nothing's perfect."

"Oh, don't tell me someone has a system for altering brand marks! Can you think of the havoc that'll cause?"

"Nope, don't want to think about it. I want to think how I can prove Todd Reeve never rustled nothing in his life, never stole nothing, never fiddled with log tapes or deviated from his registered flight plans. I want to think how ships been getting through one of the most secure security systems in the galaxy. That's what I want to think about. And this helps." He lifted his empty glass and signaled a passing barman. "Bring the bottle!"

When the bottle had been brought, he inspected the cap with a narrowed eye before he broke the seal and filled his glass. Kelly was somewhat astounded by his capacity but she kept her expression polite.

"Can't be one of the Codeps. I got them under my thumb," and he held it up, flat and broad and stained, "if you know what I mean. They know all better'n accept stolen goods 'cause it makes me mad and besides that, makes it look like the government's condoning theft. Fred Horstmann was some upset about that bundle of hides but I calmed him down. That Zapata provenance checked out genuine. So we got to go back further in this rustling-business, hide-marking, moneymaking nonsense. I do remember"—Kiachif paused thoughtfully—"carrying a feller back to Earth. He'd done his prison term. Knew all about lasers did Askell Klonski. A weasely little wart, if my memory doesn't mislead me. Claimed he could change a tattoo of a wanton, winking woman so she was blinking with the other eye and you'd never know it hadn't been that way to start."

Kelly smothered a laugh, for his words conjured up an indescribable vision. Kiachif held up his hand.

"He'd be just the sort to deftly do the deed, if you know what I mean. Now, I don't know if he was bragging or not. Those types do. He'd served his sentence, but he didn't learn it, if you understand me. The guards in the galley said he was a genius in laser techniques. Served as a trustee his last years on the Rock because he was the only one who could fix the alarm system. He was so good no slips, skips, or blips went undetected. No escapes at all during his tenure. Shortened his sentence slightly, where it shouldn't have ended at all, if you follow me. If I hadn't had orders signed by Varnorian himself, I doubt I would have carried him anywhere."

"Where is he now?" Kelly asked eagerly.

Kiachif massaged his whiskers. "Still on Earth, so I hear. No decent colony would have him. He was pushed in on a snooty section of Corridor and Aisle, to the infinite consternation of his neighbors. They say he's 'not our type, dear.' " Kiachif did a humorous imitation of a proud matron looking down her nose at Kelly. "Spending a lot of money, too. I'd like to know where he got it. With his record, the chances that it was hardly honest are high."

"Hmm," Kelly said thoughtfully. "Any chance of contacting him soon?"

Kiachif nodded his head up and down, refilling his glass again. "Strangest part is that that man was released just about ten years ago."

"Oh!"

"That's what I said. Ten years ago. Not so long before I saw that leopardy horse."

The moon played hide-and-seek with the clouds as the two girls sneaked down toward the transportation grid on the Hrruban side. A thin spot of light penetrated the clouds, striking the ground in front of them, and they ducked behind the bushes. Kelly hoped there were no small nocturnal predators abroad, not when they didn't wish to draw attention to themselves. Night critters all had mean bites.

"You do know how to set the grid, don't you?" Kelly asked Nrrna in a tone barely above a whisper.

"I do, but, Kelly," Nrrna replied, "you know this is highly illegal."

"So is what they're doing to Todd and Hrriss," was Kelly's whispered reply. "Time's running out. Ali Kiachif thinks he knows the man who could have used a laser to change animal brands and he's on Earth, so that's where I've got to go and fast. If we can just cast doubt on one of those phony charges against Todd and Hrriss, we might be able to prove that a conspiracy exists. If we can't, who knows what will happen to them—or to Doona."

Nrrna sighed. "I know, I know. But you must be very careful. If it was discovered that I assisted you to grid back . . ."

Kelly brought her face very close to Nrrna's. "I'd never tell who helped me, Nrrna. Anyway, who's going to know, if we keep to the schedule you worked out? I'll get to the medical supply warehouse on Earth. You just make sure you're here to rescue me when the pallet comes, all right?" She squeezed Nrrna's hand for confidence.

"A female shouldn't be so fearless," Nrrna said.

"Where did you get the idea I was fearless?" Kelly demanded. "I'm terrified but that doesn't keep me from doing it, because it's the only way I can help Todd." She took three deep breaths. This was worse than watching Big Mommies heading toward you. "And it's your way of helping Hrriss. So let's get it done. 'To she who dares falls the prize,' " she muttered to herself before she beckoned for Nrrna to lead the way.

When they reached the grid, there was no one in sight. Kelly didn't at all like using the Hrruban grid: it made her nauseous. Nevertheless she jumped lightly to the platform, turned to stand inside the pillars, and held on to them for support until her knuckles hurt. Silently she begged Nrrna to hurry as the slender Hrruban bent over the controls. The grid beneath her shoes started to vibrate. She barely had time to register that effect before the misting clouded her immediate vicinity.

"Good luck," came Nrrna's soft voice, and lingered as Doona dissolved around her friend.

Kelly materialized inside the transport chamber on Earth. Nrrna had carefully chosen a time when Hrringa was unlikely to be on duty. The only light was the circular glow of the

clock calendar facing the grid. It was not quite dawn here on
Earth. As Nrrna had suggested, a time when security guards of
any species are likely to be less alert. So all those excuses she
thought up for Hrringa could be forgotten. None of them had
sounded very convincing anyway. So the first hurdle was over.
Now to proceed without getting apprehended on Earth when
she wasn't supposed to be here. If she was caught, her career
as a diplomat might be over before it had properly begun.

She swallowed hard, trying to open her throat. Fortunately
she knew the floor plan of the Hrruban Center. It was in the
middle of the Alreldep block, part of the Space Services cube.
Once she got out of the building, she should have no problem finding her way around, but there might be sensors and
alarms designed to detect body heat or movement. She couldn't
remember much about the security measures in the Alreldep
block, but there was generally much more fuss about getting
in than getting out. If she was caught in the Hrruban Center,
it would be obvious that she'd had a Hrruban accomplice,
because no Human knew how to operate a Hrruban grid. And,
undoubtedly, Nrrna would come forward to share the blame.

Gingerly she moved off the grid, expecting any moment for
lights to flash and alarms to shriek. She stepped onto the floor
below the platform, her body tense, until she realized she had
broken no security circuits. She took a deep breath of relief.

She took a second and a third, forcing herself to calm down
so she could think logically how to proceed now. Pending the
end of her holiday and her return for a permanent assignment,
Kelly's privileges in the Alreldep computers had been suspend-
ed. Therefore, she needed someone else's help in finding Ali
Kiachif's clever parolee. She knew several people who had the
necessary skills, and clearance, to find that file in the central
computer complex. But first she had to contact them. She
didn't dare use the Hrruban Center's communications units.
Hrringa shouldn't have to answer questions about why calls
were made from his office in the middle of the night. A
public facility would be much more sensible, if farther from
her present position.

Her luck seemed to be holding, for the center must have
been designed to accommodate visitors appearing through the
grid at times without benefit of operator on this end. As her

eyes grew accustomed to the dark, she could see a double line of tiny low-intensity lights set into the floor leading away from the grid. Cautiously Kelly followed them to the door. She tried the handle, hoping that she hadn't come all this way only to be locked in the Hrruban Center all night long. As the handle moved without hindrance, she murmured a thanksgiving. It probably locked on the outside. It swung easily and silently open.

No alarms sounded and no lights came on. For all her apprehension, she had accomplished the transit without problems. In no time, she found an exit Aisle and was shortly in the main Corridor of Alreldep block and in the main swim of foot traffic without drawing any attention. Now to find a communications kiosk.

The hour may have favored her undetected arrival on Earth, but this was the time when late-shift workers were abroad, and a certain dangerous element of society crept out of their lairs, dens, and hiding places to catch the unwary for what they might have of value about their persons. Proper citizens were too afraid of Aisle and Corridor gossip to report assaults or robberies, so the petty criminals were bold as well as vicious. Kelly was Doonan bred as well as born, and trained to take care of herself, but she didn't want to be noticed. To deflect a would-be assailant would be easy but it would certainly identify her as a most unordinary pedestrian.

Cautiously she kept glancing right and left. No monitors were in view. The gray passage with its moving conveyor belts carried scattered traffic. It wasn't elbow-to-elbow as it was at major shift change times, though there seemed to be as many as Doona had hosted for the Snake Hunt. As she watched all the dutiful citizens in their dull muddy clothing, one mumbled an apology under his breath and his fellow passengers moved aside so he could get off without touching them.

Kelly stepped carefully onto the far edge of the belt, keeping her head down so that no one would look closely at her. She concentrated on walking in the short mincing steps she had learned to use in her years on Earth. She adjusted her usual stride, hunched her shoulders, let her arms hang listlessly at her sides, and pretended disinterest in those she passed on the faster belt. It wasn't as hard as she had feared. The greater gravity of Earth made her muscles work harder at keeping the same pace. The one precaution she had taken before leaving Doona was to alter the vibrant shade of her hair with a dulling brown rinse. It would wash right out, but she'd recognized the wisdom of that artifice. She hadn't had time to search for her old student tunics but she'd worn the dullest, grungiest clothes she owned. Even these were a little bright in comparison with the garments of shift workers at five o'clock in the morning. However, she wasn't going to be on the beltway very long and no one was paying any attention to her. She remembered to take shallower, grudging breaths, just like everyone else. That way she also avoided "tasting" some of the stink of an overcrowded city. Had the air got worse in the short time since she'd left? Or was it the shocking change from breathing the exhilarating air of Doona?

As soon as she spotted a communications kiosk, she muttered the appropriate apologies and stepped off. Her fellow riders carried past her without ever looking up. Monitors might be watching: they always were even if Earth was less restrictive than it had been a quarter century earlier. Controls remained in place to handle the offenses, both real and imagined, of the multiple billions of Humans who lived in such restricted space.

The booth provided her with complete privacy once she shut the door and activated the "engaged" signal. Now it was decision time. Which of her former friends could she positively rely on? Who was well enough placed to get the information she needed? There were rewards available to those who turned in miscreants. Returning without leave was only a misdemeanor but she didn't want to risk even that. One by one, Kelly considered a list of her fellow university students. Cara Martinek was a supply clerk in the Spacedep offices. She couldn't inquire about a former felon with impunity. Jane Kaufenberg worked as a senior researcher at the Amalgamated Worlds Library. Unfortunately Jane probably wouldn't have the necessary clearances to access Alreldep and Spacedep records. She was also rather prissy and would very likely balk at the thought of making an illegal data search. Dalkey Petersham? He was bright, and had graduated first in his class from his Section Academy before attending the university.

Kelly hesitated to approach him, even though they had once worked together on a class project—or perhaps because they had worked together. Dalkey was good, but his after-school thoughts went in one direction only, and Kelly had always told him no. Still, he did work for Landreau, in the right department, and he might even have heard office gossip.

Kelly checked her reflection in the viewscreen. With her fingers, she swiped her hair into place. It was a little earlier than was decent to make a comunit call, but she remembered that Dalkey worked first shift. He should already be awake.

The unit in Dalkey's apartment answered after the first blink. Kelly plastered on a big smile as the camera changed to live. "Dalkey! Hi!"

"Kelly!" She was right. Dalkey was up and dressed. He was still rail-thin, and his hair was brusquely chopped into the bureaucrat's unbecoming clip. He wasn't bad-looking, but there had always been something too smooth about him that turned her off. Trying to be impartial, she had to admit that there was never anyone so obviously born to wear a narrow-necked suit. "Are you back on Earth?"

"I am," Kelly said, and let out a deep breath. Once she uttered the next phrases, she was committed. "Can I come over and talk to you? I'm not far from your Aisle. I've got a favor to ask."

Dalkey looked surprised but pleased. "Sure. I've got thirty before I've got to punch in. Come and have breakfast."

Kelly paid a credit into the kiosk and accepted a receipt chit from the slot so the door would open. Then she retraced her steps to the Corridor. Dalkey lived one more Aisle over, and down to the right several hundred meters on the same level as the Hrruban Center. Several times along the way, she had to force herself to slow down and remember to bow her head like native Terrans. People were beginning to notice her. Kelly bit her lip and concentrated on the appropriate mincing steps, though it was permissible to move slightly faster in an Aisle. She couldn't take any chance that a sharp-eyed monitor might become suspicious and whisk her off the Aisle into Poldep headquarters.

Dalkey was waiting right inside the door of his apartment. He lived in a block of flats occupied mainly by government employees in the Space Services. With an elaborate bow, he escorted her inside.

"Welcome back, Kelly. May I hope that you're back on Earth for a long stay?"

"Actually not," she said, glancing around. The room was a typical bachelor pad. The Residential and Housing Administration allowed the minimum amount of space for single people. The place was sparsely furnished, the walls one of the neutral colors permitted, but it held one surprise: a very colorful tapestry in the Doonan style which brightened the room immensely. Kelly didn't recognize the weaver, but it was an excellent piece of work. In her eyes, that upgraded Dalkey a notch above the usual run of bureaucrats. "Thank you for the invitation to breakfast. Can you really spare the calories?"

"Sure can," Dalkey said, waving her to a seat. "I have more than I need. I keep some of the excess on credit for times when friends drop in, such as now." He programmed two breakfast meals out of the food machine and smiled at her as the characteristic whirring began behind the panel.

Synth-food! Kelly smiled bravely back, wondering if she could keep from gagging. The moment she left for Doona weeks ago, she had gladly put the horrors of synthesized food behind her.

The hatch opened to reveal two plates. Several different grayish or pale tan masses were arranged on each.

"Here we are," Dalkey said cheerfully, as if conferring a real treat, as he brought the steaming plates over to the table and placed one before her. "Go right ahead." He slid into the chair opposite her and began on his own food.

From long experience Kelly remembered which lump was supposed to simulate eggs, and that the next was a milled grain colloid, but the last one's origin she had never been able to figure out. Certainly it could never have been meat, and it wasn't sweet enough to be fruit. She knew that only because the saccharine dessert lump that followed the midday meal was supposed to be fruit.

Dutifully Kelly picked up her fork and started to eat. With the first mouthful the flavor, or lack of it, brought back memories of four long years of make-believe comestibles. She reminded herself that billions of Terrans started every single day with this food. It was healthy, contained every vitamin and mineral necessary for life, and was easily digested. It was still disgusting. She thought she was doing fairly well at disguising her distaste until a tiny chuckle brought her attention back up to Dalkey. He was watching her with an impish gleam in his eyes. He waggled his fork at her plate.

"Not what you got used to on holiday, is it, colony girl?"

"Well"—Kelly laughed self-deprecatingly, putting her fork down—"when you grow up eating real food, it's hard to adjust to a synthetic substitute. If you hadn't been born here, you'd know what I mean." The inadvertent use of Kiachif's favorite bridging phrase reminded her of her errand. "Look, I'd be happy to send you some fruit and things from Doona, so you can find out what you've been missing."

"From the look of you, plenty," Dalkey said, raising an eyebrow. "You don't need to finish the meal, if you can't stand it."

Gratefully Kelly got up to put the dish into the hatch. As she turned back to the table, she found Dalkey standing over her. She started around him, but he pinned her against the wall, his hands on her shoulders.

"So," Dalkey said, lowering his eyelashes seductively. "Come on. Out with it. You didn't come back here just so I can look into your beautiful eyes, although I'm always happy to have that opportunity. What's the favor you need?"

Kelly squeezed back against the synthesizer hatch so there was a few centimeters breathing room between them. The expectant expression on his face alarmed her. She had spent all that time worrying whether anyone would notice her on the street when she should have been figuring out how to fend off Dalkey's advances. He was taller than she was and thin; even his neck was thin. He needed more muscle on him. She could probably knock him down with just a good hefty push. Which wouldn't get her the favor she needed, and she didn't need a wrestling match. Resolutely, so he might realize she had other things on her mind, she folded her arms over her chest.

"All right, here it is," she blurted. "I need to find a man, housed somewhere in the blueblood Corridors. He was released from a prison planet about ten years ago. He was an expert in laser technology and he's been given some kind of annuity. I need to know why. The safety of two of my dearest friends is at stake, not to mention the continuation of the Doona colony."

He gave her a measuring look. "And in return?" he asked, running the back of his hand down her cheek. "Surely you're not going to offer me a silly case of Doona oranges for performing an illegal act with such broad-reaching consequences? Spacedep frowns on people trying to penetrate the privacy files of a former convict. I could be exiled to a mining planet, and so could you for asking. Hard labor."

Kelly nearly asked him what he did want, and realized that she didn't have to. She decided to tell him the truth, and trust to his discretion.

"Dalkey, two friends of me and my family are being framed for crimes that there's no way they could have, or would have, committed. I have it on very good authority that this man might know something about the method that was used to incriminate them. He's the right kind of expert, and he seems to have more money than someone recently paroled ought to have. It's also very odd that a man who faced a life sentence should be paroled, at just about the time we have now discovered a conspiracy was evolved to discredit my friends. He could be an essential party to that conspiracy. I always thought of you as a person with a fine sense of justice. I'm appealing to that now." And she looked Dalkey straight in the eye.

"You've got me interested, I'll say that much. Too many criminals get loose and there've been gangs that have done serious damage. So what sort of crimes are your friends supposed to have committed?"

"Horse rustling, theft of antiquities, possession of stolen goods, and breaking prohibitions set by the Treaty of Doona," Kelly replied, still keeping eye contact. "No matter what you decide, please keep this confidential."

"You just bet I will," Dalkey said with a weak laugh. "As a colonial, couldn't you have fallen for small-time offenders? I'm sure not in your class." He stepped back then, still shaking his head as he let his arms fall to his sides. Kelly gulped in relief and flushed with embarrassment.

Dalkey winked at her consternation. "You don't have to look so surprised. I may not be the man you thought I was, but I'm not the one you were afraid I was either. Ah, ah, ah, don't deny it!" He shook a finger under her nose. "On the other hand, if you're feeling grateful later on, I wouldn't refuse."

He gestured for her to sit on his couch, an old piece Kelly remembered from his student digs and a lot more comfortable than it looked.

"Now, suppose you acquaint me with all the details you've got about this mysteriously paroled felon," he said. "I don't suppose you've got a name?"

"Captain Kiachif knew him as Askell Klonski."

"He'd change his name first thing," Dalkey said, "to shield his real identity. Or maybe that was the name he changed to. Never mind. What else do you know?"

While Kelly talked, he made notes by hand on an old piece of film. "Best not to enter anything on a computer, even for immediate printout and erasure. You never know when the government monitors might choose to check for employee subversion."

Kelly was impressed by his caution. "You surprise me, Dalkey. Thank you."

"Oh, it's not such a surprise. I'm not quite the perfect cog in the machine yet. You know, I've always been attracted to you, partly because you come from Doona. You seemed so much freer than most of the other girls. A pity that freedom didn't extend to the sensual pleasures." Kelly eyed him warily, wondering if he was going to make a grope. He pursed his lips, amused by her. "I'll help you because it's one way for me to get back at the upper-up bureaucrats. There are dirty tricks being played on other people, not just your friends, and I'm getting sick of them. Are all the government services as dirty as Spacedep?" He made a face.

Kelly hurried to reassure him. "No, they're not. Alreldep isn't, otherwise I wouldn't be staying with it. Sumitral's a straightforward man, and he attracts people of a similar stripe."

"Stripe?" Dalkey asked.

"That's a Doonan compliment. You should transfer to his service. Or," Kelly said, laying a hand on Dalkey's arm, "opt for Doona the next time you hear of a residency opening. I'm a citizen. I can sponsor you if you want to come. You could work in the Treaty Center. You've got the right kind of training."

"You'd do that for me? Just like that?" Dalkey asked, snapping his fingers. Kelly nodded. "Yes, I believe you would, colony girl." Then he grinned wryly. "So it's to my advantage to help your friends clear themselves, thus keeping the Doona Experiment going. Fair deal. Look, you'd be safest staying here in my apartment while I get the data crunching. What monitors don't see, they can't report. I don't share with anyone, so you wouldn't be disturbed. If you don't feel comfortable," and Dalkey eyed her for a long moment, "I've some friends who work in Residence Administration and maybe they can let you crash somewhere. It may take a couple of days to snoop into the right files."

"A few days? I don't have that much time, Dalkey. I've got to go back to Doona tomorrow, no matter what. I don't mind sleeping on the couch either: it's not that uncomfortable."

"No, you'll sleep in the bed," Dalkey insisted. She opened her mouth to protest, and he clicked his tongue chidingly. "Ah, ah, ah, there you go again. I can sleep on the couch. Especially if my courtesy gets me out of Spacedep. Oops, five to the starting clock. I'd better go and sign in. I'll see you after shift."

Kelly's conscience stung her as Dalkey saluted her rakishly and stepped out of the door. She'd had to revise her opinion of him upward. During their years at school, she had never had the courage to brave her way past his cool façade: an impenetrable barrier to the self-effacing colonial girl she'd been. She was sorry now that she'd been so reserved that she'd missed the chance to know someone who could have been a good friend.

The time passed with maddening slowness. Kelly tried to sleep but the walls seemed to close in on her. They weren't that far apart. She was very tense during the first few hours, afraid that a friend of Dalkey's might decide to visit him. Then she reminded herself that everyone would know Dalkey was at work. She didn't dare use any of the electronics, for fear of alerting the residence monitors, who would also know that no one should be in the Petersham flat. So she didn't, for fear she might be apprehended as a burglar, taken into custody, and have to explain why she was on Earth when she wasn't supposed to be. She'd be incarcerated on Earth:

never see Doona—or Todd—again. Years of claustrophobia and synth-food! She paced out the dimensions of both of the small rooms over and over again. The apartment was about three times the size of her student studio flat. It astonished her to recall that she had actually existed for four years in a box that was smaller than Calypso's stable.

Dalkey had only a few nonfilm books on his shelf. One of them was an antiquated economy text. Another was an old, old copy of a novel about a great lover of the fifteenth century. She smiled, wondering if Dalkey considered himself a latter-day Casanova. For lack of better occupation, she began to read.

"Kelly?" a voice prodded her softly. "Shift's over."

To Kelly's drowsing unconscious, the voice was unfamiliar. Alarmed, she shook herself out of a sound sleep and sat up. Dalkey Petersham was looking down at her, smiling. She remembered then where she was: on his couch in his apartment on Earth. The swashbuckler novel was open upside down on her stomach.

"I want you to look at this," Dalkey said, nudging her over so he could sit down. "Behold the product of many hours of furtive work. I hope you appreciate this. Lucky today wasn't a busy day." He handed her a film printout of a residence document. "I'm glad you didn't want the names and addresses of a whole host of people. It took forever just to get this data. The system hasn't been debugged since ice covered the Earth. I lived in fear while the computer was processing. I wanted to climb through the screen and bang its little chips together. You're right, by the way. There is such a man who knows lasers. He is a former felon, by the name of Lesder Boronov. His name's been changed to Askell Klonski, and he does live in a fancy part of town."

"Oh, Dalkey, you're amazing!" Kelly said, devouring the closely typed sheet. "How did you find him?"

"Strange to say, he was in the Spacedep file index, bold as brass. It required a little special jimmying, because it was restricted under the Spacedep privacy seal, but I managed to push my way in."

"Spacedep?" Kelly asked, staring at him. "Why?"

Dalkey raised his hands helplessly. "Who knows? But only Landreau himself, Commander Rogitel, and a couple of other top brass normally have access to that index. See where it says that he's been retained for 'special services.' Special services covers a multitude of bureaucratic sins."

"I could cite a few right now. You didn't have the same sort of luck about his financial records?"

"I couldn't get more than a credit balance," Dalkey said with a rueful expression. "My supervisor came by, saw the kind of screen I had up, and said if I was doing my personal banking on Spacedep time I might as well go officially on break. He watched me the rest of the afternoon, but I had all I could access without generating suspicion. He got a fine big credit balance, that Boronov!"

Kelly agreed. "But did he make it the way I think he did . . . ?"

"Which is?"

"I don't want to say it for fear I'm wrong," Kelly said, not wishing to cross her luck at this juncture. "What are those other printouts?"

"More research," Dalkey told her with considerable satisfaction. "While I was in the index, I got curious. Do you know that there isn't just our laser friend here under the seal? There are several people, all listed as performing special, unspecified services, and getting paid hefty hunks of credit. I got to the initial screen, showing their profiles. There wasn't time to get more, but I'll look into it when I have half a chance. Rather a lot of them are out on early remission."

Kelly's eyes widened. "So Klonski-Boronov isn't an isolated case. They've got a fileful of dirty tricksters."

"All on file," Dalkey said, disgusted. "More than I feel comfortable knowing about, too. Makes me more fed up with Spacedep. Codep's no better. I contacted one of my pals at lunch. He ran a similar check for me in the Codep index. He found something like this there, too, before he got caught accessing forbidden files. As soon as you're safely off Earth, I'll bring him to the attention of Amalgamated Worlds Administration as a whistle-blower. They'll have to take his statement as a public document, so he doesn't unexpectedly get shipped off to a mining colony."

"I didn't intend for anyone to get in trouble," Kelly said, concerned. But she held tightly on to the film printout Dalkey had given her. It wasn't full proof, but here in her hands was the beginning of what she needed to clear Todd and Hrriss.

"Not your fault," Dalkey stated promptly. "There's more than one of us sick of the corruption. Before they took him away, he managed to get his printout to me. They're trying to trace down what he was doing and who he saw afterward, but I'll wait till you're clear. They have their dirty secrets, but you are my clean one."

"I'll keep faith with you, Dalkey," said Kelly, "as soon as ever I can. But these," and she shook the printouts, "mean that Todd was right. Landreau is involved and using Spacedep facilities. I can't take the chance that I'll get caught before I can get these to an official source. I don't like mines either."

She had Dalkey make a call to the Poldep office from a public kiosk, requesting a confidential appointment on matters concerning the Doona Experiment. Kelly prepared to leave as the hour approached. She was surprised to find that she wasn't as nervous as she had been when she arrived through the grid. In fact, she was almost looking forward to her meeting with a Poldep official.

"As soon as I get more data, I'll send it out to you," Dalkey promised. "Meanwhile, you watch out for yourself."

"I want to thank you, Dalkey," Kelly said, kissing him on the cheek. "You've been a gem."

"Just don't forget your promise to sponsor me to Doona," Dalkey said. "I'm going to be counting on it." He grinned ingenuously. "If I get caught, I'll need somewhere to go. Come back if you can or need to. And good luck."

It was not unheard-of for informants to request informal meetings with Poldep. Many cases would never have been solved if ordinary citizens, taking advantage of anonymity to protect themselves and their familes, couldn't come forward with incriminating information and data. Few did it with malice, for Poldep could turn an entirely different face toward the prankster. Dalkey had assured Kelly that Poldep wouldn't pry into her true identity, for that would defeat the purpose of anonymity. Kelly hoped that the immunity extended to no curiosity on how she had travelled to Earth.

The Poldep offices differed from those of the other government services only by the color of their uniforms: black. Even the entry operators, and the officers, bailiffs, and investigators swarming in and out of the main entrance wore black. The color was ominous and off-putting, but she supposed that was intentional.

The big man behind the desk in the little room was not unfamiliar, but he did not appear to recognize her: the hair dye had been a very smart idea. True, she had only seen him from a distance in the halls of Alreldep and once on Doona. They hadn't actually met. DeVeer made the rounds of his beat periodically in a small, fast-moving scout ship. He had a reputation for being straightforward and honest. Firmly she overcame her feelings of nervousness and gave him her hand. The Poldep captain shook it.

"I'm Sampson DeVeer, miss. What name are you using?"

So the anonymity was genuine. "I don't know how much you have to know about me to believe what I'm going to tell you," Kelly said, stalling.

DeVeer gave her a brief smile. "I find the facts often speak for themselves. How about a pseudonym for the time being? That's not incriminating."

"All right," Kelly said boldly, "call me Miss Green." That was stupid, she admonished herself, but apt. She was green enough in more than name. Imagine blurting out a name so close to her own. But she didn't really care. Kelly was surprised how calm she felt now that she was facing the Poldep man. She recognized that she was riding the high of success when she had expected none. She was surprising herself. She'd been a dutiful child, a good student, an obedient second on Snake Hunt, and a biddable employee of Alreldep. But now, for her friends' sake, she was discovering a lot about what she could dare and do.

"What can I do for you, Miss Green?" DeVeer asked.

"You're familiar with the situation on Doona?" she asked. His eyebrows lowered, and she went on quickly. "I know there's lots of situations, but I mean the one concerning the Reeve Ranch. And the son, Todd. He's being accused of horse rustling, smuggling, and entering restricted zones. And you've got to believe me when I tell you that he wouldn't do any of those things. He's innocent."

"Ah, yes," DeVeer said, tenting his fingertips. "I know the circumstances. In fact, I recently had an interview with his father. He had hides bearing freeze marks for his ranch on animals he never owned. The hides had been recycled from Zapata Three with a genuine provenance. Yet he claims the brands have to have been altered."

"They were! I think I know how it was done," Kelly blurted. "I mean, I believe I know who could have done it."

DeVeer's expression didn't change, but his moustache twitched. "Tell me more," he said.

She produced the first of her film prints and put it before him. "This man was paroled from a labor colony and returned to Earth. He's a laser expert and innovator. His name was Lesder Boronov, but he's called Askell Klonski now."

"What makes you think that he involved himself in stock theft? Name changes are not illegal."

"He might not be involved directly, but he came into a lot of money when he was released," Kelly said. She produced the printout of Klonski's credit balance.

DeVeer read over both films carefully and made notes on a pad as he scanned. He glanced at her from under beetled brows. "May I ask where you got these screens?"

"The one about Boronov is from Spacedep sealed files. I . . . would like to protect my sources but they are reliable. I expect Poldep would be able to check the information. You can see that Klonski has been paid sums for 'special services.' Now"—Kelly swallowed, because she was diving forward into conjecture—"what services could a laser expert do to earn that much money?"

"The matter could be legitimate."

"Then wouldn't he be listed in Spacedep's regular contractor file?" Kelly asked. "Why hide him under the privacy seal? And he's not the only one." She showed him Dalkey's other printouts. "These men are all ex-felons, all received early paroles, and they're all under similar privacy seals."

DeVeer didn't insist that she identify her sources, which was an immense relief to her. She hoped that he thought that she herself was the Spacedep employee who had pulled the files.

He read the third set of films with the same focused attention he had read the other two. Partway through the first page, he pulled over his computer terminal. He spent some minutes entering data and looking from the screen to the printouts. Then he became engrossed, fingers stabbing at function keys, tapping out new requests. Kelly sat with her hands clutched in her lap, her eyes pinned on the Poldep investigator.

"Interesting," he said, looking up at her after nearly an hour. He leaned back in his chair, tented his fingertips together again, and fixed his keen gaze on Kelly.

Kelly leaned across the table. "Then you believe me? Can you find out if Klonski does have a way to alter the freeze-dry brands?"

The chief investigator smiled thinly under his moustache. "I'll try to help you, Miss Green, but I have only your suspicion, based on hearsay, that this Klonski might—just might—be involved in illegal activities. Even if he admitted to developing such a process, that wouldn't automatically clear your friends. They could have made use of his 'special services' as easily as anyone else. In fact, some of that large sum in his credit account could have been paid in by them."

"But they didn't. They didn't!" In her frustration, Kelly banged her fists on his desk. "Why would he be in the Spacedep files if that bunch didn't use his 'special services'? And you surely don't think they'd let him take outside contracts!" DeVeer smiled at that remark. "This is the first real evidence to support my friends' innocence. Won't you help me prove it? Please! There's really a lot at stake!"

DeVeer tapped his fingertips together. "Yes, I will have to initiate an investigation. Not necessarily on your friends' behalf, for some of those charges do not lie in my jurisdiction. But rustling does. The problem of stock theft has recently trebled. New worlds are desperate for all kinds of stock, not just horses. Every animal must be marked and records kept of inoculations to prevent the spread of disease, and to be sure that livestock is protected against any indigenous problems on their destination planet. But if the marks can be skillfully altered, then our very complex disease control system has been bypassed. That can't be allowed to happen, especially on an increasingly larger scale. One

of my priorities is putting an end to illicit traffic in livestock."

"Then Doona isn't the only planet to have trouble with
rustlers?" Kelly asked.

"Unfortunately, it isn't. But you may just have brought me
the tip I've needed."

He smiled at her, and his face changed from an austere
mask to that of a warm and charming man. "If this Klonski
has an illegal means of altering brand marks, I can help you
clear your friends at least of that charge. And Klonski is on
parole?" DeVeer sat up and entered the identification number
from the film into his computer console. "Yes, he is. The
creation of a process used for illegal purposes is a parole
violation. That can land him right back on a penal colony
world, with or without Spacedep approval. I see he's due for
a meeting with his parole officer, should have met with her
yesterday. Didn't show. That gives me the right to have a few
words with him." DeVeer stood up, indicating the interview
was at an end.

"May I come along?" Kelly pleaded. The chief considered
the question for a long moment.

"It is not necessary for an anonymous accuser to face the
defendant prior to a hearing. In fact, it could be dangerous."

"Look, Mr. DeVeer," Kelly began earnestly, "I've risked
a lot to lay this information before you. It might even be
dangerous for me to go back out into Aisle and Corridor if anyone
guesses where I've gone. If I'm with you, I'm safe."

"I could arrange for protective custody for you . . ."

"Mr. DeVeer, I only feel safe in your presence," she said
firmly.

He considered her argument. "It is certainly not regular
procedure."

"There's been nothing regular about this whole mess," Kelly
replied tartly. "I trust you, Mr. DeVeer. I can be discreet but
I'd rather be in your company."

"Would Klonski recognize you? No? That's as well. But
there is another aspect you must consider, Miss Green, in
this compulsion of yours to stay under my protective wing.
Suppose he describes you to his contacts at Spacedep?"

"Let him," Kelly said, sticking her chin up and shoving her shoulders back resolutely.

He handed her a black tunic. "Lift your right hand"—she did—"now swear that you will obey me as your superior," which she did. He fastened a plain bar to the collar tab. "There! You are now a deputy under my direct orders." They left the office together.

The address on Klonski's file was in a block which had been occupied from before living memory by clans calling themselves the First Families. The living spaces bordered on the spacious homes of distant memory and were located in the widest Aisles Kelly had ever seen: Aisles with plants in the malls. Security devices and operatives strode slowly but alertly up and down. She was startled to see several men and women in poorer dress hurrying along between the buildings. Security didn't seem to notice them, and then Kelly realized they were undoubtedly menials, serving in the fine apartments of the wealthy and powerful families. The genuine residents of the houses swept by in much fancier dress, reminiscent of Jilamey Landreau's posh togs.

Kelly and DeVeer made their way as unobtrusively as possible to the address given for their quarry. The Poldep officer pushed a doorbell, and they waited.

"Askell Klonski, also known as Lesder Boronov?" DeVeer asked as the door edged open a crack.

"Who wants to know?" demanded a short, scrawny man through the gap. Kelly recognized him as quickly from Captain Kiachif's description of a warty weasel as from DeVeer's updated file photo.

"Poldep," DeVeer said, flashing his identification. "May we come in?"

"You can state your business first," Klonski said pugnaciously. "I've got nothing to hide from my neighbors."

"You did not keep your appointment yesterday with your parole officer, Mr. Klonski," DeVeer said, keeping his voice low. Klonski wavered for a moment and then flung the door open wide.

"I'm not a well man," and he coughed a few times to prove it. "She knows. She don't hassle me."

"A few moments of your time is all that's required, Mr. Klonski," DeVeer said smoothly.

"Well, if that's all, you can come in," he said, his eyes shifting warily from one to the other of his unwelcome guests.

Klonski's apartment was of the size intended for the use of high-ranking families with two legal children. The main room was palatial compared to Dalkey's, but it had been furnished in a totally haphazard fashion: the furnishings and decorations were obviously expensive but were placed in awkward groupings or hung without care or taste. If Klonski had intended to impress his neighbors with his wealth, he certainly had achieved that aim. Kelly glanced at a brilliant pink couch draped with a handwoven teal and red throw, and shuddered at the effect.

Klonski might be wearing expensive clothing but it could not camouflage his small stature, and the color only emphasized his gritty complexion. The padded tunic did not disguise, much less improve, his narrow chest. So he gave the impression of being held prisoner inside his clothes. The style was practically a parody of what his neighbors wore with elegance.

"I'm respectable now," the man insisted. "Gone straight and square. I'm not supposed to be bothered with parole matters. I call her up when I remember. Give me the usual blab, then you've done your duty and you can leave."

DeVeer drew himself up to his own impressive height and loomed over the little man. "Askell Klonski, not only have you violated the terms of your parole with your nonappearance, but you seem to have violated it much more seriously. We'd like you to come down to Poldep with us and to answer a few questions."

"What about? I haven't done anything wrong."

"That is what we need to determine," DeVeer said.

Klonski eyed them. "You're on a fishing trip, Officer," he said, grinning maliciously. "You haven't got a thing that could make me go anywhere with you. You're from them, out there." He jerked his thumbs toward the apartments on either side of his. "They want me to leave, but I won't. I like it here, see, and I've got a long, long lease. All paid up through the year double-dot."

"Yes, we have that data in our files. But there are other discrepancies in your record that are currently of interest to Poldep."

"Yeah? What, for instance? Ask me anything you want to . . . right here." The former felon hitched himself up into a huge, thronelike chair.

"On a routine investigation of your case," DeVeer went on, ignoring the sneering voice, "it would appear that the robbery for which you were incarcerated involved a death."

"It was an accident!" Klonski said agitatedly. "He shouldn't oughta have been there in the first place. That's all in my testimony."

"The laws are explicit in the case of death, whether accidental homicide or premeditated murder. Especially murder. You were rocketed up without the possibility of parole. So how, Askell, were you allowed back on Earth at all?"

"I was given clemency for being a sick man." Klonski essayed a few dry rasping coughs, then he looked up, his expression far more genuinely indignant. "Hey, those records were supposed to be sealed!"

"To Poldep?" DeVeer asked scornfully. "Well, they might remain sealed to the public at large, or they might not. That's up to me—and up to you. I think Poldep might ignore that anomaly if you will help us with our inquiries in another matter. Come down to my office to talk."

There was evidently something in those records which Klonski didn't want made public. Or was there someone he didn't want to know that his file had been opened? He was on his feet and standing by the door, exhibiting a marvelous agility for a man ill to dying from a cough.

"You call for a private copter, then, hear? I don't want to be seen talking to no Poldep inspector." He straightened his tunic as they stepped outside. "I got some standards."

As soon as they had arrived, Klonski made himself comfortable in a chair in DeVeer's office. When the computer recorder was turned on, he took the oath to give a true statement. (Not, Kelly thought, that the truth was likely to mean much to a man like Klonski.)

"So I'm sworn in. Let's get this over with."

DeVeer began austerely, "You're known to have unusual laser skills. We have reason to believe that you have perfected a means to alter or undo freeze-dry chemical brands on the skin of herd animals."

"*What?*" Klonski bounced up and down in his chair in amazement and began to howl with laughter, rolling from side to side, until the tears streamed down his warty face. "That is the most ridiculous thing I ever heard a Poldep say! Ohhhoo, hhahaha!" He was off again in paroxysms of mirth.

With hands lightly clasped on his desk, DeVeer regarded Klonski patiently while he enjoyed his amusement at their expense. Getting madder every moment because she knew this little weasel was a key find, Kelly wanted to box his ears or kick shins or do something to stop him laughing with such abandon. She saw her hope disappearing to the sound of his cackles. They merged into a genuine coughing fit. DeVeer poured a glass of water and passed it on to Klonski, no emotion whatever on his face.

"Me? Rustling?" Klonski demanded when he finally caught his breath. "Waste my time and know-how changing freeze marks? Mind you, that's beyond even me."

"It made a starting point," DeVeer said, not the least bit disconcerted. "A man must keep his skills up or lose them. Right?"

"Ri . . ." Klonski began, and then realized he was being indiscreet. He pressed his lips together.

"However," DeVeer continued, "you do have laser skills and we do believe that a laser technique had to be used to alter freeze marks. Therefore, if you do not wish to be charged with aiding and abetting the theft of livestock and the illegal transportation of animals, you might just clear up the point of what you are doing with your special skills."

"Now, wait a minute . . ." Klonski began, no longer so arrogant.

"You know the drill, my man. Rustling's grand larceny, and between unauthorized planets, it carries a double penalty. There'd be no possibility of parole for an offense of this magnitude." He pulled his console to him and began typing. "We'll just enter you for a preliminary, based on those unusual deposits in your credit account." DeVeer peered at Klonski from under his thick eyebrows.

"You'd never trace the source of those deposits," Klonski said with a sneer, his confidence somewhat revived.

"Really?" DeVeer asked cheerfully. "Anything on a computer tape, no matter which mainframe, can be opened for inspection—especially when a major crime is involved."

"They told me no one could crack their codes!" Klonski was mutinous with fear.

"They?" DeVeer asked softly. "You forget that Poldep has extraordinary powers to investigate any department, given sufficient cause. Rustling is an excellent example." He turned back to his keyboard.

"Stop!" Klonski cried. DeVeer's face was immutable stone. "I never rustled nothing, nor helped no rustlers."

DeVeer pushed the keyboard slightly to one side, folded his arms on his chest, and gazed at Klonski. "I'm waiting."

"I need a deal from Poldep."

"Our budget is exceedingly tight this quarter."

"I don't need credit. I need immunity. I want an undetectable change of identity and location." He paused as DeVeer nodded solemnly. "I didn't help rustlers, and I sure didn't change freeze marks, 'cause you can't. But I'll tell you what I did do. Is that enough to deal?"

"I can't say until I know," DeVeer said. "I may just consider your information sufficient to return you to your current quarters with the parole violation forgotten."

"I gotta have security." Klonski was so insistent about that point that Kelly's hopes began to rise again.

"Security you'll get for cooperating with Poldep."

"Okay," but Klonski's expression indicated he was still dubious. DeVeer just waited while Kelly found it hard to restrain herself from jumping up and shaking the truth out of the weasel. He gave a nervous cough and then said, "What I did do was a little patching and splicing of log tapes. Nothing that looked illegal."

"For that kind of credit?" DeVeer allowed his face to register disbelief.

"And . . ." Klonski hesitated, his eyes darting from DeVeer to Kelly. She tried to look encouraging. "And . . . I showed 'em how to neutralize security systems."

"Really?" DeVeer's response was mild, but Kelly had to grip the arms of the chair to keep from jumping up in exultation. "I thought your specialty was improving such systems."

Feeling slightly more confident, Klonski grinned, showing badly discolored and jagged teeth. "Improve, disimprove. Same techniques needed."

"Who?"

"You think I'm stupid, Polly? No blinding way do I name names. You find 'em yourself with all your extraordinary powers." He leered smugly. "We made a deal. And I don't say nothing more. I got rights, too, you know."

"However, for a new location, new name, and the right to retain the credits in your account, you might nod your head if I drop a familiar name or two?"

Klonski was not too pleased to be probed so deeply but he didn't deny further assistance. DeVeer pulled over a flimsy.

"Your file indicates that you worked for Spacedep before your . . . first prison term," the Poldep inspector said conversationally. Klonski gave a sharp nod of his head and darted a glance at Kelly. "You were in Research and Development, is that correct?" Klonski did not hesitate to nod, since that was known fact. "Wasn't old Bert Landreau in charge of R&D?"

Kelly hoped that DeVeer noticed the shuttered look that altered Klonski's expression.

"Isn't his son an Admiral now?" DeVeer went on in that deceptively casual fashion. This time Klonski's head moved as if physically restricted. "I think that about covers it, Klonski," DeVeer said more briskly. "You'll be moved in the morning to similar quarters in a different sector. New ID will be issued and Klonski/Boronov will be listed as deceased, cause of death, a fatal respiratory condition. Does that suit you?"

Klonski's nod was enthusiastic.

"I'll have you returned in an ambulance to your current residence. Tomorrow a reputable firm of undertakers will arrive and your 'corpse' will be removed for the benefit of any observers." DeVeer pressed a button on his communit and a uniformed constable appeared in the door. "Medical escort is to be provided for this person, Constable. Do you wish a guard?"

Klonski snorted in his arrogance. "No one could get in my place!" Then he clamped his mouth shut, shooting a quick glance at the rigidly attentive constable.

"Use the discreet exit from the block, Constable."

"Very good, sir. This way, sir," and the constable gestured courteously for Klonski to follow him.

"We got a deal, Polly," Klonski said, turning in the door and jabbing his finger at DeVeer, who nodded acknowledgment.

The door hissed shut behind him and Kelly bounced out of the chair in her elation.

"He admitted it. Those log tapes were altered. Todd and Hrriss *are* innocent."

"Do calm yourself, Miss Green," DeVeer said, flicking off the recorder. "This is only the beginning of what is going to be a very difficult investigation."

"But he said he altered log tapes and tinkered with security systems. Don't you see what that means?"

"I see what you wish it to mean, but the wish is not always parent to the proof. However, such statements do cast doubt on the authenticity of the logs in question. Nor did he give us any inkling as to which security systems he has adjusted."

"But don't you see? It has to be the Doona/Rrala satellites. That would explain how rustlers could get in and out with livestock and be undetected!"

"Oh, I take that point, Miss Green. But it doesn't solve the matter of mismarked hides, does it?"

"No, it doesn't," Kelly said, and then started to giggle, covering her mouth with her hand and shooting an anxious look at DeVeer. "Klonski was so indignant to be taken for a rustler!"

"I have discovered, Miss Green, that there is a certain form of honor among thieves."

"Well, then, honest men ought not to be discredited, should they?"

DeVeer regarded her kindly after that vehement declaration. "No, they should not. I shall consider it my prime obligation and most urgent priority to assist you in clearing the good reputations of those two young persons. *But*," and he held up his hand warningly when Kelly exclaimed her joy aloud, "to prove that Klonski did, in fact, use his skill on the tapes in question and on the Doonan security satellites is going to take time."

"We don't have time," Kelly said in a despairing wail. "The Councillors will bring Todd and Hrriss to trial any day now. And then there's the Treaty negotiations . . . The charges against Todd and Hrriss were planned to coincide with this critical period. My home is at stake, Inspector DeVeer."

"So you are a Doonan colonial?"

Kelly sighed for her indiscretion.

Not unkindly, he smiled. "Doona must fall or stand on its own merits, but clearly the odds against it have been staked by what does appear to be a genuine conspiracy. Personally I have had doubts about the Experiment, but I was old enough to experience the repercussions of the Siwanna Tragedy, so perhaps I'm not entirely without prejudice. But I try to overcome what I know to have been early conditioning. I think it's a mistake to mix two such advanced races."

"But that's the best kind to mix," Kelly exclaimed. "Equal intelligence and parallel societies with similar aims and mutual respect."

"But Hrrubans are much more powerful than we smaller Humans. And their technology more advanced."

"Not in the same direction ours is. So we've learned from each other . . ."

"They have not granted us that transportation system of theirs . . ."

"And we have not given them the right to build our more sophisticated spaceship engines, so I think we're even on the question of space travel."

"You argue well, Miss Green."

"I've specialized knowledge to back up my arguments, Mr. DeVeer."

"I trust that events will conspire to let us continue. I have never met a more devoted adherent of the Experiment. But, in my estimation, the appalling Siwanna Tragedy has not been diminished by the short period of Doona's success." He brought himself up short. "You remind me of my daughter. She argues for her causes with all her heart, too. And you've risked much to lay your case before me." He rose to his feet, signalling an end to their discussion.

"I'd risk a lot more!" Kelly got to her feet and shrugged out of Poldep black. "Can you let me know how your investigations progress? Or do you no longer consider me your special deputy?"

"That deputization will be in force for the remainder of your stay on Earth, but I'd prefer that you didn't wander into a situation where I have to notice you officially. I'll be in touch with the communications number that made your appointment with me. And by the way," he said, "next time, please obtain permission to visit Earth. If you have a legitimate reason, or an invitation, there isn't any problem."

Kelly smiled. "You are thorough."

"I like to think that I am, Miss . . . ah, Green." He actually winked at her and she wondered if he had discovered her real identity but thought better about asking. "The amnesty policy is scrupulously maintained."

"Can that cover my 'sources of information,' too?"

DeVeer frowned slightly, then his face cleared. "You did mention that there's someone about to whistle-blow, didn't you? We'll see that your friends are protected if at all possible. I expect there'll be a great deal of housecleaning before this matter is concluded. An official privacy seal is not meant to conceal capital crimes such as grand larceny and security tampering." DeVeer took her hand. "I am grateful to you for your information. Poldep does need the help of all honest citizens, otherwise where would we be? Thank you, Miss Green."

Kelly grinned at him, positive that he did know who she really was. "Thank you, sir."

She spent the night curled up on Dalkey's hard mattress, dreaming of snaking tapes with matched ends that then split apart to reattach themselves to other loose ends, and satellite spheres with the face of Askell Klonski, and each wart on his face another capped sensor.

The medical supply warehouse was in a section of Corridor and Aisle that Kelly had never visited before. She had to descend on a packed elevator through several levels, through the newer, smaller residences of Labor workers, and then pattered off the elevator into the manufacturing zone. Her fellow passengers, mostly maintenance workers for the Air Recycling Service, marched past her in a single mass, almost as if they were stuck together from being squeezed in the elevator.

The noise control standards had evidently been waived for this level, and so had the air purification ordinances. Hooting and wailing from machinery battled with the deafening thrum of turbines and the cumulative babble of Human voices. This Corridor was full of unrelieved gray and black buildings. They looked clean enough—no graffiti, no layers of dirt or filth—but they left her with the feeling that if she touched anything her fingers would come away filmed with soot.

Kelly found the address Nrrna had written down for her and slipped past the great open doors. Inside was the largest single room she had yet seen on Earth. The raftered ceiling loomed the full height of the level. Hundreds of men and women in drab bodysuits and heavy gloves passed her in pursuit of their various tasks. Pallet loaders, large, small, and staggeringly huge, rolled around the floor, picking up crates and packages from teetering stacks of merchandise. The scale of the warehouse amazed her. The entire Doona Launch Center could fit in the middle of this vast facility, and leave room for its normal day's operation on every side, and this facility only forwarded medical supplies to outer worlds.

Stinking of hot oil, the forklifts trundled great bales of goods into giant freight elevators, for conveyance to the lower levels for distribution, or to the surface, where they could be loaded into spaceships. Neither of these two destinations was appropriate for Kelly. She needed to find where a particular small delivery was being prepared. The Hrruban Center grid was only a few meters square.

She had fitted herself out with a clipboard and a small parcel, wrapped under Dalkey's instruction and sealed with a Spacedep logo they had cut out from a discarded film copy. The box was filled with food from his synthesizer. After two unappetizing meals of the stuff at Dalkey's flat, she hoped she wouldn't have to eat it, but who knew how long it would be before she could be rescued from the container? Nrrna might have to wait for solitude to open the crate.

"Is this the shipment for Doona?" Kelly asked in a bored tone, consulting her clipboard. "I've got a parcel to add to it. Spacedep," she added with a nice touch of apathy.

The man glanced up at her with equal disinterest. "Nope. Try dock sixteen."

"Is this the shipment for Doona?" Kelly inquired at dock sixteen.

"It is." The short woman directing the lowering of boxes from one side of the dock onto a pallet glanced back over her shoulder at the tall mousy-haired girl. "Why?"

Kelly's heart gave a little jolt within her. "I, uh, have a package to go on it. Spacedep."

"There's nothing in my manifest from Spacedep for Doona," the woman said, tapping the clipboard she held under her arm.

Kelly pretended disgust. "Well, it was handed over to me this morning to make sure it got aboard."

The woman stopped and flipped open the clipboard. It was full of neat documents, all sealed at the bottom by the departments of authorization. "Codep; Healthdep; Healthdep, that's not here yet; Alreldep; Healthdep . . ." She turned each one over until she came to the last one. "No, nothing from Spacedep. You must have the wrong order." The woman looked up, but her querist was gone. Shrugging, the woman turned back to her bales.

While the woman's attention was focused on the documentation, Kelly had slipped away and squeezed between two large boxes. One of the crates heading for Doona was only half full. Nrrna had arranged for Healthdep on Earth to send just enough sterile gloves to fill half a standard case but too many to be crated in a smaller container. Nrrna and Kelly calculated that there should be enough room for her to fit. Kelly began to look at labels to find the Healthdep shipment. She found it by the logo—a cross and crescent in a circle—marked on a blue crate. She tapped out the security code on the small comp, wriggled into the crate, and pulled the lid down over her, hearing the whirr as the cover locked itself again. Now all she had to do was try to make herself comfortable, and she would be home in hours.

The muffled sounds around her crate got louder, so she had a bit of warning before the box rose into the air and swung wildly from side to side. One of the cranes was doing the transfer. Kelly had the terrifying sensation of flying through the air, followed by a bump that tossed packages of the flimsy gloves all around her. The plastic envelopes stuck to her clothes, hair, and face. She peeled them off, and cupped her hands over her face to keep from being suffocated by the flying packages. As soon as the case was fastened down on the pallet, the gloves settled. She burrowed her way into the packages until only her head and her shoulders were jammed against the side of the box, her feet propped against the lower end and her knees under her chin. Not the most comfortable of positions and she tried to make herself believe that claustrophobia was a small price to pay for the success of her illegal voyage.

The crate jerked again as it started to move sideways, bumping Kelly's head. The whole pallet must be on its way to the Hrruban Center. She could hear the squeak of unoiled wheels as it was pushed onto the transportation grid which rattled under her buttocks. She had little room in which to relieve cramped muscles and half wished that she'd asked Inspector DeVeer to arrange legitimate transport for her back to Doona. But that would have required too many explanations and too much time by ordinary Human spaceship. However uncomfortable, at least this trip would be instantaneous.

Through the sides of the crate, she could hear the low rumble of Hrringa's voice, asking for the cargo manifests. She hoped he didn't have to search each package before sending it. No, she merely heard the telltale beeping of the bomb detector as it was swept over the bales, and then it trundled sideways again. Kelly hoped her bale wouldn't be sent somewhere else in error. All she could do now was wait and try not to worry.

At least she didn't see the transfer mist or feel nauseated by the dislocation amid her padding of glove packets.

CHAPTER

8

NRRNA WAITED AT THE TRANSPORT STATION. SHE was trying to appear calm, but she could not control the nervous twitching of her tail tip, a giveaway to anyone watching her. She was no longer of an age where she could have held her tail between her hands to subdue its reaction to her mood.

The Hrruban male who was in charge of the transport grid had passed a few pleasantries with her, but he had to keep his attention on his job, and not on the very attractive female hovering nearby. The timetable on transmissions and receptions was very tight. Two sendings could not be received on the grid at the same time. If one overlapped another, he had to put it on hold until the first one was entirely received.

"The medical shipment is not due from Earth for another thirty minutes," he said once again.

"I know that," Nrrna said, dropping her jaw in an appealing smile to belie her nervousness. "It is very important that I take delivery as soon as possible. There's quite a lot of fur flying over letting the supply of sterile gloves get so low."

"Hmm," grunted the technician, unimpressed. Everyone was always in a hurry. His tail began to switch impatiently.

The Treaty Controller, clad in his magnificent red robes, appeared out of a corridor and addressed the technician, who stood to attention. Nrrna slipped into the shadows of the terminal to keep from being noticed. "Hasn't the transmission from Hrruba arrived yet?" the Controller asked.

The operator made the proper bow to such an important Hrruban. "No, honored sir. It is scheduled to arrive in three dots. You do not have long to wait. I could have notified you if you had called me."

"Hmm," the Treaty Controller growled his dissatisfaction. His eyelids lowered halfway over glaring green. "I was informed that it would be here at half past the tenth hour."

The grid operator courteously gestured to the display of quartz timers, synchronized with grid transporter terminals in the other spheres of Hrruban autonomy. "That time approaches rapidly, honored sir," he said, his voice hoarse.

The Controller turned away from the nervous young Hrruban and noticed Nrrna. To distract the grid operator, she had put on some of her most attractive ornaments, and a spicy cologne which approximated the pheromones of mating. She had not counted on anyone else coming along, especially not the Treaty Controller. At once she assumed a position both humble and hardworking, hoping he would look away. To her horror, she saw his nostrils flare as he scented her.

"Rrrmmm," he purred, moving toward her. "And who is this? What is your name, lovely one?"

Flustered, she murmured her name, and was gently asked to repeat it. "Nrrna."

"Nrrna. A soft name for a soft pelt. I find you most attractive, Nrrna." He rubbed his hand along the length of her arm. Offended by the familiarity of the contact, she moved her arm, trying not to give deliberate insult. After all, she was wearing a provocative scent.

"You honor me, sir, but I am already promised."

"Surely no single male will be sufficient to relieve one as young and feminine as you, Nrrna," the Controller said, pitching his voice intimately. "I would be the one honored if you would choose to favor me with your company."

Nrrna looked to the grid operator for assistance, but he had folded his ears tight to his head in an effort not to overhear. Which was only discreet of him, Nrrna had to admit. Why had she chosen such an alluring scent? She really had left herself open to offers. The operator she could have teased, but it would be most unwise of her to lead on the Treaty Controller.

"Please, sir, I am promised as lifemate." She hadn't wanted to admit that yet. Particularly not to this old male. She edged away. He sidled closer to her, and she could feel the heat of his body against hers and the rising scent of his sensual response to her condition. "I am not yet at full cycle," she added as coolly as she could. Indeed she was a few weeks away from her season and sexual activity would be distasteful. He had no right to be harassing her.

"Really?" and the Controller looked genuinely surprised. "I think perhaps you have misjudged your readiness, soft Nrrna," the Controller suggested in a low voice. "My quarters are most comfortable." He was a much older male, with persuasive ways that should overwhelm such a young and obviously inexperienced female.

She shifted away from him, revolted by his manner. Any decent male would have desisted, but this old stoker obviously didn't recognize a genuine denial.

"The transmission from Earth," the operator announced.

With the agility of her youth, Nrrna sprang toward the pallet in a graceful leap that took the Controller totally by surprise. With her own hands, she helped the operator roll the crate off the transport grid to make room for the next transmission.

However, the Controller, not to be done out of his prize, followed her. Ignoring him, she opened the top crate, which did not contain Kelly, and began to inventory the materials very slowly, checking each box several times as she marked it off on her list.

"One box of size 00 sutures, one box of size 0 sutures, four cases of plas-skin . . ."

"You haven't answered my question yet, Nrrna," the Treaty Controller pressed.

She gave him a smile. "All thought of personal indulgence must give way to duty, honored sir." She paused to give him the most courteous and coolest of bows. "You must forgive my diligence but it is my first position and I cannot discredit my Stripe with less than my closest attention. Everything must be inventoried before it can be transported to the village center." She began her count over, glancing from the clipboard to the pallet with an anxious expression. "One box of size 00 sutures, one box of size 0 sutures . . ."

"I thought you needed to get this to the medical center as quickly as you could," complained the operator, wondering that the pretty female was silly enough to ignore a Controller.

"As soon as it is counted," Nrrna said firmly. "Earth must be notified promptly if the count is short." Once again, she began at the top of her list. Just as the Treaty Controller moved in to pursue her, the grid bell rang.

"Honored sir, the transmission from Hrruba!"

On the grid platform a cluster of small boxes appeared. The Treaty Controller bent over them and straightened up with an exclamation of self-satisfaction, one of the document cases clutched in his hands. "Yes, this will ensure the number of days is finite." He glanced at Nrrna, who was still pantomiming a diligent inventory and walked over to her. "Silly stripe," he said in a voice low enough to reach her ears only, "you would do better to accept my protection and virility so that I can provide well for you when you have to return to Hrruba. It is not too late to reconsider."

"My Stripe has a long tradition of honoring its promises," Nrrna said with a swift sideways glance toward him before returning to her inventory check. Halfway between checking off a film tape for educating small children about bacteria control and reaching for the next film in the stack, she heard an annoyed snort, and the Treaty Controller swept away, holding the small document box. She sighed with relief.

"My goods are all accounted for," she told the grid operator. "Will you transport me and this shipment now to First Village?"

The gesture with which the irritated technician directed her onto the platform showed that he would be very glad indeed to get rid of her. For her sake, he had nearly had to annoy the Treaty Controller. No male, not even a Treaty Controller, should persist when a female has made her disinterest so plain. He would be glad to see the last of both of them and the end of a possible disgraceful incident.

The moment that the village coalesced around Nrrna, she shoved the crate off the grid and tapped the code to open it. Kelly exploded up in the midst of a snowstorm of plastic packets. They were plastered all over her like wet leaves.

"Oh, my poor neck," she groaned. "This was such a good idea but neither of us counted on sweat and plastic suffocation. I hope I don't offend your nose."

"I am so glad you are all right," Nrrna said, trying hard to keep her nostrils from flaring at the reek of the Hayuman. She couldn't help her current odoriferousness and Nrrna helped Kelly out. "I would not have left you in it so long, but that wretched ol' cat"—and Kelly blinked at such an epithet coming from the gentle and polite Nrrna—"of a Controller was revoltingly offensive!" Nrrna almost spat in outrage and Kelly could see every single hair of her stripe was standing up.

Nrrna began to pick the static-charged packets off Kelly's hair and clothes. Each time she tried to put a pile down, they seemed to spring back to adhere to her fur. When Kelly tried to help, it only made matters worse. The packets merely transferred themselves from Nrrna to Kelly. Frustration gave way to laughter and then Nrrna thought of moistening her hands, and when that seemed to help, Kelly wet hers and they began to divest themselves of their unusual decorations.

"I heard him, the old tomcat," Kelly said, grinning at Nrrna. "But he's a persistent bugger, isn't he? I thought males didn't bother females without permission."

"It's partly my fault," Nrrna said. "I used too much of a provocative scent."

"Not to get his attention, I'll warrant."

Nrrna wrinkled her nose. "The operator was too well mannered to pursue me, but it kept him interested until white muzzle interfered."

"All's well that ends well. But remind me not to ride in a crate again," Kelly said when the last of the gloves were stuffed back into their container, and the top was clamped down again. "I also caught that bit about you reconsidering him so he could provide for you when you had to return to Hrruba. What's happened since I left here?"

"Nothing," Nrrna said, but she was as worried about his phraseology as Kelly was. Possibly more than Kelly was, for she had lived on Rrala all her life and the quarters of her clan on Hrruba were very crowded.

"What was he waiting to collect? Did you see?"

"A document box. Well covered with Third Speaker seals, that much I did notice."

"Neither the Treaty Controller nor Third Speaker is a supporter of the colony. Strikes me as odd that that Stripe should be in control with Treaty Renewal approaching. I wonder what kind of documents were in that box."

"I don't know how we'd find out, but I'd better complete this shipment without any more delay." Nrrna spoke into a radio unit which was hooked to her belt, contacting the Health Center's operator. "They will send a flitter for the shipment. Now, did you have any luck on Terra?"

"I sure did, Nrrna. We've got a Poldep inspector on our side, willing to look into certain oddities that came to light. I want to tell the Reeves, but I'll meet you later at Hrriss's so I only have to tell this twice, but tell him I got good news." She was stretching and working her arms and legs to relieve the kinks. "I never could have found out so much without your help, Nrrna. You've been a star! See you soon."

With a final wave, Kelly jogged off toward the Friendship Bridge on her way to collect Calypso and make her way to the Reeve Ranch.

Todd took one look at her and yelled, "What did you do to your hair?"

"My hair?" she shrieked back at him, hand to her head before she remembered the rinse. "I couldn't go back to Earth in my own hair and expect to be unnoticed!"

"To *Earth*?" he roared, white-faced with shock. When he had finished bawling her out for the risks she had taken, she got just as angry right back at him for not letting her deliver her good news.

"In the first place, I was never in danger, Todd Reeve. In the second place, I got more information than I ever thought I'd get, and thirdly, we got Inspector DeVeer actively pursuing an investigation on our behalf."

"Is that Kelly Solinari with you, Todd?" Pat called, and rushed into the room, her expression both anxious and relieved. "Young woman, where have you been? Your family's been worried sick about you. And what have you done to your hair?"

"It washes out and I left my parents a note to say I'd be away a few days. Didn't they get it?"

At the moment, Ken Reeve came bursting into the room. "Robin was right. It was Calypso tearing up the road. Where have you been? And what did you do to your hair?"

"I *dyed it*! And if you'll all drop out of panic mode, I'll tell you why I dyed it and where I've been and what I've been doing," Kelly yelled back, glaring at all of them. Then she turned less aggressively to Pat. "That is, if I can have a drink to soothe my throat after all the shouting I have to do in this house to get listened to."

It was Todd who provided the juice and then sat down at the table, where she began the recital of her inquiries.

"Nrrna helped?" Todd interrupted as she began. Then, "How well did you know this Dalkey? Can you trust him?"

"I probably shouldn't have mentioned his name," Kelly said tartly, "but I trust you not to repeat it. And not to get stupid about me approaching the only one I felt could help us. And he's still helping us, or rather Inspector DeVeer is."

"Cool it, Todd," Ken said in an aside. "Continue, Kelly."

She did but was aware that Todd was uncharacteristically morose until she got to the part about DeVeer taking her with him to interrogate Klonski.

"You see, we were all working on the wrong assumption," she said, looking at Ken, "that the brands had been altered somehow. Even Kiachif thought Klonski might be able to do that but he didn't. In fact, he burst out laughing at the very notion that he was being accused of rustling." The others didn't quite seem to see the humor in that, so she continued. "He did much worse . . . all to incriminate you," and now she turned her gaze to Todd to see the dawning of hope in his eyes. "Klonski altered the log tapes . . . By the way, which of you handed them over to Rogitel?"

"Neither of us did. He removed them from the unit himself," Todd said.

"Well, then, that's when he switched them."

Todd opened his mouth to protest. "You know, you're right. He bundled the log box into a plastic sack and carried it off in a proprietary fashion. I didn't think about it till now and I was certainly too shocked at all he was flinging at Hrriss and me to think his manner odd."

Kelly nodded. "It had to be Rogitel substituting the altered tapes and at that moment, since the ship had been properly sealed. I wonder where your real log went."

"Into the nearest vat of acid," Todd said with a deep sigh.

"Possibly not," Ken suggested thoughtfully. "Go on, Kelly. What else did Klonski do?"

Her eyes glowed. "This is sort of the best part. He altered satellite security modes."

"He what?" Ken lifted off his chair and Todd stared at her as if she had suddenly changed shape.

"Don't know how, do know why," she went on.

"To let the rustlers in and out," Ken continued, throwing both arms in the air at such an obvious explanation.

"Klonski was rather proud of that. And DeVeer has it all on tape!" Kelly said, grinning broadly.

"Is DeVeer really on our side, Kelly?" Ken asked, his expression grim.

"I think so, sir," Kelly replied. "He admitted he doesn't really like the Doona Experiment. He was alive when the Siwanna Tragedy occurred but he also admitted that colored his opinions. But," and she waggled her finger at all three Reeves, "he's out to crush the rustling because too many uninoculated animals are being transported illegally. And he said the incidents of rustling had increased all out of proportion. He couldn't figure out why."

"I brought the illegal hides to him. . ."

"And I've been squaring my eyeballs trying to match missing horses to those hides with duplicate Reeve marks."

Ken brought his fist down on the table so smartly that it startled everyone else. "Okay, we've had the wrong end of the stick. Kiachif gave me a clue in reporting Mark Aden helping to load that leopard Appie for export. He was also about the height you are now, Todd, dark-haired and blue eyes, and to Zapatans that description also fits you. Let's assume that Mark rustled while he worked for me. So he probably stashed unmarked foals, born in the pastures, in some blind canyon. He had the run of our ranch as well as our neighbors'. He could have picked up unbranded foals from all over. Every breeder expects a few mares to abort in a year or lose their foals to mdas before we round 'em up for branding. But just one or two from fifty or so ranches, and that'd make a nice shipment off-world. Especially if someone is turning off the satellite tape—or however your Klonski rigged the system, and your rustler's away with no one the wiser."

"Spacedep is involved up to its armpits," Kelly said, "and I think Inspector DeVeer is going to prove it. Which reminds me, I promised my friend Dalkey that I'd sponsor him to Doona."

"You did?" Todd gave her the queerest look she'd ever seen on his face.

"How else can we repay him for the help he's given?"

"If there is a Doona for him to come to," Todd said in a bleak tone. "Neither Hrriss nor I is cleared . . ."

"You will be!" Kelly said emphatically.

"Kelly, this family can never properly repay you," Pat said, tears of relief in her eyes. She dabbed at them with the edge of the dish towel she had had in her hand when she heard Kelly arrive.

"We're neighbors, aren't we?" Kelly replied, struggling not to get too sentimental. Wanting very much to hear Todd commend her. "And it's Hrriss and Todd who've been jeopardized. I don't let my friends get done over. How much more time do we have before the trial?" She looked at Ken Reeve because she couldn't look at Todd, who still faced that ordeal unless lots of things fell into place in the next few days.

"We've not yet been informed," Ken said in a taut voice. Then his face broke into a relieved smile and he leaned forward with his elbows on the table. "Look, we can't do much about the satellite . . ."

"Kiachif?" Todd asked, also leaning forward, his expression alert even if he wouldn't look at Kelly next to him.

"Possibly," Ken said, "and I don't know how we'd locate the genuine log tape . . ."

"Emma Sumitral?" Pat suggested, her eyes brighter with hope than with tears.

"I can ask, but now we concentrate our efforts on finding where stolen livestock could have been hidden."

"Tadpole in a tangle of tiddlers," Todd said, "but there'd have to be water, good grass, some sort of shelter . . ."

"Well off all known trails, especially snake ones," Kelly added. "But every rancher'll help now."

"They've all been helping . . ." And Todd inadvertently turned his head toward her. Kelly held her breath, not wanting to turn away from the look in his eyes, keen again and as intense as they got when he was thinking rapidly, as he did on a Snake Hunt, examining and rejecting alternatives. He was her buoyant, marvelous, alive Todd again. He lifted his body from the chair in a lithe movement. "I'll send out a revised message, for mares that ought to have foaled and didn't come in with foal at foot. Let's see how many come up missing on that data!"

"No, son," and Ken grabbed Todd's arm as he passed. "You'll saddle up Gypsy and go out hunting for likely places to stash livestock. Pat, you send out a blanket message to all ranches to be on the lookout for such storage spots, and also query folks about barren mares. Kelly, will you ask your father and brothers to help?"

"I'll go there first, but I promised Nrrna that I'd come over and give Hrriss the good news as soon as I'd told you." She dared look at Todd again.

"You were nearer Hrriss if you came in on the village grid," he said.

Kelly cocked her head at him, thought she wanted to shake him out of his stasis. Couldn't he see what her priority was? She planted her fists at her belt so she wouldn't do something drastic in front of his parents. "I've got my priorities in order, Todd Reeve. Hrriss doesn't ranch horses." With that she pushed past him and out of the house, down the steps, and vaulted to Calypso's back before she thought what she was doing.

"Hey . . . Kelly?" Todd's plaintive, puzzled call followed her down the track.

When he went back into the house, he saw the amused expressions on his parents' faces. "What'd I do to upset her?"

"For a bright man, you can be as dense as two planks," his mother said, and took herself back to the kitchen.

Todd looked at his father, who was making strangled noises.

"I think, son, it's more what you didn't do that's upset her. And you should get your priorities right. But not now. Now we got some rustler pens to find. You'll have time to apologize to Kelly later."

"Apologize?"

Ken turned his son around and shoved him toward the door. "Saddle my horse when you're tacking Gypsy. Tell Lon what

we're going to look for and let's get going!" Ken's voice raised
to a triumphant shout as Todd pitched forward and out the door
from his father's hefty push.

What he should apologize to Kelly for bothered him as
soon as he set off in the southeasterly direction his father had
appointed him to search so that he could stay within the Reeve
Ranch limits for more klicks than if he went west or north.

Perhaps he ought to have been more effusive in his thanks,
but he'd been so scared that Kelly had done something stupid—
which she had, only it worked out right—or been abducted—
which was not really a possibility, but in his anxiety he had
imagined all kinds of gory fates. She really had come up a
heroine to smuggle herself back to Earth on a Hrruban grid . . .
he ground his teeth, knowing that she had faced a sentence
of life on a penal world if she'd been caught. Why hadn't
she gone to one of those girlfriends she'd told him about?
Who was this Dalkey Petersham? Why would she sponsor
a Terran to Doona, a Terran working in Spacedep? It was
analogous to inviting Jilamey Landreau to a weekend at her
family's lake cabin.

And this DeVeer Polly! Who hadn't really listened to his
father when he reported hides that didn't match their records.
They had got the wrong end of that stick, all right. Stupid
not to have tumbled to the duplications. Kiachif once again
to the rescue. Only then did Todd become aware that Gypsy's
gallop was slowing. Gently he eased the gray to a more sedate
pace. No sense taking his frustration out on his horse. He gave
Gypsy's neck several affectionate slaps to reassure him and
kneed him toward the nearest height. It commanded a good
view over to the next range of hills. As he reined Gypsy in,
he looked out over the land, peaceful and greening up well.
More mares would be foaling . . .

An odd noise attracted both him and Gypsy at the same
time, the horse pricking his ears and turning his head to the
right. An echo it was, a bass echo, too loud for a nearby
mda. The sound gathered intensity, and suddenly, out of the
fold of the hills before him, he saw the pointed snout of a
shuttle angling upward. It pulled up above the hills, its engines
roaring, thrusters blazing.

Todd sent Gypsy down the hill at a gallop while he grabbed for his radio and called the ranch.

"Mom! Notify Martinson at once. A shuttle just illegally lifted off our property. I'm going to see if there are any traces of stock near the launch burn."

"What? Are you sure, Todd?"

"Mom! Don't argue. Tell Martinson to monitor the tracking satellites. They can catch him as he leaves the atmosphere."

Despite the clip at which he pushed Gypsy, it took him nearly an hour to reach the launch spot. What he saw there made him weep, but it was also incontrovertible truth that someone had been rustling Reeve livestock. Concealed in a fold of the hill, where trees formed a screen, a paddock had been fenced, the posts and rails so well disguised by shrubs, some of them rroamal, that Ken, or Todd, or Lon could have ridden by here every day and never noticed the setup. They wouldn't have looked past the rroamal to the glade, for horses avoided that plant as carefully as Humans did. Water had been piped into a big barrel, fitted with a stopcock. Dung dotted the little glade, enough for twenty or so horses, just the number to make a nice profit for the rustler's efforts. But not all the horses had been loaded and that's what upset Todd the most. Three yearlings, well grown, freeze-marked with the Reeve brand, lay on the ground. One had a broken neck—probably caused fighting to resist being loaded, for the rope burns on head and neck were obvious. The other two had broken legs. The nails that had been driven between their eyes into their skulls had not been removed. Todd shuddered. Circling the corral, Todd also found the bleach marks that freeze-brand chemicals made when carelessly spilled.

His radio bleeped.

"Todd?" It was Lon.

"They caught 'em?"

"Nothing, Todd," and Lon's voice sounded as savage as Todd felt. "Linc Newry says there was no alarm from the orbiters."

"But that's impossible. I saw it launch. There has to be traces of that!"

"I'll patch Linc through to you," Lon said, and Todd was too enraged to bother to hold the handset from his ear to avoid the high-pitch squeal as the patch to the Launch Center was made.

"I know you think you saw something, Todd," Newry said apologetically but firmly. "But no ships took off Doona today at all and none were scheduled to land."

"Linc, I know what I saw! I know what I see about me right now—three dead yearlings with nails driven through their skulls because one had a broken neck and two had broken legs. Check your readouts, will ya? Check your equipment . . ." Todd almost suggested that Linc check for tampering but that would be premature. He knew Linc Newry too well to suspect the man was in league with Doona's detractors, but this was the time to stand pat and let someone with clout, like DeVeer, handle that end of the business.

"Todd, I'm serious. Nothing came through the atmosphere. All readings are normal. But you can be sure I'll keep my eyes peeled to the gauges. Could be they only up-and-overed. Maybe they had another rendezvous but they won't leave Doona without my seeing 'em tonight."

"You're probably right. They up-and-overed. Thanks, Linc. Over and out!" He held the radio away from his ear as the connection ended, then dialed Lon again.

"Ouch," Lon said. "I didn't disconnect. I heard what he said, Todd, and I heard what you said. Fardling bastards! When I get my hands on 'em . . . Give me your whereabouts. We'll join you to film the evidence. Got any idea whose they were rustling?"

"The one with the broken neck is a leopard Appaloosa," Todd said, his shoulders sagging at the irony.

Uncharacteristically loud voices echoed in the Council room of the Speakers of Hrruba. Third Speaker raised his voice to be heard above them all. He was getting old, but fury gave his throat the power to shout down his opponents who were arguing over his tirade against Rrala. Only the banging of the gavel of First Speaker Hrruna put an end to the snarling and growls.

"That is enough," First Speaker said in a very soft voice. "Third Speaker, will you give substance to your demand that Rrala be disbanded?"

"You have all read the report from the Treaty Controller," Third said, raking his fellow administrators with a glare which stopped short just before it fell on First Speaker. "One of our most prominent young diplomats is involved in a disgraceful situation, in which he is accused of capital crimes, in violation both of the Treaty of Rrala and of Hrruban Law. Hrrss theft! Robbery from interdicted worlds! He has been corrupted by his Hayuman companion. I have been getting full reports from my representatives on Rrala, and none of it is good news. It would seem that this is not an isolated case. Honorable, honest citizens are being lured into a life of crime by these animals who walk like Hrrubans! Rrala must be closed to Hayumans, or all of society will suffer!"

"Surely responsibility for reporting the actions on Rrala falls to Second Speaker for External Affairs," Hrruna said, indicating Hrrto, seated to his right. The First Speaker's mane had gone entirely white, but his eyes were as keen as ever. "I have already had his report, and it gives me the same information you offer."

"This information affects Internal Affairs," Third Speaker said doggedly. "Now that the date draws near for Treaty Renewal, when the Hayumans hope to have it extended, there is a chance to painlessly end these harmful influences before they do more ill unto the youth of Hrruba. I have been besieged by special interest groups here on Hrruba. This young Hrruban, Hrriss, has been implicated in crimes committed solely to profit a Hayuman. We cannot support corruption of this kind. It is an ill example for our young people. We must withdraw our support for the continuation of the Treaty."

There was more shouting, and the First Speaker applied his gavel to its stand. "I have heard also from Hrruvula, counsel for the accused. He is adamant that his clients are innocent of the charges brought against them and must be allowed to clear their names. I find that I agree with him. Hrriss and Zodd have always acted in honor before."

"A ruse! Never did trust bareskins." Seventh Speaker for Management was the newest member of the Council, and of the narrowest stripe. As a result, he tried harder than any of the others to follow a clear mandate from his constituency rather than make risky decisions on his own. He was diligent and the trade figures continued to rise. So much so, in fact, that the higher the balance from the benefits of trading under the Treaty conditions, the more certain he was that the Hayumans were stealing profit from Hrruban interests. "They will destroy us."

"I disagree," said the Fifth Speaker for Health and Medicine. "I have close associations with many Hayuman practitioners in my specialty. They have provided us with knowledge and techniques we could not have developed on our own. They have done nothing but improve our standards. You cannot deny that mental outlook and physical health have been on the upswing since the Rrala Experiment began. Rrala has moved steadily out of what could have been a terminal situation in the younger generations, in the main due to interaction with another speaking, thinking race. Why," he said, trying to lighten the mood, "if only for the fresh food alone, the Rralan Experiment should not be ended—certainly not because of a situation involving one single Hayuman."

"He is representative of his race," Third Speaker raged, unamused. He pounded on the table and pointed a claw at First Speaker. "The one you considered to be most honorable, above all other Hayumans. Here, honor is at stake. What is cohabitation without trust? We were warned from the beginning of this unnatural colony, by this Zodd's own father, that one day Hayumans might try to take what is ours. What is more precious than honor?"

"Honor certainly is at stake," Second Speaker Hrrto agreed. "The honor of a Hrruban as well as a Hayuman. And Hrruban honor requires us to wait for the results of their trial before we condemn an entire society. That would be honorable behavior on our part."

There was more shouting, which First Speaker silenced by banging the gavel.

"Very well, we will put it to the vote," Hrruna said. "Those in favor of allowing Hrriss, son of Hrrestan, and Zodd Rrev to be proved innocent, vote aye."

Third Speaker held up a hand to stay the voting. "As a rider to this resolution, let us set a time period in which their honor must be proved. A significant date approaches: Treaty Renewal Day. If these two have not expunged the stain on their honor by that day, we must vote against renewal, for the sake of our youth. Those on Rrala will not be penalized, for other planets have been opened," he added, "and they can make homes there, safe from Hayuman influence."

No one spoke to debate that rider, though several faces reflected dismay.

"Very well, the rider is allowed," Hrruna said reluctantly, then called for the vote. It was overwhelmingly in favor of the motion. Satisfied, Hrruna nodded. His eyes were bleak as he addressed Third. "You may so notify the Treaty Controller of our decision."

Third Speaker bowed. Probably to hide his true feelings, Hrruna thought sadly.

The Launch Center bar was the perfect place to hold meetings, Ali Kiachif thought as he entered the place. It had small nooks and obscure corners where private conversations could be held—and the proprietor debugged his rooms at random intervals. Kiachif had most opportunely made a gap in his schedule for a long stopover at Doona; originally to discuss new rulings and profit principles with the captains who answered to him. He had acquired a second purpose which he diligently pursued, leading almost every conversation to topics that might help Ken Reeve and his boy.

"Well, look at you," a man said, blinking, as his eyes became accustomed to the gloom in the bar. "If I'd known you were already here, Kiachif, I'd have gone to the Centauris instead."

"What for?" asked Kiachif airily, shaking hands with Captain Feyder. "We've been there already, with all the best the colony worlds have to offer. Tell 'em, never compel 'em, and you sell 'em, that's my motto." The friendly rivalry between the independent merchant Rog Feyder and Ali Kiachif had gone on for years. Feyder sat down, and Kiachif signalled to the barman to bring bottles for them both.

"I've got a shipment of unrefined sugar for Doona. Special order. Just unloading." Feyder let Kiachif fill his glass, waited till Ali had filled his own, and then raised it courteously to his old rival. "Your health."

"Yours! Hear unrefined sugar used to make damned fine spirituous potables."

"Did it? Well, we make sure the customers get what they order, don't we? Though sometimes you wonder why they pay the freight charges."

"Oh?" Kiachif had long since learned the art of subtle prompting.

"Sugar's the most ordinary thing I have on board. The damnedest things are getting shipped these days."

"That they are," Kiachif agreed. "Last season, I carried a copper sculpture fifteen meters long to one of the outer agri-worlds from Doona. A commissioned work by the governor to commemorate ten years of the colony, engraved with the name of every colonist and his accomplishments. It was a pain up the afterburners to handle, but orders are orders! I hate to see what he'll ask for when twenty-five rolls around, like Doona's is."

"Aye, I wanted to come back for the big celebration, but I should be worlds away by then," Feyder said. "I'm just here on turnabout, starting me route over from the topside. No, when I say strange, I mean the epitome of strange, not ordinary strange. Listen to this one. Got a meteorite puncture on my way in from the outer worlds. After we sealed it up, I found a container cracked open in that bay, with the meteorite smack in the middle like a ball through a glass window. Splintered the whole damned thing into pieces. D'you know what had been inside?"

"Not an idea."

"A beacon. An orbital drone beacon," said Feyder, slapping his leg. "No assignment code. No idea where it came from. We checked its memory, and it was hollering Mayday like a pack of banshees. Did you ever hear such a thing in your life?"

"By all that's white, bright, and right," Ali said, holding on to his excitement, "that surely is a strange thing to report. Never heard its like in all my years in space. And it didn't have no ID number, you say?"

Feyder was not at all taken in by Kiachif's idle curiosity and gave him a long sly look. "Now I can't rightly remember."

"We could both take a look," Kiachif said.

"So you can see what else I'm hauling and cross-ship me? Try another one, Kiachif."

"Surely there must be a little favor I could do for you, Rog ol' boy!"

Feyder regarded him speculatively. "Well, now, there's the matter of the Eighth Sector."

"Oh?" and the single sound dove and swooped up again while Kiachif's eyes went round as ball bearings.

"Hell, Ali, you gotta leave some routes open for the independents."

"That's true enough," Kiachif said, scratching the stubble on his chin. "I don't want to appear greedy, or restrict free trade . . . You don't happen to have it still on board, do you?" He winked at Feyder.

"Happen I do. But you don't get a look at it. That amadan portmaster's gone all rules and regs on honest traders and he sealed my hatch when I told him that I was only here to refuel and get a drink or two. I can't unseal till I reach Earth, my next port o' call."

"Earth, huh? Is that where your funny gizmo's going?"

Feyder drained his glass, which Kiachif promptly refilled. "Yup, going to Earth. Spacedep's the address on the manifest."

"Is that so?"

"It is."

"That's the queerest sort of cargo to carry, I do agree. A beacon with no point of origin, screaming a Mayday, if you get what I mean."

"Do you mean to let us have some routes in Eighth, then?"

Kiachif affected hurt innocence. "Of course, I do. Soon's you can give me the beacon's ID. Give you my word," and he held up his right, bargain-making hand in promise.

Just then some of Feyder's gangers entered the bar and Kiachif had a chance to slip away to find Feyder's supercargo, who was an old friend, and called in a favor he had with that man. "When you get to Earth, just make certain you order that box opened in front of the inspectors because it was 'damaged in transit.' "

"Why?" the super wanted to know.

"I'm not going to tell you why, what, or wherefore," Kiachif insisted, fending off the man's questions. "That would be suborning the witness, if you know what I mean. I just need an official inquiry into the contents of that container! And let me know who picks it up. That's important, too."

He left the Launch Center, looking for Ken.

Only Pat was at the farm, just getting up from the computer and looking so sick to heart. Kiachif thought he'd better let her talk her worry out of her system. And a drink'd help that process.

"They should be back fairly soon, Ali," she said, still distracted and worried.

"Now, Patricia, why don't you get me a little drink and tell me all about it?"

"Ali, you haven't changed in twenty-four years," she said, but she looked at him, not around him, and he chuckled.

"Why should I?"

"I know what you mean," she capped his jovial question with his own words. "Perhaps a drink's not a bad idea what with everything that's happened today."

"You look wore out, Patricia. You sit. I'll get the bottle. Know where you keep it."

"That doesn't surprise me," she murmured, low enough so he wouldn't hear her out in the kitchen. But his low chuckle suggested that he had. He was back in no time with the bottle of mlada and two glasses. "Oh, that's too much for me, Ali."

"Not a bit of it. You're paler'n a milk stone and this'll put heart in you. Your health!"

They touched glasses and she watched in fascination as half the large tumbler disappeared down his throat while a sip was all she could swallow. Still, as it slid down, she felt its warmth easing the tension in her body.

"Now, what's been happening here today?"

So she told him, including a summary of Kelly's activities on Earth, DeVeer's assistance, and Klonski's admissions.

"Knew that feller was involved in all this. Shoulda known he'd be put to better use than changing freeze marks. Hmmm. And Todd saw the shuttle blasting off and it didn't register at the Launch Center?" Kiachif frowned deeply. "That do sort of point to the fact that Doona's security satellites might have felt the touch of Klonski's little talented digits."

Pat frowned in the act of sipping the mlada. "Linc Newry—whom we've no reason to distrust—thought maybe the shuttle up-and-overed. He promised to keep a close watch on all the orbital monitors."

"Huh! If one's been tampered with, they all have. That your men coming back now?" he asked. Ears sharp enough to hear air escaping from a pinhole caught the thud of horses' hooves and wagon wheels. Two wagons, he thought.

Pat hurried to throw open the door.

"Ali!" Ken swung his leg over the pommel and, throwing his reins to Robin with an admonition to rub Sockertwo down well, charged up the steps to greet the spacefarer. "Glad to see you. Got some questions . . ."

"Got some answers, but not necessary to your questions. Hi there, ropy," Ali added, shaking Todd's hand as he joined his father on the porch. "Need a drink? Made your wife join me in a glass and you both look like you need a swig er two to set you right before we start jawing."

Ken and Todd instantly saw the merits of that suggestion. They'd had a bad time in that hidden corral. Vic Solinari and Ben Adjei had sledded over to verify their findings. Vic had taken blood and tissue samples from the little leopard Appie— he was positive it had been foaled by his spotted mare—and Ben had done the same with the other two. One bore so many of his sire's physical traits that it was easy to identify it as having come from the Hrrel Ranch. The other, a chestnut filly, had no distinguishing marks to give clues to her origin. Ben Adjei would freeze all three carcasses in case they were needed as evidence. They had made the most careful sweep, section by section, to find any more clues. The only one they did find was a half-empty sack of ssersa seed, which proved that the rustlers must have been responsible for the proliferation of that weed on previously cleared pasturelands.

Halfway through their recital, Pat slipped from the kitchen, having been distressed enough by the details to feel that preparing food was a better occupation for her.

With a tray full of steaming bowls of stew and bread rolls as well as a fresh bottle of mlada, she returned in time to hear why Ali Kiachif had sought them out.

"I've found me a new occupation," Ali began, sipping at a freshly filled glass. "You might say I've taken to reading the future, if you know what I mean," and he winked at Robin and Inessa, who had joined those in the living room once their evening stable chores had been completed. Lon had come in, too. "If I was to say, for example, that someone in the docks on Earth is going to open a container in four days, and make an official note that he found inside it a homeless beacon drone calling Mayday, would you believe me?"

Todd and Robin let out a wild, joyous war cry. Ken pounded the old merchant on the back. "How did you discover that, you old pirate?"

"Never mind," Kiachif said, much gratified by the reaction to his news. He tapped his lips. "I have my sources, if you understand me. But I'll say that the probe's code number will be ARB-546-08, and see if it isn't."

"I'd better let Poldep know," Ken said, starting toward the computer.

Hastily Kiachif put a hand on his arm. "Easy on the retros, mate. It'll be reported to them by the appropriate authorities. It might seem as if you know something about it as you shouldn't, if you know what I mean. Just concentrate on what's near, dear, and here, and everything will work out all right. They'll soon have proof that these boys passed through into Hrrilnorr space for good and sound reasons." He winked solemnly and took another long pull on his drink. " 'Sides, Patricia's been telling me a thing or two that falls pleasantly upon the ears. It's all coming together, if you get what I mean, all coming neatly together."

"Finding that shuttle beacon'll really clear us, Dad," Todd said, his whole being revitalized. "How will we ever thank you for locating it, Captain Kiachif?"

"Well, laddie, there's such things as hidden profits. I get what you need, you keep this planet viable, and I cart off the excess and sell it. You plant it, I transplant it. Neither of us loses that way! Better get going. Can't trust those gangers of mine. Might get randy drunk er something."

A few days later, Hrruvula notified them that information about the nameless beacon had been received by Poldep and passed on to the Treaty Council. An audience with the Council was arranged immediately to plead for their release.

Rogitel appeared, representing Spacedep, followed by Varnorian of Codep, who thudded heavily into a chair and gazed without much interest at the ceiling. Sampson DeVeer, having

tendered an official copy of the supercargo's report, represented the Poldep arm of interplanetary government. Ken and
Hrrestan slipped in when the boys' attorney was admitted.
They ignored indignant, outraged, and pointed glances in their
direction; Hrrestan patiently, Ken stubbornly.

Although DeVeer also handed copies to each of the individual Councillors, they seemed to read as if spelling out each syllable in whichever language the document had been rendered.

Hrruvula finally cleared his throat several times and gained
the Controller's signal to proceed.

"As you have all had time to read and absorb the signifi-
cance of the document so kindly brought by Inspector DeVeer,
it is apparent, honored ones, that my clients have told the truth
from the very beginning." Hrruvula noted the glowers from
Rogitel and Varnorian. "I am certain we are all relieved that
two such fine young men have been cleared."

"On this one point," the Treaty Controller snapped out, "not
on the other crimes of which they still stand accused. They must
be adjudged guilty or innocent on all." The Treaty Controller
was adamant in his particularity. "More than just a simple
matter of truth or falsehood is involved here. It pivots on the
trust of one race for another in all matters concerning Rrala."

"Is that just rhetoric," Ken asked Hrrestan in an undertone,
"or is he issuing a challenge?"

"It would seem so," the village elder said. "Hrruvula tells
me that he has heard of a resolution passed in the Hrruban
Council of Speakers that will require it to withhold approval
of the Treaty if our sons are proved guilty of the charges laid
against them."

Ken felt as if the floor had dropped out from under him.
"That's ridiculous!" he exclaimed, his voice rising. He hastily
recalled where he was. "Holding up the Treaty for a pack of
trumped-up allegations? What happened to 'innocent before
being proved guilty'?"

"Silence, please!" Treaty Controller banged on the table with
his gavel.

Ken glanced up and received the chairman's full glare.
He forced himself to subside and sit quietly beside Hrrestan.
Hrruvula resumed speaking.

"If one accusation has been proved spurious, honored Council members," the attorney said, bowing gracefully so that his long red robes swayed, "and the characters of the two young men must speak for them somewhat . . ."

"Granted," Councillor Dupuis spoke up from her end of the dais. Councillor Mrrorra nodded her agreement, too.

" . . . Does that not cast significant doubt on the other incidents?" The Hrruban paused, hands extended to the board, appealingly.

"One piece of proof doesn't negate the other charges ipso facto," Rogitel said with dry contempt. His grasp of the formal court language was by no means as complete or subtly shaded as Hrruvula's, but his diction was exact. "They will have to prove their innocence on each and every count and I doubt that lies within their abilities. There is still massive evidence on the charge of illegal purchase and smuggling of controlled artifacts."

The Treaty Controller polled his Council, and the result, to Ken's dismay, was a majority requiring a total acquittal. "The Council agrees. Innocence must be proved in regards to each of the remaining charges."

"Then let them prove their innocence together," Hrruvula said in a rich, rolling purr. "Keeping them apart was perhaps an acceptable remedy when their probity was at issue. It no longer is. Therefore, I feel that the separation of these two friends of the heart perpetrates an unnecessary cruelty. They both must be proved innocent so let them both work to prove it. That is not an unreasonable," and Hrruvula's cultivated voice rolled out the word syllable by syllable, and rolled out the next word, "request to make." His voice rose slightly, not quite a question, but certainly subtly insinuating that it was too pretty a contingency to be denied. Now he made deliberate eye contact with the Treaty Controller. "There is much at stake as you, honored Controller, know."

The Controller seemed somewhat taken aback that anyone else knew about the Speakers' decision, and he stared at the tall and elegant attorney.

"We can't release them from house arrest," Rogitel protested vehemently. "If they are allowed loose, who can tell what they'll do next. Spacedep does not recommend giving that pair the freedom of the planet."

"Honored Council members, may I speak?" Sampson DeVeer rose impressively to his feet and gazed down upon Rogitel. "Poldep disagrees with Spacedep. I agree with honored counsel that to be fair the house arrest should indeed be lifted. I have only so many hands and eyes at my disposal. I would be grateful for the additional help, which I assure Spacedep I will direct most carefully." DeVeer bowed toward Rogitel, who sat staring up at him in barely concealed consternation. Ken could almost hear the wheels twirling in that machinelike brain of his. "They will be released, as it were, into my cognizance. I will know where they are at all times."

Ken and Hrrestan could have cheered for DeVeer when he sat down, but that would have annoyed the already tried Treaty Controller further.

"I cannot condone their release for any reason whatsoever," Rogitel said flatly.

"Nor I," said Varnorian, after being pointedly nudged by his companion.

"But you do not have to. You have no actual authority in these cases," DeVeer said gently. "Though you are frequently asked for advice, all misdemeanors and certainly grand larceny fall within Poldep jurisdiction. In my opinion, Codep and Spacedep are grossly overstepping their authority by attempting to investigate crimes or act as a judicial body where one is suspected." He raised his voice. "I held my tongue before this, but in light of proof represented by the beacon and other data I have recently been shown, I urgently request the Treaty council to release Todd Reeve and Hrriss, son of Hrrestan, from a home arrest which I understand neither has violated in any particular. Rather this body should applaud their humanity in answering a Mayday signal, knowing that it was an infraction of the Treaty they have both upheld and promoted."

"He should have been a barrister," Hrruvula murmured in an aside to Ken. "What a presence!"

The Treaty Controller found himself outnumbered by his own Council, who were overwhelmingly in favor of DeVeer's proposal.

"We have spent enough of our valuable time on this case," an elderly Hrruban member argued. Treaty Controller had always suspected that Second Speaker Hrrto had seen to his nomination to the Council. "Our time is limited. We should turn our attention to the matters which truly concern us and I suggest respectfully that we have the chamber cleared so that we may proceed."

Treaty Controller had no choice but to agree. He referred to the printed agenda on the table before him. "Very well. The Council will reconsider this matter four weeks from today. The allegations against the defendants and their proof for and against their guilt will be discussed before the final vote on Treaty Renewal. So moved." He banged the small hammer.

"Seconded," Madam Dupuis trumpeted. The gavel fell again. "You are excused, gentles."

Ken almost danced out of the austere chamber and he could see the violent switchings of Hrrestan's tail as he walked beside him. When the doors had closed behind Hrruvula, Ken and Hrrestan could no longer contain their roars of triumph and were shushed by Hrruvula as well as the bailiff. Ken's stride quickened to a jog, and he flat-handed open one side of the heavy door of the Treaty Building, Hrrestan doing the same to his leaf, until they were out in the open and able to cheer as loudly as they chose. Hayuman and Hrruban made for the transport grid, Hrrestan telling the startled operator to send them to the Friendship Bridge.

Once there, Ken looked at his old friend, his eyes dancing. "Shall we see which of us gets to his son first?"

Hrriss's swifter feet made the reunion just barely on the Human side of the Friendship Bridge. He and Todd slammed into each other's arms, pounding each other on the back and talking at the same time. Hrriss felt something slapping him in the legs. After a startled downward glance, he started to howl with laughter until his tear ducts overflowed.

"So, my Zodd, while we have been apart, you have grown a new tail," he said, when he could catch his breath between snorts of laughter.

"What better way to celebrate our reuniting," Todd replied, grinning until his jaw ached but not far from tears of joy himself. "It proved a talisman once before and I felt we needed all the luck we could cobble up."

With the practice of many childhood years, Todd reached for

the length of rope, carefully frayed at the end to resemble the tufted tip of the Hrruban caudal appendage. Then with a decisive gesture, he hauled it loose from his belt. "I couldn't miss a real tail more than I have missed you, friend of my heart."

"I have missed you, too," Hrriss said, giving Todd a rib-crushing hug. "Half of my life was severed from my heart, my mind, my soul. Twenty-four years we have been friends, and these last weeks have seemed far longer than those we have enjoyed together."

"We don't do as well apart as we do together," Todd said with a rueful grin. One arm about Hrriss's shoulders and he felt twice the man who'd slumped about the house and ranch, unable to concentrate, like a machine idling . . . "Whoa there!" And his hand dug into Hrriss's forearm to stop him.

Surprised, Hrriss stopped and regarded the sparkling in Todd's blue eyes and noticed the wicked grin shaping his hairless lips.

"What thought has occurred to my friend now that his brain is engaged again?"

Todd slapped a hand to his forehead. "I haven't been thinking. And it only just dawned on . . ." He turned, gripping Hrriss by both shoulders. "Okay, so they know we weren't lying about the Mayday: they found the bloody beacon, but there's other incontrovertible evidence that the *Albie* couldn't have made all those stops, and not one of us, not even Captain Ali, thought of it."

Hrriss racked his brain, shaking his head. "I do not know what you mean. Spare me more suspense, Zodd."

"The engines of the *Albie* . . . and us!" Todd's grin got broader and his eyes were so bright that Hrriss thought they would pop from his head. He fanned his fingers at his friend. "C'mon, c'mon. What effect would all that warp-jump travel have on an engine? What effect would so many warp jumps have on the crew of a ship making them?"

Hrriss's jaw dropped to his chest and his tail began to lash. "Of course! Proof that we weren't where that tape said we were has always been in front of our faces."

"*In* our faces, if you please. That sort of travel would have left us trembling wrecks. How many jumps were we supposed to have made? Nine? We're pretty fit guys, but we'd've been dragging for days after so many transfers. And the engines? They'd've been dry as old snakeskins and badly in need of realignment. Wowwee!" Todd ripped off a wild yell that echoed across the village green. "C'mon. Race you to Hu's. His is the nearest console and we want him to hear this, too."

Since their meeting on the bridge had been more on the Hayuman side than the Hrruban, their few steps brought them to the Hayuman lands.

"Rrrace me?" Hrriss demanded. "We rrrace but together, Zodd. Together!" Hrriss was so full of joy he could have run to Hrruba and back without benefit of the grid, but now he lifted his thighs to push off, Todd beside him, the friends heading toward the low bungalow that housed Hu Shih and his wife, Phyllis.

She saw the pair thundering down the path toward her house and called over her shoulder at Hu.

"Todd and Hrriss are coming at a stampede pace, Hu. Oh, dear, you don't think any more has happened, do you?"

Her husband, his age showing only in his slower movements, patted her hand as he peered out the window.

"Something good, to judge by the elation on their faces." And Hu felt the better for seeing that as well as seeing them together again. That had been such a miserable thing to do to those boys. Young men, he corrected himself.

"Mrs. Shih, good morning. Good morning, sir," Todd said, his bows as jerky as his breath from running. "Please, sir, can we use your comunit? We urgently need to contact Captain Kiachif."

Hrriss had said nothing but he was bowing and grinning his jaw off its hinges and Hu stepped aside, gesturing toward the alcove which constituted his home office and held the communications equipment.

"You'd better hear this, too, sir. Don't know why we didn't think of it sooner than this."

"You boys have always operated as a team," Phyllis said, her indignant expression showing her poor opinion of the separation.

Todd raised Captain Kiachif's ship only to be informed that the captain was asleep.

"Look, Todd Reeve here. Hrriss and I have to speak to him. I know he's probably hung over. Put a cup of malak in his hand and ask him to please come speak to me. It's urgent or you'd better believe I wouldn't bother Captain Ali so early."

Todd flung a grin over his shoulder, for it was close to midday. Hrriss chuckled, and even Hu smiled.

"That man!" Phyllis muttered, for she had never understood how anyone could consume so much hard spirits and be allowed to command a ship, much less a whole fleet of them.

"This better be good, young feller me lad," came a growl that was barely recognizable as a voice.

"Drink the malak, Captain Ali, while you listen," Todd said. He explained his theory in crisp sentences and was rewarded by a string of curses.

"Plain as the nose on my face, which has always been very plain to see," Kiachif replied, his voice rougher with chagrin than with overindulgence. "Look, laddie, this is something we don't leave to just one engineer. And that ship of yours is under Martinson's seal, isn't it? So we gotta have an order to see the condition of those engines. They ain't been touched, have they? . . . No, good! Ha! Better 'n' better. Them's as they were left but how d'you prove you and Hrriss weren't space-shattered?"

"And start organizing the Snake Hunt the very next morning?"

"Everyone saw you then?"

"Hrriss and I had day-long conferences and there'd be tapes on the whole day . . . that day and the next thirteen!"

"Ha! Best way to wake up of a morning, laddie. Good news sure sets a man up, if you know what I mean. I'll just get the DeVeer feller. He seems to know beans from bran and brawn. Leave it with me, laddie."

"Of course, of course, of course," Hu muttered to himself, past chagrin that he hadn't thought of that factor: that no one, trying to clear the boys these past weeks, had thought of it.

"Don't fret, Mr. Shih," Todd said, grinning, "Hrriss and I just thought of it ourselves! You'd have to make a lot of warp jumps to know what it does to your circadian rhythms . . . or be an engineer to know what that kind of punishment does to your engines!"

"Or the skin of the ship," Hrriss added. "The *Albatrrrosss* is remarkably unpitted and bright."

"Thanks for the use of the com, sir. We'd best be going. Got a lot more to sort out today."

"Have some . . ." Phyllis's offer of lunch trailed off as the two young men were out the door, leaping off the top of the steps and making for the village corral. Spare horses were always available for emergency use.

Hu took a deep breath. "I feel better than I have since . . ."

"Since Todd Reeve came out of the mist leading the First Speaker?" his wife teased.

He nodded, his smile nostalgic.

Todd and Hrriss didn't bother with saddles. They used bridles only because they didn't recognize any of the horses standing hipshot in the bright noonday sun. They set off at the easy ground-covering lope most Doonan-bred horses were trained to use, kind to both horse and rider.

Pat and Inessa came out onto the porch the moment they heard the horses. Ken, Robin, and Lon jogged up from the barn, warned by shrieks of welcome from the two females.

"Oh, it's so good to see you, Hrriss," Pat said, pulling his head down to rub his muzzle affectionately, squeezing his hand, for he was too massive now for her to embrace.

Inessa bounced about, clapping her hands and hooting like a hunting urfa, a habit her mother deplored, but this day was too special for reprimands.

Pat was babbling about the feast they must have to celebrate the reunion, that Mrrva and Hrrestan were coming, and . . .

"Kelly and Nrrna," Inessa said, "and half the Solinaris and most of the Adjeis, and Hrrula because that filly they killed was his."

The men arrived and they welcomed Hrriss with much back-thumping and handshaking, while Ken went so far as to rub cheeks with the young Hrruban.

"You've had no lunch!" Pat declared, suddenly noticing their hot faces, the sweat on Todd's and the dust on Hrriss's. "Get washed up this instant. Inessa, come with me."

"Dad, got some real good news for you," Todd said, interrupting the general tumult and launching into what he had asked Captain Kiachif to do.

Ken stared, as drop-jawed as a Hrruban, as he assimilated the information. Then he swung about, banging his fist against the nearest wall in self-abnegation.

"Why didn't one of us think of that aspect?"

"Calm down, Dad," Todd said, grabbing his father's fist. "You haven't warp-jumped half as much as Hrriss and me, and you haven't logged in enough spacetime to know how it disorients you. You know we didn't come into your office that day shagged."

Ken shook his head from side to side, still blaming himself for not seeing so plain a verification that they could not have been plucking items from so many different systems during that controversial Hrrethan flight.

Todd gave his father a clout with his fist. "Stop it, Dad, no time for recriminations now. If Captain Ali gets an independent, and well-witnessed, overhaul of the *Albie*'s engines, and we get statements from everyone who saw us working all hours of the day to organize the Hunt, that still only proves we couldn't have made those side trips. It doesn't prove who did. And that . . ." Todd glanced at Hrriss as he began spacing his words in an implacable tone, "is . . . what . . . we . . . have . . . to . . . find . . . out!"

"You're right about that, son," Ken said. "From the way the Treaty Controller was handling the hearing, not to mention the smug look on Rogitel's face and that sycophant Varnorian, proof that you didn't smuggle is not as important as documentation of who *did*."

"Right. Then let's figure out how to go about getting the proof." Todd pulled his father to the dining room table at which so many happier conferences had been held, snagged a chair back, and guided his father to sit. He and Hrriss sat down in the same instant beside each other while a grinning Lon Adjei and Robin joined them.

"By any chance do we have holos of those items we're supposed to have stolen?" Todd asked.

"Hrruvula should have been given copies of all the evidence against you," Ken said.

"Rrrobinn," Hrriss said, "please brrring us the star maps and the handcomp. We must calculate prrrecisssely."

"Kelly's good at that," Robin said. "And she'd want to help." He didn't glance in his brother's direction but there was a twinkle in his eye.

"Both Kelly and Nrrna will be here shortly,"' Pat said, bustling in with platters piled with sandwiches.

"We owe those girls a lot," Todd said, reaching for a sandwich. The appetite which had deserted him during his separation from Hrriss had returned, doubled.

"Well, don't tell me," his mother said archly. "Tell them!"

Astonished at her tone, Todd watched her leave the room. Then shook himself.

"We've also got to find out who could have possibly assembled such a variety of items, how much they'd cost on the black market—I figure Kiachif might know—"

"And I will inquirre of Hrruban sssourrrces for those which came from ourrr interdicted planets . . ." Hrriss was making notes, too.

"Any word from Linc Newry about launches?" Todd asked, remembering another detail.

Ken shook his head. "But all the ranchers are looking for burn-offs and other illicit corrals. Those hides aren't as important . . ."

"Oh, yes, they are, Dad," Todd replied. "Every single element has to be sifted, sorted, and sewed up."

"Could Kiachifisms be contagious?" Robin asked, his face screwed up in a grin.

Rogitel did not move from his seat when Reeve and his feline friends left the Council chamber so noisily. The bailiff closed the door and returned to his post. Once order had been restored, Poldep Officer DeVeer took up where he had left off, deferring to the Spacedep official.

"If Spacedep has any further objections, I hope it will inform Poldep," DeVeer suggested politely. "We would be happy to cooperate in any interdepartmental inquiries."

Rogitel was already considering the ramifications of the Poldep official's words. He wondered what other data Reeve had uncovered that caused Poldep to intervene on their behalf.

There might be a leak in Spacedep's own offices. Internal security checks must be promptly initiated. "None at this time. Spacedep is grateful for Poldep's interest."

"Then, honored Council members, and gentlemen, I must take my leave. There is much to do in the next four weeks." DeVeer left the chamber. It seemed larger without him there. Rogitel felt less pressured. Beside him, Varnorian had fallen asleep.

"I would not wish it to be understood that the department is unwilling to cooperate," the Spacedep subchief said, addressing the board. "Admiral Landreau will be happy to assist in any way he can to fulfill all our wishes." He met the Treaty Controller's eye, and the Hrruban nodded almost imperceptibly. Landreau was correct. The Controller was willing to form a détente to prevent the renewal of the Treaty of Doona. Little did Treaty Controller realize that his actions would displace his fellow animals and leave the entire planet in the possession of its rightful owners, the Human race.

"I am convinced that we both want the same thing," the Controller said. He will help me, the Treaty Controller thought. And then he and his bareskin cohorts will be expelled, leaving only Hrrubans here on Rrala. The unnatural colony would be disbanded. He and Rogitel smiled at each other companionably over the conference table.

CHAPTER

9

CAPTAIN HORSTMANN FOUND DEVEER AND whisked him off to Portmaster Martinson's office, where that official was in a state of dithering shock. For one thing, he had every spacefaring captain and every chief engineer of the many ships on landing pads in his facility crowding his office and the adjacent hall.

"Make way! I got 'im," Horstmann bawled, and bellies were sucked in, toes splayed, to allow the passage of two more large men. "Special delivery! Live cargo!"

"Now, will you tell me what this is all about?" DeVeer demanded, for he was unused to being manhandled without explanation, and his temper, exacerbated by the hearing, was becoming shorter with every passing second.

"They say . . . the engines will show wear and tear," Martinson said, gulping in anxiety and waving his hands about. "But I can't let them in unless I have proper authorization. They absolutely refused to let me contact Spacedep or Codep . . ." He flinched as bass and baritone rumbles reinforced that prohibition. "Inspector DeVeer, I can accept your authorization to unseal the *Albatross*?" It was more entreaty than query.

"It's like this, Inspector," and a swarthy, hook-nosed wiry man with a stubbled chin, bleary-eyed, stepped forward. He wasn't a large man, but he exuded an air of authority that DeVeer related to immediately, accepting him as spokesman for this crowd. "Ya see, Todd and Hrriss are supposed to have made these nine warp jumps in the *Albie* on their way back from that Hrrethan do. They say they didn't. The engines in a ship that has been tightly sealed since that Spacedep chair pilot charged 'em with all that piracy will show to this impartial"—and a long stained hand waved at the crowd silently listening—"jury of experts just how much wear and tear those engines took since their last service." He hauled flimsies which DeVeer recognized as maintenance records. "We got these from Martinson here and the Hrrethan Space Authority, dated, sealed, and all legal-like, as proof of the most recent service checks the aforementioned *Albatross* had. You sign the authorization. We all take a look, write up official reports, and I'd bet you credits to cookies, we'll all discover— not to our amazement but what we all know without having to check—that those engines'll prove those boys didn't take no nine warp jumps in that vessel like they're accused of doing. Whaddaya say?"

DeVeer had had to concentrate to follow the rapid-fire explanation in a hot cramped space. It took him a moment to absorb the points.

"It will not prove who did, o' course," the captain went on before DeVeer could respond, "but those engines will prove those boys didn't! Hear you got word the Mayday beacon turned up, if you know what I mean?" The captain winked. "By the way, I'm Ali Kiachif, skipper of the *White Lightning*," and he offered DeVeer his hand.

Absently DeVeer accepted and the slender fingers were as strong as his own though the hand was half the size of his.

"I believe that could prove a profitable investigation, Captain Kiachif." DeVeer turned to Martinson, who was wiping the sweat from his face, looking haggard and harassed. "Can you supply me with the proper documents, Mr. Martinson?"

"All made out, ready for your John-Cock on the dotted line," Kiachef said, wiping out a second sheaf of official-issue flimsy and spreading it out on the one clear portion of Martinson's desk.

Writing implements were offered by eight or nine different obliging hands. DeVeer, for once feeling completely overwhelmed, twitched the nearest one free and poised it over the quintuplicate form. He was far too experienced an executive to sign what he had not scanned, but he was a speed-reader. The form had been filled in properly, and when he actually started to sign, a deafening cheer resounded from office and corridor.

"You must of course be present during the unsealing and the investigation, Inspector," Kiachif said, seizing the form and separating its sheets, crumbling the first one, which he fired at Martinson, shoving a second into DeVeer's hand, and, waving the rest over his head, pushed his way out of the office while the cheers still echoed. Realizing that DeVeer was not on his heels, he paused and beckoned urgently for him to follow.

Several hours later, the truth of Captain Kiachif's allegation was proved beyond question. In all particulars, the engines were in excellent running order, no wear, tear, or abuse visible: rather no more than was consonant with a journey to and from Hrretha, and this was verified not only by the Hrrethan Space Authority maintenance check but by nine fully qualified warp-drive engineers and nine fully qualified space captains of impeccable integrity. In order to prove their qualifications and allegations, DeVeer learned more about the workings of warp-drive engines, fuel capacities, gauges, the pitting of ship skins from forced warp jumps, and the condition of lubricants, greases, flux levels, and rocket tube encrustations than he would ever again need. He fully appreciated why Martinson had looked so fraught: he felt rather wrung out himself.

"Ah, Inspector, I see you are in need of sustenance," Kiachif said, folding away the sheaf of formal declarations from captains and engineers. "Lads, we can't let this fine gentleman suffer a moment longer."

DeVeer had no option but to accompany the jovial group to the pub. He also had no memory of how he got back to the accommodations he had been assigned on the Treaty Island. Some thoughtful soul—possibly Ali Kiachif—had left a small vial and a brief note where he could not fail to see it the moment his eyes could focus. "Drink this!" the note said. He did and rather more quickly than he thought possible, his condition improved.

Others had celebrated during that evening of which DeVeer had few lucid memories. For immediately upon finishing the scrupulous inspection of the *Albatross,* Ali Kiachif had informed the Reeve family.

"Don't fret too much about the smuggling charge either," Kiachif said. "Got friends working on that, too, if you know what I mean. It'll take a bit more time 'cause we've more to check."

"Ali, you must be calling in favors by the container load," Ken said, immensely grateful.

"Give a little, take a lot's been my motto for decades, Reeve. And, like I say, we all got a lot at stake, same's you Doonans. You keep on tracking down livestock. That's where your expertise lies. I'll keep on prodding, poking, and producing where mine'll do us good. Have a drink on me, you hear me?" Kiachif hadn't waited for an answer and Ken was staring at a crackling handset.

As everyone had heard Kiachif's inimitable voice on the radio, cheers rose from around the dining table. Kelly and Nrrna executed a triumphant dance routine before careening into a table.

"One by one, the charges are being dismissed," Hrrestan said while Mrrva nodded as if she had expected no other outcome.

"Down to two—identifying who purchased the artifacts and who's playing Todd and Hrriss off-planet," Ken said.

"No, three," Todd said. "We've got to find out how the security satellites have been fixed."

"Is not Inspector DeVeer investigating that?" Hrrestan asked.

Ken and Todd both frowned, increasing the resemblance between them so much that Pat, Kelly, and Inessa grinned.

"DeVeer would need Spacedep authority to check the satellites," Ken said, shaking his head over the improbability of assistance from that source.

"Would he?" Hrrestan asked, stroking his chin. "Would he not have authority over Martinson?"

"He must have some, to get clearance for Ali to check the *Albatross* engines," Ken replied, but he wasn't all that certain that DeVeer might not press the issue. "But Linc Newry's got a separate authority and reports only to Spacedep."

"The inspector wants to help us," Kelly said. "And he practically got Klonski to admit that he had."

"You didn't mention that," Todd said bluntly.

"Well," and she shook her spread hand to indicate uncertainty, "Klonski is known to have done that sort of security tinkering—Inspector DeVeer established that—so why else was Spacedep paying him, and putting him in their restricted 'special services' category?"

"We still need more documented evidence of who's behind what we may now call a well-planned and long-standing conspiracy," Ken said, addressing everyone but looking at Hrrestan.

"I think they overdid the evidence bit," Pat said. "They might have made one charge stick but so many?"

"Ah, but that is where they have been clever, not stupid, Pat," Hrrestan said. "They have created a variety of charges, none of which can be ignored by one or the other of those departments of yourrs and ourrs that are involved. Rrala is to be torn apart by debates on which allegations are true and which might be specious. The fact that would, I fear, become lost in the morasss of true, half true, and false, is that our sons never committed any of the crimes of which they stand charged. But by the time they can be cleared of all counts, any hope of renewing the Treaty would be lost and the colony forced to decamp."

Nrrna shuddered and drew closer to Hrriss.

"But I'm positive Landreau is behind all of this," Ken said. "He's hated me and Todd since the first time you all disappeared and left us looking like first-class liars."

Hrrestan and Mrrva bowed their heads. "We had no choice."

"Oh, I know that, Hrrestan," Ken said, dismissing any implication of blame. "But it was Todd who kept us here because Hrrubans would not leave a small child in a dangerous forest. And it was Todd who brought First Speaker here, and Al Landreau has never forgiven him or me for that humiliation."

Kelly and Hrriss grinned during Todd's obvious discomfort at that summary, but Nrrna was curious, not knowing all the historic details from that period.

Hrrestan sighed. "If only Third Speaker's associate were not Treaty Controller this period . . ."

"Another piece of deft planning on Landreau's part. I gotta give him credit for that," Ken said with a hint of grudging admiration.

"Trrrue, for with another Hrruban as Controller, we would be able to lay before First Speaker the framework of this conspiracy . . ."

"Would First Speaker not be aware of that already, Hrrestan?" Mrrva asked, her hand lightly on her mate's thigh. "We know the pressures that are being exerted in the Speakers Council."

"This time," Hrrestan said, "there is no child with a tail of rope to capture the hearts and minds of our people and swing a vote in favor of a Treaty of Cohabitation."

"I know this might sound silly," Kelly began tentatively, "and forgive me if this question offends, but it's something that has never been addressed in Alreldep either: if the Treaty breaks down, which of us gets to stay on Doona? Or do we both leave, lock, stock, and block?" She tried to make a joke of it.

When everyone stared at her, she began to flush and ended up with her head down.

"No, no, Kelly," Todd said, "that's a very good question indeed. In fact, that might actually be the crux of the matter."

Kelly looked up, eyes shining and face alight with his genuine approval.

"Indeed, Kelly, that is a question which has not been asked," Hrrestan said, "and one we should have considered long before now. Have we all been looking at the forest without seeing the trees?" He leaned forward, elbows on his knees, his eyes slitting with the intensity of his thought. "You and I, Ken, like our sons, wish the Rralan Experiment to succeed. We both know in our minds that there are Hrrubans and Hayumans who do not wish that. If the Treaty is not renewed, each sees this planet as a prize for the taking. As you once confided in me, Ken, twenty-four years ago on a hilltop, Hayumans get greedy. Well, so do Hrrubans. There is indeed much more at stake than just this planet and which species gains control of it." Hrrestan paused, unwilling to follow that line of discussion to its obvious conclusion.

"An interspecies war?" Todd exclaimed, horrified.

Nrrna gave a frightened yip and clung to Hrriss's arm. Kelly and Pat Reeve turned pale.

"I could go back to Alreldep," Kelly said earnestly. "I may be only a junior but if I could present any proof whatsoever that this is what's going down on Doona . . ." Kelly's voice failed her as the permutations of a struggle between Hayumans and Hrrubans sank in. "Oh, no! We can't let that happen!" she said in a whisper.

Todd jumped to his feet, glaring about him. "You just bet we won't." His words rang in the frightened silence.

"By all that's holy, we won't," Ken added, rising from his chair.

"We will not!" Hrrestan and Hrriss spoke at the same moment, springing to their feet.

"Rralans forever!" Kelly shouted in Middle Hrruban, jumping up and down, fists clenched.

Todd grinned at her, proud of her for using that language, and more moved than he could say by her offer to help, by returning to Earth and the Alreldep job he knew she must hate. But, then, she was as Doonan—no, Rralan—as he.

"All right, now then, folks," Ken said, rubbing his hands together as he would before taking on any difficult task. "We've got more to do than we thought. But we've got help. I don't think we'd better let tonight's conclusions loose on the planet. There's enough panic and crazy-minded speculation as it is, with rustling and false accusations and suchlike just before Treaty Renewal. So, while we're knocking down the accusations against the boys, we'll see if we can also find any clues that might show us that the scope of the conspiracy goes beyond Landreau and—" He looked at Hrrestan.

"And Third Speaker," the Hrruban added for him.

"Too bad we can't use their techniques against them," Kelly said, "and start finding the tadpoles in their ponds. Get that Treaty Controller impeached or something."

"Oh!" Nrrna's little cry of surprise focused attention on her.

"Yes, Nrrna?" Hrriss prompted, and that was when Todd really began to notice how tender his friend was toward the pretty female and how often she seemed to rely on him for reassurance.

"The Treaty Controller," and she bowed her head slightly, keeping her eyes averted from Kelly's sudden grin of comprehension, "received delivery of a document box the day Kelly returned. It must have been very important for him not to send an assistant or secretary."

Kelly snapped her fingers. "I've got a memory like a sieve. I got a coded comp-line message today from Dalkey Petersham. He was very cagey even in code. He's got something he needs to get to me and he doesn't trust the comp-mail lines."

"Did he say what?" Todd asked, aware of an unusual uneasiness with a guy comp-lining Kelly all the time. But that was silly. They needed help from whatever quarter it came.

"What I got from the code was that, as a very junior official, he was supposed to check over and delete some ancient accounting tapes. They were for the Spacedep slush fund. There seemed to be large financial disbursements about ten years ago from that fund and all of them were paid to accounts off-Earth. He thought they might be useful to me, but he won't send it comp-line and wants to know how he can get it to us in . . . as they say . . . a rapid irregular fashion."

"Isn't Captain Feyder back on Earth?" Todd asked.

"Been and gone, according to Kiachif," Ken replied. "He'd done us all the favor we can ask of him with that Mayday beacon."

"We could get in another medical shipment," Kelly said, glancing sideways at Nrrna.

Her eyes went into slits of anxiety. "Oh, no. I was in trouble over the gloves when they saw how many packets had been trampled on. My superior was going to send a harsh message to our office on Terra. So I told them that I had opened the box outside, to take inventory, and a wind had come up and scattered them."

"The wind was named Kelly," the redhead said, giggling at the memory of the trouble she and Nrrna had had to get the static-charged packets back into the carton. "I even found one inside my tunic."

"The count was off so I had to say that some had blown away," Nrrna dropped her jaw and purred her pretty laugh.

"You've got a resourceful female here, Hrriss," Kelly said. "And you nearly wouldn't let her help."

"I shall not again be so foolish as to interfere with her good plans," he said, pulling a solemn face that made Kelly laugh.

Todd looked from Kelly to Hrriss and Nrrna, and then at Hrrestan and Mrrva, who seemed quietly pleased about the behavior of Nrrna and their son.

"Hey, friend, did you forget to tell me something this morning?" Todd asked.

"Nrrna and I plan to be lifemates," Hrriss said, his eyes glowing as he glanced down at Nrrna. "The joining is due to take place about the time of Treaty Renewal."

Todd dropped his jaw, so like a Hrruban that Kelly smothered her giggles. "Oh, really? Well, you didn't waste any time while I was gone, did you?" But his eyes were glowing with pleasure and approval. "Why, you old tomcat, you! Congratulations!" He gave Hrriss a hearty punch on the arm and took one of Nrrna's hands, lifting it to touch his forehead in the Hrruban gesture of well-wishing and congratulation. "To think you went out and did that all by yourself," he said, unable to leave off teasing Hrriss. He could see that Hrrestan and Mrrva were delighted and his parents seemed to have known. He felt a little silly that he hadn't twigged to it.

"We plan a celebratory feast on the occasion," Hrriss said, "and we would be honored if you would stand as master of ceremonies."

"The honor is mine," Todd said, falling back into his chair and letting out a hoot of relieved laughter. "Well, I feel lots better. I admit I wondered why Nrrna was suddenly so much a part of the investigation. I thought she was a friend Kelly had brought in to help her."

"Of all the . . ." Kelly jumped to her feet and ran out of the room.

"What got her so uptight?" Todd inquired of everyone in the room.

"Kelly has been helping *you,* you numskull," his mother said with a weary sigh of exasperation for her son's obtuseness. "She's the main reason you and Hrriss have been reunited."

"I know she's been helping me," Todd said, still perplexed.

"Then do not sit like a mda in warm mud contemplating its toes," Hrriss said. He rose and gave Todd a shove toward the door. "I have had the opportunity to make plain to her my gratitude. It is time that you adequately express your own. Do it suitably in the style of Hayumans, but do it now!"

Half stumbling onto the porch because Hrriss had put considerable strength into that push, Todd corrected himself and looked about for Kelly. Twilight made it difficult to see, but he spotted Calypso's hide and saw the mare moving before he realized Kelly was astride her.

"Kelly! Kelllleeee! Wait a minute!"

He knew she had seen him, for he saw her white face turned in his direction, but she cantered off anyhow. Piqued, Todd took the nearest horse from the tie rail, Robin's fleet racer Fargo, and started after her.

Todd was just gaining on the cantering Calypso when Kelly realized that she was being pursued, and kicked the mare into a gallop.

"Kelly! Pull up!" Todd yelled angrily.

She bent low in the saddle and urged Calypso faster.

Todd had half a mind to pull up right then and there. He hadn't meant to insult her. Didn't she know him well enough by now to know he liked her? Why, she was as moody as a Hrruban female in estrus.

In shocked surprise, Todd almost pulled up Fargo as he suddenly understood what he'd been too self-involved, first in the Hunt and then in clearing his name, to recognize. His heart seemed to expand in a peculiarly painful but marvelous way . . . as it had when he had embraced Hriss on the bridge . . . but not quite the same way. Stunned by the intensity of his feelings for Kelly, he clapped his heels into Fargo's sides and sped after his girl.

For Kelly was, and she had proved her love for him over and over again, only he'd been dense as two planks not to realize that his former friend and willing cohort had turned into a lovely girl, who could wear frilly wide skirts imported specially from Earth to look her best at the Hunt dance. For stupid him! Why she bothered with such a lunkhead he couldn't understand, but he had to catch up with her and see if he couldn't set matters straight between them.

A girl who had ridden between his home and Hriss's doing her best to say to each what they weren't permitted to say to each other. And she had even gone to the extreme of dyeing her gorgeous red hair, risked her safety on Earth's slideways and sleazy Aisles, bearded inspectors with purloined documentation and . . . And he hadn't the sense to realize what any Hrruban male would have known—that Kelly wanted him just as much as Nrrna wanted Hriss.

Now he exercised his wits and saw the turn off the main road that would give him the jump on their head start.

He drove the bay up the hill and down, hauling him to a dead stop across the narrow trail. Calypso was travelling at such a speed that she did a stiff-legged stop to avoid crashing into Fargo. Kelly, who'd been looking over her shoulder, came tumbling out of the saddle, right into Todd's arms. He caught her before she could slide out of his grasp and pulled her sideways across the low pommel.

"Gotcha! Fair and square," he said, grinning because it had been a close thing. But he hadn't been about to let Kelly go now he realized how much she meant to him. And before she could say or do anything to put him off his intended action, he kissed her hard.

The shock that coursed through his body at the touch of their lips was totally unexpected. Briefly he held her off so he could see her face, see if she could possibly be feeling the same way he did about that kiss. But her eyes were closed and there was an incredibly dreamy look about her face. So he gathered her to him more tenderly and found that their second kiss was even sweeter than the first and so he didn't break it off in any hurry at all. Especially when he felt her arms clasping him, one around his ribs and the other pressing at the nape of his neck so he couldn't have released her even if he'd wanted to.

The feel of Kelly in his arms was something magical. Much better than dancing with her had been, so he pressed her as close to him as he could. Until he felt Fargo—who was not up to the weight of the pair of them—buckle a bit on the forehand.

"Robin'll kill us if we lame Fargo," she murmured. "But Calypso could carry us both a long time."

"I think we'll rest both horses after that mad race," he said, managing to dismount with her still in his arms. Then he clipped an arm under her knees and carried her to the nearest clear patch of grass. "I love you, Kelly Solinari. Will you forgive me for being dumb blind stupid iggerant not to realize how precious you are to me?"

"I might, but it could take a long time—like forever," she replied in a lilting voice.

Sometime later, Fargo decided that he'd make his way back to his stable. Calypso had better manners. She wouldn't leave her rider and grazed contentedly until she was needed again.

CHAPTER

10

THE NEXT MORNING, THE TWO YOUNG COUPLES composed a carefully worded message to Dalkey, containing instructions on where to hide the information he wanted to send. They posted it signed with Kelly's key-code. Couched in the chatty phrases about their years together in college was the fact that several pallets of medical supplies were being transported to Doona in two days. Dalkey swiftly responded with an ardent note, the tone of which made Todd frown and Kelly blush.

"But it sounds genuine, Toddy," Kelly said soothingly. Then she giggled. "You're here and he's parsecs away. Don't be silly. Besides, he does say that he understands the instructions and I get the impression that he accessed more data than he originally promised."

Todd apologized for acting silly, but the truth was, they were all nervous. Something could delay the shipment, or Dalkey might be seen where he had no reasonable explanation to be. Both Nrrna and Kelly arranged to be on hand to receive the supplies. This time Nrrna did not wear any scent.

The grid operator flinched when he recognized Nrrna appearing on the platform from First Village. He still found her attractive, though not as strongly, and especially not when she was accompanied by a Hayuman female. He only hoped that the Treaty Controller was not expecting another shipment, but a quick glance at the manifest told him he didn't need to worry about that tonight.

Kelly was relieved that the operator seemed too busy to chat them up. She and Nrrna managed a desultory conversation while they waited, but they were so keyed up they'd forget what the other had just said. Kelly kept imagining problems: What if the envelope didn't come or got torn loose in the transfer? What if Dalkey got caught? They needed to have genuine, hard documentation. Well, maybe if Dalkey didn't come through for them, they might have some luck with the documents that the Treaty Controller had personally awaited. Anything that pleased an associate of Third Speaker was likely to be bad for Doona.

When the suspense became so great that Kelly was prepared to dive right through the pillars and drag the shipment up from Earth, the air thickened over the gridwork and the pallets materialized. She and Nrrna let out sighs of relief.

"Will you check it now so I may clear the grid?" the operator asked.

"That's why we're here," she said, handing a sheaf of papers from her clipboard to Kelly and peremptorily gesturing her to go to the back of the grid.

They'd planned this so Kelly would be screened from the operator and could feel under the pallet for the envelope. Then she thought of a better stratagem than blind groping.

She let her clipboard drop. "Ooops," she said gaily, and, in attempting to pick it up, kicked it under the pallet. "Wouldn't you know?" she said with cheerful self-disgust. She got down, peering under the shipment, trying to see Dalkey's envelope. He'd been instructed to use a gray one which wouldn't be so readily visible to anyone casually glancing under the plastic pallet. She shook her wrist so the small torch would fall out of her sleeve where she'd hidden it, and played its dim beam around, but she saw absolutely nothing, not even cobwebs.

"Does your friend need help rising?" the operator asked rather irritably.

"Probably," Nrrna said in intimate pitch, trying to stall. "Her balance is very poor. Hayumans have weak inner ears."

"I had noticed that their ears are abnormally small," he said, and came round to help Kelly to her feet. She feigned momentary weakness before she met Nrrna's eyes over the boxes and gave a shake to her head.

"Thank you, sir," she said to the operator, reaching out suddenly to grab his arm, swaying in a fashion that alarmed him. "My balance is none too good."

That had given Nrrna sufficient time to look underneath on her side. But she shook her head, too.

"Is this all we're supposed to get today?" Nrrna asked, checking over the number of boxes on her board. "I am missing several cartons."

He leaned over to examine her list. "No, you do not have all. Those sizes have to be broken down into two shipments. Second lot will come through in"—he paused to check his own schedule—"two hours. A shipment of ore from one of the mining worlds is due in next. Come back."

"Very well," Nrrna said, masking her relief in a cool response, "I will accompany this lot to the Health Center. Will you stay on the island and wait for the rest?" she asked Kelly.

"Oh, I don't mind. I've got a few things I can do while I wait. See you in the village." Kelly threw a good-luck gesture to Nrrna.

Once the characteristic mist rose around the crates and Nrrna, whisking them from sight, Kelly left the reception area. As she departed, she heard the operator's audible sigh of relief.

She'd been to the Treaty Island often enough to know the general layout, which was another reason why she had the best chance of accomplishing her second, and possibly more important, errand. But she stopped for a long moment to reread the inaugural plaque outside the main administration building.

"This Treaty Center was constructed in the fourth year of the Colony by the people of Hrruba, Earth, and Doona/Rrala in the spirit of cooperation represented by the Treaty of Doona."

Kelly felt a tingle of pride and renewed determination that the colony world, the turning point in the histories of both civilizations, would not become a future battleground. She knew where the Councillors' quarters were but she didn't want to blunder into the Controller's rooms if he was present. From the look of so many lights in the low Administration Building, there might be late meetings that would solve that problem.

She strode right up to the information desk where two Humans and a Hrruban, wearing official guide badges, were drinking malak.

"I've a message for the Treaty Controller," she said brightly, addressing all three.

One of the Humans peered at a list on the desk. "He should still be in the Council chamber. They've got an all-day session. Back the way you came and around the corner to the right at the T-junction."

"Oh! But I was told to take it to him at his personal quarters, sir."

The guide exchanged a glance with the other two. "Well, they'd be due for a break soon." He pointed out the glass door facing the desk. "Across the courtyard there, and along the garden walk. Treaty Controller's apartment is the last on the right."

"Thank you so much," Kelly said, and followed the directions, swinging her arms and striding off as if she hadn't a care in the world.

Several blocks on the left of the Administration Building housed visitors to the island, mostly researchers there to consult the ever-increasing Archives. To the right were the residences assigned to members of the Treaty Council. Each species, Hayuman and Hrruban, sent three delegates to the Council. Of those three, one was chosen from the species' homeworld, one from Doona/Rrala, and the third could be from either of those or from a colony world. The seventh member, the Treaty Controller, was nominated every three years in turn from the Hayuman or Hrruban side. Most frequently the Councillors were justiciars by profession.

The seven apartments were actually small detached houses abutting the formal garden and maintained by Treaty staff. Kelly followed the row to the end and found the modest home of the Treaty Councillor. Swallowing her nervousness, she slipped through the gate and approached the door, which was shaded by a stand of fringed palms. It wasn't just the tropical sun that was making Kelly sweat. She had no idea what excuse she could give if the Controller should find her here.

Following the spirit of openness and trust fostered on Doona, nothing was locked. Doors had fastenings and fences with strong latches to keep animals from wandering in or out. Irreplaceables and valuables were locked up safely out of sight, but few residences on Treaty Island were ever secured.

She hoped the Treaty Controller, not known for his acceptance of Doonan traditions, followed the local custom.

The door opened without resistance.

"Sir?" she called out tentatively. There was no answer, and indeed, as she stepped inside, the apartment had the silence of an uninhabited space. Gently she pushed the door almost shut. She ought to hear footsteps on the shell-lined walk.

The Treaty Controller lived in style. The fine green carpet was deep and soft, and took footprints all too easily. Her sandals made smaller impressions in it than slender Hrruban feet would. Would the nap spring up to erase her inward path? Or would he notice? His furnishings were lavishly decorated and suited to Hrruban anatomy. Not a single Hayuman-style chair or stool. The walls were hung with warmly colored Hrruban tapestries. All manner of Rralan-made crafts were displayed in wall niches and on small stone-topped pedestals, presents from Hrruban villages on the planet. Grudgingly she admitted that the old tom had good taste, but the furnishings also afforded numerous hiding places for the document box she sought.

As the tapestries were fastened to the wall from rods on a picture rail, she could look beneath them and tap the bright orange-dyed rla wall for hollow places. She found nothing and was examining the walls in the sleeping chamber when she heard the front door swing open and bounce against its hinges.

She froze and listened, hearing with great relief the sighing of a breeze. She tiptoed back to the door and peered around the corner, trying to keep out of sight. Someone stared right at her. Shocked and still in a half-crouch, Kelly stared back. But it wasn't the Treaty Controller. It was a small, coffee-skinned Hayuman with gray hair twisted into a coronet on her head. A Councillor's robe was slung casually over one arm.

"Who . . . who are you?" Kelly asked meekly.

"I was going to ask you the very same question, girl," the woman replied in a stern voice. "I thought the wind had blown the door open but I see he has a snooper going through his possessions. A thief on Treaty Island itself! Disgraceful! Give me your name this instant and your business here."

"Please, Madam Dupuis," for Kelly recognized her, "I'm not stealing anything. I'm Kelly Solinari of First Hayuman Village and I'm trying to help Todd Reeve."

"In the Controller's bedroom?" Madam Dupuis's eyebrows rose in amused query. "He doesn't like Hayumans, you know."

"Don't I just!" Sensing a sympathetic relaxation of the Councillor's disapproval, Kelly decided the truth would do her more good than any invention. So she summarized her illegal return to Earth and approaching Inspector DeVeer for assistance, and how she had overheard mention of a very special document box from Hrruba anxiously awaited by the Treaty Controller. "We've got Todd and Hrriss cleared of one charge," and Madam Dupuis nodded, so Kelly didn't bother to explain other matters of which the Councillor would have more intimate knowledge than she did. "But it's more than just an attempt to ruin the Treaty, Madam Dupuis. We think it's a conspiracy between certain Hayuman and Hrruban elements that might lead"—this was the hardest part to say aloud—"might lead to an interspecies war . . ." Madam Dupuis's hand went to her throat and her complexion paled noticeably. "A war that is meant to leave only one species on Doona and only one dominant species in the known galaxy."

Madam Dupuis regarded her for a very long moment with eyes dulled with sorrow.

"I fear you may be right, Kelly Solinari, though I have not had the courage to admit it to myself. I have always known that our current Controller was one of Third Speaker's nominees, but he has, until recently, been scrupulously fair in his judgments during our negotiations." She bowed her head for a long moment, her hand idly stroking her robe. "I have suspected a subtle alteration in his mien. You don't live for twelve years in close contact with someone, even of another species, and not notice"—her fingers flickered—"little things. I've wondered about his much-vaunted impartiality, but then," and she gave Kelly a rueful grin, "mine has been slipping somewhat, too. With all of my heart I want Doona to remain as it is." Her manner altered abruptly. "It is extraordinary behavior for a born and bred Doonan to break and enter, but if you can keep it to yourself and can find what you seek, I shall forget I've seen you."

"You will?" Kelly couldn't believe her escape.

"Hmm," Madam Dupuis murmured in an absent fashion. "I just came over to shut his door. I had noticed that the wind must have blown it ajar. Surprising how strong the breeze can be when the temperature starts to fall at this time of day." She started back to the door then turned, hand on the knob. "Have you found what you're looking for?"

Kelly shook her head. "I only just got here."

"Then for the sake of us all, find it," she said in a voice of command. "I'd help you myself because I believe you have seen the true reason behind all this maneuvering. I've got a boondoggle that I've been waiting to raise before the copies of the Treaty are written up. A Human outpost on Hrruba, similar to the facility Hrringa occupies on Earth. I want to see equal treatment for our species, but it's a sticking point I haven't been able to maneuver that old tomcat past. That should make a good long point to argue. I will make certain that you have an hour to search, but that is all I can hope to extend the argument. His patience isn't infinite. Will that suffice?"

"It will have to," Kelly said, her tone expressing her intense gratitude for understanding and assistance.

Just as Madam Dupuis was about to close the door behind her, she added, "If you need a haven, my office is on the first floor above the commissary." Then she closed the door firmly behind her.

The first thing Kelly did was to look about the sleeping quarters for a hiding place for herself. The heavy curtains would do and they gave onto a small shrub-lined yard but the bushes would be nothing for her to scale.

His closets yielded nothing except that the Controller was a fastidious person, for everything was neatly hung and arranged in outfits for lounging, public appearances, and ceremonial receptions. Nothing among the films and flimsies in his desk looked like official documents or reports. She read Hrruban, High, Low, and Middle, but a quick scan told her there was nothing incriminating in the drawers.

The communications unit was like any other on Doona or Earth, with no place for concealment in, on, or under the console. Brushing her hands on her legs to dry nervous perspiration, she started on the other furnishings.

She was halfway through her hour's dispensation when she found her prize. The document box was hidden underneath the last drawer in the bedroom bureau. The Treaty Controller had sawn out and removed half of the supporting board under the drawer, leaving a large hiding place accessible without turning the heavy chest over. Kelly drew the box out and rested it on her knees.

It was a very ordinary document box, like any other used for conveying official papers back and forth between offices. Kelly had seen, and handled, dozens like it at Alreldep. She hefted it: light, couldn't be much inside. But then she didn't need much, only the right sort of document.

She examined the lock and here the resemblance to ordinary courier boxes ended. It was fitted with a custom lock intended to·discourage unauthorized entry. The lock was flat, but a glance inside the keyhole with her tiny torch showed that it was made to accept a key with multiple wards each as narrow as a strand of hair. Box in hand, she looked about the room for something she could use to manipulate the lock. She found a straight pin but it was no use. She didn't dare try to force the box or break it open and her time was nearly up.

She started to put the box back into its place of concealment, but stopped when she noticed the remains of an official seal on the untied tapes that dangled from the sides of the container. It reminded her of something, and the memory tickled at the back of her mind. She had seen a seal used by the High Council of Speakers of Hrruba. This one was a lot like it, but not as complex. Using the point of a pin and an old scrap of film she found in a wastebin, she copied down as much of the seal as she could.

Madam Dupuis's gift of an uninterrupted hour was definitely over. Not daring to try the lock any longer lest she be caught there fiddling with it when the Treaty Controller returned, Kelly put the box away and replaced the drawer.

On her knees, she backed out of the room, fluffing up the woolly carpet with her hands. At the door, she stopped, and tried to remember if there was anything she had left open or out of place. No, she had been thorough, if unsuccessful.

"There," she said. "I hope he doesn't check for fingerprints."

Striding with as much nonchalance as she could, Kelly made her way to the research quarters where she knew Hrruvula was quartered for the hearings. Without explaining her presence or her occupation the past hour, she showed him her drawing of the seal. He gave her a startled glance and peered at it closely. When she opened her mouth to explain, he held up his hand, his eyes dark and inscrutable.

"You are not my client, Kelly Solinari, so anything you might wish to impart to me would not be done under the cloak of confidentiality," he said, still studying the scrap of film. "You have not been here. We have not talked of anything, especially about a replica of the private insignia of the Third Speaker."

He handed it back to her, gestured politely for her to exit as quickly as she had entered, and turned his back on her.

She left Hrruvula's office at a trot, heading for the transport grid. So that was it! The Treaty Controller was, against all the precepts of his current position, actively collaborating with his sponsor to prevent the renewal of the Treaty! She hoped the evidence Dalkey had found was indeed on the next shipment. There wouldn't be another medical shipment for weeks, and by then Doona might be just a memory. The thought scared her so much she ran all the way back to the grid station.

The grid operator transferred Kelly and the remaining pallet directly to the transport station in First Village. She all but fell off the platform into Todd's waiting arms and let him sustain the embrace to restore her self-confidence. Hrriss watched the salutation with glowing eyes, Nrrna beside him, delicate hands nervously clasped together.

"It's here," Kelly said excitedly, thrusting the dark gray envelope into their hands. "He came through. I just love Dalkey. He did it."

Todd eagerly opened the packet which contained a sheaf of printouts, folded neatly in half. To the top a note in Dalkey's precise, impersonal handwriting was attached, which Todd read aloud. "None of these account numbers Earth-based. Good luck. D." Todd's fingers fumbled as he opened the sheets and glanced quickly through them. "He's done it. We've got it!"

Hrriss hissed softly. "This will take time to decipher," Hrriss said, reading over Todd's shoulder. "First it must be determined which numeric prefixes pertain to which worlds."

"A lot of money changed hands," Todd said, and whistled at the size of separate amounts. "I don't think it'll be that hard with so many good minds"—he grinned about him—"focused on the job. Look. The numbers repeat. Some of these accounts have had several deposits. With what we already know, we ought to be able to figure out which worlds are involved. We can start by checking the amounts against what we've got in Klonski's."

"Shouldn't we take this right to Poldep?" Kelly asked.

"Call me paranoid if you want, Kelly, but I want to decipher this for ourselves first before we show it to anyone else."

"Yeah, if they turned out to be legitimate supply payments," Kelly said with a grimace, "we'd damage our cause. We can't afford to do that! And"—her voice strengthened and her eyes flashed up at him—"you're not paranoid—not any more than you have reason to be."

Todd grinned down at her, really enjoying their newfound intimacy. "These could turn out to be quite legitimate remittances to free-lancers on infrequent invoices."

"I think Dalkey would know if that's what they were," Kelly said, slightly defensive. Dalkey had taken risks to get these to her, and he wasn't stupid. "But you're right. Let's divvy them up among us so it'll go faster."

"All for one and one for all," Nrrna startled Todd and Kelly by saying. Seeing their surprise, she smiled in pleasure at the effect. "I found that quote in one of your Earth classics."

Todd grinned. "I think a more appropriate quote might be 'If we don't hang together, we will most assuredly hang separately.' Any luck on the other half of Project Infiltrate?" he asked Kelly, his arm still lightly about her shoulders.

Kelly rolled her eyes over that little escapade and then gave her friends a quick summary.

"Madam Dupuis is on our side?" Todd exclaimed when she had finished. "That's a real plus." Then he shook his head. "It's just tough luck that you couldn't get inside the document box, but the seal's incriminating. The Treaty Controller is supposed to be impartial. He certainly shouldn't be receiving documents from Third Speaker. No wonder he collected the shipment himself. Let's get cracking on what we do have."

They quickly determined that what Dalkey had sent was the complete printout of all transactions within the slush fund account for a period of fifteen years, ending two years before the present date. Once decoded, it might provide the hard documentation they needed.

"Three eight one is the prefix for Zapata Three," Todd said, referring to the printout that had been presented to the Treaty Council by Landreau. "So shall we assume that this first number is the account opened by 'Rikard Baliff'?" He compared the dates with missions he and Hrriss had been on: those which Rogitel had intimated had included nefarious side trips. "Well, whaddya know? Every single transaction date matches with one of our trips, Hrriss."

The Hrruban hissed softly between his teeth. "Someone has most scrupulously kept track of our journeys. But that could be anyone on Rrala. We made no secret of our departures and of our estimated time of return."

"And told their Zapatan contact just when to make lodgments," Kelly said, seething at the complicity and the way it had been turned against her friends. "Isn't that a second Zapatan account?" and she tapped her stylus on another 381 listing. "Is that our rustler being paid off? It's too neat to be mere coincidence, especially when all the figures match all that incriminating junk Rogitel was waffling on about. Sure looks like a connection between Spacedep and that rustler to me. Let's take it to Inspector DeVeer."

Todd grinned at her for her enthusiasm. "Not yet," he said, ticking off the entries they had identified. "I'd rather find out where all these other entries fit in." He held up his index finger. "One correlation is not sufficient. We present the entire package and they have to believe us. Someone has gone to a lot of trouble to make us look as guilty as possible. We have to shoot down all the brrnas in the flock."

Rogitel left the official chamber as soon as the Treaty Council adjourned for the day and transferred by grid back to Earth. Without a word to Hrringa in the Hrruban Center, he made his way swiftly out of the Alreldep block and directly to Landreau's office at Spacedep. The secretary silently admitted him to the director's small private office.

He stood vector-straight before Landreau's desk while his superior finished a comp call.

"I have information from our contact in the Archives," Rogitel reported as soon as Landreau had completed the call. "Inquiries are being made through to Zapata and several of the other worlds where the Reeve accounts are being maintained. They are in possession of specific deposit information, so they must have a source, within Spacedep, providing them with data from our records."

"So that is what's going on," Landreau said, his face suffusing with anger. He began scrolling through his console, his finger hard on the key. "A report came to my notice a few days back but I couldn't see why I should be bothered with minor infractions. Here it is!" And he gestured for Rogitel to scan it. "Trivial matters must never be ignored: even something so insignificant as a junior making copies of old screens. Take this Dalkey Petersham into custody, for illegal copying of official documents. Find out who he's been working for, if he's sent on the documents and to whom. Take his brain apart if you need to. Use querastrin if you must. But get a full confession from him." Landreau sprang out of his seat, pacing up and down, his stocky body quivering with fury.

"A confession under duress, sir? That's not altogether prudent. Nor can we obtain permission to use the truth drug on him for copying old, declassified accounting records. Wouldn't it be wiser, Admiral, to leave him in place and watch him? If he thinks he has gotten away with this first foray, he'll feel bolder about repeating his success. If you catch him in the process of committing a crime, you have far more latitude in extracting information from him."

"I don't like it," Landreau said, sitting down again, and flicking his fingers at the damning report on the screen. "I don't like it in the least." He pressed hard on the scroll key, stopping it and rewinding to position a new document, bearing the Poldep seal. "Reeve has had the damnedest luck. Couldn't you have done something to keep that beacon from being discovered?"

"Admiral, we had to get it out of the way as fast as possible and that meant using the most accessible transport, a merchant ship. Safe enough under most circumstances."

"But it wasn't! And that Mayday has removed one of our weapons against the Reeves. How did they find that shipment, Rogitel? That beacon should never have seen the light of day and it surfaces . . . plainly marked to Spacedep."

"Freak accident, sir," Rogitel replied calmly. He had often discovered that the calmer he remained, the sooner the Admiral's rages cooled. "Meteorite hole penetrated the hull and the carton, setting off the Mayday. I interviewed the captain himself. He was eager to talk about it. He appears to have been 'dining out' on it. Fortunately I was able to cancel the pickup and the crate remains unclaimed. If someone inquires, we say that it could well be an attempt on the part of the Reeves to implicate Spacedep to clear themselves of complicity."

"Good thinking, Rogitel, good thinking," and Landreau began to relax, even to smile. "But we'd better find out if there's any connection between this Petersham clerk and Doona. They can't slip out of any other charges or our plans will be ruined." He rattled his fingers on the desktop. "And I've an unsettling report from Varnorian's contacts in Codep. A Dr. Walter Tylanio from Prueba V was hired for a special job by someone from Doona." Landreau's eyes narrowed. "The only laser technology that Doona has is in its security satellites."

Rogitel could well appreciate how serious that could be, but he didn't know how anyone had discovered Klonski. Surely not the Petersham clerk. Maybe he had better acquire a vial of querastrin from his sources. Then an angry thump brought his attention right back to Landreau.

"I want Doona to be totally discredited. I want our plans to succeed in every particular, and for that to happen, the Doonan Experiment has to fail. Fail! Be wiped clean of its contaminated Humans and especially those misbegotten animals."

"Sir, calm yourself," Rogitel said, leaning across the desk toward his superior. "Your plans will succeed. While it's too late for subtlety, it's not too late," and he paused to smile reassuringly at Landreau, "to remove the primary cause of the entire problem."

"What?" Landreau said, staring fiercely up at his subordinate.

"Really quite simple. Remove the Reeves from Doona. I think they are at the bottom of much unfavorable publicity about Doona. Surely they should report—in person—to their Codep superiors here on Earth."

Landreau's ruddy face slowly broke into a smile. "See to it," he ordered. "Varnorian will oblige. Get them here and get them eliminated!"

Admiral Landreau was the epitome of regret and sorrow when he informed the Amalgamated Worlds Congress of the dreadful situation which existed on Doona when so much was at stake in the renewal of the Treaty. He stood in the beam of a pinpoint spotlight, addressing the half-seen figures illuminated by twelve identical cones of light in the vast chamber. In the blackness between was the faint peeping sound of the court reporter's machine.

"The Reeves are threatening the very safety of your design to form a Federation of Sentient Planets. Their activities destroy the very integrity and credibility of the Amalgamated Worlds and our dream for a united galaxy! Once the models of probity and dedication, both father and son have conspired to seize Doona for their own, and, had it not been for the discovery of their heinous infractions of the most basic Treaty stipulations, they might have succeeded in their scheming."

"Treaty Councillors are supposed to deal with such infractions, aren't they?" one of the panel inquired.

"Not when the crimes have such far-reaching consequences. No, honored sirs, this matter goes far beyond the Doonan system. It has most certainly raised awkward questions in the Hrruban Speakers Council and the Treaty Council as well!" Landreau shook his head sadly to add that detail. "I am deeply concerned that the Hrrubans will feel obliged to alter their opinions of us all, if these deplorable men remain in so public a position on Doona. The least that will happen is for the Hrrubans to pull out of the Federation or, worse, decide that we Humans must be rigorously schooled in their ways. They will undoubtedly impede our reach for the stars, cut short our explorations, confine us to the few planets we already own. Since Todd Reeve has not, cannot be cleared of his alleged crimes, I call for the removal of the Reeves from Doona to Earth for being detrimental to the renewal of the Treaty of Doona. I am sure your counterpart on Hrruba will also withdraw their, er, embarrassment from the colony, for that young male causes his people great sorrow. You must surely understand why we cannot have people of questionable integrity involved in high-level positions in the colony at this critical time. Remove the Reeves from Doona and let that situation resolve itself without further detriment."

There was a lot of muttering among the panel as Landreau's suggestion was discussed. He waited patiently, knowing that he had presented a valid and timely argument. He was rather pleased by his eloquence and the way he had deftly emphasized the salient points.

Landreau was even more pleased when the prevailing sentiment favored his solution. He had also counted on the fact that trade agreements had been drawn up and were awaiting the renewal of the Treaty before Hrruban ratification. That factor had probably contributed to the necessity of removing such controversial persons.

"You have made a plain case of a disgraceful situation," the chairman said. "At such a critical stage, nothing may be permitted to jeopardize the Treaty Renewal. Bailiff, give orders for Ken Reeve and his son Todd to be immediately brought to Earth to appear before this panel. Make the necessary representations to the Hrruban Center for the use of grid transportation of these two." Then the chairman inclined his head toward Landreau. "You may, of course, be present at the hearing, Admiral."

"Gladly," Landreau said. "I wish to further the cause of justice in every way within my power."

With some effort he restrained his elation. He must now make arrangements so that when that pair arrived, the Hrrubans on duty at that wretched grid would be those who would deliver the Reeves into his keeping. Soon, soon, he thought, rubbing his hands together in smug anticipation, he would be rid of Ken Reeve and that hyperactive son of his forever. Then his most ambitious plan could be initiated. Instead of the panel of inquiry meeting them, there would be an entirely different kind of reception committee awaiting the Reeves. Landreau smiled.

"My eyes will be ruined reading this small print," Todd said, briefly knuckling his eye sockets as he wearily turned over another one of Dalkey's printouts. "Some of these entries date back from when we were kids. Have you found anything relevant?" he asked Hrriss, who was as diligently examining his share of the packet. He paused, stretching his arms above his head to release the tension across his shoulders.

"They may be old but we have decided that the conspiracy against us was very carefully put into motion long before there was any reason to suspect one," Hrriss replied, but he also took a moment to stretch cramped muscles. "These entries," and he tapped a claw tip on the sheets, "are all from Darwin II-MF-4, a very remote colony world, not yet qualified for full status."

"Could be a place to ship stolen livestock," Todd said. He bent to his task again, stylus poised to cross off an entry, as he peered at the next line. "Whoa! Here's an account number right here on Doona!"

"Whose?" Hrriss asked. Todd swung around to the computer and instituted a name search. Madam Dupuis had arranged for them to use Archival records to match numbers with names, providing they limited their inquiries to that.

"Dunno yet. The last payment in these records is two years old. The person it belongs to might have left Doona in the interim." He drummed his nails irritably on the tabletop, waiting for the data to appear. When the screen scrolled up in answer to his query, Todd just stared at it, his face turning into a cold mask. Without a word, he rose, snatched up the printout, and started for the door.

"Whose number is it? Zodd? Where are you going?"

Todd kept walking. "To the Launch Center."

"Why?" the Hrruban demanded.

"To skin a snake."

Hrriss glanced at the name on the screen and hurried after his friend. "Lincoln Newry! How very convenient!"

"Todd!" Lincoln Newry said pleasantly as they marched into the circle of light cast by the single spot set into the ceiling. Martinson's assistant had his feet up on a desk in the Launch Center office, watching the tape of an entertainment program on the comunit screen while keeping half an eye on his scopes. "Hrriss! Nice to see you both. We don't get many visitors way out here. It's lonely in the evenings. Can I offer you something to drink? Nice warm night for this time of year."

"Your boss isn't here?" Todd asked expressionlessly. "I'd like him to hear what I've got to say."

"Nope," said Newry gaily. "He's gallivanting around the galaxy with old Kiachif. Some people have all the fun. I get to mind the store while he's gone."

Todd nodded. "How convenient, but that does fit another piece into the puzzle. We'd no reason to suspect either you or Martinson."

"Suspect? Me or Martinson? Of what?"

"Of helping Doona's enemies."

"Ah, c'mon, now, Todd. You're imagining weeds into snakes," Newry said in a soothing tone, but Todd noticed a wariness in his eyes despite his rallying words.

"Someone knew when and where Hrriss and I went on the *Albatross,* knew our flight plans and where we'd warp-jump. Someone also had to be here, in this office," and Todd had Newry's complete attention now, "to let rustlers lift from the surface. Whaddya want to bet that we can prove that every time a heist was made, you, Linc Newry, just happened to be on duty?"

With an incredulous laugh, Newry shook his head. "No way, son . . ."

"I'm not your son," Todd said, his face hard and implacable with suppressed anger. Hrriss had never seen him so furious. He moved to the balls of his feet in readiness. "And you know a ship launched the other night and somehow you can turn the security satellites off so they don't record either launches or landings of rustler shuttles."

"Hold on, hold on, there!" Newry said, raising his hands to pacify Todd and shooting Hrriss an indignant look that suggested Hrriss should calm his friend down. "You can't run around accusing people of doing this or that just to clear yourselves."

"I think I can," Todd said in an icy certain voice. "I figured it out. If Martinson's not here, you're the one who creates legitimate documentation for export shipments from Doona. You mind the shop, as you said yourself. And no one could have missed that atmospheric insertion the other night. You were probably looking at its trail as you assured me that no one had blasted off-planet with a load of horses rustled from Dad's ranch."

Newry was still waving his hands and shaking his head incredulously at Todd's accusations.

"You can look at my records. You'll find there was no insertion that night, Todd!" Newry turned to Hrriss, hands open to emphasize his innocence and disbelief.

"Oh, I believe we'll find no blips on the security satellites. That I do believe, Newry," Todd said, and then smiled. "Ever heard of a man named Askell Klonski?"

Newry shook his head, his reaction genuine.

"Or maybe you knew him better as Lesder Boronov?"

The change in Linc Newry was dramatic despite the man's attempt to cover that momentary lapse.

Seeing that Newry was rattled, Todd sat on the edge of the desk, folding his arms on his chest, his gaze never leaving Newry's face.

"Boronov is a genius with security systems. How'd he fix Doona's? D'you use a code so the satellite recorders blank? Or maybe just a convenient function key that isn't supposed to be programmed at all? Ah, yes, so it is a function key!" He twisted so he could reach the console that Newry had pushed to one side of the desk, making circles with his index finger over the ranks of spare keys. "Now . . . eeny meeny tipsy teeny . . ." he said in a singsong voice.

"Enough!" Newry cried, sinking dispiritedly back into his chair and burying his anguished face in his hands. "How'd you know about Boronov?"

"Amazing the things you can learn when you've been falsely accused, Newry. So what's your story? Martinson in on this with you?"

Newry shook his head from side to side. "No, he never knew a thing about it. He's too damned honest. And he gets paid what he's worth."

"Spacedep pays well," Todd said, his voice now a soothing coaxing one.

Newry looked up at him, his expression sour. "Not at my level. And nothing to make up for hours of sitting here night after night, day after day, doing double shifts when Martinson's away. I'd only two more years to go.

What I got for pressing a key now and then would be far more than that ridiculous pension Spacedep pays you. I wanted enough to buy into Doona. I saw my chance and I took it. And I was nearly there. So nearly there!" He buried his face in his hands again and his shoulders began to shake.

Todd looked away from the broken man, moved by contempt as well as pity.

"Who is the rustler, Newry?" Hrriss asked.

"You haven't figured it all out, then, have you?" Newry's muffled voice was bitter.

"Cooperation could mitigate your guilt," Hrriss added gently. "You can repair some of the damage you have caused."

Newry kept shaking his head in the cradle of his hands. "You're so smart, Reeve, you should know who it is."

Todd racked his brain. Who "it" is? Newry couldn't mean Landreau. He meant someone much nearer, someone who knew enough about the management of their ranch and . . . "Mark Aden?" He could scarcely believe that the young assistant manager whom he had so admired as a youngster could have turned against the people who had trusted him and encouraged him to learn as much as he could so he'd be able to start up his own spread on Doona. "Why would Mark turn on us? Dad paid him well. He gave him excellent references when he said he wanted to leave us. No one really wanted him to leave."

"That's not the way he told it," Newry said, his voice blurred by his hands. "That sister of yours thought herself too good for a ranch manager."

"Inessa?" Todd remembered that his sister had been infatuated with Mark Aden at one point, although she hadn't been unduly upset when Mark had suddenly decided to leave. But Todd did remember that Mark had a vindictive streak in him: he never forgot a grudge and he'd wait months to pay back an imagined slight that anyone else would have forgotten. Only Mark Aden would have been vindictive enough to sow ssersa in pastures used by horses. "He manages the rustling operation by himself? He didn't have the kind of money that would buy him any kind of a space vehicle. Certainly not one large enough to make rustling pay."

"Did he not perhaps have assistance from those who have been adding to your pension fund?" Hrriss asked Newry, pulling on his shoulders to make him look up.

Slowly Newry raised his head, and then his eyes began to widen, his whole face brightened, and a smile of unexpected salvation parted his lips.

"Todd Reeve?" a stern voice said.

In a swift move, Todd was off the desk and looking into the shadows beyond the console, trying to locate the newcomer.

Rogitel emerged from the darkness, Todd's father behind him, Spacedep marines flanking him.

"You are always found in the most incriminating situations. Harassing a Spacedep employee, were you?" Rogitel let out a patient sigh. "You will come with me. Now."

"With you, Commander? Dad?"

Todd stared at the lack of expression on his father's face. "But Dad . . ." Todd began before taking his cue. "Linc was explaining to us how the security satellites record incoming and outgoing traffic." It might sound lame but it covered the surreptitious sign he made to Hrriss. Just let Hrriss get free. "Weren't you, Linc?" And let Linc prefer to keep silent about the last few moments in front of one of his Spacedep superiors. Commander Rogitel dealt harshly with failures . . . and probably drastically with informers.

"That's right, Commander," Newry said in a drawl that almost disguised the tremors in his voice.

"Let's go, Reeve," Rogitel said, motioning to one of the marines. "You have to report in an hour to the transport station." He caught sight of Hrriss, edging farther into the shadows. "You! You've no business in a Spacedep installation. Out of here!"

Todd had the satisfaction of hearing Hrriss's low and menacing growl as he swung around the marines and out the door.

Ken shot Rogitel a furious glare for his uncalled-for incivility to the Hrruban, but the commander paid no notice as he took his place in front of the detail.

"I've some things for you in the one bag we were allowed," Ken murmured to his son. "I don't think we'll be gone long for all the precipitousness of our departure."

"What's up, then?"

"We're to appear before a panel of the Amalgamated Worlds in their Terran offices."

Todd was seething to tell his father what he and Hrriss had got out of Newry. More pieces had fallen into place, pieces he never would have considered as part of the conspiracy. And yet they fit!

They had no chance to talk on the way to the Treaty Island, not with Rogitel looking so smug and well pleased with himself. At the grid, though, Todd began to worry. The Treaty Controller and two strange male Hrrubans wearing sidearms awaited their arrival.

"Send them to Earth," Rogitel ordered the grid operator.

The Hrruban glanced nervously at the Treaty Controller, who nodded, and the Hrruban had no option but to manipulate the controls. Todd watched the bright room around him dissolve and vanish. In a moment, the features of their destination started to coalesce around him. He could see the posts of the transport station becoming solid at the four corners of the grid, and the blank walls of a corridor beyond them.

As soon as the Reeves had fully materialized, they were attacked from behind.

CHAPTER

11

IN HIGH SPIRITS, ALI KIACHIF TAPPED AT THE DOOR of the Reeve residence. He and the other two men had debarked so hastily from the *White Lightning* they were still in shipsuits.

"Now, this will just take a minute," the Codep captain assured his two companions. "Hello-oo?" he called out, and rapped with his knuckles on the window. "Reeve, are you home? Ah, hello, Patricia. Surprised to see me so soon? Rank has its privileges, I always say. I brought someone by for your husband to meet. May I introduce Dr. Walter Tylanio? He's the best laser expert in the whole galaxy. What he don't know about 'em, no one does, if you see what I mean. Martinson you know." The tall, bearded man behind Kiachif bowed.

"How do you do?" Pat asked. Her daughter Inessa and Kelly were crowded behind her in the doorway. The merchant tipped them a little wink. Their faces fell when they didn't see the figures they expected.

"Good afternoon, Mrs. Reeve," Martinson said impatiently. "Kiachif, I have to get back to my office."

"Patience, patience," Kiachif said chidingly. "Surely you can give the man one moment to crow over all of you who thought so ill of him. *Honi soit qui mal y pense,* if you know what I mean."

"Neither Todd nor Ken is here, Captain," Pat said, her anxiety increasing because she thought it just possible that the captain might know where they were. "They were supposed to see an Amalgamated Worlds panel."

Kiachif clicked his tongue. "That's bad luck. I guessed he'd want to see my smiling face, soon's my expert here had a chance to unreel that doctored log tape that was on the *Albatross*."

"Come in, come in," Kelly said, usurping Pat's prerogative, but Hrriss had told her and Nrrna all about Newry. And if this expert was so good, maybe he could figure out which function key controlled the security satellite bypass and how Klonski-Boronov had managed to scramble supposedly tamperproof chips.

"Martinson here," Kiachif said, stepping lightly inside and peering about as if he hoped Ken and Todd were only hiding in their own home, "wouldn't let me bring the tape to Tylanio, so I brought the mountain to the prophet." He caught Kelly's grin. "Well, I alter to suit m'purpose, girl, if you get my drift. Martinson kept his word of honor like the fine upstanding man he is, and the log was never out of his sight for a moment. So we have returned with the news and Martinson maybe has returned to Doona a wiser man."

"What did you find, Dr. Tylanio?" Pat asked, absently gesturing for them to be seated. She signalled for Inessa to get refreshments.

"To give you the tall, small, and all of it," Kiachif said, still dominating the conversation, "the log was some messed with." Dr. Tylanio, who apparently took no umbrage from Kiachif's ebullience, nodded agreement.

Martinson cleared his throat and shot a quelling look at Kiachif. "Let the expert explain, Captain. I thought that's why you insisted he return with us."

"The tapes had clearly been extensively altered, Mrs. Reeve," Dr. Tylanio said. He had a pleasant tenor voice and spoke in the measured phrases of a born lecturer. "It was apparent from the tape that it was not recording anything on its homeward-bound journey: certainly not when they paused outside the Hrrilnorr system. Internal recordings were being taped. I would guess that the VU and transmitter had been tampered with."

"But that doesn't prove it was altered by an outsider," Martinson said, obviously unsettled by Tylanio's report.

"It does to me," Kiachif said, accepting a glass from Inessa. "And there's more. Oh, how I wish Todd and Ken were here right now. Walt says the box was only diddled once. That puts paid to that Spacedep stringy bean's charge that the boys had been wiping the memory clean every time they were ex-Doona while committing all those piracies and smugglings."

"That's right, Mrs. Reeve," Tylanio said. "The alteration could only have been made before or after their latest mission. Since the ship was sealed, that would mean it would have to have been done before. The inserted material was masterfully done, very carefully filmed to present such a single continuous record of multiple warp jumps and atmospheric insertions and launches. The most masterful piece of logging I've ever seen."

"But couldn't it have been substituted for the real log?" Kelly asked diffidently, for they had figured out how such a switch could have been made.

"Now, how could that possibly have been done, young woman?" Martinson demanded, irate. "I was present the entire time. I saw Commander Rogitel remove the log box myself, package it very carefully, and carry it off the ship. No one could have substituted this . . . this . . ."

Kiachif was waving a finger under Martinson's nose. "That lassie has made a very good point, Martinson, so don't get hot under your collar, which you aren't wearing, but you're getting riled."

"Commander Rogitel . . ." Martinson began again with greater indignation, but Kiachif's crow of exultation totally disconcerted him.

"I wouldn't trust an Amalgamated Bond, sealed, signed, secured, if that Spacedep stringy bean gave it me. Ah, no," Kiachif said. "I'll bet my *White Lightning* herself that that's when a switch occurred. Found the real log, lassie?"

Kelly shook her head. "We only figured out how and when the other day." She wanted desperately to get Dr. Tylanio and Kiachif to herself to tell them about Newry, which she couldn't quite do in front of Martinson. For all that she knew Martinson was respected and seemed straight as a die, she wasn't going to take any chances. Especially as he seemed to think Commander Rogitel was such an upright type.

"So when d' you expect your men back, Patricia?" Kiachif asked easily.

"I don't know, Ali," she said, and began to wring her hands. "They should have been back the next day. And now there's

this awful rumor that they never appeared before the panel
at all. That they've . . . they've skipped out of an untenable
situation." Pat blurted the slander out and then began to weep.
Kelly put her arm around her protectively.

"Never!" Kiachif said in a voice that would have been heard
from stem to stern of the *White Lightning* through closed safety
hatches.

"Commander Rogitel escorted them," Kelly said in a caustic
voice, her eyes on the captain. "With marines. I heard," and
while she couldn't mention Madam Dupuis, she was certainly
the most reliable source, "that two strange and armed Hrrubans
took over from the marines when they got on the grid."

"Did they, now?" Kiachif's eyes went wide. "Now, that's a
nasty turn-up. And I'll tell you one thing." He swerved toward
Martinson, his long stained finger almost in the man's nostrils.
"I don't want to hear one more word from anyone that Ken
Reeve, or Todd, skipped out of any obligation—to Doona, to
Amalgamated Worlds, even to ol' Terra! You see that gets put
about right smart, Martinson. I've known Ken Reeve a quarter
century. He's run *at* a lot of stuff *I'd* never be caught charging,
but he's done it and won out over odds that would have pipped
plenty on this planet. If he didn't show up when and where he
was supposed to, then he was prevented, if you understand me.
Now, you dry those tears, Patricia Reeve, and stand up proud
for your man and that fine son of yours," he said, somewhat
awkwardly but kindly patting her shoulder. "Your man is a
fighter. Your boy, too. They'll be back, sure enough, before
you've any more time to miss them."

"Thank you, Ali," Pat said gratefully. "You know him in
ways I don't. You've given me new hope. And so have you,
Dr. Tylanio. You were so good to come all this way for us."

The laser expert took an envelope from his pocket. "This is
a copy of my report, signed and sworn to by an accredited
Amalgamated Worlds notary. Your son and your husband
will doubtless find this useful. I will, of course, be happy
to testify in person to the authenticity of my investigations."
Tylanio handed it to Pat and bowed. With Martinson at his
side, he left the room.

"You see, signed, sealed, and sworn to. Proof positive of no
perjury, Patricia," Kiachif said in a low voice. He gave her

one more squeeze and started for the door.

With the pretext of courtesy, Kelly followed him, touching his arm and bending close to his ear. "I gotta see you, Captain, and preferably before that expert leaves the planet." Kiachif gave an almost imperceptible nod of acknowledgment, not so much as altering his stride as he continued on out of the house. Then she turned back to Pat, Inessa and Robin comforting her, and said in her normal tone, "I'd better get on home now but I'll be back tomorrow."

She clattered down the steps, whipped Calypso's reins free from the rail as the men piled into the flitter. As it took off, it wallowed from side to side and she grinned. Trust Kiachif. Which she did.

Kelly had been looking over the last charges against the boys that still had to be cleared before Treaty Renewal Day. And the valuables and interdictables they were supposed to have stolen and secreted on the *Albie* would be the hardest part. Having Dr. Tylanio's proof that the log tape had been altered, or even a carefully edited one substituted, was a real relief. If only they could somehow prove that Commander Rogitel had switched the doctored tape for the genuine log record . . . He'd had more opportunity than anyone else. And reason.

But if the tapes of alleged visits to collect valuable artifacts, including the Byzanian Glow Stone, were adjudged a simulation, then they hadn't been where they were accused of stealing things. They hadn't stolen anything. As Todd and Hrriss maintained, all that junk had been planted on the *Albatross* and that had to have been done while the *Albie* was on the pad at Hrretha. Rogitel had been there.

But where were Todd and his father? Thank goodness, Captain Ali had soothed Patricia Reeve on that score. Maybe the word that they were detained would get out and Robin wouldn't be sporting black eyes for defending the family honor. She knew Hrriss was lying low. Which was smart of him. Rogitel might not have considered the young Hrruban dangerous when he shooed him out of the Launch Center, but Newry knew different. Why hadn't Todd come out with an accusation right then? In front of the marines. Surely they could be made to testify . . . or could they?

A tiny noise penetrated her cogitations. Looking up from her desk, she nearly fell off her chair at the face grinning outside her window.

"You scared me to death, Captain Ali," she whispered hoarsely at him.

"Your manner did suggest a need for caution, lassie."

It wasn't the first time Kelly had crawled through that window, and taking the captain's hand, she ran with him to the deep shadows of the barn where no one was likely to look for them.

"You hit the nail on the head with Klonski, you know," she said, "though I daren't even get in touch with Inspector DeVeer right now."

"And which nailhead would that be, lassie?" Kiachif asked. "Though Tylanio agrees privately with me that the work on the tape is exactly the sort of thing Klonski would do so well."

"You also said he was a genius at fixing security systems." Kiachif nodded, his eyes glinting in the dark. "And Dalkey's records show he got paid several huge hunks of credit. I think some of it went to pay for him hobbling Doona's security satellites."

"Oh-ho-ho! I've been away too long."

"You have. Todd and Hrriss found payments to a Doonan account . . . and it belongs to Lincoln Newry."

"Martinson's assistant?" The whites of Kiachif's eyes, for once, Kelly noted, without bloodshot cobwebs, were visible in the shadow. "No wonder you wouldn't speak out in his presence. Does Patricia know?"

Kelly shook her head. "She's got enough to fret over right now. 'Sides, I didn't think it would cheer her up."

"Not a mite nor a moment, if her men are missing. Go on."

"Hrriss said Todd broke Newry down into admitting that he'd been letting the rustlers in and out of Doona, only when he was on duty. The ship Todd saw the other night was probably registering on Linc's screens while he was denying an atmospheric insertion."

"But the beacons . . ."

"Klonski's fixed them. Hrriss said there's an unprogrammed function key on the launch board that interferes with satellite recording. Furthermore, Linc Newry can authorize export documentation . . . like for Reeve freeze-marked livestock going off-planet to unknown destinations. And the rustler is Mark Aden."

"That young lad? Hmmm, isn't often someone fools Ali Kiachif." The captain frowned. "The nerve of him, making me transport rustled animals! And all that scud about making a new life."

"Apparently he's made a very profitable one," Kelly said drolly. "At the Reeves' expense."

"But they always treated him well. He even said so."

"Inessa didn't," Kelly said. "She had a flirt with him but she gave up on him because he always wanted her to get her father to help him get a ranch of his own. He was a funny guy, never forgave a hasty word or a silly joke on him. Hrriss thinks he's the one seeded the ssersa. Todd found a half-empty sack of it by the corral he found. It'd be just the sort of rotten trick Mark Aden would do, to make Inessa sorry she ditched him."

"Fascinating, lassie, fascinating. I think Dr. Tylanio has one more job before I return him to the quiet rectangles of his hall of learning."

And between one breath and another, Captain Ali Kiachif disappeared. That night Kelly slept well for the first time since Todd and Ken had been hauled off to Earth.

The very next morning, Kelly had a call from a frantic Nrrna.

"Kelly, they are hunting Hrriss." The girl was sputtering so badly that Kelly at first didn't understand the import of her words.

"Hunting? Hrriss?"

"The Treaty Controller has demanded his presence immediately on the Island. He sent four of the Third Speaker's special force for Hrriss."

"So where's Hrriss?"

"He has made himself scarce. Hrrestan told him that is what he must do. Oh, Kelly, I am so frightened."

"Don't be," Kelly said as firmly as she could. "I've got official confirmation that the *Albie* log tape was a fraud. Tampered with, fixed, altered. And that means that neither Todd nor Hrriss was where they're charged with being, so they couldn't have stolen those things. And illegal possession of those artifacts is really the last charge against them. And we'll soon have proof, too, of what Todd and Hrriss discovered talking to Linc Newry."

"But what good does all this proof do when Zodd is missing and Hrriss is, too?"

"A good point that, Nrrna," Kelly said. "You just keep your cool, friend. It's up to us now."

She stopped by the Reeves', just in the crazy hope that Todd and his father had returned home. They hadn't and the gloom that hung over the ranch house was depressing. Kelly did ask to have a copy of Dr. Tylanio's document.

"To keep with all the rest of the evidence, Mrs. Reeve," she said in an offhanded manner.

"You've got all these mysterious sources, Kelly," Inessa accused Kelly, her face and eyes showing the strain that affected the entire family. "Why can't you find out about Dad and Todd?"

Kelly suppressed her annoyance with the girl whose flirtation with Mark Aden was having such a long-range effect. Then, generously, Kelly reminded herself that Inessa had been just a kid at the time. Perhaps this would all sort itself out and Inessa would never realize that her childish infatuation was part of this dreadful affair.

Kelly left for Nrrna's house in First Village. She had all the proof they had so painstakingly gathered, including Hrriss's summary of Newry's disclosures. Surely that was enough! Surely Nrrna would see how terribly urgent it was that they stop messing with underlings and go to the top!

"Go to Hrruba? To First Speaker?" Nrrna's voice broke into a startled squeak and Kelly shushed her.

On her way into First Village, Kelly'd noticed some strangely accoutred Hrrubans milling around the clearing in the center: the biggest specimens of their species she'd ever seen. Deciding they were not in First Village for census taking, she ducked around, taking a narrow little track to the fenced-in pasture where the village horses grazed. Unsaddling Calypso, Kelly turned her out and lugging saddle and the bulging pouches, finally reached Nrrna's house, entering by the back flap.

"We should have gone to First Speaker in the beginning, as Todd wanted to," she said, a trifle annoyed with Nrrna's timidity.

"Oh, Kelly, no! I dare not!" Nrrna said. "It is absolutely forbidden to convey Hayumans to Hrruba."

"Now! But Todd's been there and he thought seeing Hrruna was his best chance."

"Todd went to Hrruba before the Treaty was written and the Treaty has a clause utterly prohibiting visits from Hayumans. Todd was held in high honor by the Council of Speakers . . ."

Kelly flicked her eyebrows up in disgust. "Was held."

"He is honorable. He would say that he must obey that prohibition."

"Yes, but no one has specifically prohibited me and, where Todd is concerned, honor can go out the window for all the good it's done him lately!" Kelly scowled fiercely. "Look, both Todd and his father are missing. Some nasty minds say they've done a flit because there's too much evidence against them."

Nrrna was shaking her head now in staunch disagreement.

"Right. So something's happened to them. And it's up to you and me to get them released. *Before* the Treaty gets signed. So we go to Hrruba and sort things out."

"We can't do that."

"Why not? You know how to work the grid controls. You sent me to Earth."

"But that was different," Nrrna replied, aghast at Kelly's daring plan. "You are of Terran stock. It is not forbidden under the Treaty for you to travel to your homeworld. It would be as impossible for me to send you to Hrruba as it would be for me to go to Earth."

"You'd be with me. I'd be your guest, as Todd was the guest of Hrrestan and Mrrva twenty-odd years ago. And it's for the same important reason. To save both our planets." She paused, watching Nrrna shake her head, her eyes mournfully big as she struggled with her principles—her honor. "This is the time to dare all. All for one and one for all."

Nrrna smiled wanly at Kelly's joke, but it took two hours of solid persuasion to get the Hrruban to see that Kelly's daring plan was the only option open. Kelly ruefully insisted that this scheme also went against everything she had been brought up to believe sacred and binding. But sometimes one had to make exceptions. As Hrrestan and Mrrva, and Hrrula, had made an exception of the six-year-old Todd.

Nrrna still experienced pangs of deep guilt over telling Dalkey when the medical shipment was being sent out.

"This is the time for stouthearted females to save their menfolk, Nrrna. Or didn't you see those Hrruban heavies prowling around the village center?"

"What?"

"Go have a look," Kelly said. "They're Third Speaker's or I don't know my Hrruban insignias. And they're armed."

As a terrified Nrrna sidled cautiously out the back flap, Kelly decided that if this wouldn't persuade the female, she'd have to think of some other plan. Only nothing, absolutely nothing, would come to mind.

When Nrrna returned, she was shivering and the fur along her entire stripe stood up.

"They are very powerful males. They are dangerous. They look for Hrriss." She took Kelly by the hand. "We must go to First Speaker. Such males should not be on Rrala. They should not be in our village."

There wasn't time to wait until dark, for males might take to searching the houses and Kelly didn't think they'd like finding a Hayuman in a Hrruban village right then. She covered her bright hair with an edge of a sleeping fur and wrapped herself in Nrrna's big winter cloak, the all-important dossier clutched to her chest with one arm.

"We don't have to go to the Treaty Island grid to get to Hrruba, do we?" Kelly asked, suddenly realizing that her mad scheme had a few large holes in it.

"No, we can reach Hrruba from here," Nrrna reassured her. For once the little female had made up her mind, she was capable of as much cool resolution as Kelly. "Until the Island grid was established, all shipping and travel were done through the village grids. It is only to satisfy the Controller of what is being sent in and out of Rrala that all goods now go first to the Island."

"Where are we likely to find the First Speaker?"

"First we will go to the Executive Cube which houses the Speakers' chambers. Someone there will direct us to First Speaker Hrruna." Nrrna was pressing the appropriate codes into the transport controls. She gestured for Kelly to step up onto the grid. "If they do not arrest us first."

Their first bit of good luck was that they arrived late in the Hrruban night. No one was immediately visible, although they heard the rumble of several voices issuing from a side corridor. Together they raced down the nearest aisle until they spotted a curtained alcove. They dove behind this and sank to the floor, their knees cocked so that they would not disturb the fall of the draperies.

When light began to filter through the soot-covered window, Nrrna carefully crept out to find out where she might find the First Speaker's quarters. She returned to Kelly, who had been fearful of discovery, that at any moment, a functionary would arrive to pull back the curtains.

"The Council is not in session today," Nrrna whispered to Kelly. "The First Speaker has expressed a wish to be alone in his retreat." Kelly's hopes crashed about her. Nrrna gave her hand a little pat, her eyes gleaming. "The chief of the Council chamber told me how beautiful was the First Speaker's retreat and I do not think he realized that he also told me exactly where it is. We must go swiftly while there are not too many using the slidewalks." Then she wrinkled her nose. "Even in that cloak, Kelly, you do not stand or walk or even smell like a Hrruban."

"It's too late to worry about a minor detail like that," Kelly said, nervousness making her snappish. "What about me limping and crouching over like I'm ancient or hurt?"

"That is a very good idea, Kelly," and Nrrna nodded approvingly. "I am your dutiful daughter, taking you to see the beauties of the countryside. It is fortuitous that the fur you took is a white pelt. Here."

Nrrna made some rapid adjustments with her delicate hands, and, although Kelly felt she was more in danger of suffocation than discovery, she let Nrrna's strong hands guide her as she settled into a limping gait which she felt suggested advanced age and decrepitude.

With corridors and aisles separating blocklike buildings many levels deep, Hrruba was not unlike Earth, which surprised Kelly, though she managed only a few glimpses behind the folds of the pelt. They rode a slow-moving beltway to a remote section of the capital city of Hrruba. Around them, Hrruban workers, clad in tool belts or robes to denote profession and status, passed them on every side. The only differences between the Human workers of Earth and the Hrrubans were the preponderance of bright colors in the latter's dress, the inborn grace with which they moved, and the scent. Scent, not smell, for although it was just as strong as the odors of Earth's passages, it was different.

"Do not speak if anyone bumps you," Nrrna whispered. "Your Hrruban is good, but your accent would inform anyone that you are from a colony."

"I couldn't talk if I wanted to. Is it much farther?" Kelly murmured. Her right hip was protesting the unnatural gait, and she ached to stretch her back up.

Nrrna peered at the lettering on the block they were passing, and her pupils contracted to slits in the strong light. "Not very far. We are nearing the passageway. We must get off as soon as we see a lift. First Speaker lives on the top floor."

Hrruna's retreat was in a well-soundproofed block of the Hrruban residential complex. To the surprise of both Kelly and Nrrna, no one guarded the entrance or any of the lifts. Though only one, Nrrna discovered, went as far as the twenty-second story. When the lift stopped, the door slid back and, to their utter consternation, the First Speaker faced them. Later Kelly would remember that a green light blinked above the lift, informing the First Speaker that someone was coming to his retreat.

"By the first mother, what brings such a lovely young one to the door of such an old man? Is this your mother who comes to entreat me? Or to protect her cub?" He beckoned them to leave the protection of the lift.

Once they had moved on into the first of the boxlike rooms that comprised the retreat, Kelly opened her hood. Hrruna's eyes widened with surprise and the barest trace of amusement.

"Not an aged and grieving mother, but a redheaded Hayuman. I have heard that such hair color is possible but never have I seen it." His wise eyes twinkled at her.

What surprised her most was his voice, clear and musical, and young! She could not believe that the greatest Hrruban of all would sound so young. She had met some of the other Speakers who came to New Home Weeks or other celebrations of importance on Rrala, but First rarely left Hrruba. He had been old when the Treaty was first signed, but, in the intervening years, he seemed to have changed little from his image in the old tapes. His mane was as white as snow, and the fur on his face and chest was faded, too, making a striking setting for the characteristic bright green eyes of his kind. First's eyes, under fluffy frontal crests which served the catlike race for eyebrows, were kindly and wise. Kelly felt quite shy under his scrutiny, but she knew immediately that she could trust him. So she fell to her knees, threw back her cloak, and deposited the precious pouch of documents on the floor before him.

As Nrrna appeared to be speechless, Kelly began in her best High Hrruban. "My name is Kelly Solinari. This is Nrrna, daughter of Urrda. We came from Rrala seeking an audience with you. We apologize most profoundly for disturbing you in the privacy of your retreat but we had no option save an appeal directly at your feet."

The old Hrruban's jaw dropped with pleasure. "That sort of posture is all very well for formal occasions, young Kelly Solinari," he said, responding in Middle Hrruban, "but this is not an official visit or I should have been informed of it by the appropriate underling. Please, raise yourself and walk as a Hayuman should, tall and proud. And be welcome in my home."

This was evidently the dayroom, furnished in a fashion similar to that of the Treaty Controller's apartments on Doona. A translucent panel gave onto a terrace, open to the sky and surrounded on all sides by high walls. The rarefied air had the chill of the mountains, though none could be distinguished because of the walls. If Hrruba was anything like Earth, many of its original heights had been terraformed into plateaus, to provide solid building bases for residences and factories. All the view Hrruna had was an unending plain of buildings. No wonder the Hrrubans were as desperate as the Terrans to find suitable colony worlds on which to expand.

Someone (and quite likely, Kelly thought, Hrruna) had filled this little space with colorful flowering plants from the hydroponics laboratories deep inside his planet, and from the wild plains of Rrala. The effect was the equivalent of a miniature Square Mile park. Overhead, though neither heard nor seen, a forcescreen kept out the choking pollution that stained the air above a sickly gray. The atmosphere inside the conservatory was sweet with the scent of the plants.

Hrruna beckoned to the girls to sit down in the garden. Kelly hadn't been born yet when he accompanied Todd back to Doona to save the Human colonists from deportation, and to negotiate the Treaty of Doona. She had no idea how he would receive the information she had for him now.

"So what is it that makes two lovely young ladies risk safety and freedom to visit an old man?" Hrruna asked. He glanced warmly at Nrrna, who was made somewhat uncomfortable by his openly ardent expression.

With a deep breath, Kelly began. She had rehearsed what she would say to Hrruna, if they got to him. "It is of the greatest importance to us, sir, that the Treaty of Rrala is renewed in two days. To cohabit and cooperate with your people on that world a joy to all us Hayumans is," Kelly said. Despite Hrruna's use of Middle Hrruban, she couldn't switch from what she had so carefully memorized. And she was certain she had the right rhythm, the pitch and inflection to say what was needed in High Hrruban, which was as difficult as singing opera. "There may be a difficulty to the Renewal of the Treaty. We come to you to prevent that difficulty. The First Speaker Hrruna is the only personage to prevent rapidly approaching disaster."

"You are perhaps a friend of the young Zodd?" Hrruna asked in his kind young-sounding voice. "I seem to have had several visits from and on the behalf of that young man. What is it this time? And do not worry about the form of address. We speak as friends."

With great relief, Kelly lapsed into the more familiar idiom to relate the events of the past several weeks. When appropriate, she handed him the relevant documentation. He read through Hrriss's translations, sheet by sheet. Although not all Dalkey's lists had been done in Hrruban, there was more than enough in Hrruban script to show First Speaker sufficient proof of illegal payments out of Spacedep funds. That is, if he chose to believe that neither Todd nor Hrriss was guilty.

The First Speaker was skilled at posing questions in a natural progression, making the conversation a comfortable chat instead of a headlong plea for help. Kelly hardly felt she was speaking to him of planet-shaking matters in which the safety of her friends and her home was at stake. He considered everything she told him with a gentle gravity, nodding as she pointed out items that had seemed to Todd to be the most important.

"Why are you emissaries of Zodd?" Hrruna asked at last, his jaw dropping in a smile. "Why did he not come himself?"

"He and his father have disappeared. They are not the sort of people who run from trouble," Kelly said, once again feeling her crushing worry for Todd's safety.

"Neither son nor father is craven or thin-striped," Hrruna said encouragingly.

"We're afraid they've been abducted."

Saying that aloud in Hrruna's presence made it sound so horribly true that Kelly burst into tears. She was exhausted and worried. Nrrna sat beside her, holding her hand and muttering soothing phrases. Hrruna offered her a small glass of clear water and she sipped it, determined to control herself. This was no time to show weakness. The water helped. Then she could tell Hrruna what Todd and Hrriss had learned at the Launch Center, what Kiachif had discovered about the incriminating tapes, and if the tapes had been falsified, that neither Todd nor Hrriss could have stolen anything they were accused of stealing, including that awful Byzanian Glow Stone.

"But Mr. Reeve was taken from his house, and Todd from the Launch Center, by Commander Rogitel. They were taken by aircraft to the Treaty Island to go by the grid to speak before the Amalgamated Worlds panel and they never got there." Kelly forced back tears. "They wanted to clear their reputations. But they didn't even get that chance!" And then she stuck her fists against her mouth so she wouldn't disgrace herself with more tears.

"I do not like what you have told me," Hrruna said, his voice suddenly sounding very old.

"It is the truth, most honored Speaker," Nrrna said, speaking for the first time.

Kelly hiccupped back her sobs. "You're the only one we know who can demand an investigation into their disappearance. No one on Earth even cares what happens to them!" she added bitterly.

"Please, please, most honored First Speaker, help us! Help Rrala!" Nrrna's voice was low but so sweetly imploring that Hrruna leaned down to pat her cheek.

"I must assist you," Hrruna said, his voice kindly but firm. "I have known much of what you related, but you have also brought me the proofs which were withheld, or falsified, or conveniently misplaced." Hrruna chuckled, a series of throaty grunts. "I was truly unable to interfere until now. The continuation of the Rralan colony is far more important to me, as Hrruna, and as First Speaker, than I am willing to let any of my colleagues realize. If, however, I tried to interfere, that would give leave to others who are less altruistic to meddle in their own fashions and for their own reasons, which would not be as benevolent as mine. So I sheathe my claws to give others no excuse to sharpen theirs. They are compelled to show restraint, or suffer censure. A subtle means to an end but sometimes a more potent weapon than it first appears. When reputation and honor are more important than life, it becomes a greater lever." He sighed. "Perhaps not long enough a lever, for it does not appear to have unbalanced Rrala's greatest foes. I have been watching this contest from a distance. The players are not only fearful Hayumans. Some are very powerfully connected Hrruban xenophobes, including ones living on Rrala, who are trying to abort the Treaty."

"You know all this?" Kelly asked, and then bit her tongue for such impudence. "I beg your pardon, honored sir," she said humbly. She hadn't learned quite enough at Alreldep. She really had no business dealing at such a level.

First Speaker took no offense. "I have my sources," he said. "Young Hrrula has not been idle throughout all this, reporting directly to me. He is intelligent and most discreet. I value his observations enormously. He is devoted to Rrala, as well as to his world of birth. If you had asked him, he might have been able to bring you directly to me. Hrrestan knows of my trust in Hrrula."

Kelly and Nrrna looked at one another in amazement. "I didn't know that. Neither of us knew that. And with Hrriss gone . . ." She broke off.

"Exceptions have been made before now," Hrruna said enigmatically. "But someone has lowered himself to the dishonorable practice of kidnapping. I see the ramifications of that clearly. If Zodd and Hrriss do not appear in court with the proofs you have shown me, they are guilty by default. One more tool has been used by the hands of those without honor who would see Rrala fail. The involvement of Admiral Landreau, Commander Rogitel, and Codep Varnorian is known. The dishonorable Hrruban is not."

"It's the Treaty Controller working under Third Speaker's orders," Kelly said, and then closed her eyes because now she had to admit to her own dishonorable sins. "I, um, I sneaked into Treaty Controller's rooms to look for that document box Nrrna and I knew he had received and which he was so fussed about. Well, we had to know what he meant by the days being numbered," she said, defending herself, but Hrruna merely looked amused. "I couldn't unlock it, but it had been sealed by Third Speaker's personal sigil."

"There is no crime in his receiving such a package," Hrruna reminded them. "Third is his sponsor, after all."

"Yes, but why did he feel it necessary to hide that case in a specially made place at the bottom of a chest instead of putting it in the safe in his office or in the Archives? If the documents were innocuous, why didn't they arrive in a courier pouch?"

"You took out all the drawers in his bureau?" Hrruna asked, chuckling merrily. Kelly turned red. "I am not judging your actions, child. But I do see the point of your suspicions. Third may indeed be involved in this conspiracy. It is not beyond him when he feels thwarted. Yes, I am sure he is not uninvolved. Rrala is a nightmare to him. If the Treaty is not renewed, he would be unimaginably relieved."

"Please, honored sir. Don't let them scuttle the Treaty! Surely you can keep Treaty Controller from listening to the pessimists on Hrruba?" Kelly begged.

"Rralans are no threat to Hrruban society," Nrrna said. "We want to live our own life in peace."

Hrruna nodded his approval. "I think it would be best if Rrala continued as it is, I agree. But there are those who feel that once we unleash the ocelot, we will cease to be master of the hunt, and one day may even become prey. An all-Hrruban colony will behave as any Hrrubans will anywhere else. When you add in the Hayuman factor, behavior becomes more uncertain. I prefer to trust, but others cannot. It is not in their natures. I must not interfere in the negotiations or decisions of the Council, or it would not be a genuine agreement. It would be forced. But I will see what I can do to keep others from meddling so deeply."

With some difficulty, First Speaker rose stiffly to his feet. "A line of inquiry will be initiated immediately, even though I said I would spend my day in private. I hope, pretty one," he addressed Nrrna, "that you will stay, so we can get to know one another better. Though I am old, I would be entirely at your assistance, should you care to remain with me."

Nrrna shot Kelly a black-pupilled look of entreaty and the fur stood up on the backs of her forearms and on her tail. Such an invitation from the First Speaker was a high honor and Nrrna could not think of how to answer in a polite but negative way. It had been one thing for her to vie with other females for Hrriss's notice, but to diplomatically extricate herself from the attention of another, more assertive male, especially one of the broadest Stripe on Hrruba was more than she could handle. Kelly had noticed how fascinated Hrruna was with Nrrna's dainty beauty and realized it was now her turn to rescue her friend before Nrrna really panicked.

"O most honorable First Speaker, how we wish we could stay, both of us." Kelly ignored the glance he flicked at her that suggested the Hayuman had not been included in his invitation. She rose to her feet. "But we will be missed and awkward questions might arise from our disappearance—especially as we are known to be the promised mates of Todd and Hrriss."

Giving Kelly a long and somewhat amused look, Hrruna shook his head. "I suggest both of you remain with me, for safety's sake, my dear Hayuman. A tactful message will be sent to Hrrula to settle disquiet in both your houses. But should any whisper fall upon the breezes near Treaty Island that you have come to the First Speaker, you would be in mortal danger if you returned to Rrala."

"Oh," Kelly said in a very small voice. She sat down again and exchanged looks of alarm with Nrrna. Put in that light, neither of them was eager to go. Hrruna's jaw dropped as he watched the byplay between them.

"I was preparing food when the lift light flashed that visitors were on their way to me. Come, we will eat together, for we will need our strength. You may even assist me. Then we will set to work, for there is more to be done than I thought and I will need your assistance."

"That's what we came to get," Kelly said, and grinned broadly at him. Nrrna even managed a soft purr.

Hrriss had found a safe haven with the Reeve family, keeping out of sight in the house and trying to piece together from them what Kelly and Nrrna might have learned that had sent them into hiding, too. According to his betrothed's mother, Kelly had arrived to see Nrrna. She had left Calypso in the village pasture and her saddle was still in Nrrna's room. Marva had been busy with her tasks, somewhat worried by the strangers in the village center, and when she had gone to call the girls to eat at midday, they were gone. No one had seen them since.

"I've called all the nearby ranches and no one has seen either Kelly or Nrrna," Pat Reeve told Hrriss. "Did you have any luck?"

Hrriss had contacted every Hrruban he knew to be trustworthy, and some had set out discreet search groups to the farms around Nrrna's home village and some of the ranches where Nrrna had friends, but no one remembered seeing the girls.

"If she left Calypso, she's not anywhere a horse could go," Pat said. She was past worry, and into numbness, but she could still sense others' pain. Hrriss had only just been reunited with Todd after a traumatic separation, and now he had more troubles to concern him. Hrruvula had told Pat discreetly that if she saw either Todd or Hrriss, they must be prepared to appear before the Councillors or be judged guilty by default. He devoutly hoped that one or both would appear at the appointed time.

Robin came home from school with another black eye and many scratches and bruises.

"They're saying my brother's too much of a coward and he's flitted. They say Hrriss has run, too, which proves both of them are guilty as sin!" Robin was nearly in tears and refused to let his mother or his sister touch his injuries. "And I can't even tell 'em you haven't run. And they won't listen when I tell 'em my brother wouldn't! It's not fair. They weren't saying such things about Todd and you and Kelly at the Snake Hunt, and that wasn't that long ago." Robin didn't quite succumb to tears in front of Hrriss but it was touch and go.

"There are as many whom you have not seen today who do not believe that of either of us, Robin," Hrriss said. "Hrrula is one. Vic Solinari is another. And Lon Adjei."

"And Captain Ali Kiachif!" And, light-footed as ever, the spacefarer stood in the doorway.

Hearing his voice, Pat ran out from the kitchen. "Any news?"

"If you call no news good news, Patricia, then I've plenty of good tidings," the swarthy spacer said, shaking his head. "I've been listening in among my captains. No one reports transshipping any mystery guests off this planet in the dead of night, or knowing anyone who did. Any package that looks big enough to hold an unwilling prisoner, or one past caring, if you understand and forgive me, has been opened, turned over, and shaken. There's no trace of either of your men, either heading toward Earth or going in the exact opposite direction." Kiachif grimaced apologetically. "I've been on to Murphy, the supercargo at Main Station, Earth. No one's come by to claim that beacon yet. I'm still hoping someone might so I can tie a can to his tail. No offense meant, Hrriss."

"None zaken, Captain. I have sent more messages to our friends on Earth," Hrriss said. "My father was there when they left to Zreaty Island. We have so little time left, but I believe they are on Earth."

"Earth's a damned big place to find two Humans, laddie," Kiachif said grimly. "I'd have more luck searching space."

The radio buzzed and Pat grabbed up the handset, her face wild with her desperate hope for good news.

"Yes, Vic? . . . They are? But where? . . . You don't know? Then how can you be sure . . . Oh, Hrrula . . . Well, yes, I do trust him as you do . . . Yes, yes, I understand. Oh, I think I do understand!" There was a glow on her worn face when she turned to the rest of the room. "Vic Solinari has had a message from Hrrula. Kelly is safe, and Nrrna." Pat reached out to grip Hrriss's arm reassuringly.

"Where did they get to, then?" Kiachif asked.

"Hrruna would only say that they are in the safest place they could possibly be. We're not to worry about them."

Hrriss threw his head up, his shoulders back, and his eyes began to gleam. "Zzoo! Zat Kelly," and his laughter was a loud purr of mixed satisfaction and surprise.

"Where are they, Hrriss?" Pat asked, giving his arm a shake as she peered up into his face.

"With the best friend we could have right now."

"I think I get what you mean, m'lad," Kiachif said, and winked.

Dalkey Petersham straightened his narrow collar before answering his comlink line's signal. Six hundred hours was an odd time for a call, but fortunately he was already up and dressed. Kelly again? She was always turning up at odd times. Dalkey switched on the unit. The screen displayed the face of a man he'd never seen before, but he certainly recognized the uniform: Poldep. Dalkey gulped. He knew he was being watched in the office now, but pretended he didn't. Partly because he really didn't want to be under observation. That only resulted in unpleasantness sooner or later. Fortunately he'd sent all he could to Kelly without breaking into the current data banks, so perhaps they'd stop watching him if he went strictly about his proper business. He still didn't know how Kelly had talked him into stripping those old files, but Kelly had a way with her. And it had been fun, delving into files, showing how cleverly he could penetrate massive files and extract just the information he needed. If only someone else would realize that Dalkey Petersham had untapped potential. But why was a Poldep inspector calling him at this hour? Spacedep had their own—and Dalkey gulped again—disciplinary branch. Then he remembered that Kelly had gone to Poldep, so this call might have more to do with Kelly Solinari than Dalkey Petersham.

"This is Sampson DeVeer," the moustachioed man said. "This is the communications number left by a young woman who has been assisting me in one of my inquiries. A Miss Green."

Kelly! Then he had lulled suspicion in his office. Relieved, Dalkey wondered if he should try to look dashing and piratical, suitable for the acquaintance of a police informant, or as harmless as possible. Harmless seemed more sensible. You lived longer if no one felt threatened by you. He let his shoulders hunch forward a little bit and tried to look clerkish. "Yes, sir?"

"I have received a request from another quarter to locate one of the subjects concerned in that investigation," DeVeer said obscurely. He waited, and Dalkey realized that he wanted Dalkey to prove he knew what the officer was talking about.

"That wouldn't be a member of the Reeve family, would it?" Dalkey asked, and DeVeer nodded. "Has that party been found?"

"Ahem, how did you know the party was missing?" DeVeer asked.

"Mrs. Reeve inquired by way of comp-line if by any chance one of her relatives had been in touch with me," Dalkey replied, thinking there was no harm in that. "She doesn't think they got as far as here."

The man sighed gently and smoothed his moustache with a fingertip. "That is a possibility which this office has been investigating. We thought you might help."

"If I should hear from either of them, I will contact you immediately." Dalkey felt that was safe to say.

"Please be sure to."

There was something ominous about that phrasing but the call was disconnected.

Hrringa didn't often leave the Hrruban Center. Hayumans should be accustomed to Hrrubans by now, but he was always conscious of stares, discreet, indirect observations. Nor could he tell if this was mere curiosity, bad manners, or outright hostility. The last seemed unlikely, judging by what he had observed of *Them*. Their lack of expression bothered him most, for he could not tell, as he could of any Hrruban countenance, what they felt: their eyes black dots in the center of oblong white orbs. Without another of his kind to keep him company, he often felt himself a hostage on Earth. Should something go very wrong with the Treaty, he might be eliminated by a tribe of these expressionless white-eyed folk, even if physically he was larger than most, and certainly stronger. That he might be faced with death on this posting had been subtly suggested to him in his original briefing. He had been chosen from the young applicants of many distinguished stripes because of his calm nature, excellent bearing, and diplomatic training.

"The Zreaty is at a crucial stage, as I am certain you are awarrre," Hrringa said to Rogitel when he was finally admitted to the Spacedep subchief's office. With Terran officials, he spoke Terran. "I have juzt been approached by an official of yrrr Poldep. He asks is it possible zat I wass given the wrrong date and hourr for the arrival of the Rrevs? I was zold to expect zem. Zey have not come. I waited all that night for zeir appearrance, and set the alarrrms so that I would be awakened zereafter by the activation of the grrid."

"Alarms?" Rogitel asked. His face remained still, but he felt agitated. He had been waiting for a report from the men he had hired to wait for the Reeves outside Alreldep block, and was concerned at the delay. This was a snag he had not anticipated, that the Reeves had failed to appear inside the Hrruban Center.

The Hrruban's tail lashed once in dismay. "Yes, motion alarrms. I do not usually set zem because no otherrs of my species are perrmitted on Arrth, and the only Hayuman outpost with a grid is Rrala, so I do not see much trraffic. There is no need to arrise in the off-shifts to rrceive a nonsentient shipment, the most frrquent use of the grrid."

"True." Rogitel wasted few words, especially ones that might be misconstrued.

"The alarrms are very sensizive. Nothing set zem off, not yesterday, and not zoday. I tessted zem mysself just beforre I came to be certain that they were in worrking orrder and zey are. Zo I must ask you, onorred sir, has something happened to delay the Rrevs? Surely if they were summoned by the court, zey would have come? Zey are known to be honorrrable men. Am I in error?"

"You are not," the commander said. "The Amalgamated Worlds court was waiting for them." Rogitel stood up and nodded curtly to the Hrruban. "Thank you for coming to see me, honored sir. I will look into the matter, and bring it to the attention of my superior."

Hrringa bowed and left.

Within the hour, Admiral Landreau appeared in the Hrruban Center and demanded instantaneous transport to Doona. He was upset. He had been expecting to hear in bloody detail how Rogitel's hired toughs disposed of the Reeves and found out that the damned nuisances had not even reached Earth! Rogitel was in trouble, for not verifying that the prisoners had not been taken into custody by his hirelings and disposed of as arranged. There was only the one fast way back to Earth—by the Hrruban Center's grid. Had someone tipped off the Reeves as to the reception awaiting them?

Landreau had thoroughly enjoyed listening to the furor among the Doonan colonists, caused by the midnight summons of the Reeves to appear before the Amalgamated Worlds panel. What had happened? Rogitel had seen them safely to the Treaty Island grid. They had been transferred by that abominable mechanism, but the men waiting outside the Hrruban Center swore blind that neither Reeve had left the block. None of the corner monitors at each angle of the building recorded anyone passing, in either direction. Could the rumormongers on Doona be correct? The cowards had done a flit? Unless, and Landreau considered this possibility, they had been in cahoots with the grid operator on Doona and got themselves transported to some village where they were no doubt lying low until after the Treaty was ratified.

Landreau swore under his breath. Damned cats couldn't be trusted to do even the simplest things: like key in a proper grid destination. The wretched felines had been a thorn in his side all along. If those Reeves were hidden somewhere on Doona, he'd find them if it was the last thing that he ever did in his life.

He continued muttering to himself while Hrringa hastened to set the controls for transmission to Treaty Island. The engulfing smoke rose around him and blotted out the Hrruban's expressionless cat face.

Landreau grunted in relief as he recognized the Treaty Island facility and strode off the platform. Yes, that was what had happened. The bedamned grid operator had redirected the Reeves somewhere on Doona. Why hadn't Rogitel checked the settings? Or had the Treaty Controller do so? Slack discipline, that! You had to do everything yourself to see it done properly. Landreau wheeled, confronting the grid operator directly.

"What is your name?" he demanded of the astonished Hrruban. All grid operators understood Standard. Had to.

"Hrrenya," the Hrruban replied, surprised.

"Who is your superior?"

"Zreaty Controllerr," the catman answered, backing away from Landreau and blinking his eyes. "He is seniorr diplomaz on Rrala."

"You were on duty three nights back? When the Treaty Controller and Commander Rogitel brought the Reeves here? D'you know the Reeves?" The Hrruban nodded quickly. "Where did you send them?"

"To Arrth as I was inzructed, honorred sir."

"You didn't!" Landreau shouted. "You didn't! They never arrived on Earth. Where *did* you send them? Someplace right here on Doona. Isn't that right?"

Landreau's rising voice had attracted attention. Out of a nearby corridor, three of the Treaty Councillors hurried toward the grid, the Controller among them. The grid operator tried to keep his dignity, tried to remain calm, but the Hayuman's face was growing very red and, without fur to cover it, it was a terrifying sight. Grid operators were not trained in diplomatic matters, so Hrrenya was intensely relieved to see assistance near at hand.

"Admiral Landreau," the Treaty Controller snapped out in Hrruban. "Why are you berating our operator? You should report any insubordination or impudence to me."

"Where are Ken and Todd Reeve?" Landreau turned on the Controller as perhaps the genuinely guilty party in this absurd miscarriage. He stubbornly kept to his own language,

too enraged to exercise any courtesy until he had the answers
he had come to find.

"What?" the Controller demanded, as stubbornly replying
in Hrruban. "Are they not on Terra? You demanded their
presence there three days ago. I myself witnessed their departure."

"What do you mean, they're not here? Your drone there,"
and Landreau swung an arm toward the grid operator, whose
tail was between his legs in fear, "sent them somewhere here
on Doona instead of back to Earth so they could answer for
their crimes. They are my prisoners. I demand that the Reeves
be produced and sent immediately to stand trial."

"You demand?" the Hrruban snarled, the points of his teeth
exposed. Treaty Controller flew into a rage. "You have dishonored our people who live on Rrala, by using these Humans,
whom you have yourself misplaced, to commit foul crimes
against the Treaty which you pretend to support. If you cannot
find them on your planet, then that is no fault of ours. Seek
to set your own tribe in order without falsely accusing those
of another."

Landreau's momentum came to a dead halt. The Treaty Controller's anger was too genuine to have been faked. Landreau
was a fair judge of knowing truth from lie and the Treaty
Controller obviously told the truth—or what he thought was
the truth. If the Reeves had transported, why hadn't Rogitel's
men detained them? Or did that fur-faced Hrringa assist them
and send them out of the Hrruban Center a secret way? He'd
never been too happy with the secrecy shielding the Hrruban
Center from outside interference.

"Naturally you would defend your employee," Landreau
began, trying another tack. "How do you know that he was
not got at? Bribed? Those men should have been sent to Earth
to answer for their offenses. They did not arrive. They are still
on Doona!"

Treaty Controller drew himself up indignantly, looking down
with great condescension on the stocky smaller Human. "We
have more important matters to debate than the whereabouts
of two troublesome Hayumans. If the young Reeve does not
appear at his trial, he is by default guilty and so is his partner
in crime. We are constrained to continue for the next two days

to work out details which may, indeed, be irrelevant. But we are by honor bound to continue."

He swept magnificently away, though the other Councillors did not immediately follow. The small woman who had met the Admiral on his last visit, Madam Dupuis, gazed at him steadily, as if she was trying to read his mind. Did she know something of his secret plans?

"You have no jurisdiction to search Doona, Admiral," she said in a cold expressionless voice. "Go back to Earth. Where you belong." She signalled to the grid operator, repeating her order in her fluent Hrruban and waited, arms folded, to see that her order was obeyed.

Uncomfortable on many counts, Landreau had to step back on the grid and hope that the presence of Madam Dupuis meant that the grid operator would explicity follow his orders.

When Ken tried to move, his head hurt, and his wrists were pressed against the small of his back. His hands were numb. He tried to turn over and pull them apart to restore circulation, but he couldn't move. He opened his eyes to the unencouraging sight of a dull gray wall. Squirming, he tried to free his hands, but they were tied by a taut binding that allowed no slack he could use to free them. He turned his head in a quick survey. There wasn't much light, but sufficient to see Todd's limp body on a flat plank of wood similar to the one under him.

"Todd?" Ken said, trying his voice.

Todd was on a flat plank of a bed that was identical to his own. As Ken's eyes grew accustomed to the dim light, he saw the bruises on the boy's face, blood on his nose, cheeks, and chin, but old blood, dried. Torn clothes revealed bloody scratches and more discoloring bruises. But at least the blood was clotted and dried. Todd was breathing heavily through his mouth, not surprising, for his nose was probably broken. At least he was breathing. Ken remembered the two of them standing back-to-back, fighting for their lives against too numerous assailants.

When the transport mist had cleared after their departure from Treaty Island, Ken had been struck across the back with something hard, like a bar. The force of the blow had dropped him to his knees. Gasping with pain and surprise, Ken struggled to his feet to defend himself against the attacking Hrrubans. Demanding that they identify themselves and repeating his own name brought no answer save for grunts at the punches he landed wherever he could. Ken Reeve had wrestled a few steers in his day and, bigger though the Hrrubans were, they only had two legs. With a well-aimed kick, he forced one attacker to his knees, kicking the sheath knife out of his hand and ducking the claws that swiped at him as the Hrruban sprang up.

Then the prehensile tail wrapped around Ken's waist like a snake. Their caudal appendages weren't really very strong. They were made for holding, not subduing. Ken jerked an elbow down hard over the joint between two of the small bones under the fur. The Hrruban let out a wail of pain and whipped his tail out of reach. But then someone jumped Ken from behind, trying to throttle him. He kicked out at another who leaped at him in a frontal attack, catching him in the throat, snapping the fringed jaw shut, and knocking him unconscious.

Another Hrruban merely lifted both Ken's legs off the ground while the one behind him forced his hands together. Ken knew from sounds beyond him that Todd had been acquitting himself well against such overwhelming numbers of assailants. As Ken waited bravely for his neck to be broken, he felt only that his hands and legs were being tied tightly. So they weren't trying to kill him, just capture him. He looked toward Todd, struggling in the hands of three Hrrubans. One thing was certain with so many Hrrubans around: they were not on Earth. Had they been diverted to Hrruba?

Though Todd had the height and heft of his attackers, he couldn't quite fight free. Years of riding and hard work had given him the strength of a mule, and the Hrrubans couldn't pull him down. While Todd was still on his feet, Ken had hope, and filling his lungs, he started to yell at the top of his voice in Hrruban.

"Help! Someone! Help us! We are being denied honorable treatment!"

Todd added his voice, shouting in High Hrruban for the Speakers. Whether or not they were on Hrruba, such a cry should raise an alarm nearby. Their yelling upset their assailants. The one behind Ken began to clout him across the mouth to silence him. Ken writhed, trying to evade the blows with his bound arms. Suddenly he heard Todd's shouts end abruptly. Then a pair of fists caught him on the point of his chin, and that was the end of his fight.

Now Ken squirmed and rolled until he got himself into a sitting position. The sound of a throat being cleared told him that the two of them were not alone in their small, gray prison. Ken glanced over to the far corner of the room. Two Hrrubans in the harness of official guards sat in chairs beyond the end of the small chamber, closed off to the corridor by a wall of bars. Ken peered at them. They were both of a very narrow Stripe. They looked unmarked, so they were unlikely to be part of the gang that had attacked them. The narrow Stripes wore only bare harnesses, giving Ken no idea of where they were and which faction had captured them. However, he could rule out Earth because of the presence of so many Hrrubans, though the corridors beyond the chamber reminded him of Earth. They could have been taken to any one of several dozen Hrruban-settled worlds.

"Todd? Wake up, son!" Ken whispered. He eased himself slowly along the bench until he was sitting opposite Todd's head. Neither of the guards moved, either to help him or to make him lie down again. Trussed up as he was, guards were no more than a formality. His movement had been noticed and the Hrrubans muttered between them in Low Hrruban.

Todd stirred, and his eyes opened. Ken noticed that his chin was dark with stubble. They had been unconscious a long time, perhaps even a day. Todd started to sit up, and winced at the pain of his bruised muscles. "Where are we, Dad?"

"I don't know, Todd," Ken said. He caught Todd's eye and then looked significantly toward the barred wall. "But it sure isn't Earth."

Todd turned his head and opened his mouth but Ken intervened.

"No, son, don't. Don't speak Hrruban. Just before you woke up, one of them said to the other, 'They're a lot more docile than Third said they'd be.'"

"Oh?" Todd raised his eyebrows at that indiscretion.

"This pair obviously don't know we understand their language." Ken smiled grimly. "If we keep listening, we may hear something even more valuable. Here, move toward me and I'll see if I can't undo your bindings. Hey, untie us, would you?" he asked the guards loudly in Terran. The two Hrrubans stared at Ken without saying a word and then went back to their own conversation.

"I don't think they understand Terran," Ken said with satisfaction.

"So does Third plan to kill us?" Todd asked with commendable detachment.

"I think not or they'd have done so during the fight on the grid," Ken said grimly. "No, they want us alive and I'd give anything to know why."

"So I can't appear at that trial and Hrriss and I are judged guilty by my default?" Todd suggested.

"Could be, son, since it was Third Speaker who made your innocence a sticking point for Treaty Renewal."

Both kept working surreptitiously to release their hands. If the guards thought them docile, so much the better for the success of their efforts to free themselves.

Plainly bored by a long stretch, the two guards leaned together and began to speak. They didn't bother to lower their voices, believing that their bareskin prisoners did not understand Hrruban. Their conversation was less than complimentary about the cravens they had no real need to guard. When one said that the bareskins would be easy to subdue, after all, Ken and Todd redoubled their efforts to free themselves.

Todd got his hands loose first. He stifled an inadvertent gasp as blood rushed to his fingers, causing excruciating pain. As soon as they worked again, he moved closer to his father and unbound him. They'd have to be very careful getting their legs free. Perhaps if they pretended to sleep . . . It was when Todd shifted cautiously onto one side that he realized what had been taken from him.

"Dad! They've taken it."

"What?"

"All the documents we were going to show the panel, to prove me innocent, to prove Landreau's conspiracy."

Ken's groan was genuine. In Third Speaker's possession, those documents were pure gelignite! He closed his eyes, knowing total defeat of all he'd strived to build, all he hoped for the future of the Doona/Rrala Experiment. He couldn't look at Todd, but the boy's soft anguished moan told him that Todd understood the scope of the disaster.

CHAPTER

12

ON THE DAIS OF THE ASSEMBLY HALL, ELDERS FROM all ten villages of Doona waited for the huge crowd of colonists to come to order. The transportation grid on the Hrruban side of the Friendship Bridge had been busy all day, bringing in anyone and everyone from all over the planet who wanted to help organize the celebration for Treaty Renewal Day. Carts and flitters full of food and decorations lined the paths outside and spilled over into the garden. Children caught the mood of excitement from their parents, who whispered among themselves about the upcoming great event.

"Please!" Hrrestan shouted over the din. "We have much to do before tomorrow. May we have your attention, please?"

"I'm glad I lived to see this day," said Hu Shih, smiling through his spectacles at his friends, both Human and Hrruban. "The celebration tomorrow will be both a tribute to all the hard work we have put in and an acknowledgment of the cooperation between our races."

"If there is any celebration to look forward to," Anne Boncyk said sourly, from just in front of the dais. She had been passing on the whispers she heard to anyone who'd listen that Ken Reeve and his son Todd had disappeared rather than appear in court to defend allegations against them. "They're probably headed for one of the outer worlds where they have all that money hidden away," she confided out loud to Randall McKee.

But she picked the wrong target for such a statement.

"You know better than that, Anne," Randall replied, rising to the defense of both Reeves.

"Yes, indeed," and Vic Solinari joined McKee, facing down

the woman's gossip. "There'll be a bloody damned good explanation for their disappearance, just you wait and see."

"I'll wait but I don't think I'll see," she replied tauntingly. "Those Reeves never could run things right."

"Confound it, Anne Boncyk," and now Ben Adjei confronted the small woman, "if you mean how they run the Snake Hunt, I've told you three times for every pig you own, Anne, if you'd have chosen a different homestead than the one you did, the snakes wouldn't come anywhere near your spread."

"They're supposed to make sure all livestock is safe all along the way," Anne retorted, getting angrier.

"Those reptiles have been sliding up and back between the dunes and the marshes along that stretch since before your acres had even surfaced out of the sea. I showed you a dozen better sites when you came here. You'd be better off if you moved."

"I might not have a choice, thanks to those Perfect Twins you all think so much of." Anne sniffed, turning away from the burly veterinarian and looking around to make sure Hrriss was not within earshot. "What I've heard is, if they're judged guilty, then the Treaty won't be renewed. All along, you thought they were such saints, and look what they're doing to us!"

"Todd and Hrriss are innocent," Vic Solinari said. "Most of the charges against them have been proved bogus. You know that as well as anyone else here, Anne Boncyk, so stop acting the maggot."

"If they're so innocent, why isn't Todd here to stand beside Hrriss and prove it? Because if they don't, we're off Doona! The Hrrubans will confiscate our homes, our stock, everything we've worked for."

"Hrrubans do not intend to confiscate Hayuman homes," said Hrrula, stepping through the crowd around them. "I, Hrrula, know that Zodd Rrev is innocent."

"Well, we're not sure of that," a Human woman cried out.

"Yet your system of justice, like ours, clearly states that one is innocent until proved guilty. If, after knowing how hard both Todd and Hrriss have worked to make this colony succeed, you think they are guilty, then this great Experiment is already over."

There was a moment's stunned silence as Hrrula's words condemned many for their lack of faith. Hrriss, standing well back in the crowd, lowered his head in shame. He had endured much calumny and heard his dearest friend slandered. Nothing he had said, or proved with the precious documents they had worked so hard to gather, would change the minds of many of these distressed folk, Hrruban and Hayuman, when they realized that all their hard work could be swept away at any moment by the dissolution of the Treaty and the Doona/Rrala Experiment.

"No, the Experiment has not failed," cried Hu Shih, struggling to the dais. "Not if we, Hayuman and Hrruban alike, present a unified front. We must be of one mind now, more than ever, putting aside petty questions of innocence or guilt. The Colonial Department and the Speakers will have to realize that we, Hayumans and Hrrubans, are sincere and dedicated to the principles of the Decision at Doona and the Cohabitation Treaty."

"Well said, well said!" Clapping his hands above his head in Hayuman fashion, Hrrestan jumped to the dais to stand beside the slender little Hu Shih. "This colony is a state of mind as well as a place for both species to live and prosper. It was founded on hope. Let us keep that hope alive. Now! Let us hope that our faith in those young men is vindicated as I know it will be!" And to the surprise of everyone listening, Hrrestan threw his head back and uttered an ancient Hrruban challenge.

It had barely died away when others repeated the challenge, Hrrubans with their uncanny howl and Hayumans with wild ululating cheers.

"Okay, folks," and Vic Solinari leaped to the dais. "No one's called off the ceremonies so let's make sure they start on time. Senior dignitaries from Earth and Hrruba are due in shortly. Let's show them as united a front as we did twenty-five years ago. They didn't believe us then, and we made them. Let's revive that spirit and show 'em now, today! We're here to stay, Hrrubans and Hayumans, equal and together." He waited through long seconds of renewed cheers and then held up his hands for silence. "We got a lot of work to do now, everybody, so let's hop to it. First Village has sent rails of brrnas for roasting, Wayne Boncyk's given us four of his boars to roast. Norris has donated a hundredweight of those special sausages he makes, Phyllis here has ssliss eggs by the cartload, and I dunno how many women have been baking. Let's get organized, folks!"

He sprang down from the dais, genially pushing one group one way, another toward the doors, gesturing at the fire pits that were already glowing.

"We have the crop of our berry harvest to offer," called out Hrrmova of the Third Hrruban Village. "A bounty of blackberries and drroilanas."

"The Launch Bar will donate beer, mlada, and wine," the owner called. "If any spacers come wanting a drink, they'll have to find me here. I don't want to miss a minute of the celebration."

"That's the spirit," Vic Solinari cheered him. "Hrrestan, where should I put my two hundred kilos of good aged urfa cheese?"

"We shall find a place, my friend," the Hrruban said, "for I know that many Hrrubans are particularly fond of that commodity."

"And the hunters of First Village," Hu Shih said, "have made a record catch of the hatchlings. Snake stew must be on the menu."

"We're doing all this for nothing!" Martinson of the Launch Center shouted, pushing through a crowd which had recovered its hope. "We'll all be off this planet before that food can be cooked, much less served."

But his warning elicited more jeers than agreement.

"You may leave now, if that is how you feel, Martinson," Hrrestan replied, letting his eyes slit as he looked at the portmaster. He didn't show the irritation he felt at this attempt to puncture the delicate mood of optimism that was beginning to build. "Go if you do not share our hopes. We will not miss you." And resolutely he turned away.

Martinson stared after him, looked around the room, but others had turned away, too. He stamped out of the Hall, cursing fools and fatheads and men who wouldn't face reality.

Soon even the most pessimistic caught the growing spirit of hope and resolve. There was a lot to be done, however the events of the next day turned out. After all, twenty-five years ago, there had been less hope for those who remembered that fateful day. Was it wrong to expect a second miracle?

Hrrestan hoped that he sounded more convinced than he felt. If some worked only because it was something to do, that was better than doing nothing. And so the preparations for the feast began, Hrrubans and Hayumans working side by side.

The next day dawned, for better or for worse. Pat forced herself out of bed and set about kneading bread dough which had risen during the night. She put the loaf pans on the sun porch to rise again. Deftly she put fancy touches on each, spread glazes on some and sprinkled seed on others. For someone who had never baked a loaf of bread before she came to Doona, over time Pat had mastered the skill until she had pride in it. If she worked, she didn't think about how frightened she was. Once again she was alone on Doona without Ken: she hadn't liked it the first time it had happened twenty-five years ago and she didn't like it now. He should be here with her. Where was he? Where was Todd? And where were Kelly and Nrrna? Safe, they said, but where *was* safe these days? Kelly had given her so much support, ever since Todd had woken up to what everyone else had seen—that he and Kelly were so well suited to each other. The bread made, she had only to wait until it was ready to bake. Only to wait? That was the hardest part of all. Wait for what?

The handle of the front door rattled, and Pat flew to answer it. On the doorstep was her daughter Ilsa, and her two small daughters.

"Oh, sweetheart," Pat gasped. "I'd almost forgotten you were coming."

Ilsa put down her bags and threw her arms around her mother.

"Happy Treaty Renewal Day, Mom," she said happily, embracing Pat, and then stood back at her expression. "If it is. What's wrong?"

Pat bent to cuddle her two small granddaughters, four and seven they were now.

"How would you two like to help me make bread?" she asked, diverting them as well as herself. "Wash your hands now," and when they had, she showed them how to shape spare scraps of dough into little loaves and left them to it.

With them happily occupied, she explained to Ilsa what had been happening since their last contact.

Ilsa listened quietly and thoughtfully to the most recent troubles. Knowing her brother's sense of honor, Ilsa had expected Todd to have cleared up all that nonsense about smuggling and stealing and things. She kept to herself her anxiety when she learned of the disappearance of both her father and brother.

"Why didn't you comp-line me, Mother? If Dad and Todd are on Earth, we could have gone to Poldep to instigate a search for them."

"I didn't want to worry you, dear," Pat replied, knowing that she hadn't considered her gentle daughter could be much help in such circumstances. "Every minute I expect them back, to walk in that door and explain where they've been. And there's no time left now. Nothing they could do even if they do make it back today."

"Now, now, Mother, I'll just make us a nice cup of tea and think what to do."

When the baking was done, the two women put the still-steaming loaves and buns in the flitter and went to the Assembly Hall kitchen. The room was uncomfortably silent. The previous day's ebullience had dissipated when dawn brought no sign of the missing Reeves. Preparations for the feast were proceeding, but the mood was of people performing chores by rote or by sheer and dogged obstinacy, with none of the laughter and joking and excitement that should infect such a task on a day of such historic importance.

Those who would cling to their hope and faith until the bitter end of all expectation tried to resist the spread of despair. Some of the faces were stunned and incredulous, others resentful. A few doomsayers murmured to any who would listen that there was no way to avoid or escape the inexorable end of this sad day.

Hrrula, Hrrestan, Mrrva, the Solinaris, and the Shihs moved constantly about the work parties, encouraging, complimenting, urging people to greater efforts. The preparations continued in spite of the general depression. It looked like it would be a magnificent feast, in the very best tradition of Doona. Even if it did turn out to be the last one, the condemned would eat heartily.

"You always present food so beautifully, Miranda," Pat told one of the young women who had just been carving Doona blossoms out of root vegetables. Smiling, the girl glanced up at the compliment and her smile turned to a sneer as she swiftly moved away.

Pat felt as if she had been slapped. She glanced up and met the eyes of one of the Hrruban males who were helping trim roasts, and he too turned his head, without changing expression. Pat cast wildly about for Ilsa and found she'd watched the whole thing. The young woman's eyes were full of shocked hurt. Pat was embarrassed that her daughter had to be witness to her mother's humiliation. It was so obvious that people unconsciously blamed Todd, and Ken, for their predicament.

"Pat, I'd appreciate your help outside," Dr. Kate Moody said, wrapping an arm around her shoulders and escorting her firmly to the door. Once they were hidden behind a cultivated hedge which separated the rear of the kitchen from plain view, Pat let go and sobbed bitterly on Kate's shoulder.

"You've been a model of fortitude, Pat, don't spoil it now," the colony pediatrician murmured to her, patting her on the back. "This isn't a personal rejection of you, you know. Everyone's tense, frustrated. I don't have a notion what happened to Ken or Todd but I'm damned sure they'd be here if they could! And I keep hoping any minute now they'll come striding over that bridge and set everything straight. Mind you, they may be cutting their timing a bit close, but they'll come."

"If I could believe that . . ." Pat wiped her eyes with the doctor's handkerchief and let out a sigh. She wanted that very scene to take place, and soon. She looked over at the bridge, hoping against hope that Ken and Todd would materialize from the grid. "I can't blame people, Kate. If . . . We'll all lose our homes and everything we've worked for and we really don't belong anywhere now but Doona. And why is it that both Todd and Hrriss have to be at the hearing? Hrriss has almost all the evidence. Why, that Mayday beacon being found on Earth, and Dr. Tylanio proving the log tape was doctored beyond recognition. That proves that the boys didn't steal those things because they weren't even near those planets, just as they've always said." Pat had to stop to blow her nose. "And if Hrriss is innocent, then Todd is, too. Or that's what Hrruvula assured me. And that's how he's going to present the documentation we have!"

Kate smiled at her. "Well, you're a lot more generous with the fools than I'd be. Come on back inside. There's a lot left to be done, and we need you. I know they've got almost all the evidence, but they may hang us all on the specific wording of the Speakers' resolution. Both boys and all charges dismissed. No one could ever keep either Ken or Todd down for long. And you know it." Kate lifted Pat's chin and smiled at her. "So hold your head up and shame the devil."

Pat managed a weak laugh. "My grandmother used to say that. If I just knew that they were both . . . okay . . ." She couldn't bring herself to use any other word. "I feel so lost without them."

"Well, you're not lost, and you're not alone. You have all of us. Let's see if I can remind these doubting fainthearts of that."

Kate pushed through the door and escorted Pat back to the cake-decorating station. With a firm hand, she sat her down on a stool and put tools in front of her. To the others who glanced at them in surprise, the pediatrician stated in a loud voice:

"Now let's get something straight, you gaggle of gossiping grannies. No, you're acting like pre-teens, and I've the right to kick sense into that age group. You know where to lay the blame for all the anxiety we're experiencing, and it isn't on Pat Reeve's shoulders. It's because her husband and her son haven't turned up. Do you know them so little after twenty-five years that you'd honestly believe they'd leave us in a lurch?

"Well, I don't, and there're plenty of others who agree with me. Someone, or some group of ones, made sure Ken and Todd never made it to Earth. 'Cause there's no way they'd go unnoticed there! Not those big-striding, proud-walking men. Can you imagine them mincy-mincing," and she mimicked the short polite stride of the Terran natives, drawing a giggle from some quarters, "along Corridors and Aisles without being noticed? We know they're not on Doona because where we

Hayumans haven't looked, we Hrrubans have! And any of us silly enough to believe that there aren't some Hayumans and Hrrubans who'd both prefer never to set eyes on the Reeves again better take the next shuttle out of here."

"We'll have to anyhow, won't we, if the Reeves don't show up?" a woman murmured.

"Well, I got hopes on that score, too. We've got Hrruvula, no narrow-stripe mince-stepped poseur either, to present the documentation that has been assembled. And if Hrriss can be proved innocent, then ipso facto, Todd Reeve is. And that ought to be good enough for everyone here and good enough to sway the Councillors. *And*, I don't want to hear another sour word from anyone." She clapped her hands vigorously. "We got a lot to do. Let's do it. And with a few smiles to make the work go quicker."

Few could argue with her facts or the good sense for which Kate Moody had always been noted. Flagging hopes revived again and soon a few smiles appeared on faces. Several people deliberately came up to Pat, giving her affectionate squeezes on her forearm or apologizing for their unkindness. Instead of seeking for something or someone new to blame, long glances passed between friends who were fearful that they would never see one another again. Work resumed at a more energetic pace with the renewed sense of solidarity.

Old Abe Dautrish, carefully decanting wines of his own recipes from herbs and local berries, spoke in reminiscence. "Remember that first winter? Ten months of misery. Living in one miserable plastic hut until we could get the others up. Remember what that was like? Who'd believe we could come so far?"

"And together," said Lee Lawrence, smacking Hrrula on the back.

"All was bezzer when we became frriends," a Hrruban woman said, with dropped jaw.

"We'll fight this," Phyllis Shih stated, whipping a bowlful of eggs with a vengeance. "They can't throw us out of here. This is our home. We'll take the appeal to the Amalgamated Worlds court ourselves if we need to."

"That's the old Doona spirit," Kate Moody said with satisfaction. She winked at Pat.

All the preparations were complete by midafternoon. The First Village's hunters, following Hrriss, returned with dozens of young snakes and a few wild fowl for the stewpot. Carcasses of dozens of urfas, pigs, and cows rotated over coals in the many roasting pits downwind of the kitchen.

The transportation grid was brought over the bridge from the Hrruban side and laid in front of the Assembly Hall's big double doors. Its posts had been draped with floral streamers. Not long thereafter, diplomats of both races began to appear and were escorted into the Hall with much attendant dignity.

The weather was cheerful and bright. Doona's long winter would arrive within two months, but there was no early chill which the organizers feared might mar the celebration. Some colonists from warmer climates shivered a little in the autumnal air. Every settlement, including Treaty Island, had lobbied to hold the celebration, but the honor was eventually returned to First Village, where the original accord had been signed twenty-five years before.

Depressing any misgivings, the population of the planet turned out in its best. All the Hrrubans wore the formal red robes: the males in heavy, opaque garments that fell to the tips of shiny black boots; the females in filmier garments of jewel-spangled gauze. The Humans wore monochromatic tunics with touches of white, and beautifully cut but simple ankle-length gowns. There was none of the cheerful cross-cultural dressing that was usually prevalent at most other big events. Today's garments unexpectedly became a restatement of racial identity.

Hrriss stood tall beside his father just below the dais inside the Hall, hiding his emotions. In a few moments, he must present evidence to prove his and Todd's innocence of the crimes of which they were accused. On the basis of that proof or lack of it, the Treaty Controller might refuse to ratify the Treaty, and the colony would be dissolved.

What Hrriss had not been able to tell anyone was that the carefully gathered documentation had vanished from the Rrev home at about the same time Kelly had. He had worked night and day to duplicate the evidence from the files still remaining in his home. Dr. Tylanio had supplied him with a copy of his report on the tape's alteration. He had the latter half of the

Spacedep slush fund dispersals which Dalkey had procured but not the more important entries. Tylanio had gone off with Kiachif and so the expert was not available to present direct testimony to the Councillors. To be sure, the Mayday beacon had been discovered but the Speakers' resolution required a total clearance of all charges—and Zodd's presence! Would Hrruvula be able to make what they did have sufficient to clear all those charges even in the face of Zodd's nonappearance?

One by one, the high-ranking officials of Earth emerged from the grid, some looking puzzled and taken aback by the process of transportation which they were experiencing for the first time. Most of them, nervous about suddenly being bereft of walls and ceilings around them, walked as quickly into the Hall as dignity permitted, without so much as a quick glance around at the beauties of the village green.

The settlers clustered in and around the building, their bows and smiles becoming more and more mechanical as time went on. Sampson DeVeer of Poldep, wearing the dress uniform of black with silver touches, emerged from the chest-high fog, accompanied by a slim, pale man wearing a plain uniform.

"My heart isn't in this," Lee Lawrence muttered, feeling the strain of smiling when he hadn't any reason to do so.

"I am still determined to put the best face on the day," Hu Shih said. Then he arranged his most benevolent smile on his face as he stepped forward to introduce the newly arrived Treaty Island Archivist to the other village elders.

"Perhaps the Treaty Council will still take what is best for Doona into account," Abe Dautrish said quietly to Lee. "They shouldn't pay too much attention to overworld councils, since we are supposed to be independent of both governments. We have proved ourselves capable and worthy of self-governance."

"After all the accusations of the last few days, can you genuinely say that?" Lawrence asked.

"I want to," the old man said humbly. "I keep it closely in mind. Ah, here is Admiral Sumitral and his daughter."

"Good day, my friends," Sumitral said, mounting the ramp with quick strides and taking Hu Shih's hand. Age had done nothing to bow his proud carriage, but he bore the same heavy expression of concern that troubled the Doonan elders. He was still the greatest friend Doona had in the Terran government. "You know my daughter, Emma?" The tall girl smiled and nodded to each of them, then took her place among the colonists in the audience.

"Hrrestan, it is good to see you," Sumitral said, turning to the younger Hrruban. "Hrriss, have you had any word from Todd?"

"No, sirr," Hrriss said.

"It looks very bad that they haven't returned yet," Sumitral said. "Where could they have gone? And why? The Amalgamated Worlds court was well disposed to give them a fair hearing on the basis of their achievements."

Hrriss burned with shame. "They would come if they could," he insisted.

Sumitral eyed him curiously. "Do you know where they went?"

"No. But they would have returned if they could. Of that I am certain. They are held somewhere against their will." He placed his hand on his heart, his upper lip, and his forehead to emphasize his stated belief.

"I fear you may be right. Neither has ever betrayed an ounce of cowardice. Defection does not fit their characters," Sumitral declared. "You have searched Rrala?" Hrriss nodded. "I alerted all Alreldep offices. Can none of you Hrrubans search your own planet? They have to be somewhere."

"If they are alive," Hrriss murmured, for he had denied that possibility as long as he could.

Then he saw the slender frame of Admiral Sumitral stiffen. A hand touched his arm in apology and Sumitral moved toward Hu Shih.

"Come, Hu," the Admiral said as he urged the man toward the platform where a small, thin, clean-shaven Terran in a white tunic descended from the grid. "May I introduce you to the representative of the Amalgamated Worlds Congress? Hrrestan, I am pleased to make you known to Dorem Naruti, of the AWC." He continued to make introductions among the village elders.

At a signal from the Hrruban grid operator, Sumitral took his place beside the other Terran delegates. Third Speaker appeared from the mist surrounding the transport grid and, looking neither left nor right at those who bowed courteously to him, marched majestically into the Hall. The glow of triumph in his eyes was absolutely indecent. Many Rralans, seeing that look, growled quietly under their breath at his lack of restraint and the implications for them.

The rumors of dissolution spread from Rralans to Hayuman friends and neighbors. Hrriss fielded glares and blatant animosity from longtime acquaintances. Who was holding the Rrevs captive? No, which of the known antagonists to the Treaty had succeeded in denying the Rrevs the dignity of facing their enemies and confounding them?

As if in answer to his thoughts, Admiral Landreau in gleaming dress whites and an almost garish display of medals materialized on the grid. A moment earlier and he might have tread on Third's tail. The Admiral was accompanied by Rogitel and two other aides. Landreau had arranged his features in an expression of pious serenity which would fool no one on Rrala, certainly not Hrriss. His demeanor added more discouragement to Hrriss's depressed morale. Why didn't Zodd appear, through the grid or out of the underbrush, with his document case in his hands, to wipe the smugness from the faces of Third and Landreau?

At last, Second Speaker Hrrto made his way from the grid through the hanging garlands of flowers to the platform. With his arrival, the complement of delegates from both sides was complete. Only the Treaty Council was yet to arrive before the ceremony would begin.

As the assembly of settlers held its collective breath, the Council appeared, clustered together on the grid behind the Treaty Controller, magnificent in flowing red robes. On his breast hung a medallion of two intertwined gold suns, studded with sapphires mined and cut from native crystals. It represented the interweaving on Doona of Human and Hrruban cultures. The light reflected from the jewel vanished abruptly as soon as the Treaty Controller stepped inside the Assembly Hall. Immediately behind the Council came two clerks, one Human and one Hrruban, each of whom carried a large leather-bound and gem-studded book.

Solemnly the Council ascended to the dais. Each member bowed to the assembled dignitaries. The Treaty Controller was the last to do so. He made an especially deep obeisance to Third Speaker, who returned a curt nod. The clerks moved silently to lay the huge books side by side on the table in the center of the stage. Without further hesitation, the Treaty Controller held up one hand.

"Hrriss, son of Hrrestan and Mrrva, stand forth! Zodd Rrev, son of Ken and Patrricia, stand forth!" he intoned. The purrs and growls of High Hrruban had never sounded so severe.

Hrriss stepped forward, holding his spine straight, and willing his tail to refrain from twitching with his inner turmoil. Hrruvula, clad in his official professional garments, joined Hrriss.

"Sir, Zodd Rrev has been unavoidably detained," Hrriss said. "I speak for us both."

The Treaty Controller's tail twitched once from side to side behind him. "Both of the accused must face this Council. Have you, perhaps, a document of the ill-health of your codefendant?" At that moment, Hrriss was very certain who had detained Zodd and his father. His heart sank but he raised his chin just enough to show that he knew the sordid game the Controller was playing out. "Be that as it may, you and your absent accomplice stand accused of crimes which violate the laws of the Hrruban League, the laws of the Amalgamated Worlds, and the Treaty of Doona. These are serious crimes, which shake the very fabric of trust which made the Treaty possible twenty-five years ago. What proof can you present to attest to your innocence?"

"There is documentation," Hrruvula said, stepping forward and pulling one flimsy after another from his case, "to prove that the Mayday beacon was heard by Zodd Rrev and Hrriss, son of Hrrestan, said beacon being found among cargo shipped to Earth and designated to be delivered to a minor office connected with Space Department. And here is a declaration from a noted laser expert stating that the log tapes of the *Albatross* had been skillfully tampered with to show landings and launchings never made by the *Albatross*, as further testified to the signatories of the documents that the condition of its engines, rocket tubes, and other equipment showed no sign of the abuse such a hegira would have done to said equipment. I have these documents stating the health and energy of both defendants, who would have suffered even more physical deterioration than engines, rocket tubes, and other equipment from a medical condition known as journey lag, which is known to affect unwary travellers making as many different landings and launchings as the defendants are alleged to have done." Hrruvula paused for breath. "Also available are documents," and the attorney spread the Spacedep slush fund flimsies, "that prove that deposits ostentively made into an account purported to have been initiated by a Terran of Zodd Rrev's general description in fact tally with sums and deposits from a slush fund. There is a signed and attested declaration by an ex-criminal known as Askell Klonski . . ."

"You overwhelm us," said the Treaty Controller with broad sarcasm.

Hrruvula bowed. "Even as my clients were overwhelmed with evidence which we have conclusively proved to be a massive conspiracy to discredit Zodd Rrev, Hrriss, and in their names the integrity of the entire population of this lovely planet." Hrruvula took another breath. "With such overwhelming evidence to sustain my clients' plea of innocence, these charges must, in all conscience, be dismissed and their reputations and honors returned to them." He bowed low in deep respect toward the other members of the Council, but noticeably not in the Controller's direction.

Behind Hrruvula, an entire planet's population held its breath.

Third Speaker's eyes narrowed and glittered. He stepped forward. "You have defended your clients well, Hrruvula," and the attorney executed another courteous bow. "But it was clearly stated, and so resolved by the Council of Speakers, that both young men must be present to clear their names. One is clearly not present. The reason for his absence is immaterial. The conditions of that resolution have not been met. Therefore the Council of Speakers must withhold ratification of a permanent Treaty of Rrala."

There was a silence that nothing in the Hall disturbed. Third Speaker, his manner patronizing and smug, turned to Second Speaker Hrrto. Second Speaker seemed to rise with great difficulty, his shoulders slumped beneath the weight of his robes.

"It was so resolved and must be maintained." He sat down

heavily, head bent, arms limp at his sides.

"No!" a woman wailed from the depths of the crowd. "No. That's not fair. Not fair at all! They were innocent."

"You can't use that as an out, Third Speaker!" a Hrruban called.

Dorem Naruti of the Amalgamated Worlds Congress rose then, holding up his arms for silence. "It was resolved. In honor we must abide. Our Congress is constrained to comply with that resolution, much as it pains me to do so. The Congress cannot sanction the colony any longer. We would be glad and proud to trade with the Hrruban League under a new treaty, but the Decision at Doona must be considered annulled. The Cohabitation Principle is herewith invoked."

Protests were yelled from all directions then until Dorem Naruti, not wishing to be a target for anyone's frustration, took refuge behind Third Speaker.

Landreau was all but jumping up and down in jubilation. He, Rogitel, and their assistants kept calling for silence, for order, for good manners. But it was Admiral Sumitral whose amazing voice was heard above the babel and restored order.

"Dear friends, Hrruban and Hayuman, we are all persons of honorable intent. Having entered into an honorable agreement, we must indeed recognize the commitment we undertook twenty-five years ago, and abide by this very, very painful conclusion to what has been an experiment of cohabitation of . . ." He paused, craning his neck to see through the open doors of the Hall. His attentiveness, the surprise that began to wreathe his features with new hope, caused everyone to turn to discover what he saw.

The grid was misted, indicating a transportation, and as it cleared, three figures became visible: a bent figure in ornate red robes supported on either side by two others, one tall, straight, and proud, one slender, delicate, and equally proud. The central personage could only be First Speaker Hrruna! His companions, dressed in diaphanous red gauze spangled with gems, were Nrrna and Kelly.

Hrriss felt joy nearly bursting his heart. The girls had reached him, after all, and with the remaining evidence that Hrriss had felt lost forever. A reverent silence settled on the green and the Hall as if noise was snuffed out like a candle flame. Everyone watched the aged Hrruban walk into the Hall and slowly toward the dais, leaning heavily on the arms of the two girls.

He looked kindly at the colonists and gave an especial smile to Hrriss, who was gawking like a cub at the First Speaker.

"This is an occasion for which I have waited long," First Speaker said in High Hrruban, mounting the ramp to touch hands with Sumitral.

"Sir," Sumitral said, replying in the same tongue, "we did not think to expect you."

"Your accent has improved so very much over the last years, Admirrrl. You no longer need your young translator," Hrruna said, dropping his jaw in a smile and glancing around at the crowd. "But I miss his presence. He has been a joy to me. Where is my young friend? Where is Zodd?"

With a surprising swiftness that belied his age, he rounded on Treaty Controller, and his tone, no longer kindly or gentle, rang with conviction. The Controller was so startled, he backed up a pace.

Hrruna's eyes narrowed to fierce slits, though his clear voice was calm and even-toned. "I believe that you know precisely where Zodd and his father, Rrev, are to be found," Hrruna said. "You are to produce them instantly, or your Stripe will be forever dishonored. If harm has come to two Hayumans of indisputable integrity and honor, you and your immediate family will be transported to the most primitive mining colony in the galaxy, and allowed only the most meager of rations."

Hrriss listened with awe. Few of the settlers could understand Hrruna's speech, but they could easily see the effect it had on the Treaty Controller. From a haughty administrator, he was reduced to snivelling like a cub, protesting that his actions had been taken in the best interests of Hrruba.

"The return of the Rrevs at this point would have made it impossible to avoid the ratification of the Treaty," the Controller babbled. "I meant no harm to them. They are unhurt. They would have been returned to Earth with everyone else of their species."

"You kidnapped my friend?" Hrriss demanded in a snarl. He felt the savage blood of his ancestors coursing through his veins and he forgot his upbringing, the position he held as a scion of a civilized race. Claws and teeth bared, he gathered himself to leap and strike, as he had leaped at the Momma Snake. Without a moment's hesitation, Hrrestan knocked his feet out from under him, and signalled to several others to drag his infuriated son away from the cowering Treaty Controller.

"Produce the Rrevs, father and son!" Hrruna commanded, his eyes ablaze with green fury. Cringing, the Treaty Controller signalled to his grid operator in the audience, who ran to the transporter. Making a few deft adjustments to the controls, the operator stepped onto the platform and vanished. In a few moments, the Hrruban reappeared, no longer alone. With him were two very large Hrruban males in guard harness, and Ken and Todd, clothes torn, faces empurpled here and there with bruises and long scratches, but alive and smiling as they recognized their destination.

"Come here, my friends," Hrruna beckoned them. His voice, soft again, nevertheless penetrated the ringing cheers that reverberated inside and outside the Hall at this much-longed-for reappearance. ——

Together Todd and his father marched smartly up the steps and into the Hall. When Todd saw who occupied the dais, he smiled in amazement and, shaking his head, continued through the parting crowd. When Hrrubans and Hayumans alike reached out to slap his back or grab his hand, Todd became aware of the deficiencies of his appearance in such a gathering. Still walking forward, he brushed at the dirt on his tunic and combed back his hair with his fingers. Ken, similarly embarrassed, straightened tunic and hair. Crying with relief, Pat ignored protocol and pushed through the crowd to embrace husband and son just as they reached the foot of the dais.

"It is good to have you back," Hrruna said, as if Todd and his father had only been off on some minor errand. With Pat between them, they climbed the ramp to the dais. The old Hrruban signalled for Hrrestan to release his son. In two leaps, Hrriss was beside his dear friend, wrapping his tail firmly around Todd's nearer thigh. "This silly cub"—Hrruna pointed to the Treaty Controller—"is not the only dishonorable one among Hrrubans to sow discord on Rrala."

"The discord was not solely Hrruban," Ken said. "And during our incarceration, our guards spoke freely, not being aware that we bareskins understood what they said."

"Whatever is pertinent to sustain the Treaty and this colony must be related so that all may hear," Hrruna said at his most austere, "although I am aware of much that has happened of late, of false accusations and tamperings and alterings that would have greatly strained my patience had they not been delivered by such charming couriers."

Todd had not failed to notice that his Kelly and Hrriss's Nrrna were Hrruna's attendants. Kelly was grinning at him with a total lack of discretion, which gladdened his heart immensely, but at least Nrrna had cast her eyes down modestly despite Hrriss's attempts to make eye contact.

Then Todd saw Hrruna's peremptory gesture to Ken. "Be so good as to explain what you overheard, Rrev."

"While it was the Treaty Controller who had our destination altered from Earth and our appointment with the AWC panel, he received his orders from another, high in the Speakers Council," Ken said. "In good plain Low Hrruban, they mentioned his name frequently: the Third Speaker for Internal Affairs." Ken looked pleasantly at Third Speaker. "We can repeat what was said in our presence . . ."

"Lies!" Third Speaker hissed. "All lies. These Hayumans mean to dishonor me."

Hrruna gestured for those on the dais to move aside so that he could confront Third face-to-face. His eyes had narrowed to implacable slits, and the hem of his heavy robes flicked with the lashing of his tail.

"I will believe the words of Rrev and Zodd even over those of my own Stripe," Hrruna said in an ominously calm tone. "Deceit is not in them. Any dishonor on your stripe has been brought there by you. You have forsaken the objectivity necessary to just administration, Third. You have sought to interfere in a matter which is outside your commission. You were also one who insisted that Rrala would stand or fall on its own merit. You have not abided by your own decree. I invite you to resign your post."

Third opened and closed his mouth a couple of times, but at last nodded curtly at Hrruna.

"Very well," Third Speaker said, his own eyes closed to vindictive slits. "I tender my resignation."

"I accept it, effective now! But we have waited long enough to discover whether Rrala may continue. In view of what you have heard in these past minutes, do the Treaty Council and the representative of the Amalgamated Worlds Congress wish to alter their decision?" Hrruna asked pleasantly, turning firmly away from the dismissed Speaker. "I surely see no bar to the continuation of this colony nor to the ratification of the Treaty Renewal so anxiously awaited by us all. What say you?"

Madam Dupuis smiled as she stepped forward, assuming the position of Controller. She bowed with great reverence to the First Speaker. "Most honored of persons," she said in perfect High Hrruban, "the Council must indeed overturn the recent verdict, and clear the defendants of all charges against them, including nonappearance."

Dorem Naruti was jittering with relief at being able to rescind the verdict he had been forced, by the previous circumstances, to announce.

"Then let us adjourn all this formal talk and harangue and let the festivities begin," said Hrruna, dropping into Middle language and leaning toward Nrrna in a paternal fashion. "The smell of roasted meat is making this old belly rumble."

Few heard that comment, for cheers had erupted as he ordered the festivities to begin. Colonists of both species were hugging each other, weeping or purring in an excess of relief after the dramatic scenes that had first dashed then restored their hopes.

Robin and Inessa were shrieking for their father and brother to come down so they could be suitably welcomed. Ilsa was trying to calm them down but she was smiling and crying at the same time, upsetting her daughters, who began to fret, too.

"We should take an official vote, you know," Sumitral said, looking out over the jigging, whirling mass of colonists.

"Oh, don't be so hidebound," Madam Dupuis told him, waving at the jubilation below them. "That's the loudest, most unanimous 'aye' I've ever witnessed."

"I'd agree to that," Dorem Naruti said, beaming from ear to ear. "I've never seen anything quite so official as this! Must be something in the air here, I think."

Sumitral chuckled. "Then we shall record that the vote was unanimous. And I'm hungry, too. Naruti, they have the most delicious little birds here, covered with a sweet spice, that simply melts in your mouth. You really must try some, mustn't he, Nesfa dear friend?"

"Indeed, and although the suggestion might seem bizarre, the snake stew they make is exceedingly tasty. We shall tell you what to sample first, Dorem, if you will accompany us."

While they were settling the voting issue, First Speaker's escorts had guided him to his place at the Treaty table set in exactly the same place it had rested twenty-five years before, under the trees that clustered just beyond the Hall. Hrruna gestured for Naruti to be seated to his right and Sumitral to his left. Both senior diplomats, with the precision of long practice, sat down at the same moment. The gemmed and tooled volumes containing the Treaty of Doona were opened before them.

"There's a lot of work, many years of negotiation in the document," Madam Dupuis said, "but it is as fair as it could be made."

"A thing of beauty, outside as well as inside, these are," Naruti said in flawlessly inflected High Hrruban. "As handsome as the ideals they represent."

Hrruna's jaw dropped in pleasure. "So they are," First Speaker agreed.

Each signed one, and the volumes were exchanged. One by one, the Treaty Councillors stood by to affix their signatures to the documents. Hrrestan placed heavy seals on the signature pages and closed the books. Bowing, he presented one to each of the principals.

Sumitral looked to Hrruna for permission to speak and it was graciously given with a nod of the dignified and graying head.

"The Treaty of Doona/Rrala is now officially extended indefinitely. May I extend the congratulations of my service to Hrrubans and Hayumans alike!" His last syllables were drowned out by wild cheering.

When the noise began to abate, Todd approached the Treaty table. Someone had found him a decent tunic to replace his torn one, and he'd been able to wash his face and comb his hair so that he looked considerably more presentable.

"May I be permitted to speak?" Todd asked in High Hrruban executing a deeply reverent bow to the First Speaker.

"Pray listen to the first Hayuman ambassador to the Hrruban people," Hrruna said, his voice carrying over excited conversations and laughter, and immediately silence prevailed again.

Sumitral, leaning across to Hrruna, chuckled. "And that was a day! About a meter tall, dressed in mda skins with a rope tail hanging behind and the dignity of a dozen judges for all he was six years old. He and Hrriss have done great service for Alreldep since then. I hope they'll continue to do so."

Todd glanced at Hrriss, who nodded, jaw dropped humorously. "As long as we can, sir."

With Hrriss beside him, Todd stood forward to address his friends and neighbors. "I feel like I got thrown from a bucking stallion into a compost heap, so I hope you'll forgive my appearance." The assembled settlers chuckled. "I've dreamed of this day since I was a small boy. I was afraid for a while that the day wouldn't come, and then I feared I wouldn't be able to be here. Now"—he grinned, throwing an arm around Hrriss's shoulders— "all we have dreamed of has happened. Doona is now a permanent reality. As long as we live, we can live here together.

"Today is not just a continuation of Doona but the start of a brand-new era for Hrrubans and Hayumans. From the trust that has been built here, both species can spread out, can make new homes on new planets together and separately." He smiled around at all the faces, bare and furred. "Honored folk, Doona has taught us all the most important lesson: that we both can make friends, firm friends, trusted friends, of each other and of other species. The Siwannese example must never be forgotten, but it mustn't stop us from keeping an open mind and extending an open hand. The generations that will be born on this planet," and with that he sent a glowing look at Kelly, "will meet others, strong in the practice of Cohabitation. So long as they remember what we have all learned here, the stars beckon. Long live Doona/Rrala!" Todd shot his fist toward the sky and Hrriss's joined it in the next second.

When other arms tired of holding fists aloft and throats turned hoarse with cheering, Hrruna turned plaintively to Sumitral. "Now do you think we can eat?"

• • •

Totally reunited and in the best of harmonious spirits, the entire population of Doona and its guests began the long-awaited feast. Platters of food poured out of the kitchen to tables inside and outside the Hall. Beer, wine, mlada, and even wild-berry juices flowed to every cup as friend toasted friend and the success of the Doona Experiment was drunk to over and over again. The members of the Doona/Rrala Ad Hoc Band rarely got time for more than a few mouthfuls of food, so much in demand was celebratory dance music.

Hrriss tried repeatedly to extract Nrrna from attendance on the First Speaker, but he couldn't get any nearer her than Todd could get to Kelly. If it hadn't been Hrruna who monopolized the attentions of their promised ladies, the two friends would have snagged them away at the very first opportunity, but Hrruna seemed to require that they serve him the various delicacies prepared by the colonists' best cooks.

"Damn it, Hrriss, I'm the one who was on short rations. Couldn't Kelly come feed me?"

"I'm doing my best, Todd," his sister Ilsa said, her knees buckling under the laden tray she was bringing them.

"Urfa steak *and* snake stew?" he said, salivating. "Sis, you know how to treat a brother."

"When he remembers to come home to eat," Ilsa tossed at him as she went away to see to the needs of her children. Todd stared after her.

"Marriage has done her good," he muttered to Hrriss, and dug into the stew. "I never thought I'd eat any of this again." Then he had to swallow without truly savoring the fine flavor, for Sampson DeVeer approached their table.

"You cut that mighty fine," DeVeer said, and then drew up the young man in the plain uniform hovering beside him. "You might like to meet my companion, Reeve. Dalkey Petersham."

"Really?" And Todd realized in one second that the man he had feared as a rival to Kelly's affection was no real competition. So he pumped the young man's hand energetically. "We owe you a lot, Dalkey, for putting out your neck for people you didn't know. Come, sit down."

"Well, I did know Kelly and I sure discovered a lot of real creative accounting. Which . . ."

"Which what?" Todd prompted, gesturing for Dalkey to fill a plate from the food on the freshly filled tray.

"Which actually lost me my job."

"You haven't really lost a job, Dalkey," Todd said, "you've just been transferred. An accountant who could uncover that Spacedep slush fund is just the sort of fellow we need to set up a system here on Doona that can't be diddled."

After Dalkey had expressed his deep appreciation of the offer and accepted with considerable alacrity, Todd turned to DeVeer.

"Which reminds me. Just before Dad and I got kidnapped, Hrriss and I got Linc Newry to admit he'd been falsifying export documents and disarming Doona's security satellites to let rustlers in and out. What's happened to him?"

"He gave himself up," DeVeer said with a note of satisfaction in his voice, "after I had a most interesting chat with a Dr. Walter Tylanio. Once he was in custody, Newry gave me more information which led me to the real rustler."

"You got Mark Aden?" Todd's eyes flashed, remembering the score he had to settle with that bastard for his vindictive use of ssersa.

"He is under arrest on Zapata Three, awaiting transport back to Earth for trial. It would seem that he kept a computer file of the layout of each ranch on Doona and the best secluded spots to secrete the livestock pens. He's the one who planted the artifacts on your ship while you were occupied by your mission on Hrretha. He did so with Spacedep credentials to pass by Hrrethan security guards. Newry was the one who switched log tapes."

"I always thought Rogitel had done it when his men were busy hauling artifacts out of the *Albie*'s panels," Todd said.

"No, I have Newry's confession." DeVeer nodded at the grim looks that Todd and Hrriss exchanged. "It couldn't have been Rogitel. He did the shopping for the artifacts with the illicit traders on Hrretha. Remember, Newry had asked you to give him your flight plans nearly two weeks before your actual departure. So he sent them to Klonski, who's rather proud of the way he handled that assignment. Took him thirty-six hours of intensive work. He shipped it back to Newry in an authorized Spacedep courier run and put it in the *Albatross* before you launched. Klonski had left gaps for your legitimate stops, triggered by signals from the beacons orbiting Doona and Hrretha. Aden is the one who made the insertions into the interdicted systems in a ship with identification codes altered to match yours."

Todd let out a long sigh. "So we're cleared of everything? Then why was the Treaty so nearly cancelled?"

"Third Speaker had also rigged that resolution so that your presence was absolutely essential to the Renewal of the Treaty."

"And Hrruna waited until he knew he had Third right where he needed him," Todd said thoughtfully. "It was close!"

DeVeer nodded. "However, you both might like to accompany . . . that is, if you can leave off eating that delicious food for a short time?" he asked them. "You rather deserve to be in on this. I've one more criminal to bring to book."

Todd and Hrriss hastily dashed their fingers into bowls set on all the tables to cleanse hands. DeVeer led them to the head table where they waited respectfully until Sumitral and Naruti concluded their conversation with Second Speaker Hrrto. When Ken and Hrrestan were beckoned by DeVeer to join them, the group advanced on Landreau and Rogitel who were seated as inconspicuously as possible for men in brilliant white uniforms. They were the only two ignoring both the food and the merrymaking going on around them.

"Well, what do you want?" Landreau asked sourly, glaring at the Reeves. "You have everything you claim you value. This abominable colony has a permanent charter, and your so-called honor is restored."

"Admiral Allen Landreau?" DeVeer said formally. "As an inspector of Poldep and in the presence of a representative of Amalgamated Worlds Congress and a senior officer of Spacedep, I arrest you on the following charges: conspiracy, fraud, misuse of public funds, attempted kidnapping, suborning of witnesses, aiding and abetting grand larceny and felony theft, aiding and abetting violation of Treaty Law, and conduct unbecoming a senior officer of the Space Department."

"Have you quite finished with this fairy tale?" Landreau snapped. "I am about to return to Earth and pressing duties there—unlike other officials who seem to have infinite time to play."

"This is scarcely a laughing matter, Landreau," Sumitral said.

"Don't attempt to instruct me," the head of Spacedep growled, his face turning red. "You're my equal, not my superior. You don't outrank me in any way. In fact, Spacedep is a larger department than Alreldep and takes precedence over yours. If we didn't exist, there would be no aliens for your department to relate to, not the Siwannese, not your tame pussycat people!"

"Sir," DeVeer said, "I must suggest that you not make any more statements until you have engaged a counsel for your defense. We have impounded your records, and I am obliged to remind you that anything you say now can and may be used in evidence against you."

"Read me—Admiral Landreau—my rights?" Landreau shouted.

Nearby Doonans turned to look. Once they identified Landreau, they continued to stare.

"How dare you even question a senior official of the government, when these damned Reeves are the real troublemakers?" He flung a contemptuous hand in Todd's direction before he planted a fingertip in the middle of the Poldep chief's black tunic and pushed. "You, a jumped-up little Aisle constable, have the unmitigated gall to interfere with Spacedep, to access Spacedep files, to snoop into my department! I have a good mind—I have—!" Landreau suddenly clutched at his chest. His eyes protruded in DeVeer's direction and then rolled up into his head as he slid to the floor.

"Get a doctor!" Todd shouted, dropping to his knees beside the man. Rogitel knelt down and bent his head to Landreau's chest.

"His heart has stopped," Rogitel said, his voice more expressionless than ever.

"He doesn't get out of it this easily," Todd said, and flattened a hand over Landreau's sternum. He hit it a short rap with the other fist and then started cardiopulmonary resuscitation.

Mike Solinari was beside them in a moment. "Dr. Moody is coming." He looked at Landreau. "I don't think anything can be done, Todd. Look at all that blood in his face. I think he had an apoplexy."

"What?" Rogitel demanded. "Can't you revive him?"

"Not from that sort of a fit," the young veterinarian said, exhibiting only a clinical detachment. "He burst a blood vessel. Embolism. Instantly fatal. People with high blood pressure are prone to it. Probably had it coming for years."

"You can say that again," said a new voice, and Ali Kiachif pushed his way to the group looking down at the Admiral's prone body. "No one had it coming to him longer, stronger, or wronger than he did, if you know what I mean." He pulled at Todd's shoulder. "You might as well stop that, laddie. It won't do him a bit of good. Don't waste any more breath on him. I know a deader when I see one."

Kate Moody arrived a moment later and confirmed young Solinari's and Kiachif's diagnoses. "There's nothing I can do for him. Here, some of you help me get him out of here. We'll take him to the Health Center. My skimmer's outside."

"Commander Rogitel," DeVeer said, laying a hand on the assistant's arm and bringing him to his feet. "If you are not going to indulge in a medical emergency of your own, I have a list of charges that have been laid against you. Will you come with me now?"

Rogitel rose silently. DeVeer turned back to the Reeves. "Oh, and save me some punch, won't you?" he asked with a twinkle in his eye. "I'll be back as soon as I shut this fellow up." He marched his prisoner away toward the grid, accompanied by Hrrula to operate the controls.

"I don't believe he's dead," said Todd, watching the stretcher team leave the Hall with their burden. Someone had spread a tablecloth over Landreau's body before they carried it away.

"Believe it," Kiachif said firmly, slapping him on the shoulder. "Well, that's that, if you know what I mean. The end of all your troubles, trials, and tribulations. Well, this set! Third's gone, Landreau's sputtered his last, and the Treaty's signed. Nothing to stand in the way of you living happily ever after, is there?"

Todd and Hrriss exchanged meaningful glances. "Now that you mention it, no," Todd said, "particularly the 'happily ever after' bit. C'mon, Hrriss, Hrruna's had our girls far too long."

"We owe you so much, sir, for coming in when you did," Hu Shih was saying to First Speaker Hrruna as Todd and Hrriss approached.

"If it is not an imposition, honored sir," Hrriss asked Hrruna politely, "I would like to dance with my betrothed." He reached out a hand to Nrrna.

Nrrna glanced appealingly at the First Speaker, who patted the female's hand. "Yes, of course. Such a charming young lady. You are most fortunate, young Hrriss."

"You are so kind, sir," Nrrna said, lowering her eyelids prettily at First Speaker.

"And when is the joining to be?" Hrruna asked.

"Soon!" Hrriss said emphatically.

"Very soon," Nrrna agreed, looking lovingly at Hrriss. "Possibly tomorrow."

The old man sighed as the couple slipped through the crowd. "Ah, if I was thirty years younger! But it is always the lady's choice, isn't it? I must say, he is a fine young cub."

"I couldn't agree more," Second Speaker Hrrto said, watching the couple swirl gracefully onto the dance floor. "He is one of the hopes for Hrruba's future."

"Kelly?" Todd asked, bowing to her. "May I have the honor of this dance."

"May I, sir?" Kelly asked Hrruna sweetly.

"Yes, do. Enjoy yourselves, young ones!" Hrruna said, jaw dropped. "Ah, youth."

"That's a very pretty dress you have on," Todd said as with a firm hand he guided Kelly out among the dancers.

"Almost have on," Kelly grimaced, tugging at the filmy swags of cloth and settling them more securely across her nicely developed chest. "Red's not really my color."

"I think you can wear any color," Todd said with genuine gallantry.

"But I'm really not sure I should be dancing with you," she said, with such a firm arm around his neck and such a firm grip on his other hand that he stared at her in surprise. "For one thing, you're not really suitably dressed for the occasion."

"Kelly, that's not fair . . ." he began, and then saw the merry devilment in her sparkling eyes. "All right, I'll bite, how should I be dressed?"

Suddenly she took the lead from him and danced him over to a window ledge.

"You're not wearing tails," she said, waving a coil of rope in front of him that she must have somehow secreted on the ledge. "Imagine you forgetting an old Rraladoonian custom like that!"

Enchanted by his lover's gesture, he let her tie the rope around his waist and proceed to tie the other end around hers, completely ruining the line of her gown.

"Hey, that's not how to make a rope tail!" he said, laughing.

"No, it's to keep you from going off somewhere without taking me with you!" Now she backed him into the curtains of the window and whirled a length around him, before she pulled his head down to hers and kissed him long and lovingly. Not at all surprising, especially since he had never hoped to see her again, he responded passionately. Kiachif had been right—there was nothing at all to stop them living happily ever after.

"Friends, feasting, and fine firewater," Ali Kiachif said, carefully enunciating each word to Ken Reeve, swigging the last of the mlada from his glass. "That's the elements that make the best parties, if you know what I mean! No, don't take that bottle away, Reeve," he implored Ken as he swept dirty dishes off the table in front of him so he could prop up his elbows. "Pour me another portion, if you please."

"Nothing left in it, Kiachif." Ken upended the crock to show that it was empty. "See?"

Kiachif looked mournfully at the bottom of his glass. "You couldn't find another bottle somewhere nearby, could you? I always thought you were a merry mate of mine."

From long experience, Ken judged the old captain was only a few minutes from falling asleep when the power of the mlada hit. "Oh, I suppose there's one more in the kitchen. You wait here, Kiachif, and I'll see if I can't find it."

"That's fine, fair, and friendly of you," he said with satisfaction, and propped himself up to wait, tapping his fingers to the slow dance music and watching the couples swaying rhythmically. Ken went into the kitchen and peeped out through the door until he saw the old spacefarer sag over onto folded arms at the table. It had only taken a moment when he wasn't moving or talking for the liquor to relax him completely.

"Hrrestan, give me a hand, will you?" Ken asked, getting under one of Kiachif's arms and heaving upward. "We'd better put him to bed."

"With pleasurrre, my friend," the Hrruban said, taking the other arm. Together, they hoisted the Codep captain upright and started to walk him toward the guest cabins at the far side of the common.

Kiachif woke up partway there and glanced at each of his escorts in turn from under his bushy brows. "That's what I like to see," he said, nodding approvingly. "Cooperation between happy Human and Hrruban. Long may it continue."

Ken and Hrrestan got Kiachif onto the bunk in one of the rooms and considerately pulled his boots off. "So long as we can help it," Ken said, glancing at his old friend, as they lowered the lights in the cabin behind them, "it always will."

They left the old pilot snoring and went out together to rejoin the celebration.